ALSO BY JACK TODD

Desertion

Sun Going Down

Come Again No More

RAIN
FALLS
LIKE MERCY

JACK TODD

A TOUCHSTONE BOOK
Published by Simon & Schuster
New York London Toronto Sydney New Delhi

Touchstone
A Division of Simon & Schuster, Inc.
1230 Avenue of the Americas
New York, NY 10020

First Touchstone hardcover edition November 2011

TOUCHSTONE and colophon are registered trademarks of Simon & Schuster, Inc.

For information about special discounts for bulk purchases, please contact Simon & Schuster Special Sales at 1-866-506-1949 or business@simonandschuster.com.

The Simon & Schuster Speakers Bureau can bring authors to your live event. For more information or to book an event contact the Simon & Schuster Speakers Bureau at 1-866-248-3049 or visit our website at www.simonspeakers.com.

Designed by Renata Di Biase

Manufactured in the United States of America

10 9 8 7 6 5 4 3 2 1

Library of Congress Cataloging-in-Publication Data
Todd, Jack.
    Rain falls like mercy / Jack Todd.
        p. cm.
    I. Title.
PS3620.O318R35   2011
813'.6—dc22   2011004721

ISBN 978-1-4165-9851-0
ISBN 978-1-4391-0952-6 (ebook)

For Mick Lowe,
who kept the faith

In memoriam:
Gunner's Mate James D. Wilson,
USS Tennessee, Pearl Harbor to Tokyo

Ten? That's all you know? I've killed eleven.

—Charles Starkweather

Rain is to wet and fire to burn . . .

—William Shakespeare, *As You Like It*

RAIN
FALLS
LIKE MERCY

PART I

The Girl in the Blue Dress

I.

Wyoming
May 1941

S ATURDAY NIGHT, ALMOST TIME FOR THE SALOONS
to close. The girl lies on her narrow bed, waiting, her body tense
as a whiplash. Knowing what is to come, her body weak with
dread, a useless prayer frozen on the tip of her tongue. She tugs the
curtain back, watches the slow wheel of the cold and distant stars, the
quarter-moon like a dancer slipping through a skirt of thin cloud. Seeking mercy in its slender light, finding none.

At the stroke of midnight, she tiptoes into the kitchen and pours a
teacup half full of whiskey. It burns like fire going down, but the booze
will make things easier. She touches the thin wall next to the bed with
her fingertips. It vibrates in rhythm to her mother's snores. The woman
has had a snootful. She could sleep through a cyclone.

This night, what is about to happen, will be the last time. Her grandmother's letter is hidden under her mattress. *If it's that bad, honey, you
just come on to Grandma's and I'll look after you. I wish I could send you
the bus fare, but I don't have a dime to spare. If you can figure out how to get
here, we'll get along just swell. Go to the bus station and tell them you want to
buy a one-way ticket to Thermopolis. If I have my druthers, you won't need
a return.*

She doesn't have long to wait. She hears him coming a block away,
bellowing a drunken song from his homeland. He urinates noisily
against the side of the house, fumbles his way through the front door,
makes straight for her room. He gets tangled in his overalls trying to
undress and falls heavily on the floor. Something crashes in the next
room. She tenses for a moment, hoping, but her mother snores on. He
struggles to his feet, cursing her for making him fall. She hears buttons

popping as he rips his shirt off. He will expect her to sew them back on. Then she is pinned by his suffocating weight, the rough callused hand over her mouth, the whispered threat. *If you say goddam word, I break your neck like fucking chicken.*

She lies rigid as a board. He tells her that he loves her, which makes it worse, and he covers her mouth with his, pushes his tongue between her teeth. He tastes of whiskey fumes and stale tobacco and she thinks that she might vomit right down his throat. There is a moment of pain and then dirty fingernails claw at her buttocks. He thrashes like a dying chicken and makes a gagging sound in his throat. His body goes slack, his rough beard scrapes her neck. He mumbles something in his language which she doesn't understand, then a long, ripping snore shakes the bed. When she's certain he's asleep, she tiptoes to the outhouse. She throws up and cleans herself and comes back in to pack what clothes she can stuff into her mother's valise. Then she stretches out on the floor next to the bed in her nightgown, wide awake in the darkness, listening to the rasp of his breathing. Wishing he would have a heart attack and die in the night.

Near dawn, she takes the money from his billfold and the cigarettes and lighter from his shirt pocket. She dresses in the dark, slips on her good blue Sunday dress, picks up the valise, slings her coat over her arm, and walks the four miles into Gillette, where she waits two hours for the bus station to open. She's not afraid. He'll sleep until noon and so will her mother. She'll be long gone by the time they wake. When the station opens, she buys her ticket. Her bus is due any minute, but she'll have to wait in Sheridan and transfer to the night bus to Thermopolis. When she boards the bus, she feels lighter than air, like a beam of light. The driver smiles at her and says *Good morning, miss.* It's the farthest she's ever been from home. More than a hundred miles, the driver says. She watches the countryside flow past, a colt running in a pasture, a family standing around waiting while the father changes a tire on an old jalopy, cowpokes working cattle on a ranch that seems to go on forever.

When the bus arrives in Sheridan, she goes for a long walk. She passes three or four cafes without stopping. The smell of frying bacon makes her hungry. She sits on a park bench and eats two apples and some dry biscuits from a paper bag and drinks from a water fountain. She follows the sound of bells and finds a little white church. She sits in the back pew with her valise beside her, watching the working men with their big square hands trail their worn-out wives into church. They sing "The Old Rugged Cross" and "Nearer My God to Thee" and the girl sings a high harmony in a clear, pretty voice. A woman in a beaded blue pillbox hat with a black lace veil turns and smiles at her. She tries to listen to the sermon, but the preacher wanders off the subject. Her mind drifts. When the service ends, she leaves quickly.

Three blocks from the church, she finds a lunch counter that is open and pays a nickel for a glass of milk. She sits there as long as she feels she can sit without ordering something to eat. She is about to leave when the heavyset waitress places a tuna-fish sandwich with pickles in front of her.

The girl blushes. "I'm sorry, ma'am, I didn't order this."

"I know you didn't, honey, but you look a trifle peckish. I got extra tuna fish I'll never get rid of today, so this one's on me."

She eats the sandwich quickly, as though fearful the waitress will change her mind. The woman brings her a second glass of milk. The girl drinks it with the last crumbs of the sandwich. Before she can finish, there is a slice of apple pie with a big scoop of ice cream in front of her.

The waitress winks. "Pie and ice cream comes with the tuna fish. I made that pie myself, fresh this morning. Now do you drink coffee, honey, or are you too young for that?"

It's the best pie she has ever tasted. She savors every bite and sips the hot coffee loaded with milk and sugar and nearly weeps to think a person could be so kind to a stranger.

When the pie and coffee are finished, she thanks the waitress and dawdles back to the bus station to wait. The meal makes her feel sleepy in spite of the coffee, and she falls asleep sitting erect on one of the stiff wooden benches. When she wakes, it is 7:17 in the evening and the bus to Thermopolis is not due until 8:47, so she has exactly ninety minutes to wait. She promises herself a smoke at 7:30. She picks up a few of the tattered magazines scattered around and looks at the advertisements for things she might want to buy someday, like a Sunbeam Mixmaster or an

RCA Victor radio. She studies the photo of Veronica Lake on the cover of *Hollywood* magazine. It's the May issue, but the magazine is falling apart. When the cover comes off as she is reading it, she slips it into her bag.

At 7:25, she goes to the ladies' room and uses the facilities and stands in front of the mirror, primping her hair, trying to look like Veronica Lake. She is a pretty girl, even if her hair is long and dark and not blond at all. The blue dress is looking a little rumpled, so she smooths it over her good figure, her breasts that seem larger every day and her hips that are filling out. When she is satisfied, she steps outside for a smoke. She takes her coat and valise and steps into the ring of light cast by a single yellow bulb outside the station door. With the sun down, the mountain air is cool. She slips her coat on and lights a cigarette, inhales deeply and blows three perfect smoke rings, a trick she learned from her father. Thinking of him, she crosses herself and whispers: "May he rest in peace." Out of habit, but also because she really hopes that he has found eternal rest. He was the best person she has ever known. When he died, she was left to the mercy of a man without mercy.

There is a woman waiting in a car parked across the road. The woman stares at her, making her feel like an actress on a stage. She moves back into the shadows near the wall, where the woman will be able to see nothing but the red glow of her cigarette.

An automobile eases along the street in second gear and turns in to the parking lot behind the bus station. She hears a car door slam and a man comes around the corner of the station. He strolls up to her, his boot heels echoing on the sidewalk, and asks if he can bum a cigarette. He is beautiful, the most beautiful man she has ever seen. As though God has sent down an angel.

She rummages in her purse and finds her Lucky Strikes. She is reluctant, because she has only nine left now, but she wants him to linger. She draws a cigarette from the pack and hands it to him. He takes a box of wooden matches out of his shirt pocket and strikes a match on the heel of his boot, lights the cigarette and tosses the burnt match away. The cigarette dangles from his lower lip. When he draws it away, it leaves a fleck of tobacco on his lip. They stand talking, his voice so soft that she has to move closer to him to hear, into the circle of light from the streetlamp. When he speaks, she watches his mouth, his lips moving, as though she can lip-read what he is saying.

The last glow of the day vanishes. Night falls like a shroud. They stand like tango dancers, swaying in silhouette. He leans closer and whispers something in her ear. She nods. She takes one last drag and flicks the butt of her cigarette toward the street. Sparks fly as it cartwheels into the gutter. He lifts her valise and leads the way. She follows, her coat slung over one arm. At the corner, she trails the fingertips of her left hand along the wall as she steps into the darkness.

FTER YEARS OF DROUGHT, RAIN FALLS LIKE mercy on the parched land, where ragged, low-running clouds hug the prairie. A three-day downpour has turned the bunchgrass a deep green, coaxed wildflowers out of rock and sand to flare pink and yellow and indigo for miles in every direction. There is scarlet paintbrush, beardtongue, balsamroot, pink shooting stars, Rocky Mountain thistle, a stand of poisonous indigo lupine in a low-lying stretch of pasture.

The Choctaw rides with his eyes on the ground. Wet snow mixes with the rain, and a stiff north wind drives it into his face. Cold rain pours off the brim of his hat, sluices down his oilskin slicker, and turns his bay horse black. He pays it no attention. He's tracking, following a single rider on a fresh-shod horse along the barbed-wire fence that marks the northern boundary of the 8T8 ranch. Every quarter mile or so, the rider has jumped down to cut all three strands of barbed wire. Where the wire is cut, there are clear boot prints in the wet ground. Next to his own size twelve, the boots look as though they belong to a child. The Choctaw calls him Baby Foot.

The Choctaw's name is Hanchitubbe, although no one but Jenny Hoot Owl calls him that. The way he translates it from the Choctaw, Hanchitubbe means either "Kill the Sun" or "Sun-Killer." Sun-Killer is a name he likes, but no one calls him Sun-Killer, either. They call him Two Spuds, for his habit of asking a stingy roundup cook for more potatoes. When Eli Paint asks if he minds the name, he says it's better than being called a fuckin redskin.

He has ridden four miles along the fence line when he hears a cow bawling off to his right. He rides on until he sees her through the rain, a white face with one horn, standing over her dead calf and bawling like doom. He trots over for a closer look. Three magpies rise and wheel away, followed by a dark buzzard reluctant to leave the feast, its wet black wings skimming the tall grass as it flaps out of reach. The bay horse shies. He has to tighten his hold on the reins and dig his heels into its flanks to urge it into a crabwise, head-slinging dance, prancing side-long over the wet sage and the mesquite brushed with rain.

The bay is almost on top of the calf when the Choctaw sees that it has been killed and left to rot. He dismounts and squats on his boot heels, keeping an eye on the one-horned cow in case she decides to put that horn to use. Baby Foot's boot prints are all around the cow and the dead calf. He has cut the calf's throat with a single deep slash. The knife has some heft to it, to cut as it does, like a big Bowie knife, and it is sharp enough to split a man's belly like a can opener. Baby Foot has cut the calf's head off and spiked it on a fence post. The black tongue lolls, the eyes have been pecked out. The Choctaw feels goose bumps, a tightening in the scrotum. He is back in the Ardennes during the Great War, German patrols creeping through the dark trees, phantoms in the fog. Every fiber in his skin alive, trying to sense where they will strike next. He knows the feeling: something is badly askew here.

He draws the carbine from its scabbard, wipes it dry with a handkerchief tucked inside his poncho, breaks it open to be sure there is a round in the chamber. He walks the ground in a hundred-foot circle, leading the bay with his free hand. He swivels the carbine in all directions, drawing a bead on mist, fog, sheets of rain. He swings back into the saddle, digs his spurs into the bay, and heads west at a canter, with the carbine braced across the pommel of the saddle. He knows what Jenny Hoot Owl would say about this. *If you had the sense God gave a goose, you'd turn around and head home right now. Go straight to Eli, let him figure out what to do. He owns the damned ranch, it's his problem.* Baby Foot could be out there with a Winchester, waiting to put a bullet in his heart. But as far as he knows, he's the only pureblood Indian ranch foreman in Wyoming. He can't afford to quit. He rides on and finds six more dead calves. Two of the cows are still bawling next to their calves, the others have drifted off or rejoined the herd.

The rain turns to wet snow. The lone rider's trail veers north, through the last of the gaps cut in the fence, onto the neighboring ranch, land that Eli sold to a Scottish lord back in '33. It's snowing hard now. The rider seems to be headed toward an old sheepherder's shack. The Choctaw's outfit uses the cabin as a line shack and restocks the supplies twice a year, spring and fall. When the rider's trail veers off to the west and then vanishes under the snow, Two Spuds decides to make straight for the shack to build a fire and thaw out, maybe have something to eat. He's dreaming of hot soup, not paying attention to what lies ahead, when the bay stumbles heavily over the edge of a draw that is half-obscured by a drift. He's thrown hard on his left shoulder, feels a thunderbolt of pain. He lies still for a moment, winded, trying to figure out what is broke. Then he rolls onto his knees and fumbles in the snow for the carbine, cursing the horse and the weather and that calf-killing sonofabitch Baby Foot.

He fears that the bay horse might have broken a leg in the fall, but it has already struggled to its feet, steady on all four legs. It stands, blowing hard, reins trailing in the snow. It's a two-year-old, no better than half-broke. He leans heavily on the carbine and manages to stand, although it feels as though his left arm has been yanked from the socket. The pain is like a lightning strike each time he moves. He starts toward the bay. The horse waits until he's almost within reach, then takes off at a swinging trot, the empty stirrups flapping. The same thing happens three more times, until he gives up on the horse and trudges on in wet boots, shivery-legged with pain, until he finds the slope that leads down to the cabin. There is no sign of smoke from the chimney. He heads straight to the shelter, hoping he won't lose his wet feet to frostbite. The horse seems reluctant to see him go. It shambles along behind like an obedient dog. He stumbles the last fifty yards to the cabin, kicks the door open, and pushes the muzzle of the carbine in first. He is not yet through the door when the smell hits him. Sweet and sickening, a scent that clings like fog to low ground. He fumbles his way toward the one table barely visible in the watery light that filters through the single narrow window, finds the coal-oil lantern and the matches next to it, right where they are supposed to be. He lays the carbine on the table, lifts the glass from the lantern, tilts the lamp to soak the wick in kerosene, lights the match and holds it and waits for the flame, replaces the glass, twists the knob to extend the wick until the lantern casts a yellowish glow. He shines the yellow light onto spiderwebs, mouse droppings, empty tuna-fish cans, cigarette butts, spat lumps of chewing tobacco, engravings and photographs of comely girls torn from old magazines, bits and pieces of rope and harness, the careless mess left by men tarrying a single night in a place they do not figure to see again. There is no firewood, the coal bucket is empty, there is not so much as a solitary can of beans on the shelves. He has cold biscuits and a little bacon with him, but they are in the saddlebags on the bay horse. He twists the knob on the lantern again to get more light and turns to find the source of that infernal smell.

The dead girl lies in the shadows, on the narrow cot tucked against the far wall of the cabin. She faces him, her head dangling half off the bed, her face the color of suet. She looks to be no more than sixteen. She has long dark hair, which hangs off the bed, and she wears a pretty blue dress, which is up around her waist. She is naked from the waist down and there is a dark pool of blood between her legs and another on the floor next to the cot, where her throat has been cut and she has been left to bleed out like a butchered hog. Her hands are trussed up above her head, the loop of a rawhide pigging string in a double half hitch around her wrists, a second pigging string used to bind the first loop to a leg of the heavy potbelly stove. Two more strips of rawhide bind her ankles, one tied to another rusty iron spike driven into a post of the shack, the other stretched taut and wound around a nail next to the door which holds a lucky horseshoe, gone to rust. He crosses the room in two strides, stands beside her and holds her wrist, mistaking for a moment the sound of his own heartbeat for the race of blood through her veins. The fingertips of her left hand are smeared black, as though they were dipped in soot. He takes out his jackknife thinking to cut loose the bonds that hold her, but slips it back into his pocket. The sheriff will want things in the shack just as they are.

The Choctaw holds his breath, hearing no sound except the lazy buzzing of a fat fly, trapped indoors and nearly paralyzed with cold. He

casts about for something to cover the girl, finds a pile of empty gunnysacks in one corner, and spreads them over her tenderly. He hides her
face last, the eyes staring through and beyond him, to a spot somewhere
on the far side of eternity. He stands with his hat held over his heart.
White men will bury this poor girl in the cold earth. Better to wrap her
on a scaffold under the sky, but that is not the white man's way. He snuffs
out the kerosene lamp, takes up the carbine, steps out into the driving
snow and the cold air with the tang of wet sage, relieved to be away from
the clinging odor of the dead girl. He is trying to peer through the snow
to get his bearings for the long walk home when the bay horse sidles
up and nudges him. He gathers the reins. *You are one pitiful excuse for a
horse. Only thing that's keeping you from the glue factory is that you got to
get me home.* He slips the carbine back into its scabbard and leads the
bay around so that he can mount from the right side, the horse skittish,
rolling its eyes.

It takes him four tries to climb into the saddle. Twice the horse
dances away, leaving him dangling from the reins. The third time, he gets
partway up and the pain comes like a jolt from a cattle prod. His legs
turn to water and he slides back down. On the fourth try, he swings into
the saddle. He teeters with pain, but hangs on. He hauls the bay around
and taps it with his spurs.

Okay, you bastard. Let's go home.

ELI PAINT SITS FRAMED AGAINST THE GREAT stone fireplace in the main parlor of the house on the 8T8 ranch, waiting for the photographer from the *Rocky Mountain News* to set up the big Speed Graphic camera mounted on a tripod. While the photographer works, the reporter Roland Taggart takes careful notes. *Noble visage. Like Indian chief. Black hair just beginning to turn gray. Eyes an odd shade of gray-green. Not talkative.* The photographer uses the steel, brass, and black enamel film holders, flipping them to expose his four-by-five-inch film, one exposure on each side. He has already made a dozen meticulous exposures, but he is not yet satisfied. The reporter watches and worries. He can feel his subject getting edgy. If the photographer doesn't hurry up, Eli will not have the patience for an interview.

The newspapermen have done profiles of a former governor of Montana, a hangman, a suffragette, and a Cheyenne warrior who fought at the Battle of the Little Bighorn. Now they're in Wyoming to do a piece on the Paint brothers. The reporter has interviewed Eli's twin brother, Ezra, who runs what he calls the Appaloosa ranch on one corner of the 8T8 with Eli's grandson Ben Paint. Ezra talked away an afternoon, filling two of the reporter's notebooks. Now it's Eli's turn, but he figures to be a more reluctant subject.

The photographer finishes taking his twenty exposures and begins to pack away his gear. Eli sits stiffly in his straight-backed chair, his face expressionless. He points to the overstuffed armchair at his side. Roland Taggart sinks into it, feeling embarrassed and off balance. Juanita, Eli's Mexican-born wife, comes in to introduce herself and see if the newspaper people want anything. She's at least thirty years younger than her husband. The reporter finds her achingly beautiful. He tries to figure out what she sees in the old man. Money, has to be. When she leaves the room, he can't help gazing after her. His longing must show in his face, because he is met with a flinty, gray-eyed glare from Eli Paint. The reporter coughs, averts his eyes, flips through his notes trying to remember what he wanted to ask. The only sound is the ticking of the big grandfather clock in the hall. No time limit has been set for the interview, but he has the sense that fifteen minutes is about all he is likely to get. He clears his throat.

"You understand that we're doing a series of pieces on legends of the Old West?"

"I do. Makes it sound like I ought to be settin in a museum someplace. Like a goddamned stuffed owl."

"Well, you don't look one bit like a fella that belongs in a museum."

The reporter sees that Eli Paint will not be moved by flattery. Maybe he won't mind talking about his younger days. Most old men liked to reminisce until it makes a fellow sick.

"When you first came to Wyoming in 1886, you were how old?"

"Sixteen."

"And this is the time period when you took a blacksnake whip to the hide of an outlaw name of O. T. Yonkee?"

"Who told you that?"

"Your brother. Ezra."

"Uh-huh."

"Ezra says you gave that outlaw a good hiding for mistreating mustangs."

"If that's what Ezra says, it must be true. I've not known him to lie."

"Do you remember any details of that encounter?"

"I expect Ezra already told you."

"He did, but I'd like to hear it from you."

"I'm sure you would."

Taggart waits hopefully, but the subject is closed. He knows that Eli started out as a penniless cowboy and built a ranching empire, lost much of it during the Great Depression and recovered so quickly that now, they say, he is wealthier than ever. The trick is to get him to tell some part of the story in his own words.

"How would you describe the blizzard of 1887?"

"It was perilous cold."

"It was after that winter, they say, that you rustled a thousand head of horses from this very ranch, when it was known as the O-Bar, and you were hung by a gunslinger named Dermott Cull."

"They say a thousand head, do they?"

"They do."

"That's a heap of horseflesh."

"It is. What I'm asking, is it true?"

"What?"

"That you and Ezra and two or three others rustled those horses and ran them to Montana, where you sold them to a half-breed trader named Joe Kipp?"

"Ezra must have told you."

"Nosir, he did not. He said that was one story I would have to get direct from you."

"Is that a fact. Sounds like a tall tale."

"That's my point, sir. I need you to help me separate the tall tales from the truth."

"I can't do that."

"How's that?"

"I can't do that. You want to write about the West, you have to know the truth about this country. The truth is in the tall tales. Take away the yarns that stretch the truth, and all you have left is the East with better scenery."

"But I'm a reporter. We have to stick to the facts."

"And you always do that, is that right? You never turn things around, fudge a little, make a man look better or worse than he is?"

Taggart has the kind of pale fish-belly skin that looks as though it has never seen the sun. Now he flushes a bright red. "Maybe I make a fella look better. Never worse, unless he's a criminal."

"So you tell tall tales, is that what you're saying?"

"No, it's not that. It's just that sometimes, you want to please a fellow . . ."

He trails off, miserable with embarrassment. Eli leans forward to look him square in the eye.

"You're the fella wrote that piece on Big Bill Bury, aint you?"

Taggart smiles. His feature on the tycoon William Bury drew more attention than anything he has ever written.

"I am."

"You are. Then I guess you didn't know that Big Bill is just about the nastiest piece of work west of the Mississippi? Old Bill would stake his mama to an anthill and pour syrup over her if there was profit to be made, but you made him sound like Abe Lincoln. If that wasn't a tall tale, then Paul Bunyan is the real article."

Taggart clears his throat. "That's your view."

"Taint my view, son. It's the truth. But hell, if you didn't tell tall tales, you couldn't write about the West. You want to get a subject as big as the West in your sights, the whole shebang, with Indians and cavalry and wild horses and outlaws who would eat your liver, then you got to be able to tell a story as big as this country. That's the only way to get at the truth."

"Can I quote you on that?"

"I expect you will, on my say-so or otherwise."

"If you could just clear up the bit about the theft of those horses."

"I believe Ezra already did that. If that aint tall tale enough for you, you'll have to make up another one. You don't need my help for that."

The reporter waits. The only sounds he hears are the ticking clock and his own belly growling. Outside, it's raining harder than ever. The photographer has finished packing his gear and is drinking a beer that Juanita opened for him. Taggart wishes he had asked for a beer to steady his nerves. He clears his throat and tries again. "You got your start as a rancher in Brown County, Nebraska."

"Yep."

"During the 1890s. That was a time much like the one we've been through, depression and drought, is that right?"

"That's right."

"It must have been tough to start out as a rancher, not knowing if you could make it or not."

"Yep."

The reporter tries another tack. "I believe you have a son in the Navy?"

"Leo, my youngest boy. He went to school for this thing they call radar, but he got seasick something awful, trying to look at a radar screen out on the ocean. Now he's Shore Patrol, stationed on dry land in Hawaii. And I have a grandson who enlisted with Leo, my daughter Velma's boy. Bobby Watson. He's an antiaircraft gunner on the battleship *Tennessee*."

"You must be fearful for Bobby and Leo, the world the way it is."

"How do you mean that?"

"I mean the war in Europe. The Krauts and all. They say we're going to get into this thing any day now."

"So I've heard."

Eli looks out the window, sees that the rain is turning to snow. Juanita reappears with a big wedge of apple pie. The reporter can't resist. He puts down his pen to pick up the fork. Eli takes that as his cue that the interview is over. He reaches for his hat. "I expect you've got what you need. If you don't, you'll just have to make it up. It's getting dark out there and I have places to go and things to do."

J UANITA IS LEFT TO SEE THE MEN OUT. SHE STANDS
shivering in the cold, watching their car slew up the driveway
toward the county road, then hurries back inside, to the oppressive
silence of the big, empty house. She takes a clean dish towel and wipes
the mist from the kitchen window, leaving a neat rectangle so that she
can peer out through the snow. Her cheek presses against the cool glass.
She can barely see Eli's kerosene lantern, bobbing in the darkness down
toward the corrals, like a light dangling from the mast of a ship far out
to sea. It has taken the spark out of her, this snowstorm in May, with the
grass already green and the prairie sprinkled with wildflowers. With Eli's
children all grown and gone, she feels isolated and lonely during the long
winters. Her spirits rose with the spring, but with the snowstorm she is
once again in need of the comfort of that flickering lantern, the reassurance that her man will be back soon, stamping the snow from his boots,
teasing her with his cold fingers down her neck, wanting to know what's
keeping supper.

It's weakness to feel as she does. There is always work to be done, yet
she sometimes sits for hours, listening to the ticking of the big grandfather clock in the hall, feeling her life slipping by and herself a tiny, lost
figure in a cold and impenetrable universe.

She scoops more coal onto the stove and turns on the radio in time
for the news. A Nazi named Rudolf Hess has been captured after parachuting into Scotland. The Japanese are making more demands in the
Pacific. The Luftwaffe has hit London again, this time with the biggest
raid of the war so far. Hundreds are dead; the House of Commons, the
British Museum, and Westminster Abbey are all badly damaged. Her
stomach churns at the savagery of it. She has never been to London, but
she has seen the effects of the Blitz on the newsreels: those poor people,
huddled in terror in basements and cellars and Underground stations as

the bombs whistle down. The war has something to do with her anxiety. It takes her back to her childhood, growing up in the midst of a civil war, her father and brothers hanged in the plaza of her village by Pancho Villa's men. She knows how capricious war can be, how it can hit one town and spare the next. The only constant is fear. Her instinct is to turn away from the war news, as though turning off the radio or tossing the newspaper in the fireplace will make it go away. She tries to keep at bay the horrors of a world gone wobbly on its axis, but with Leo and Bobby already in the service, the war is like a hungry wolf, scratching at the door.

To take her mind off it, she starts supper. The warm smells of biscuits and gravy and roast beef always banish the shadows. She has just taken the biscuits from the oven when she peers out again and sees Eli striding through the snow on the way back from the barn, flanked on one side by his big dog, Rufus, and on the other by Zeke Ketcham's enormous Poland China boar, which shuffles along a half pace off the heel of Eli's right boot. The boar follows as far as the steps to the veranda, where he flops down in the mud. Rufus follows Eli into the house, shaking mud and snow off his shaggy coat before he curls up on the hooked rug in front of the big stone fireplace. Eli builds a fire so the mutt can lie there, happily lost in the rising odor of wet dog, until she has dinner on the table. Then he takes his usual place, with his big head almost under Eli's chair. Juanita tells Eli not to feed the dog at the table, Rufus whimpers, Eli slips him a few scraps when he thinks Juanita isn't looking, she glares at him, and Rufus rolls his big wet eyes at her until she laughs and shakes her head and slips him what is left of her roast beef, which he devours, bones and all.

They talk about the weather and the war. Because of the snow, Eli says they might have to put off the spring roundup for another week. It's wet, but it isn't all that cold, so the spring calves should be all right. Juanita tells him the war news, the Nazi bigwig whose name she has forgotten parachuting into Scotland, the Luftwaffe raid on London. They finish eating. Eli picks up a week-old copy of *The Denver Post* and Juanita starts the washing up. Out of habit, she wipes away the mist on the window again and sees Two Spuds riding in through the snow, slumped over the neck of a horse that is staggering with fatigue. She calls to Eli, who yanks his jacket and boots on. Juanita watches from the veranda as he wraps the horse's reins around the hitching post nearest to the house. Two Spuds slides out of the saddle and Eli gets an arm around his waist. Juanita slips on her overshoes and hurries out. They boost Two Spuds up the steps and onto the porch and help him out of his boots and coat. His lips are blue with cold, and he's in so much pain that his eyes are rolling back in his head. Juanita wants to soothe him, but he will not be soothed.

"We have to call the law," he says. "There's a dead girl in the old sheep-herder's shack. Somebody killed her and left her there."

Juanita holds his wet boot, too stunned to speak. Eli hangs the foreman's coat on a hook. "I'm going to look after your horse," he says. "Juanita will take a look at your shoulder. When we've got you fixed up, you can tell me what happened."

"What about that poor girl?" Juanita asks. "We can't leave her there."

"Nobody but the good Lord can help her now. If we try to get through in this snowstorm, she won't be the only one dead."

He leaves Two Spuds in Juanita's care and goes to look after the bay horse. The Choctaw, bent with pain and supporting his left arm with his good hand, follows Juanita into the kitchen. She is a trained nurse. For a nurse with her experience, it's not a difficult diagnosis: the left shoulder looks deformed and the pain is extreme. He has a dislocated shoulder. The trick is to get it back in place. As gently as she can, she peels off his work shirt. The wet union suit underneath is another matter. She has to get a pair of scissors from her sewing basket and cut it off. By the time Two Spuds is stripped to the waist, Eli is back. Juanita asks him to pour a double shot of whiskey for her patient. The Choctaw downs it and Eli pours him another.

"The best place is right there on the kitchen table," Juanita says. "I need you to lie flat and relax as much as you can. We can't get it back in place unless you can relax the muscles."

"Might be easier said than done."

"You can do it. You rode all the way here in this state. Finish that whiskey and lie back." He does as he's told. Juanita takes his left arm and stretches it out to the side, lifting it slowly until it is above the joint. She has Eli stand near the Choctaw's head to support the elbow. When the pain is too much, she eases up to let him catch his breath.

"All right. Now bend your elbow and reach back, like you were going to scratch your neck, nice and slow." The Choctaw follows her instructions. "Now stretch the arm as far as you can. Reach like you're trying to touch your other shoulder."

Two Spuds quivers with the effort. Juanita has him take a deep breath, let it all the way out, and force himself to relax the muscles. He stretches the arm one last time, as far as he can reach, and the shoulder slips back into place. The effect is immediate. Juanita can see the relief in the Choctaw's face as the intense pain gives way to a mild ache. She helps him to sit up. There are beads of sweat on his forehead and he looks pale and drawn, but the worst of it is over. She massages the shoulder briskly to rub a little warmth into it.

Juanita fashions a sling for him. "That should take care of it for now. If it starts to hurt again, I'm going to get you to a doctor. Now I'm going to get you some supper while you tell Eli what happened up there."

Eli sets another glass of whiskey in front of his foreman. They go through it all, from the time Two Spuds found the tracks of the man he calls Baby Foot until he stumbled on the girl's body. Eli asks a few questions, but mostly he just listens. When he's sure that he understands it all as well as he ever will, he picks up the telephone and asks the operator to put him through to the county sheriff.

5

THE OFFICE CLOCK STRIKES SEVEN TIMES. SHER-
iff Tom Call throws his pencil down. Between the ticking and
the striking, the clock sounds like a whole damned symphony
orchestra. One of these days, he is going to go down to the dime store,
see is it possible for a man to buy a quiet clock.

It isn't his job to work the four-to-midnight shift, but it's a Saturday
and they're working with a skeleton staff. Early Porter's wife is expecting
their first baby any day, so Call sent him home. He has paperwork to do,
and it's better to do it when the office is quiet. He turns on the radio to
get the news and the weather report. It's all bad. A Nazi named Hess has
parachuted into Scotland. The Germans have bombed London again.
The snow will turn back to rain overnight before it clears in the morning.
By Sunday afternoon the temperature is supposed to hit sixty degrees,
meaning the roads will be a helluva mess. He leaves the radio on, tuned
to a dance-music show out of Chicago. He isn't in the mood for dance
music, but it drowns out the clock.

It's one of those days when he wishes he'd never given up flying. He's
a pilot, and a good one. He flew a Boeing B-80 trimotor for the United
Aircraft and Transport Corporation. Carrying the mail and fourteen
passengers at 115 miles an hour. Folks said he could fly through a thunderstorm and land with dry wings. One of these days, he's going to go
back to the sky and leave all this behind.

Call forces himself to quit daydreaming and go back to filling out the
missing-persons report on his desk. He prints in neat block letters:

NAME: MILDRED STOJKO, KNOWN AS MILLIE
AGE: 15
HEIGHT: 5 FEET, 2 INCHES
WEIGHT: 110 POUNDS

HAIR: LIGHT BROWN

EYES: BROWN

DISTINGUISHING MARKS: APPENDECTOMY SCAR

LAST SEEN WEARING: BLUE SUNDAY DRESS

HOME: GILLETTE, WYOMING

MISSING SINCE: MAY 4, 1941

REPORTED MISSING BY: HELENA PETROVIC

RELATIONSHIP TO MISSING PERSON: GRANDMOTHER

He keeps a dictionary on his desk. A judge once made fun of the spelling mistakes in one of his reports. He wanted to shoot the man, but he has since been careful of his spelling. He has to look up *distinguishing* and *appendectomy*. He checks the calendar on the wall, provided by a fertilizer company. The picture for May shows an alfalfa field all lit up with purple flowers, not a snowflake in sight. The date is Saturday, May 10. The girl has been missing since Sunday evening. At the bottom of the form is a box for comments. He fills it in:

> *Mother and stepfather are drinkers. Girl a runaway. Stole money from stepfather. Called her grandmother in Thermopolis to say she was on her way, didn't show. Bus driver from Gillette remembers her. Pretty girl in a blue dress. Driver of the Sheridan–Thermopolis bus is sure she never boarded. Night cashier at the bus station says he saw her waiting. Cashier can't recall whether she was around when the bus boarded. Grandmother met bus in Thermopolis, girl wasn't on it. Probably mixed up with a boyfriend somewhere.*

Most of what he knows about the Stojko girl comes from Sheriff Bill Brower, over in Gillette. They talked after the grandmother reported the girl missing. Brower paid a visit to the mother and stepfather, who were both so drunk that they had barely noticed the girl was missing. Brower says he didn't blame the girl one damned bit for running away.

Tom thought he might have a lead when a preacher's wife named Jeanine Rubottom saw the item about the missing girl in *The Sheridan*

Press and called to say that she had seen a young woman answering Mildred Stojko's description, talking to a man outside the bus station the night the girl disappeared. He drove to the parsonage to talk to her. Mrs. Rubottom said that the Reverend Rubottom had taken the bus to Cheyenne to deliver a guest sermon that weekend. She was waiting to pick him up at the station when she saw a girl in a blue dress standing outside, smoking a cigarette.

"I noticed because that just burned me up, to see a girl that young smoking. It makes them look so cheap. Smoking and chewing gum. There's a teller at the bank, I go in to make a deposit, she's got a wad of Juicy Fruit in her mouth and she has a cigarette going at the same time. I gave her a piece of my mind, I don't mind saying so. But if the bank president won't make her quit, there's nothing a customer can do. Anyhow, I was about to march right over and give this girl at the bus station what-for, but then a fellow came along and started talking to her. She gave him a cigarette and he lit it and they stood there talking. Then he picked up her suitcase and they disappeared around back of the station. I figured he knew her, for her to go off with him that quick. A minute later, a car came out from behind the bus station and drove off. I didn't get a real good look, but I think she was in it."

"Did you happen to notice the make of the automobile?"

"I did not. I didn't think much of it at the time. I thought it was her boyfriend picking her up, see."

"Was the car new? Old?"

"I really couldn't say. It seems to me it was shiny."

"Do you remember a color?"

"Black. I'm sure it was black. And shiny."

"So it was new?"

"I wouldn't say that. I don't know the first thing about cars, except our old Dodge. That's the only one I can recognize."

"So it wasn't a Dodge?"

"I couldn't say for sure."

"What about the license plate? Did you catch any part of that?"

"Oh, no. I wasn't looking at the license plate. But it had those special tires. You know, white-and-black."

"You mean whitewall tires?"

"Yes. I think it had whitewall tires."

"You're not sure."

"I can't say for sure, but I see these tires in my mind. Whitewall tires."

"Which way was that car headed when it came out from behind the bus station?"

"West. I'm sure it was headed west. Toward the mountains. I think. Unless it headed east. It could be it headed east."

"What about the man? Can you describe him?"

"Well, no. They were standing in the shadows outside the station, see. There was the streetlight and I could see her well at first, but then she stepped out of the light. I think he was wearing a big cowboy hat, so I couldn't see his face."

"Do you remember the color of the hat?"

"No, I'm sorry. It might have been gray. Or black or maybe brown. I don't think it was white, but I'm not sure."

"Can you recall if he was tall or short?"

"I'm sorry, I don't. I don't even know if *she* was tall or short. She was a pretty girl in a blue dress, that's all I can say for sure."

"She isn't very big. Five foot two. Can you say if he was taller than she is?"

"I'm sorry, Sheriff. I really can't. I wish I had paid more attention, but I only looked because she was smoking. I don't approve of young girls smoking."

"Yes, ma'am. Is there anything else you can remember? Was he wearing cowboy boots?"

"I think he was, but I only noticed the hat."

"Could you say whether he was young or old?"

"I couldn't."

"Fat or thin?"

She shook her head.

"But you're sure about the hat."

"Now that you mention it, I'm not sure. I *think* he was wearing a cowboy hat. He was wearing a hat, but I'm not sure it was a cowboy hat. I had the impression she knew the man."

"Why did you think that?"

"Well, to go off with him so quick like that. A girl who is well brought up would never go off with a stranger, would she?"

"I expect not." Tom closed his notebook. On the witness stand, the woman would wreck any case. Her version of events got more wobbly the more she talked.

When he got back to the office, he kicked a wastebasket, waking Deputy Strother Leach from his nap.

"Everything all right, Sheriff?"

"Everything's just fine. Only I just talked to the only witness we got in the case of that missing Stojko girl, and she wouldn't notice if a army tank drove over her front lawn."

"Aint that a shame."

Tom isn't too concerned about the girl. It happens all the time. People go missing. A girl like this Mildred Stojko decides to light out, meets a fellow somewhere, loses her virtue, ends up three hundred miles away, needing a Western Union wire for five dollars so she can afford the bus fare home. The missing person almost always turns up alive and well, although sometimes a little the worse for wear.

Jeanine Rubottom did put the girl with a man, the two of them walking away from the bus station. They had talked for a while, so it seemed unlikely the man was a boyfriend, because if he was, they would have left immediately. And if she had planned to meet a boyfriend in Sheridan, why would she buy a bus ticket for Thermopolis? The Stojko girl hadn't simply fallen off the end of the earth. She had walked away with a stranger.

The telephone rings. It's 7:38. Tom makes a note of the time, out of habit. "Tom Call."

"Sheriff, this is Eli Paint, out at the 8T8 ranch."

6.

TOM SPLASHES A LITTLE COLD WATER ON HIS FACE and leaves town an hour before dawn. The snow has changed to rain, but the rain has real weight to it and the gravel roads are a mire. At the edge of the paved highway, he stops to put on tire chains. Even with the chains, the cruiser is up to its hubcaps in mud and he has to fight to keep it out of the barrow pit. He takes two wrong turns and has to double back and doesn't make it to the ranch until after daylight, just as the rain begins to ease. Eli, who was up and out of the house at four o'clock, has finished his chores and is waiting, wearing a long yellow rain slicker and trailed by a big dog and an enormous boar. The sheriff steps out of the patrol car into mud six inches deep.

"The hell this weather."

"Aint it the truth."

Eli leads the way to the house. Tom follows. "That hog always follow you around?"

"Pretty much. Used to belong to a cowhand named Zeke Ketcham, but Zeke don't work here no more. Him nor Willie Thaw."

"I heard that story. Something about you running a bunch of mustangs off to Montana, getting Bill Bury mad as a hornet."

"I expect you have."

Juanita, watching from the window, sees a tall, spare man. Young and lean, not at all her idea of a sheriff. She meets them at the door. Eli introduces them and the sheriff greets her with a handshake and a little bow. For about as long as it takes to shake his hand, she is flustered. Cornflower blue eyes, curly dark blond hair, a wide mouth, a trace of pale stubble on his unshaven cheeks. She is not in the habit of gazing at strange men, but Tom Call is so uncommonly handsome that she wonders why he isn't in the motion pictures.

"I hope you won't say no to a little breakfast," she says. "You fellows have an awful day ahead."

"I won't say no, ma'am. I barely had time for a cup of coffee this morning."

She pours coffee for Tom Call and Eli before starting breakfast. The men talk in low voices until the telephone rings and Eli goes to answer it. When she turns, she catches the sheriff looking at her. He looks away, embarrassed. "Beg your pardon, ma'am. I didn't expect to find such a beautiful lady way out here."

"Where do you generally find beautiful ladies, Sheriff? Closer to town? Is that where they grow?"

"You're making fun of me."

"Yes, I am. And call me Juanita, please. I'm not that much older than you are."

"No, ma'am."

"How old are you, Sheriff?"

"Thirty-one, ma'am."

"Well, I am forty. I think our ages are close enough that you can stop calling me ma'am, don't you?"

"Yes, ma'am."

"Anyway, I'm glad you're here. I had an awful night, thinking about that girl."

"I expect you did. I didn't sleep none too good myself."

She glances at him, surprised that a lawman would make such an admission. "You're awfully young to be a sheriff, aren't you?"

"Well, yes. But old Gale Gupton decided he was done right before the election and nobody else wanted the job."

"That's not what I heard. I heard that you were a very smart lawman and folks were so impressed with you they wanted you to take Gupton's job, and he figured that if you ran against him he couldn't win, so he decided to quit."

"Well, if that's what you heard, I'm not going to contradict you, ma'am."

Eli walks in on the tail end of the conversation and gives Juanita a quizzical look. "That was my brother Ezra on the phone," he says. "He's on the way over with my grandson Ben. They're bringing a team and wagon."

"I meant to ask if you had a team. I don't think we can get her out of there any other way. I hate to put you folks out like this."

"Taint you putting us out. It's the sonofabitch that killed that poor girl."

"I've got a deputy bringing Doc Pritchard out later. He's the medical examiner. We can't move her until he gets here, but I'd sooner not wait. He's going to be at the hospital until near noon. You have somebody who can show them the way?"

"Any one of the hands can find that shack. There will be somebody around the bunkhouse."

The men eat quickly, not saying much. Juanita wishes they would linger. It's not a day when she wants to be alone. She sees the wagon roll in, Ezra on the seat driving a matched team of Percherons, Ben riding alongside on a pale Appaloosa mare with a spray of cast-iron blotches on her flanks. Tom shakes hands all around. Ezra is Eli, recast in a less serious mold: twin brothers alike in every other way, with their graying hair and dark skin and hawklike features. Ben Paint, grandson to Eli and adopted son to Ezra, is a younger and taller version of the twins, taller than Tom Call himself and about two of him across. Ezra's wife, Jolene, has already fed them, but Ezra and Ben down steaming cups of coffee while Call and Eli finish up. When Eli stands and reaches for his hat, the others follow.

There is a stiff breeze, but it's fresh and warm. Clouds roll over the prairie, but the rain has swept off toward the mountains. The sun breaks through as Eli saddles the horses, the big sorrel Monte for himself, a gentle bay mare for Sheriff Call. Ezra climbs onto the wagon box, eases the brake off, and clucks to the Percherons. Their muscular haunches strain and the tall thin wagon wheels slice through the mud. Eli leads the way with Tom beside him on the mare. Ben's Appaloosa trots alongside the wagon. The rain has melted most of the snow except in the shady spots, but the ground is muddy underfoot and the horses throw up big gobs of mud with every stride. Barn swallows dip and rise, chasing the no-see-um bugs that always come out in thick droves after a rain. Tom has never thought of Wyoming as a place for flowers, but the prairie is splashed with color from one horizon to the other. Meadowlarks sing, a couple of high-flying hawks circle overhead. The ground climbs steadily as they ride. When they rein up at the top of a long rise to wait for the wagon, they can see the way the country opens up, all the way from the Powder River east toward the Black Hills.

They ride for two miles before Eli breaks the silence. "Helluva thing," he says.

"It is."

"Spring bustin out all over and a dead girl waiting up there. Aint right. Is this the first murder on your watch?"

"No, but the other one was no big mystery. Two oil roughnecks got into it in a saloon. One went out to the truck and got a ball-peen hammer and beat the other one's brains out. Don't take much law to untangle that."

"This could be a different sort of knot."

"I know that, and I can't say I look forward to it. Anyone you know match this fella that your foreman calls Baby Foot? I couldn't sleep last night, trying to think of men I know of with little feet."

"There's only Willie Thaw, the foreman I had to fire. Willie has the smallest feet I ever saw."

"Where's Willie now?"

"Working for Bill Bury down on the Crazy Woman."

"William Bury. From what I know, that man is one hundred percent purebred sonofabitch."

"Aw, I think he might be about a quarter polecat."

"You twisted his tail with them mustangs. Sooner or later, Bill is going to come at you."

"Maybe. But I don't see him killing that girl as a way to get at me. The calves, maybe, but that's awful penny-ante for an operator that owns land and banks and oil refineries from Mexico to Montana."

Tom listens to the creak of the harness behind them. The last rags of cloud drift away, leaving the prairie green and burnished as far as a man can see. "Bill is a vindictive sonofabitch. The whole state knows you made a fool of him."

"I'd say he made a fool of himself."

"That aint how he would see it. He isn't a man to take an insult kindly. They say he was thrown through a hotel window down in Midland when he was a young oil wildcatter. That's why he's got all them scars all over his head. The three old boys that done the throwing, they were hard cases. It took two years, but they all met with one sort of accident or another. They could never tie any of it to Bill. Seems he was always in another state when it happened."

"That would be Bill's way," Eli says. "Keep himself out of it, but no pussyfooting around. He'd fix it for me to get tangled up in a threshing machine, but I don't believe he'd fool around with skinning calves."

"Was there something personal between you two?"

Eli shakes his head. "Other than the mustangs, no. I met the man a time or two, and I have about the same affection for him that I have for a rattlesnake, but it wasn't personal. We turned those mustangs loose because there were some fine animals in the bunch. We didn't want to see them turned into dog food."

"That makes sense."

"It seemed right at the time. If you want to understand Bill Bury, you got to go up to Butte, Montana."

"Why's that?"

"The Anaconda mine. You see that place once, you never get over it. It's the ugliest thing I've ever laid eyes on. Miles and miles of ugly. There's that big smokestack of the Washoe Smelter, six hundred feet high. For miles around the smelter, it's like the belly of hell. Sulfur fumes and charcoal fires, gray hills stripped of every last living thing, dumps of yellow ore, trees stripped of their leaves, dingy little houses where the miners try to live with their families on five dollars a day. The company fights like hell to avoid paying a dime in taxes to the state of Montana, and Bill

Bury owns a big piece of the Anaconda Copper Company. Every time I hear his name, I think of that mine."

They climb a long hill and as they top the crest, they see beneath them a green meadow more than a mile across. In the center of it is a cluster of a half dozen stock tanks linked to as many windmills. As they jog down toward the tanks, Two Spuds catches up on his pinto, his arm still in the sling. With his good hand, he points to the tanks, where a hundred head of cattle are milling around. They are bawling, but they aren't drinking.

"Sonofabitch shot holes in the water tanks."

The tiny boot tracks are plain in the muddy ground: Baby Foot walked around each tank, firing holes into it. Two Spuds shows that he can put one of his thick fingers through the bullet holes. Ben jumps down and picks up two or three ejected cartridges and hands them to Tom.

"These here are .45-caliber," the sheriff says. "Heavy slugs. Somebody wanted to leave you with some thirsty cows."

They find dozens of cartridges on the ground and a few flattened, misshapen lead slugs left in the tanks. They ride on along the fence line and climb down for a closer look at the gap where the wire has been cut. The rain has melted most of the snow and washed away some of the tracks, but there are still a half dozen clear prints. Tom points to the angle of the cuts in the wire. "There's something else we can take to the bank. Your wire cutter is left-handed."

When they come to the remnants of the first slaughtered calf, the sheriff calls a halt and walks over the site with some care. Predators have been at the remains. The bones have been scattered, some already picked white. Eli confers briefly with Ezra, out of earshot of the others.

They ride on, through the last gap in the wire, onto the ten-thousand-acre parcel of land that Eli sold when he had to give up half the ranch in order to save the other half. Five hundred feet from the sheepherder's cabin, they see clearly where Baby Foot veered off to the west, toward the mountains.

The Percherons plod on; the wagon rolls downhill toward the shack. Call tries to remember a prayer from his childhood, but the only thing that comes to him is *Now I lay me down to sleep, I pray the Lord my soul to keep.* At times like this, he thinks, a man needs God. Or something like Him.

Eli sets the brake on the wagon. Two Spuds dismounts and ties the pinto to the hitching post. He starts to lead the way into the shack, but Call waves him back.

"I'd best do this alone," the sheriff says. "I don't want too many folks disturbing whatever evidence we've got in there."

He sets his hat squarely on his head and pushes the door open. He's met by a horde of buzzing flies. Overnight, the warm weather has brought the flies. The sweet, sickening smell claws at his throat. He reaches into his shirt pocket for a handkerchief, holds it to his nose, steps into the dark of the cabin. Inside, he avoids looking at the cot until he has lit the kerosene lantern. Once he has it burning well, he sets it on a high shelf and delicately plucks away the burlap bags Two Spuds used to cover the body. He sees the dark, yawning wound, the flies, the young face that now has no age but the age of death. Then he's reeling out the door, vomiting until he's empty, gasping for fresh air.

Two Spuds reaches into the wagon and hands the sheriff a canvas water bag. He rinses his mouth and face and hands and drinks deeply. He's a fair-skinned man at the best of times, but now he is as pale as a sack of flour.

"Maybe I should have gone easy on the bacon and eggs," he says.

Eli shrugs. "Maybe so. You want us to come in with you now?"

"Thank you kindly, but I can do this. I have to. You don't."

Tom takes another sip of water and a deep breath of fresh air and steps back indoors. He removes a notebook and a stub of pencil from his pants pocket and notes the position of the body, the pigging strings used to tie the girl, the nature of the wound, the detritus in the cabin: the spiderwebs, mouse droppings, empty tuna-fish cans, cigarette butts, lumps of chewing tobacco, a yellowed newspaper photograph of Jean Harlow in an evening gown. There are engravings of bathing beauties on the walls so ancient that the young women who posed for the artist must be old ladies by now. Worn lariats, a jumble of bits and bridles, old harness straps, empty boxes of patent medicines. He removes the remaining burlap bags from the girl's body and notes that she wears a blue dress, which is pulled up around her waist, and that there is a pool of blackened blood between her thighs that matches in shade and texture the blood on the pine floor where her throat has been cut.

Doing his work thoroughly keeps the horror at bay. He takes care to leave everything in the cabin just as it is, except for the gunnysacks, which he replaces when he is through. He lifts the lantern and turns in a slow circle, sweeping it high and low to see if there is anything he has missed. He turns the wick until the flame gutters out. Outside, he pauses to mop his brow. Then he walks around the cabin in a slow circle. Two Spuds, seeing what he is about, does the same in the opposite direction, casting for sign. They each make three circuits of the shack and find the same thing: the only visible boot prints belong to Two Spuds and the sheriff himself. Anything else has been washed away by the rain. There is no sign that Baby Foot or anyone else has been here.

Tom squats next to Eli in the shade of the wagon. "I don't believe there's anything more we can do until Doc Pritchard gets here," he says. "There will be more folks tomorrow. Highway patrol investigators, the county attorney. You'll have rubberneckers, too, once word gets out. If you want, I can try to route everybody from the county road, keep them off your place."

"I won't allow rubberneckers to trespass, but folks like yourself who have a job to do are welcome to use the house and anything else you need." Eli squints at the horizon, as though he might find an answer out there somewhere. "Seems to me we don't have much of anything, except those little boots."

"Little boots and a dead girl. That's about it. The highway patrol will send an investigator. Maybe he'll find something we missed."

"I wish I believed that."

* * *

It's after dark when the wagon pulls up in front of the big house on the 8T8. Juanita watches from the veranda as the men work by the light of two kerosene lanterns to transfer the body to Doc Pritchard's morgue ambulance. The ambulance leaves with Strother Leach driving. Tom Call waves before he climbs back behind the wheel of his cruiser. Juanita waves back, timidly, and watches until the taillights vanish.

Tom Call is back at the 8T8 the next morning and the morning after that. He has to escort the county attorney, two investigators from the highway patrol, Sheriff Bill Brower from Gillette, and an FBI agent named Turlington Watt, who insists that the agency should be on the case because of the Mann Act, which prohibits the interstate transport of females for immoral purposes. Tom points out that as far as anyone knows, the Stojko girl was abducted from the Sheridan bus station in Wyoming and found just north of the 8T8 ranch, also in Wyoming, and that there's no reason to suspect her killer had so much as crossed the Montana line while traveling from one point to another. There are also reporters around. The sheriff tries to say as little as possible, but they are pesky as deerflies. Turlington Watt tells one of them about the killer's small feet, how Two Spuds calls him Baby Foot. The next morning, "Baby Foot" is splashed all over the headlines. Tom has taken some pains to point out that there is nothing to link the man who killed the calves on the 8T8 with the suspect who murdered Millie Stojko, but the newspapermen are happy to make the connection for him.

Eli keeps the lawmen supplied with horses, and Juanita feeds them. She worries about Tom. He seems more gaunt by the day. She can see from the dark circles under his eyes that he's not sleeping. She wants to feed him, listen to his trials, rub his shoulders at the end of a long day. She tries not to think about any possibility beyond that, but it is as though he has her wired to an electrical current. Whenever he's around, every nerve ending is alive.

When he can get away, Tom drives down to the Crazy Woman outfit to see Willie Thaw. It's roundup time on the Crazy Woman, as it is on the 8T8, and he loses the better part of the morning chasing around from one pasture to another before he locates Willie and his sidekick,

Zeke Ketcham, squatting in the shade of a stock tank with their backs resting against the cool metal, eating their noontime biscuits and beans.

Word of the strange doings on the 8T8 has reached the Crazy Woman. When Willie sees the sheriff step out of his patrol car, he holds up his right boot. "What do you think, Sheriff? Boots small enough for ya? You want to see how quick I can skin a calf?"

"That aint funny, Willie."

"Aw, I think it's about the funniest thing I heard this year. That old skinflint Eli Paint getting what he has coming, that's funny. Don't you think so, Zeke?"

Zeke Ketcham has a grin that is about six teeth short of a smile. "Doggone right. That sonofabitch stole my hog. Is this where I go to report a stole hog, Sheriff?"

Tom squats next to Willie. There are a dozen other cowboys lounging around, some sprawled for a nap with their hats pulled down over their eyes, three or four playing cards on a saddle blanket, all of them pretending they aren't watching to see how the sheriff will handle this.

"Eli says you're welcome to come get your hog any time. He's tired of the damned thing following him around all day."

"It's fifty, sixty miles to the 8T8. How am I supposed to get a boar all the way down here? Drive it? Like you would a steer?"

"Might work. That thing is big as a steer. Or you could ride it. Anyhow, that's your lookout. You can't claim it was stolen if you left it behind."

He turns his attention to Willie. "If you know what this is about, Willie, why don't you tell me where you were around the time we got those three days of rain."

"Wet. That's where I was. I was definitely wet."

"Wet behind the ears, maybe. Since you've got about the smallest feet around, I'd like to know where you were."

"Why are you down here after me? What about Shorty Dix? I couldn't squeeze my foot into Shorty's boot. I talked to Shorty's old woman one time. She told me his feet is so little because they had to save it all for his pecker. She claims that little man has a pecker like a donkey."

"I'll talk to Shorty Dix, but he doesn't have a beef with Eli. You do. Now you haven't answered my question, so let's try it one more time. Tell me what I need to know, and we'll get this over with. Where were you?"

"I was right here on the Crazy Woman through all that rain. Settin in the bunkhouse, mostly, losing money to Hank Boyd over there. Man is a card player. Must of took me for fifty, sixty dollars."

"That true, Hank?"

Boyd nods. "We hardly stuck our noses outside. Too busy moving buckets around to all the places where that bunkhouse roof leaks."

Tom looks back to Willie. "So which one is your roping hand, Willie? Right or left?"

"Right. I don't even whack my peter with my left hand."

"What about your boots? What size are they?"

"Size six. Been the same since I was thirteen years old. You want to measure my foot?"

Before Tom can answer, Willie pulls his left boot off and hands it over. There are a half dozen holes in his sock, and it looks as though Willie hasn't washed his feet in a year. Tom doesn't need a tape measure to know that this boot is a good two sizes bigger than the prints left on the 8T8.

"Well, Sheriff?"

"Don't appear to be a match." Tom tips his hat. "Thank you kindly for your time. I'm just as glad I don't have to run you in. Your feet stink to high heaven. Don't know how I'd ever get that smell out of my automobile."

He heads back to the office, feeling grumpy and frustrated. He barely has time to sit down before the phone rings. It's Bill Brower, the sheriff of Campbell County, calling to say that he has Bosko Markovic in custody. Markovic is Millie Stojko's stepfather, a miner who worked with Millie's father before he was killed in a mine accident. Brower has talked to a girl named Susanna Fowler, Millie's best friend at the high school in Gillette. The girl says that the stepfather was in the habit of climbing into Millie's bed and that he threatened to kill her if she told anyone. Brower asks if Tom might want to drive over to Gillette, help sweat

Markovic for a while, see if he won't confess and save them a whole lot of trouble.

"There's nothing I'd rather do. I'll be there inside of two hours."

The drive is pleasant enough, but Gillette is a sorry little mining town of two thousand souls eighty miles southeast of Sheridan. He never visits the place without thinking how fortunate he is to have gone to work in Sheridan. Sheridan has better than ten thousand people, paved streets, and a conspicuous lack of miners. Not a single street in Gillette is paved. The red scoria that is the prevailing rock around the town has been ground to red dust, so the streets are either dust or mud. With all the rain, it's mud this season. Red mud, sticky as chewing gum. Tom's boots are stuck with it before he is three steps from the patrol car.

Sheriff Brower has the weariness of a man who has been enforcing the law in a tough town way too long. He has a wad of chewing tobacco tucked in one cheek, his lips are flecked with tobacco, and there are spots on his shirt where he's aimed a little short when he spat his chaw. Some folks take him for a slovenly old fool, but Tom knows that Brower is one of the best lawmen in Wyoming. Before the prisoner is brought in, Tom sits in Brower's office, sipping a mug of bitter black coffee while Brower fills him on the character he is about to meet.

"Typical Bohemian miner," Brower says. "Tough as whalebone. I don't expect he'll have anything to say, but it's always worth a shot."

"You think he's our man?"

"I know he did one thing to her, on a regular basis. And he threatened to kill her. I'd say that makes him a pretty good suspect."

A deputy brings Bosko Markovic into the office. Brower directs him to a seat, asks if he wants a cup of coffee.

"Fuck you. Turn me loose."

"We might do that, Bosko. We might. Or we might hang you. First I want you to talk with this man. This here is Tom Call. He's the sheriff over in Sheridan County, where your stepdaughter went missing. He's going to ask you some questions, and I'd be much obliged if you told the truth."

"I told you the truth yesterday. I don't know what happen to that little bitch."

"Then you can tell Sheriff Call the same thing."

Tom slides his chair up where he can get a better look at Markovic's pockmarked face.

"How long have you been in Wyoming, Bosko?"

"Seven years. Three more years, I go home to Belgrade."

"Are you in cahoots with the Nazis? They're running Yugoslavia these days, aren't they? How long did that war last? Eleven days, I believe."

"Fuck you. One more year, we throw them out."

"If you say so. Does your wife know about this little plan?"

"Fuck her. She's a drunk and her daughter is a bitch."

"Was, Bosko. Was. Let's show a little respect for the dead. Is that why you came here? To make money?"

"Why else come here? It's like miners say. This place is asshole of the earth."

"If I spent all my time working the mine, I might say the same thing. Where were you when Millie disappeared, Bosko?"

"How the fuck I know? I am in the mine or in the saloon. Noplace else. I don't give a shit what happen to her."

"Were you asleep when she left home?"

"In my bed."

"Not in the girl's bed?"

"Fuck you. She is a lying bitch."

"If you hate her that much, you might have driven over to Sheridan and grabbed her at the bus station."

"I don't know nothing about her. Somebody kill her, maybe you should ask the man that did it."

"Maybe I am asking him."

"Fuck you."

"Have you ever been around the bus station in Sheridan, Bosko?"

"Never. I take the train from Chicago to Wyoming, I come to Gillette, I work in the mines. I know this miner, Herman Stojko. We are friends. Nice man, but he is killed in the mine. Chain break, a big bucket of coal falls down. Crush him like a bug. I marry his woman, raise his daughter like my own. Feed the little bitch. She eat a lot. I got no automobile, I got no money to go nowhere."

Brower interrupts. "The county records say you own a 1929 Ford. You could have driven to Sheridan and grabbed her at the bus station."

"Fuck you. Go to my house. You find that Ford out back, sitting on blocks. It don't run."

Tom leans a little closer to the man, wanting to see his reaction. "When was the last time you saw Millie, Bosko?"

"How many times I got to tell you? She was in bed when I come home from the saloon. Next day, she is gone. With my money and my smokes. Next day after that, she is still gone. I don't give a shit. I go again to the saloon, but I have no money. Drink on credit. She is thief, that one."

"She stole from you, she told her friend that you were doing terrible things to her. Seems that could be reason enough to kill her, Bosko."

"I told you. I don't touch this little bitch. I go to work, I go to saloon, I come home and screw the old lady, I sleep. Nothing else."

"What if I had a witness who puts you in the Sheridan bus station the night she disappeared?"

"Witness is lying pig."

They go around in circles for another fifteen minutes. Tom starts counting the number of times Markovic says *fuck you*. He is past twenty when he loses track. They get nothing at all out of the man. There are other methods, but Tom doesn't believe in beating a confession out of a suspect and Bosko Markovic is a hard man. They could knock him around all night without learning a thing. Tom nods to Brower and the deputy comes to take Markovic back to his cell. Brower stares out the window at the muddy street as he works a fresh chaw of Beechnut tobacco in his jaw.

"I don't believe he killed the girl," Brower says.

"What makes you say that?"

"He says so."

"Is that all it takes?"

"When you been in this long enough, you get an itch when a man is guilty. We're not going to sweat it out of him. It's like he said, he was either in the mine, or at home with the wife, or drinking at the saloon. I don't think he could find Sheridan with a road map, if he was sober enough to drive when he wasn't in the mines. Then he would have to get her from Sheridan to that shack where she was found, and how would he know that cabin was there in the first place? Then we get the sixty-four-dollar question—where would he get a car?"

"Another miner?"

"I could count on the fingers of one hand the miners who own an automobile good enough to make it to Sheridan and back."

"There are days when I think flying planes was easier than this. I wish that preacher's wife was a better witness."

"Didn't she say the fellow wore a cowboy hat? That's something."

"She said that at first. Then she wasn't so sure. She wasn't sure about a damned thing, that was the trouble. A man came up and talked to the girl, then the two of them disappeared around the corner behind the bus station. She's about the worst witness I ever talked to."

"Well, I don't believe Bosko is our man. He's a bastard, but he aint that kind of bastard. I don't doubt that he molested that little girl, but we'd never be able to prove it. He's a mean drunk, he was surely taking advantage of her, and I wish I could keep him in jail on general principles. But I can't. He had no car, no easy way to get to Sheridan. He'd have to be missing from here for at least a day if he killed her, and he never missed an hour of work or an hour of drinking, far as I know. I'm going to have to turn him loose."

Tom shrugs. "I can't object. I wish to hell it was him, though. Otherwise, we might never find out what happened to that girl."

"That's the kind of thing you have to get used to in this business. There are always things you can't settle, like an itch inside a cast that you can't scratch. You'll go to bed and something that happened thirty years ago will come back at you, and at three o'clock in the morning, you're still layin there tryin to sort it all out."

"Jesus, I hope not."

"Could be that every lawman carries one of those around. I wasn't yet thirty years old when Dora Tanner was killed. Wife of a mining big-shot name of Woodrow Tanner. Pretty young thing, had a baby girl six months old. Tanner claimed that he went on a trip to Denver, came home to find his wife beat to death, baby bawling in her crib. Murder weapon was an old flatiron, heavy as hell. Window had been busted in the back of the house, like it might have been a robbery, except nothing was stole. I went at it night and day for a month, I couldn't get no farther than that. Right from the get-go, I thought Tanner done it and that he busted the window to throw us off the track. At the time she was killed, Tanner was supposedly on a train back from Denver. I couldn't come up with a witness who could prove he wasn't on that train. He didn't have his ticket and the conductor didn't remember him and the only man willing to say he rode that train was old Digger Boudreaux, a drunk who was on Tanner's payroll. Not much of a witness, but one more witness than I had. No prosecutor is going to try a case against a millionaire with no more to go on than that. That's where it died. For twenty-five years after Dora Tanner was killed, I had to see that rich weasel almost every day, driving around town in his Cadillac like he owned the god-damn world. It wasn't six months before he had another young wife. I had nightmares about Dora, thought she would haunt me to my dying day unless I brought him in. I never got the chance, but his car stalled on a railroad track about ten years ago. An eastbound freight train did what the hangman ought to have done, took care of Woodrow Tanner, once and for all. I've slept some better since."

8.

I T IS NOT A GOOD NIGHT FOR HUNTING. ANOTHER May snowstorm, most folks indoors. He has been to the bus station three times and the train station once, with no luck. Now he's simply driving, aimlessly, the big black 1940 Packard with the whitewall tires gliding up and down. He doesn't mind. He has all the time in the world. He prefers it this way, not knowing. Not knowing if he will see someone, not knowing if she'll get in the car, not knowing what he'll do with her if she does. It's better not to know until the last moment, when it all becomes clear. It's the moment of clarity that he seeks. The moment when he knows. Life is such a muddle, a man is pulled this way and that. There are few times when he can be absolutely clear about anything at all, but in this, when it happens, he is absolutely clear. Clear and powerful, secure in his power. Until then, he waits to see what will happen, like a man sitting in the back row during the last reel of a motion-picture show. Jittery, biting his fingernails, waiting for that one pure moment, before the credits begin to roll and people start putting on their coats, talking about the hero and the heroine and the villain. Siding with the hero, because that's the way people are. But remembering the villain. It's always the villain he remembers.

He was twelve years old when his mother took him to see Peter Lorre in a picture show called *M*. She had already left his father and they were living in Denver then. She had only three years to live, although they didn't know it. They were as close as lovers, they did everything together. When she saw how much he liked the movie, she took him back every day for a week. They would finish their popcorn during the cartoons and then settle down in the darkness to watch. When it got too scary for her, she would hold tight to his hand and press her breast against his arm. Sometimes they would stay and watch it twice, with the cartoons and the newsreels and the B movie. As they left the theater, he would try to whistle like Peter Lorre. He repeated over and over one of Lorre's lines from the film, which he read in the subtitles on the screen. *Who knows what it's like to be me?* At night she would tell him she was too frightened to be alone and invite him into her bed. Then she would say it was too hot with him there and she would pull her gown off and push him down between her legs. Later, she would hold him tight, his bare chest against her naked breasts, and she would tell him that he was becoming a real man and that he was the one she could turn to when she was afraid in the darkness.

He tries to remember the tune Peter Lorre whistled. It won't come to him, and anyway, it's too cold to whistle. He takes a right turn and a left. There's a light on in a little yellow house on South Custer Street. He can see a young woman at the stove. He glides by once, twice, three times. There's a boy there, too, sitting at the kitchen table. She won't come out. Why would she, on a night like this?

In the house on South Custer Street, the dishes have been washed and stacked, the leftovers put away. The boy they call Red is at the kitchen table, bent over his multiplication tables. Emaline can smell the freshness of the wet snow through the open window above the sink. It's the kind of warm, snowy evening when she loves to go for a walk. Red still has pages of his math to do. She always makes him finish his homework on Friday night, so they will have the weekend free. She will have plenty of time to walk.

She tousles his hair. "It's such a lovely snowfall. I'm going out for a walk, honey. I won't go far. I'll be back in an hour, maybe less."

"Sure, Mom. I'd come with you if I didn't have homework." He grins up at her. She is not his mother, not biologically or even legally, but she is his mother in the ways that matter and she adores the boy. He is nine years old and he is everything she could want in a son, even if he isn't legally hers.

She puts on her coat, ties a wool scarf over her hair, pulls overshoes onto her stocking feet, buckles them all the way up, and starts out. The overshoes are a size too big for her, and they flop as she walks, but they will keep her feet dry. As she steps onto the sidewalk, a dark form emerges from the snow and startles her. She steps back and puts a hand to her heart, then laughs in relief. It's just her neighbor, Evan Connell, out walking his big dog. Connell tips his hat. "How do, Emaline?"

"I'm doing just dandy, Mr. Connell. How bout you?"

"Just fine, ma'am. That Zane Grey you told me to read is the best one I've read yet. I'll be back for a new one on Tuesday."

"I'll see you then," she sings out over her shoulder. "This time, I'm going to make you check out *Riders of the Purple Sage*." If she lingers, Mr. Connell will talk her ear off about western history, especially anything to do with General Custer, and western novels. Emaline has read a few westerns, simply because the patrons at the library most often want them, but the only one she genuinely likes is Owen Wister's *The Virginian*, and even that is too long by half. For her own reading, she prefers Chekhov or Balzac.

From Custer Street, she walks up North Main and follows West Alger Street along the curve of Whitney Commons. The Commons is lovely with the fresh snow falling. She lingers in the park longer than usual, breathing the fresh mountain air, feeling happy to be alive. There is a streetlight at the far corner of the park and she walks toward it, her face tilted up, letting the snow fall on her eyelashes and her tongue, feeling as though she is ten years old. There is a cluster of aspen and birch and lodgepole pine near the corner, a hint of forest in the way they stand together. She strolls through the trees, playing a kid's game, grabbing the narrow trunk of one tree and pulling herself around, then taking the next tree with her free hand and circling it, around and around, from one tree to the next, laughing and shaking herself when a pine bough dumps a load of wet snow down her neck. Once out of the park, she walks on, heading north along the western outskirts of the town, intending to turn back soon, too entranced by the snow to give up her walk just yet.

She has walked perhaps a half dozen blocks past the Commons when she hears an automobile engine behind her and turns to look. It's a hundred yards back, crawling along the street as though the driver were searching for an address. She walks more quickly, but the car remains at about the same distance behind her. She shrugs, tells herself not to worry. It could be an elderly driver. There are old folks in town who drive everywhere without shifting out of first gear.

She is on a narrow road without streetlights. The houses here are more like tumbledown shacks, half of them abandoned behind rusting wire fence. The hulks of old automobiles crouch on blocks in yards that in summer are nothing but weeds and dust. Snow drifts through shattered windows. In one of the few occupied houses, an old man sits at the window next to a bright lamp, staring out, so motionless he might be dead. She waves anxiously, wanting a response, but he does not wave back. She hurries a little, looking for a street where she can turn back to the east, spooked by the darkness and the dead houses and the dark car still purring along behind her, its tires crunching in the snow. She turns her head, trying to see if the driver is someone she might know, but in the glare of the headlights, she can tell only that it is a large black automobile with whitewall tires. When she looks again a moment later, the car has vanished. She presses her palm to her chest. She can feel her heart beating against her ribs. *Silly woman*, she thinks. This is Sheridan, not Chicago or New York or Denver.

She is about to turn to the east when she sees what appears to be the same car, a black Packard, at the stop sign a block down. The headlights are off, but she can hear the engine running. She hesitates a moment, then turns back the way she has come. Now she is jogging, almost running, the rubber overshoes awkward and heavy. She rounds a curve and reaches a lot which is a jumble of old farm machinery, harrows and plows and ancient tractors, ghostly in the snow. She keeps her head down and slows to a walk. She has almost reached the edge of the lot when she sees the automobile again, parked next to an old combine. She has to stifle a scream. She is about to run when she hears a voice behind her.

Are you at peace with the Lord?

He steps out of the shadows of the rusty combine, a man in a long, dark coat, a black cowboy hat covered with oilskin pulled low over his face. She turns to face him.

"What did you say?"

Are you at peace with the Lord?

"I don't know who you are, mister, but I don't believe that's any of your business."

"Seems a reasonable question. Most folks know the answer. *Are you at peace with the Lord?*"

She stands motionless, willing herself to run. All the strength seems to have gone from her legs. He pulls something out of the pocket of the slicker. A box of wooden matches. He strikes one and holds it to her face, so close she can feel the heat on her cheek. She tries to get a look at his face, but his features are hidden under the brim of the hat.

"Leave me alone."

"Maybe I will, but you aint answered my question. *Are you at peace with the Lord?*"

"I told you. That's none of your business."

"And the priest shall take of the blood of the sin offering with his finger, and put it upon the horns of the altar of burnt offering, and shall pour out all the blood thereof . . ."

His voice has changed. It's now deep and sonorous, as though the devil himself has taken to spouting scripture. He's trying to frighten her. It makes her angry. "What are you babbling about?"

"Maybe you aint been to church enough, lady. Maybe that's why you aint at peace with the Lord. It's the word of God. It's right there in Leviticus: *And if he bring a lamb for a sin offering, he shall bring it a female without blemish. And he shall lay his hand upon the head of the sin offering, and slay it . . ."*

She sees something flash in his hand. It could be a knife blade, held low against his thigh. She doesn't wait to be certain. She turns and runs, runs as she hasn't run in years, slipping and sliding through the snow, desperate to get away. She makes it a hundred feet before she trips on the overshoes and falls heavily, hurting her elbow. She kicks the overshoes away and is off again, running in her stocking feet, across North Main and Gould Street to Broadway, south to First Street and across the Burlington Railroad tracks. She does not look back until she has crossed the tracks. Then she risks a glance: there is no one behind her.

She slows to a walk, angry that in her flight she has lost her overshoes and her best scarf. On wet feet, she pads around the corner, turns south, and walks the last block to home, gasping for breath. She sees Red in the window, still bent over his homework. She opens the door and steps into the warmth of the house. She stoops and peels off her wet stockings and bends over with her hands on her thighs, gasping for breath, her hair wild and disheveled.

Red looks up from his schoolwork. "Mom! What happened to you?"

"It's nothing, sweetie," she says. "It's really nothing."

"You look like you're scared to death. What happened to your over-shoes?"

"I was running. I lost them."

"Why were you running?"

"I ran into a strange man who started quoting scripture at me. He frightened me a bit. I'm sure it was nothing."

Red stands to hug her. "I'm sorry he scared you. I finished my arithmetic and now I have to write a paragraph about the Blitz. Can you help me?"

"Just a minute. Let me dry my feet and wash my face and warm up a bit. Do you want some hot cocoa?"

"Sure."

"I'll put some milk on to warm." She starts toward the kitchen, then turns back and locks the bolt on the front door. It's the first time since they moved into the house that she has even thought of locking the bolt.

When she pours Red's cocoa, her hand is shaking so badly that she slops the hot liquid all over the table and has to wipe it up. She is sipping her own cocoa when she remembers the dead girl, the one who disappeared from the bus station and was found near the 8T8.

Emaline waits until Red is asleep to call the sheriff. She doesn't want to frighten the boy. A deputy answers, says his name is Strother Leach. She tells him about the man who confronted her. She can't say for sure whether he had a knife in his hand, but he has frightened her badly.

Strother yawns. "I wouldn't worry about it, ma'am," he says. "We've had all kinds of calls since that girl was took. Don't amount to a hill of beans. Sounds like you ran into some kind of religious nut. I wouldn't lose any sleep over it."

"Aren't you going to send someone over?"

"I'm the only one here just now. Sheriff Call, he had to drive over to Gillette today. He's been workin so hard on all this, he's just about played out. He went home and left me in charge. I'm alone here, so I can't just up and leave."

"What if the man I saw is a killer?"

"Now, now. People get to thinking all sorts of things at a time like this. Don't you worry your pretty little head. We'll catch the fella who killed that girl and that will be an end to it."

Strother hangs up. Emaline paces a bit, then picks up the telephone and asks the operator to put her through to the 8T8. When she tells Juanita what has happened, Juanita is furious. "Strother Leach is lazy and incompetent," she says. "You should call Tom at home, tell him what happened."

"I can't do that."

"Why not? He's the sheriff. He wants to catch this guy."

"It's late now. I'll call tomorrow, when he's at work."

"If you're too shy, I'll call him myself. If I know Tom, he'll want to talk to you right away."

Tom Call is trying to read a bad western, hoping it will help him get to sleep. When the telephone rings, he has to run out to the kitchen to answer it.

"Tom Call."

"Tom, it's Juanita Paint."

Her name. It's lovely. He feels the energy crackling between them along the telephone line, wants to ask her to say it again just so he can hear it. *Juanita.*

"Hello, Juanita. It's good to hear your voice."

It slips out, but then it was bound to happen sooner or later. She might as well know. He feels her hesitate before she explains the reason for her call.

"Tom, I need a favor. I know it's late, but I was wondering if you could go speak to my friend Emaline tonight. She lives over on Custer Street."

"I know Emaline. She works at the library, right? I'm dog tired, but I'll go." He stopped himself before he could say *if it's important to you.* "What's wrong?"

"Emaline and I are really close. I know her very well and I trust her. She's a tough farm lady, she's not one to get scared over nothing. She went out for a walk tonight and she saw a big black car following her. Then a man scared her half to death, spouting scripture at her. She thinks he might have had a knife. She called Strother Leach, but he wouldn't do a thing. He said he couldn't leave the office because he's alone."

"Strother Leach is the laziest man alive. You can tell her I'll be there in ten minutes."

"Thanks, Tom. The thing is, I thought it might be the same guy who killed the girl from the bus station."

"That's why Strother should have gotten his hind end over there. I'm on my way."

By the time Tom reaches the house on Custer Street, Red is already asleep and Emaline is waiting for him at the door. "I wouldn't have bothered you at home," she says, "but when I told Juanita what happened, she wanted to call you."

"It's a good thing you called. This could be important."

Emaline offers to make him a late supper, but he has already eaten. She brews tea for them instead and they sit at the table in her tidy little kitchen, Tom with his notebook out. She is an attractive woman, maybe thirty years old, with black hair and dark eyes and high cheekbones. He thinks he can see a family resemblance to Eli. She seems very serious, like someone who has had a hard life and doesn't expect any favors.

Tom takes careful notes as Emaline goes through the story. Unlike the Rubottom woman, she is a good witness. She is certain the car was a black Packard with whitewall tires.

"Why were you way out there on a night like this anyhow?"

"I go for walks four or five nights a week. Usually Red goes with me, or Juanita if she's in town, or sometimes one of the ladies from the library. Tonight Red had homework, but it was such a beautiful snowfall I wanted to walk."

Tom knows the lot with the rusting farm machinery. It's owned by a mechanic named Russell Hills, who likes to tinker with machinery. There have been complaints from neighbors who think it's an eyesore, but the town has never done anything about it.

Emaline remembers word for word what the man had said. She has even found the passage in Leviticus and underlined it. She's able to give a pretty good description of the stranger, except that she hasn't seen his face. Something about his mouth and jaw and the way he carries himself left her with the impression he is handsome, but she can't say for sure. She is sure about his height.

"I'm five foot six," she says. "He was wearing cowboy boots, but he was still an inch or two shorter than I am."

"Did he have small feet? Did you notice?"

"I looked down. All I saw was the toes of his boots. I don't know how big they were. Not big, I'm sure of that."

"Do you remember anything else?"

"He talked very softly. I had the feeling it was deliberate, like he's almost whispering, so you have to lean forward to hear what he's saying. And he sounded young. Not more than twenty-five, probably younger than that. He has a southern accent, but not like yours. Where are you from, originally?"

"Louisiana."

"He's more western, I think. Texas, maybe. One of those accents that makes a person sound dumb, no matter how smart he is."

Tom smiles. "Sounds like Texas to me."

When they have gone through it all twice, he puts his notebook away.

"I don't want to pry, ma'am, but where is your husband? Wasn't he a boxer? He could offer you some protection here."

"You're right, he was a boxer. But I left him. He's a hard man to live with."

"As long as this stranger is on the prowl, I wish you had a man staying here."

"I can look out for myself."

"I'll bet. We'll give you what help we can, but we're going to be awful busy investigating this thing."

"I know that. I don't expect any help."

Before he leaves, Tom checks the locks on Emaline's doors. The previous tenant was a fearful soul who installed heavy locks on the front and back doors, unusual for Sheridan. Emaline has rarely locked up, but Tom suggests that she get in the habit.

"Do you own a gun?"

"Just Red's old single-shot .22."

"That's better than nothing. I'd normally advise against it with a youngster in the house, but please keep it loaded and handy. I don't think he'd come after you again, but I'd feel better if you had some protection."

"Don't worry about me. You just catch the man who killed that girl."

"We'll do our best. Ma'am, if it would make you feel better, I could just stretch out on your davenport for tonight."

"Thank you, but we'll be fine. I'll make sure the rifle is loaded, like you said."

"All right, then. But I'd rather you didn't take any more solitary walks for a while, until we catch this fella. I'll call Strother now, tell him to get his lazy behind out of the office. He'll drive by here every so often, just in case."

When Tom leaves, he hears Emaline slide the lock into the door behind him. He's a block from her house when a woman in a green Pontiac waves him down. As he slows, he sees that Juanita is behind the wheel. They sit for a moment with their windows open, trying to talk, and then Juanita parks her car and gets into the big black-and-orange Dodge cruiser and sits next to him.

"I came in to stay with Emaline," she says. "At least for tonight. She sounded pretty scared on the phone."

"I believe she's all right now. She has a rifle with her, and I told her to lock all her doors. It doesn't hurt to be safe."

"That's what I thought. I'll feel better staying with her, at least for tonight. Did she help you?"

"Well, that depends whether it's the same fella that grabbed the girl or not. She did tell me that he's short and that he sounds young, he has a Texas accent and he drives a pretty new black Packard with whitewall tires. I can start by checking all the Packards in the county. If I find one that is owned by a young man with small feet, we'll be on the right track."

"I'll be so relieved when you catch him."

"You sound awful confident that we will."

She puts a hand on his harm. "I am. I think you're very good at what you do. When I first saw you, I thought you were too young to be a sheriff, but you're very careful and very thorough. You don't try to bully people, so they tell you more."

"That's what I try to do, anyhow. Sometimes you get angry. I wanted to hit a prisoner today. We were talking to Bosko Markovic. That's the girl's stepfather, over in Gillette. Appears he was molesting her, but he's an awful tough cookie. All he did was cuss us out. But it don't look like he killed her. He was in Gillette the whole time."

They are silent for a bit, Juanita still resting her hand on his arm. She knows that it's wrong, but it feels right. "This is the first time I've ever been in a police car," she says.

"It's just a car," he says. "Except for the siren and the lights on top."

"Someday I'd like you to run the siren for me. It must be exciting."

"Nothing like flying a plane. I'll take you flying one day. That is exciting."

"I'd love that."

"Then it's a date."

"I should go see to Emaline now."

"I suppose you should."

"It was good talking to you."

She squeezes his arm. She wants to do something else, wants to do everything else, but she forces herself to get out of his car and start the Pontiac and drive on to Emaline's house. As she pulls into the driveway, she can see that Tom is still sitting in the cruiser, watching her in the rearview mirror.

Juanita falls asleep in Emaline's bed. Emaline stays awake, reading Bobby's letters from the Navy. He writes two or three times a week, and she writes to him almost daily. They are only a little more than ten years apart, but Emaline has always been as much a mother to him as a sister and she misses him awfully. His jokes, his sweet tenor voice, his constant good humor. She worries about him, too. There are rumors that if the United States gets into the war against Germany, the *Tennessee* will be sent to the Atlantic to help protect the shipping routes to England. She assumes that the huge battleship is about the safest place a man could be if war breaks out, but she'd feel better if he was back in Wyoming, helping Eli and Ezra on the ranch.

When she sleeps, a strange man in a long, black coat pursues her in her dreams, driving a rusty combine through an endless field of wheat. She runs and runs, but she can never escape the great, slashing blades of the combine. When she wakes, it's barely light and the snow has changed to rain. She hears it pouring off the roof. She rushes to the window, pulls back the blind, and peeks out anxiously. South Custer Street is empty. There is no sign of the black Packard.

LON BURY IS ASLEEP IN THE BIG OLD FEATHER BED in what was once his grandmother's home in Sheridan, and he's having a beautiful dream. He's dreaming of a thick sirloin steak, extra well-done the way he likes it. He's holding his knife and fork and he wants to start eating, but somebody in the kitchen is beating on a countertop with a hammer. The steak looks so good, sitting there on a great big plate surrounded by baked potatoes and carrots and beans and a big hunk of fresh-baked bread. It's a sorry world when a guy can't even eat a steak in peace. He's about to go ahead and eat the steak anyway and to hell with the hammering, but then he hears somebody calling his name.

"Lon! Open the goddamned door. You gonna leave me standing out here all night? Open the door!"

He sits up, looks at the clock. It's two o'clock in the morning. The pounding begins again. "Lon! Open the door! What's wrong with you?"

Pardo. Goddamned Pardo. It's Pardo hammering on the door. The steak was just a dream. He stumbles to the door, jerks it open. Then he remembers that he is stark naked and that when he wakes in the night, he always wakes with a hard-on. It's bobbing in front of him, like a puppet on a string.

"Jesus, Lon, put that thing away before it bites somebody. What the hell's the matter with you? I got to beat the goddamned door down to get you to answer?"

"It's two o'clock in the morning. You was out with my car, so I went to bed. How come you don't have a key to the house?"

"I got a key, but it's still on the ring in your car. C'mon now, let's get going. Bed is for when you're dead." Pardo pushes Lon out of the way. "Get some clothes on, will you? I don't want to look at your peter, and

I don't want to look at your fat, hairy ass. The old man called when you was out this afternoon. He wants to see us, first thing in the morning."

"In Casper?"

"No, you dumb fuck. He wants to see us in Paris. Course he wants to see us in Casper. That's where his office is, aint it?"

"Well, yeah, but we're in Sheridan."

"That's good, Lon. That's real good. You're making progress. You know where you are. Now get your clothes on. We'll stop at the all-night diner on the way out of town."

"Sweet Jesus. If he called this afternoon, why didn't you tell me before?"

"Because I had business, all right? You ask too many dumb questions. Now we got an audience with the man himself. At dawn. Maybe he's gonna have us executed or something, ya think?"

"Geez, don't say that."

"Just get dressed, okay? Naked, you are just about the ugliest thing I ever saw. And pack some clothes, in case we got to stay over."

"How come you know that he wants to see us, anyhow? Why didn't he call here?"

"Cause he thought we'd both be out at the hunting lodge, so he called out there. I told him I'd come get you on the way."

"Is that where you been all this time? The hunting lodge?"

"That's none of your goddamned business, Lon, where I've been." Pardo heads to the refrigerator, helps himself to a Pabst Blue Ribbon, and paces back and forth, drinking the beer and cursing his brother. Ten minutes later, they're out of the house. Lon wants to drive, but Pardo won't let him.

"You aint awake enough to drive. You'll fall asleep before we get out of town."

Pardo knows the waitress at the Bighorn Diner. She's sweet on him, so she throws in a bag of donuts with the coffees. They get back into the car and Pardo drops it into gear and floors it. Lon spills coffee all over his testicles. He is still screaming when they hit the city limits.

Pardo has a canvas water bag under the seat. He opens it and pours water over Lon's steaming crotch.

"Cool down, Brother. Cool down. You got to take better care of a cup of coffee."

"Shit, Pardo. You got to drive better, you asshole. Now it looks like I pissed my pants. This is my car. I get to drive this car. You got that little red roadster. How come you don't take that? You always want my car."

"Shut up, Lon. I drive your car because it's comfortable. We got a long ways to go."

"This aint the way to Casper. This here is the way to Cody. Are we goin to Cody?"

"Nope. We're goin to Casper. Through the mountains."

"But that aint the way, Pardo."

"I know that. I just got the urge to drive through them mountains, is all."

"Fuck the mountains. If we aint at the old man's office in Casper first thing tomorrow morning, he'll just about skin us alive."

"What's wrong with you? You afraid of that old bastard? You're as big as he is."

"Maybe, but I aint as mean. I still remember the time he took a length of cable, like to beat me to death with it."

"You were twelve years old then."

"Damned right I was. Thing like that stays with a fella."

"You weren't big enough to lick him then. You're big enough now."

"Don't matter. Any time I get around him, I start shakin in my boots."

"Not me. He don't scare me one damned bit."

"Maybe not, Pardo. But you're crazy. You aint like most folks."

Pardo giggles, a high-pitched, insane giggle. "I know I aint. Isn't it wonderful, Lon? Aint you glad you got a little brother who aint like all the dumb fucks you meet every day of your life?"

"I dunno, Pardo. You're pretty damned strange, you want to know the truth. Pretty damned strange. You done things, even when you was a kid when we lived in Texas, scare the hell out of everybody."

"Only a scaredy-cat like you. You always was chickenshit, Lon. You're big as a house and strong as a bull, but you're chickenshit. All them muscles aint never gonna do you no good, cause you're chickenshit."

"Maybe it's just that I aint dumb, you ever think of that? I aint dumb enough to do some of the shit you do, is all."

"Oh, no. You're dumb, Lon. You're as dumb as they come. I've known hammers smarter than you. But you don't have to be smart, cause you got me."

Pardo is driving in fourth gear when they hit the first stretch of mountain road. He downshifts into second and the engine screams like it wants to throw a rod. They're fishtailing on loose gravel. Pardo goes into the first turn at fifty miles an hour and floors the gas pedal through the turn, downshifts into the straightaway, and accelerates to near ninety before they hit the next curve. He slams on the brakes and they slide into it sideways. For three or four seconds, Lon can see the headlights trained on the edge of the road, where it drops away to nothing. It looks like they're about to go over the edge, into a drop that will send them tumbling through space, when the tires catch and they're into a hard left turn and then another right and a left. Apart from the slashing beam of the headlights, it is pitch dark. There is no moon, low-hanging clouds obscure the stars. As they round a bend, things pop up in the headlights and vanish almost before they register. A pine tree, a shrub, a startled deer, a boulder big as the car, a road sign warning of another curve. On a sharp left-hand turn, the wheels go into a long skid and the rear end hangs out over a drop that might go down forever. Then the tires bite again. They are around the bend and Pardo runs it up through the gears, accelerating for a quarter mile before they go into the next hairpin turn.

Lon yells until his throat is raw. He curses. He calls Pardo every name he can think of, until he's jabbering, random syllables, sounds coming from his throat that have never been heard before. His neck aches from fighting against the pull of gravity on the turns. He grabs anything he can grab to keep from being flung into Pardo or out the door. If he could get enough purchase, he would punch his brother in the jaw, knock him out and take the wheel, except that in the second or two it would take him to get control of the car they might slam into a boulder or sail off a cliff. Pardo never even gives him a chance to catch his breath. Every time the road is straight for even a hundred yards, Pardo has the throttle wide open and he is going hell for leather into the next bend. Twice, Lon sees the speedometer top a hundred miles an hour. He has come through here in daylight, when fifty feels too fast, and Pardo is doing a hundred.

They top the crest of a hill and hit the western slope, going down faster than they came up. A dozen times, Lon is sure that Pardo has lost it and they're about to plunge to a fiery death. But Pardo somehow rescues it, through skill or blind luck or divine intervention. When they make a last, tight turn and head into a long downward grade on a straightaway, Pardo has to swing over at the last second to avoid a head-on collision with a big cattle truck. If they had met him anywhere in that wild trip over the mountain, they would have piled head-on into the truck and they would both be dead.

At the bottom of the hill, Pardo slams on the brakes. The car fishtails to a halt. He kills the engine and jumps out, vaults onto the hood and stands there in his cowboy boots, strutting back and forth, leaving marks all over the metal. Lon stumbles out and crouches on his knees, vomiting into the underbrush. Pardo ignores him, raises his arms like a boxer basking in the cheers of the crowd. Then he tilts his head back and howls like a wolf. When the last echoes of the howl die out, he is still prancing.

"Sonofabitch!" Pardo roars. "Sonofabitch! Goddamn, that was fun! You ever have so much fun, Lon? Did you piss your pants?"

"You know I did, you crazy sonofabitch. I ought to beat you half to death for that."

"You wouldn't want to try it, Lon. You know you wouldn't. I'd cut your belly open, leave you for the coyotes."

"You're a bastard, Pardo. Nothin but a bastard. You're meaner'n the old man, I swear."

"Fuckin right, I am. And don't you forget it. Now if you're done pissin and pukin, can we get on to Casper?"

"I got to change clothes."

"So change your clothes. You got a bag in the trunk."

Lon opens the trunk, takes out his suitcase, rummages around, finds a change of underwear, clean blue jeans, and a clean shirt. He manages to get his wet jeans and underpants off without removing his boots and is standing there, buck naked except for the boots, when Pardo jumps down and gets behind the wheel and takes off, the back tires throwing gravel against Lon's bare skin. He drives a quarter of a mile with Lon cursing and running after him, slams on the brakes, backs up, waits until his brother has almost caught up, and takes off again. After the third time, he staggers out of the car, laughing so hard he can barely stand.

"Damn, that's the funniest damned thing I ever seen! I look in the mirror and there's old Lon, running down the mountain shakin his fist, with his pecker floppin all over the place. Goddamn, that is funny. Y'know, for such a big sonofabitch, you got a little pecker."

"It's all shrunk up because it's cold out here, you cocksucker. Helluva way to treat your brother. Helluva way."

"You aint more than half my brother."

"The hell I aint."

"You aint. Half. That's all. Look at us. We aint one goddamn bit alike. I aint dumb, for one thing."

"Sweet Jesus. I wish you wasn't my brother. I surely do. I wish you wasn't. I wish you'd never been born."

"Oh, shut it, Lon. Just shut it. Get your damned clothes on and get in the car. And this time, try not to piss yourself."

"Promise me you'll drive like you aint plumb crazy?"

"All right, you big baby. I promise. Get your fat ass in here. I'll drive like a old lady, rest of the way to Casper."

Lon pulls on dry clothes, and they get back in the car. They've driven ten miles at almost normal speeds when Pardo gives him a strange look.

"You ever fuck a virgin, Lon?"

"I have, time or two."

"Feels good, don't it?"

"I guess. I had my druthers, I prefer a girl that knows how it's done."

"Not me. I like 'em tight. I like to feel it when it gives. I had a virgin a while back, or I should have had. I was sure she was virgin. She looked virgin. She smelled virgin. Only she wasn't."

"So what did you do, Pardo?"

"I shacked with her, is all. She was a nice shack job, for about a week. Only she knew a whole lot more than a girl that age ought to know. She was always tryin to please me, thinking I'd be nice to her if she did. It wasn't right. A girl who knows some of the things she knew, she oughtn't to dress like a virgin, you know what I mean? She ought to dress like what she is."

Lon shrugs. He's about to drift off to sleep. "Whatever you say, Pardo. Whatever you say."

The sky is turning pale in the east. They are on paved road now. Pardo waits until Lon is asleep, then he floors it and watches the needle climb. Ninety, a hundred, a hundred and twenty. He tilts his head back and howls again. Howl of the wolf. Lon is so tired, he doesn't hear.

WILLIAM C. BURY SITS IN HIS OFFICE IN Casper, hundred-dollar alligator-hide cowboy boots propped on the glistening mahogany of a ten-foot desk, thinking that there is on this entire earth no solitary thing as beautiful as an oil refinery at sunrise. It is a view to stir a man's heart: the holding tanks, the chain-link fences topped with barbed wire, the smokestacks and catwalks and towers, the long lines of pipe curving in all directions, the earth blackened here and there where oil has gushed or dripped or poured. Above it all, a sign you can read for miles: X-BURY REFINERY.

Bury is a massive man, a half foot over six feet and well over three hundred pounds, with a head like a bull buffalo. His hair is cropped close to a skull that is crosshatched with scars, the result of that dustup in Midland. Another man might grow his hair to hide the scars. Bury shaves his head carefully, so that all the world can see every scar and understand the lengths to which he will go to acquire the things he wants.

Lon and Pardo Bury stand with their hats in their hands, waiting for their father to tell them to sit. The old man leaves them standing while he runs his fingertips up and down the razor-sharp creases in his gabardine trousers, looking for flaws in the ironing so he can humiliate the Chinaman when he gets home. "Well? Are you girls going to stand there all day, or are you going to sit down?"

They sit, Lon so awkwardly that he almost falls out of the chair. They are an unlikely pair: Lon looks exactly like his father, minus the scars. Pardo takes after his mother, a petite blonde who had been considered the prettiest girl in Midland. He's so pretty that the cowpokes on one of Bill's ranches called him "honey," until one of them went too far and woke with a pair of rattlesnakes in his bedroll.

Pardo is smart, but he's about a half bubble off plumb. It leaves the old man with a dilemma. Lon is his firstborn, so there should come a day when he takes over the Bury empire, but there are steers in Wyoming that are smarter than Lon. Lon got the muscles and Pardo got the brains, but with Pardo, it's all twisted around. Twenty years old and he's mean as a weasel. If you let Pardo start getting notions, there's no telling what he might do.

"You girls got a lesson to learn," Bill says. "When I decide to hit a man, I don't tiptoe around. I hit him right between the eyes with a two-by-four. Once you go after a man, you want to ruin him. You want to mess him up, so's the next time he sees you coming, he starts blubbering about his mama with snot running outa his nose. What you don't want to do is to piss him off. You do little things—skin his knees, fuck his woman—all that does is rile him. What you done was to poke a bear with a stick, for no reason at all."

Lon's big moon face is a blank slate. He stares at the floor. "What'd ah do?" he asks. "Ah didn't do nothin." Bill looks Pardo in the eye. "What you done, Pardo, was to get me into a situation here. You done just enough to rile that fellow, without putting him down. Now most times, I welcome trouble. Hell, I love it. But there's a war coming. A world war, not a range war. I aint got time for pissant trouble."

Pardo grins, starts to roll a cigarette, spilling tobacco on the floor. "Hell, I was just throwin a little scare into him."

"That's what you were up to, is it? Kill a few calves, shoot up some water tanks. You think that's apt to scare Eli Paint? Let me tell you a little story, Son. There used to be an outlaw that operated in this part of the country. Big fella, mean as hell. Name of O. T. Yonkee. The way I heard it, Yonkee mistreated some wild horses. Eli took a blacksnake whip to O.T., like to killed him. Eli was seventeen years old at the time. You aim to scare him, you got to be ready to take a licking, just like that outlaw took."

Pardo lights his cigarette. "He's an old man now."

"So am I. And either one of us could give you a whupping you'd never forget."

Pardo laughs. Big Bill rises from his seat, rests both paws on the young man's shoulders, stares at him up close, then backhands him across the face. Pardo sails out of his chair and lands on his back with his head against the wall. The way his neck is bent, Lon thinks maybe it's broke, but Pardo rolls to his knees, with blood gushing from his nose over the thick pile of the carpet. He picks up his chair and sits with his head in his hands, blood pouring into his handkerchief. Bill pays him no mind.

"I was trying to decide which one of you jackasses to send to Texas. Now I made up my mind. You're both going, first thing tomorrow morning. There's a fellow in Galveston, name of Hewlitt Monroe. Owes me a whole lot of money. You'll collect and bring it home, safe and sound."

Pardo, his voice thick with his own blood, objects. "I'll go to Texas, but I don't want to go with Lon. He's dumber than fertilizer."

"Talk that way about your brother again and I'll break your other nose. Lon is going with you."

"What if Hewlitt don't want to pay?"

"Burn his house down, if you got to. I said you're to collect. I don't care how you go about it, long as Hewlitt Monroe is able to hand you the money when you're through. You'll figure it out. Now get the fuck out of my office. You're bleeding all over my carpet."

As soon as the door is shut, Bill Bury forgets Pardo and Lon. He has other things on his mind. The war in Europe is already making him a fortune. The United States will have to jump into it soon. A great big goddamned shooting war, the kind of thing that won't be over in a month or two. Most folks see war as a disaster, like an earthquake or a hurricane or a volcano. But like any natural disaster, a tragedy for some will be an opportunity for others. In a war, a lot of people get dead and a few people get rich. A modern army runs on gasoline, which means oil. He has oil. He has coal. He has copper. He has beef. He has a piece of five different railroads, all of which will be needed to haul the beef and wheat and coal and oil to the seaports, where it can be shipped where it's needed, sometimes on transports owned by Bill Bury. It would be easier to cash in with a Republican in the White House, but even that arrogant Roosevelt can't wage a war without oil.

He stands and watches from his window as his sons cross the

parking lot to Lon's car. Pardo is still holding the handkerchief to his face, but he gets behind the wheel. Bury can never look at Pardo without seeing the face of that hurricane bitch he married, the one human being on earth who got the better of him.

There are a dozen men on the Bury payroll who could deal with Hewlitt Monroe, but the boys need to be taught a lesson. Either they will learn something and collect what's owing, or they'll end up dead in a Texas bar ditch, which would be be no great loss. Lon is no use at all unless you have an anvil to lift, and Pardo specializes in havoc, always has. He has wrecked three expensive automobiles, turned a dozen prize bulls loose to watch them fight, scared a Mexican maid so bad she left without waiting to collect her pay, kept a pet wolf and fed it domestic pets he caught around town, mainly cats. If something happens to this young man, the cats won't miss him.

There's a light knock at the door. Milo Stroud steps into the office and helps himself to a chair. Stroud is dressed the way he always dresses, in an old-fashioned black wool suit with a high white collar and a bowler hat. Bury thinks he might be English. If he is, his accent is a stone that has carried a thousand miles downstream and worn off around the edges. Stroud comes and goes with impunity at all the Bury companies, where he's taken for some sort of accountant. Officials bustle around at the sight of Milo Stroud, making sure that all the books are in order, a benefit which Bill Bury himself has not foreseen.

He has other uses for Stroud. Watching the man prepare for an assignment is like observing the growth of an especially malignant variety of shrub. He fairly blossoms with instruments of destruction.

"You wanted to see me," Stroud says.

"I need you to do a little job, Milo. Pack a bag. You'll be heading down to Texas."

"Is it a removal you'll be wanting this time?"

"Nope. More like babysitting. But it has to be done so them two that's being babysat don't notice you're around. I don't give a damn if the little snotnoses end up as roadkill. I just don't want to have to clean up one of their messes."

12

Iᴛ's ᴀ ǫᴜɪᴇᴛ ɴɪɢʜᴛ ɪɴ ᴛʜᴇ ᴊᴏɪɴᴛ ᴏɴ ꜱᴀʟᴏᴏɴ ʀᴏᴡ on South Center Street in Casper. A dozen customers, all of them regulars except for a slender young fellow at the end of the bar. He's been drinking steadily, whiskey doubles with a beer chaser. He has two black eyes and a bandage over his nose. Lost a fight, drowning his sorrows. Dwight Roe, the bartender, has worked dives like this one for thirty years. After a man takes a whupping, he needs a drink. It's not so much the pain, it's the embarrassment. He tries once to start a conversation, but the stranger gives him a look cold as ice cubes in a gin glass. He steps away, polishing the bar, and does not go back again except when the stranger signals for another drink. He pays as he goes and he tips well. No bartender could ask for more.

Around nine o'clock, Dwight takes the sports section from the *Casper Daily Tribune* and steps out back. When he returns to the bar, Maggie Cotant has come in for her shift, and she's already deep in conversation with the stranger. Maggie is a little thing, but she's cute as a button. Dwight Roe hired her to wait tables four nights a week when he didn't need the help. In the back of his mind, he hopes that one of these nights after the last drunken customer has staggered out, he and Maggie will be polishing tables and he'll catch her looking at him in a certain way and two minutes later she'll be up on a table with her legs open. It hasn't happened, or anything like it, but Dwight is not a man to give up.

Maggie clucks over the stranger like a mother hen. The bartender shakes his head. This pretty boy draws women like a dead rat draws flies. Once Maggie starts talking to him, she's pretty much useless for the rest of the night. The joint gets busy around eleven, but Maggie keeps drifting back to the man at the end of the bar, leaving Dwight to look after her tables. Dwight catches her eye, nods toward the back. He wants to talk. She meanders back reluctantly.

"What do you want?"

"You're not doing your job."

"Yes, I am. I'm talking to a customer."

"One customer. You're ignoring everybody else."

"So what? This one is a good tipper."

"He's trouble."

"How do you know?"

"I've been in this business since before you were born. If this guy isn't trouble, I'm Eleanor Roosevelt."

"You're just jealous."

"Why would I be jealous?"

"Because you want some, and you're not going to get any because you're too old, and I'm talking to him because he's young and good-looking."

"Okay, you can have all the time you want for him. You're fired."

"You can't fire me, I quit."

Maggie turns on her heel and stalks back to the stranger. He downs his last beer and leaves a dollar on the bar. She takes his arm and leads him out, proudly, like she has just caught the biggest fish in her life. At the door she pauses long enough to stick out her tongue at Dwight Roe.

It starts out just like any other night with a fella, the two of them entwined on the narrow bed in her apartment, kissing and getting warmed up. She tells him she wants to go to the washroom to freshen up. *Sure, doll,* he says. *You do what you got to do. I'll be right here waiting.* When she comes out of the bathroom wearing nothing but her shift, the lights are off and it's pitch dark. She walks into the room, calling him. It's awkward, she doesn't even know his name. *Are you here? Don't play tricks on me.* Her voice a little nervous. Then he rushes at her out of the darkness, tackles her from behind. She falls heavily on the floor with his weight bearing her down. When she resists and tries to twist away, she feels something icy against her throat. The blade of a knife. A trickle of something hot down her neck, her own blood. Then he is taking her, not in the place where a man is supposed to do it with a woman, but in the other place, with nothing to make it go in easy. It hurts so that she wants to scream, but she doesn't dare.

At three o'clock in the morning, she is down on her knees. She's more frightened than she has ever been in her life. So frightened that she has peed on the linoleum floor and she's kneeling in her own urine and he will not let her get up. She's crying, tears and snot washing into her mouth. Begging him. Begging him for her life one minute. Begging him to end it the next. To put her out of her misery.

She waits for it to end. He has done it to her three times in the roughest way, kicked her in the stomach so hard she puked, choked her almost to death twice. In between, he makes her listen while he quotes verses from the Bible, all of which seem to have something to do with the blood of the lamb. A dozen times he asks her the same question. *Are you at peace with the Lord?* She tries all kinds of answers, yes and no and maybe, but no matter what she says, it's not the right answer. He grabs her hair and pulls her head back and when she feels the blade at her throat she tries to pray, but he tells her she is too late, that it's too late to find peace with the Lord if a person doesn't have it, that she is a terrible sinner and now she is going to pay for her sins.

Sometimes he gets up and paces around the room. She hears him in the bathroom, then she hears the toilet flushing. She thinks of making a run for the door, but even if she can get through it, she'll be naked in the hallway, and what can she do then? Her landlady is deaf as a post, there's no one else in the building. Anyway, it's too late. He's back. The blade of the knife traces her nipples, one and then the other, then it trails down her belly and she feels it, icy cold between her legs. She waits for the thing he is going to do, but he moves away. She hears a door open and close. It sounds like the door to her apartment, but she can't be sure.

She remains on her knees, whimpering and sobbing and praying for dawn, until she hears traffic outside. When the light comes, she takes it as a sign from God that she has been spared to do good works. He's gone. Surely, he is gone. She tiptoes into the bathroom, but he isn't there. He's not in the tiny kitchen. He is not in the one room that serves as her living room and bedroom. She rushes to the door and bolts the lock and struggles for five minutes to push a heavy dresser up against it. An hour later, she has packed all her things. She is much too frightened to call the police. All she can think is that she has to get away. She peers out the curtain, cautiously, sees no one on the street, just cars going by, early birds going to work. She hurries down the stairs with her suitcases, walks the six blocks to the train station, and buys a one-way ticket to Spokane. She has said some awful things to her mother, but she is sure the woman will take her back. She'll have to. Maggie has nowhere else to go.

13

Hewlitt Monroe's truculence over his debt to Big Bill Bury has nothing to do with his ability to cover a sum as paltry as fifty-two thousand dollars. Monroe lost the money to Bury during an all-night, high-stakes poker game on a yacht out on the Gulf of Mexico. Bury accepted his marker, but Monroe knows that Bury was cheating. He can't quite figure out *how* he was cheating, but he has no doubt the game was crooked. After thirty years playing poker, he knows when a game is rigged and when it's on the up-and-up. He knows that Big Bill will come calling. When he does, Monroe plans to pay up, provided Bury is willing to admit that he cheated and to show him exactly how he did it.

When Bury's sons turn up at his office in Galveston, Monroe plays for time. There are three ways he can go at this. He can pay up and forget about it. He can have the boys roughed up bad and send them back north empty-handed, starting a war with the meanest sonofabitch he knows. Or he can stall until old Bill blows his stack and comes down to Texas to sort things out himself. Hewlitt is the kind of man who stalls instinctively. It's been his experience that when you have a problem, if you just sit tight and wait, a solution will come to you. He looks them over, hulking Lon and this pretty boy Pardo with his movie-star looks, and decides to let them cool their heels for a while. First he steps out and leaves the Bury boys to sit for nearly an hour in his office, under the glassy stares of animals he has slaughtered from Montana to Kenya: a water buffalo next to an American bison, an ibex and a pronghorn antelope, a pair of gazelles, an African lion and a cougar, a bighorn sheep and a tahr from New Zealand. Finally, Monroe saunters back and offers them brandy and cigars. Lon accepts. Pardo, edgy as a coyote in a cage, declines.

Lon clears his throat. "I expect you know why we're here," he says.

Monroe raises his eyebrows. "Matter of a little poker debt, I expect."

"Fifty-two thousand dollars. The old man says we're not to go back to Wyoming without it. In cash."

"Y'see, boys, it aint a problem of money. Me and your dad go way back, to when we was both young wildcatters in West Texas. We understand each other. I was hoping Bill would come to collect himself. Give me a shot with a fresh deck of cards."

"He aint got the time."

"No, I suppose he don't. He must go like hellfire around the clock to make that much money. I've got no objection to paying my debts. Never have. You ask anybody in Texas, Hewlitt Monroe pays up. But fifty-two thousand dollars, that's a heap of cash. Might take me a few days to pull it together. Why don't you boys just have yourselves a good time in Galveston while you wait?"

Lon grins. "We can do that." Monroe scrawls the address of a good hotel on a slip of paper, says that, as long as they have to wait, the tab is on him.

A week goes by and Lon and Pardo are still lounging in separate rooms in the red-roofed Hotel Galvez, enjoying the spectacular view of the Gulf of Mexico. Monroe also loans them one of his cars, a blue 1940 Mercury. He does everything except hand them the money. Big Bill sends daily telegrams, demanding to know what's going on. Pardo burns the telegrams, then takes the Mercury and steps out every evening, leaving Lon to entertain himself.

Lon doesn't mind too much. He likes easy living, and the hotel is as easy as life is likely to get. If he feels bored, he strolls down to the beach and sits staring out at the Gulf of Mexico. The water is a pale, delicate green except nearer the shore, where he can wade along the sand with his trousers rolled up and let the breakers wash around his calves. Pardo went to France and Italy with his mother before she died. He keeps saying that the Gulf is nothing but a mud puddle compared with the Atlantic Ocean, but Lon has never seen so much water in his life. He has promised himself that he will go to California and dip his toes in the Pacific someday, but this is almost as good. He watches the wheeling gulls and the pelicans, the shrimp boats heading out, the banana boats unloading their cargo, the waves rolling in.

When Pardo is around the hotel, he's edgy and restless. He'll sit down to breakfast, jump up to make a telephone call, return to the table, fidget and crack his knuckles and play drumsticks with the silverware. Lon wonders how a grown man can have so much nervous energy.

"I swear, Pardo, you're as jumpy as a Mexican bean."

"I can't help it if you just sit there on your fat ass. You're like these rich old men around here. All you want to do is scratch your nuts and watch the waves roll in."

"We aint got nothin else to do until we get the money."

"You don't have anything else to do, maybe. I got plenty."

"That reminds me, I been meaning to ask. Where do you go every night?"

"Out."

"I bet you found a Mexican whorehouse. You're screwing some sweet Mexican *puta* while I'm watching rich ladies with their mint juleps."

"The places I go aint your kind of place, Lon."

"Hell you say. If you're goin out tonight, I am, too."

They're sitting at a dingy waterfront saloon frequented by sailors, shrimp fishermen, and rummies who work just enough to buy the next drink. Pouring down shots of mescal from a bottle with a worm in it, getting drunker by the minute. Someone plays a Mexican tune on the jukebox. The shadows lengthen. A couple of the deepwater shrimp-boat crews come in. The men drink with a weariness which will not be erased until the third or fourth drink has gone down, after which a man becomes either jubilant or belligerent, depending on his nature.

Pardo always drinks the same way. For a slender man who is small of bone, he has an apparently endless capacity for drink. The only visible change (visible to Lon, at least) is that his brother becomes more danger-ous the more he drinks. When one of the shrimpers seated behind them scrapes his chair back into Pardo's seat, Lon sees the open switchblade appear in Pardo's hand as though conjured from thin air.

"Pardo!"

Pardo gives him the ice blue stare, but he snaps the blade closed and slips the knife back in his pocket. The shrimpers don't see the knife, or they would find themselves in a brawl with thirty-to-one odds.

"You're a dumb-ass, Lon. Don't stick your nose where it don't belong."

"I wish you'd stop callin me dumb."

"I'll stop callin you dumb when you aint dumb no more. You let me know if you feel somethin strange happening inside your head, like you're beginning to get smart. Then I'll stop callin you dumb." Pardo waves the empty mescal bottle over his head. "Barkeep! Bring us another bottle of that *mezcal.*"

"I think we ought to get back to the hotel, Pardo. We're drunk as skunks."

"Hush, Lon. I'm buying."

The barkeep, a squat and cheerful Hispanic with elaborate mustaches curling like black tusks on either side of a sharp nose, brings another bottle and two fresh glasses. Pardo pays. The barkeep shuffles away.

Lon stares at his glass. "You see how he washes these things?"

"Nope. And I don't want to."

"He spits on his finger and wipes it around the inside of the glass. Then he dries it with that apron, that aint been washed since the Alamo. I seen him do it, right in front of my face. Anyhow, I guess the *mezcal* pretty much kills every little thing."

"I wish the *mezcal* would kill your mouth. You talk too much."

Pardo lifts his glass and drains another shot, chases it with half a beer. The wind picks up over the bay, the sun bloats into an overripe tomato slipping into blue-black water. Two of the shrimpers start an argument. The proprietor levels a sawed-off shotgun in their direction, orders them to take it outside. Lon puts his head down and dozes. Pardo calls for more *mezcal*. It's somewhere on the wrong side of full dark when Pardo stands and scratches himself. "It's time to find some whores," he says.

Lon has to grab his hat and run to catch up. They move so fast that they catch Milo Stroud napping in his car, parked a discreet hundred

feet away from the door of the saloon. Stroud wakes to the squeal of
tires as the blue Mercury makes a left turn on two wheels. He starts his
Chevy and roars after them.

Pardo drives as though he grew up in Galveston, roaring through the
narrow streets at speeds that leave Lon feeling queasy. They head north,
along streets without a single light, past cotton compresses and the iron
and gasworks, the railroad yards, rusted-out factories that rise spectral in
the darkness, rows of small dark houses. They pull up in front of a narrow yellow house with a lone candle burning in the window.

"Here we go, Brother," Pardo says. "I hope you're ready for this."

The madam is a crone who appears to be at least a hundred years old.
She sits near the door, under a cage where a huge red-and-blue parrot
croaks *chinga tu madre* when a customer walked in. A massive, coal black
bouncer greets Pardo, then grunts in the direction of his brother.

"Who he?"

"That's my brother, Lon. Lon, meet Sailor. Sailor can crush your
sorry ass with one hand."

The girls inside are all Mexican nationals. They sprawl on couches
or stand in doorways down a long, narrow corridor. As his eyes adjust
to the light, Lon sees that the girls are all very young. The oldest are no
more than sixteen, the youngest ten or eleven, flat-chested little girls. It
makes Lon uneasy. Pardo picks out two of the youngest, takes one on
each knee and strokes their thin brown thighs while the crone brings
another *mezcal*.

"Which one you want, Lon?"

"Neither one. I'd rather fuck a gal that's growed tits, at least."

"Then grab one of them old ladies over there. I'll take these two."

Pardo shoos the girls down the corridor in front of him. Lon sits and
drinks his *mezcal*, trying not to hear the sounds from the back. One of
Pardo's girls is squealing like he is hurting her bad. Between that and the
mezcal, Lon finds it hard to focus. Finally he chooses a girl with ample
breasts and buttocks and a triangle of hair visible through her thin dress.
That doesn't mean she is old enough, necessarily, but at least she has tits
and pubic hair.

She smells of grease and perspiration, semen and woodsmoke. She's missing two teeth. Her breasts are so hard, her nipples seem to strain through the skin. Lon isn't used to drinking *mezcal*. It makes his head throb, like he's getting a hangover while he is still drunk. His pecker feels numb, his whole body feels numb. The girl hauls away at his equipment until she is panting and perspiring. At last, it begins to rise and throb. She moves astride him and with deft fingers massages his balls while she pumps up and down, urging him to finish. Lon is about to attain his moment of glory when he hears an unearthly scream from down the hall. The girl slips off, leaving him to spend all over the sheets.

"Goddamnit," he swears. "I wasn't done yet."

Lon's girl is cursing Pardo. *Cabrón! Hijo de puta!* She runs out into the corridor naked, with Lon staggering behind her as he tries to pull on his pants. Suddenly, the house is ablaze with electric light, illuminating a scene Lon will never forget. One of Pardo's young harlots staggers naked and shrieking along the center of the corridor, blood pouring from one gash high on her cheek and another across her breasts. The other girl, with a long cut trailing blood down her thigh, has jumped onto Pardo's back stark naked and is trying to choke him with an arm around his windpipe. Pardo, also naked, has the switchblade in his left hand and is slashing wildly, the glittering blade dripping blood, yelling that the girls are trying to rob him. Bearing down on Pardo from behind is Sailor the bouncer, a coal shovel in both hands. Sailor yanks the girl off Pardo's neck and brings the shovel down on the back of his head. He drops as though he has been shot, out cold. Lon's girl jumps on the unconscious Pardo and rakes his face with her fingernails. Lon goes to pull her off and the coal shovel descends again, this time on Lon's head. The last sound he hears before he passes out is the wail of a police siren. When he comes to, Pardo is gone. A thin and shaky Mexican doctor with a black bag between his knees is sewing up the gashes on the two girls, while two Galveston cops who can't speak a word of Spanish take statements from the girls, with the doctor translating sporadically as he stitches.

A man in a bowler hat and an old-fashioned black wool suit appears and helps Lon to his feet.

"Get dressed," he says in Lon's ear. "It's time to leave."

Lon does as he's told and follows the man out to his car.

"I seen you someplace before," he says. "I just can't place you."

"It doesn't matter," the man says. "I'm not here."

Lon nods as though he understands. It makes as much sense as anything else that has happened since they fetched up in Galveston. The man in the bowler hat drives him back to the Hotel Galvez. Lon wonders vaguely, through the fog of mescal and the pain in his head, how the fellow happens to know where he is staying.

"Get a good night's sleep," the man says as a doorman rushes to help Lon out. "You'll be on the eight-forty train to Dallas. You can change there for Denver."

Lon rubs his head. He has a bump the size of a walnut where Sailor busted him with the coal shovel. "I don't know as I can wake up that early."

"You'll be up. I'll see to it you get to the station."

"I can't go yet. We don't got that money from Hewlitt Monroe."

"I'll take care of Mr. Monroe."

"What about Pardo?"

"I'll look after Pardo, too. Don't forget now—I wasn't here."

"Sorry, I didn't catch your name."

"No," the man says. "You didn't."

Judge Oakley B. LaMontagne is eating a poached egg when his maid Louise sticks her nose into his den to announce that he has a visitor.

"You know I don't see visitors here, Louise. He can call at my office."

"He says it's all-fired important. Somethin about a rich boy what got himself arrested."

Judge LaMontagne smiles and pushes aside the half-eaten egg. "Don't keep the man waiting," he says. "Show him in."

It's the judge's lucky day. He has been expecting this visit since he learned of the arrest of a millionaire's son in a Galveston whorehouse. It isn't a serious offense. The whores the young man cut up were nothing but Mexican illegals. Another fellow, the judge might have released him already. But when Oakley B. LaMontagne sees the little item in the Galveston paper saying the accused is the son of the oil tycoon William C. Bury, he decides to deny bail and hold on to his prize until someone turns up with an envelope of cash.

Louise waddles into the room, leading one of the odder specimens the judge has ever seen, a fellow who belongs in an old daguerreotype. He is clad in a stiff black wool suit despite the Texas heat, with a high white collar and a bowler hat, which he holds tucked under one arm. He does not give his name, nor does the judge ask for it, although he does shake the man's clammy little hand.

"Louise, you can run along now," he says.

The big woman vanishes, waiting until she is out of earshot to mutter her opinion of the judge's doings: "That man always tell me 'run along' when he's up to somethin crooked."

The judge waves his guest to a chair. Stroud perches on the edge, watching the judge with eyes like coal pits.

"I represent Mr. William C. Bury," he says. "He's concerned about his son Pardo. I believe you have the young man in custody."

"Pardo Bury, is that the name?" the judge says, feigning ignorance. He peruses a list on his desk. Pardo's name is there, almost blotted out by a yellow stain of egg yolk. "Yes, here it is. Pardo, yes. Unusual name. Nasty business with a knife and two young Mexican girls. We don't normally interfere when a man cuts a greaser whore. But these two were awfully young, and they were cut up pretty bad. I'm told that if the bouncer hadn't interfered, they would both have been killed. The charges are two counts of attempted murder, but that can be less with the right inducement."

"Their age doesn't concern me, nor the charges. It's just that Mr. Bury wishes to make a donation." Stroud places an envelope on a corner of the judge's desk with exaggerated care. "You'll find enclosed a sum intended to help with the judge's retirement fund."

"Thank you kindly, sir. It's true that the state provides far too little for those such as myself, who do the most necessary tasks in our society."

"I couldn't agree more."

"I assume that your client will require a service in return?"

"He will. What is the maximum prison sentence young Master Bury could receive for this offense?"

"Ten years. He would have to serve at least five before he's eligible for parole."

"Then you'll find enclosed one thousand dollars for each year. The agreement is that you will apply the maximum sentence."

"How's that?"

"The maximum. No time off. He does at least five years, every minute of it. His father believes it's time the boy learned a lesson."

"With those jackals in an institution such as Huntsville, I can't vouch for his safety. He'll be mighty popular, if you get my drift."

"I understand you precisely. We are not asking for guarantees as to his safety. All my client wants is that you apply the weight of the law to the full extent."

"That's an unusual request. It's usually the opposite."

"This is what my client requires."

"Hell, it will be my pleasure. See how the little bastard likes the view of them East Texas piney woods around Huntsville."

"I'm told it's not a place where a man wants to spend a night."

"Not an hour, my friend. They should erect a glowing neon sign outside that establishment: ABANDON ALL HOPE. It is a species of hell. But your young man can count himself fortunate. If one of the girls had died, he might be facing a date with Old Sparky."

"I suspect he'll get there yet, by hook or by crook."

"I wouldn't be so pessimistic, my friend. Perhaps he'll learn his lesson."

"Pardo? I'm afraid Pardo Bury is not the learning kind."

The item runs in *The Sheridan Press*, under the headline MILLIONAIRE'S SON SENTENCED IN TEXAS. Pardo Bury, sent up to Huntsville Penitentiary for ten years for cutting a young female in a house of ill repute. Sheriff Tom Call reads it over three times, wondering. Remembering a run-in with Pardo when he was still a deputy. Pardo had roughed up a woman he met in a saloon. When she called to complain, the sheriff sent Tom to have a talk with the young man, to warn him that if it happened again, they'd have to run him in no matter how rich his daddy was. Pardo smirked through the whole thing. A nasty piece of work. Not very big, either, as Tom remembers him, though he can't remember anything about the size of the man's feet.

Still, there's no point wondering about Pardo. If he was in Texas, he couldn't be linked to the murder of Millie Stojko. Tom cuts the story out carefully and adds it to his file, because you never know when a bit of information might come in handy.

14.

TOM CALL TRACKS DOWN EVERY ONE OF THE late-model black Packards registered in Sheridan County, eighteen in all. Every one leads to a dead end. There's nothing left to be done. The only way they're going to solve this one is to catch a lucky break—and luck is a capricious thing.

Tom decides to head out to the 8T8 one last time, to make one more search around the sheepherder's shack. He has no real hope for this visit, but it makes him feel better to try and he figures the fresh air might help clear his head. The weather is hot and dry, very different from the way it was when he made his first trip out to the ranch. The road is dry enough that he can take the dirt track all the way to the sheepherder's cabin. On the southern horizon, he can see the cloud of dust where the cowhands work the roundup in a swirl of heat, bawling cattle, the acrid stench of burning hair from the branded calves. Where he is, the sky is blue, he can hear the meadowlarks and, with the door and window of the shack left open, the stench of a young girl's decomposing body has been cleansed by the wind. He wonders if Juanita is working with the roundup crew. She stays with a man, that one. There is a stillness to her that he finds soothing. Beneath her beauty, which any man can see, she is a deep pool.

He pokes around in the rubble of tin cans and coffee grounds behind the shack. He has been through this stinking garbage pile a dozen times, alone and with other lawmen. It's futile, like picking at a scab. If this killing ground has any more information to yield, someone else will have to find it.

On the way back to town, he detours three miles out of his way to stop at the ranch house. It's a long shot: she's most likely with the roundup crew. He knocks and waits. He's about to head back to his car when the door opens. Juanita is alone. She looks radiant. She was out riding all morning, then came in to get an early start on supper.

Tom is apologetic. "I came out to have one more look," he says. "I thought I ought to stop in, since I was in the neighborhood."

"I'm glad you did. Come in, I'll fix you something to eat."

"Sounds like you've got enough cooking to do."

"Don't be silly. We're feeding twenty here, it won't hurt to feed one more."

When Tom lifts his hat, she sees a bandage. She reaches up to touch it.

"What happened?"

"Flying bottle in a saloon. Old story."

"Tell me anyway."

"I went out with Early Porter to try to cool out some boys who were tearin up a roadhouse south of town. I caught a broken bottle as quick as I stepped inside."

"Heavens! They expect you to do that, too? Stop barroom brawls?"

"It's part of the job. That and getting cats out of trees."

"And chasing killers."

"All comes with the badge. Whatever folks toss your way."

"It doesn't seem right. We expect too much."

"I don't know about that. I knew what the job was when I ran for sheriff. Older sheriffs, they leave more to their deputies. I tend to do more of the work myself. My own fault."

"Those stitches must be ready to come out."

"They are. I haven't had time."

"I could take them out. Save you a visit to the hospital. I'm probably gentler than those doctors."

"How is it you know how to take out stitches?"

"I was a nurse in Mexico for fifteen years. I worked for my first husband, Dr. Hodgson. He died shortly after we came to Wyoming."

Tom sits in a kitchen chair. Juanita stands over him with her sewing scissors. He focuses on a vein in her neck, beating just inches from his face.

"Say, Mr. Call, weren't you going to take me up in an airplane someday?"

"I will," Tom says. "I've got a buddy, Farley Parris. He has an Aeronca

Defender at the airport, uses it to teach folks how to fly. We were to-gether in the Flying Fandangos. I can take it up any time I want."

"What were the Flying Fandangos?"

"A bunch of Louisiana boys that loved to fly, that's all it ever was. We started down in Baton Rouge, where I grew up. My daddy was a pilot in the Great War. Taught me to fly when I was fourteen. Me and five or six others, we put together the Flying Fandangos. Traveled around the country, doing stunts at county fairs and such. It was a good living for a while."

"Wasn't it dangerous?"

"It was. We were doing a show in Colorado Springs when two of the boys got tangled up on a stunt and they were both killed. That was the end of the Flying Fandangos. I went to work for United Aircraft and Transport out of Cheyenne, carrying passengers and mail. Wasn't as glamorous, but a whole lot safer."

"You love flying so much. Why did you quit?"

"Doreen Cody. Claimed to be the great-granddaughter of Buffalo Bill. She batted her baby blues at me after a rough flight, thanked me for saving her life. Six months later, she told me I had to make a choice: her or airplanes. Said she didn't want to hear someday that her man had slammed an airplane into the side of a mountain. I gave up flying and went to work as a deputy sheriff. Worst mistake I ever made."

"Why do you say that?"

"We were okay for two, three years, but Doreen made it pretty clear that she wanted a man who made more money. I ran for sheriff and won and I was making a little more, but that wasn't good enough. A month after I was elected, she lit out for California with a tourist in the real es-tate business. Six months later, she wanted to come back, but I told her I'd sooner swallow battery acid."

"You didn't!"

"I sure did. I don't give a woman a chance to do a thing like that twice."

"Do you miss flying?"

"Something awful. I'm going to go back, soon as my term as sheriff is up. I don't know how or where, but I'm going back to flying airplanes."

"It must be wonderful to be up there. I've never been on a plane."

"It is, as long as you don't get weather. You'll see. As soon as you can get away, I'll take you up."

Suddenly, they are awkward with each other. They both feel that a promise has been made. At the door, they shake hands.

"You call me when you can get loose," Tom says.

She nods, squeezes his hand, not trusting herself to say another word.

15

I T'S MID-JULY BEFORE JUANITA PAINT CAN GET AWAY to go flying with Tom Call. Eli and Ezra have taken Emaline and Red to the Frontier Days rodeo in Cheyenne and Juanita will be alone for a week. She usually goes along, but this year she begs off. Too much heat and dust, she says, and all those bawling calves getting yanked around and thrown for no reason, and cowboys risking their lives on Brahma bulls. All that is true: she finds the rodeo cruel, hot, and pointless. But another year, she would have gone anyway, to avoid being alone, to be with Emaline and Red and Eli. Now, in the summer of 1941, the only thing she can think of is that, if she doesn't go to Frontier Days, she'll have time to spend with Tom.

Eli and Ezra leave before dawn Saturday morning. They will pick up Emaline and Red in Sheridan on the way. Eli asks one last time if she is sure she doesn't want to go.

"Not this year," she says. "Maybe next year. I want to clean the house and do lots of things. Oh, and tomorrow I'm going flying with Tom Call. He said he would take me up in an airplane."

Eli, already thinking of the long drive ahead and the deals he wants to make at the rodeo, simply nods. She isn't even sure if it has registered with him. Another man might not like his wife going up in a plane with a handsome young sheriff, but Eli always has other things on his mind. She sometimes wishes that he would treat her as though she is more important than a stallion or another slice of ranchland. But each year, her wishes seem to matter less. And now there is Tom Call, waiting to take her flying.

She's up early Sunday morning. It's a clear, brilliant day, a day she imagines will be perfect for flying. She has a very light breakfast because Tom says it's better if she doesn't have too much in her stomach. She offers to make them a picnic lunch. As an afterthought, she tiptoes into the cellar and takes a bottle of red wine from a case that Eli received after buying a Charolais bull from France. She drinks wine no more than two or three times a year, but this will be an occasion. Her first airplane flight.

As she approaches the airport along a dusty gravel road, she feels apprehensive. These airplanes are so small and frail. They will be up so high. What if something happens? What if they run out of gas? What if she can't keep her stomach down? Then she is around a bend in the road and there is Tom Call, tall and lean, standing in the shadow of the bright yellow Aeronca with the navy blue lettering on its wings, waiting for her. As she parks her car next to his, she stares at it. Surely it's too small to fly? Too fragile? She has seen dozens of planes fly over the ranch, but now that she's about to go aloft herself, she's not sure that she believes in the miracle of flight.

"Howdy, Juanita," Tom takes her hand. "You all ready to come up?"

"I think so."

"Don't worry. Most folks feel a little nervous, first time. It's like a carnival ride. Once you're on, it's more fun than a barrel of monkeys."

"I've never been on a carnival ride."

"Then this will be twice as much fun. I've checked her out. She's all set to go. Farley uses this plane as a trainer, so the rear seat is a little higher than the front seat. You'll be able to see what I'm doing."

He gives her a hand and she climbs into the passenger seat, self-conscious, wishing she had worn pants instead of a skirt, knowing what Tom can see from beneath. Then she is in the narrow seat, the warm leather scorching her legs. Tom leans over her, buckling the harness. "We'll have to taxi down that way first," he says. "Then we head back into the wind for takeoff. All you have to do is sit back and enjoy yourself."

She nods. Tom stoops and gives her a peck on the lips. He shows her how to hold the brakes while he stands in front of the propeller to prop the plane. The sixty-five-horsepower Lycoming engine is underpowered, so it doesn't take much effort to make the propeller spin. He climbs into the front seat, sitting low so she can see over his shoulders as he taxis to the runway. A little more power and more agile controls would help, but he plans to give her the ride of her life anyway. He eases the stick forward to raise the tail and then brings it back, slowly lifting the plane into the air. At this elevation it takes a good five miles beyond the end of the runway to reach a thousand feet. Tom takes his time, waiting for the plane to make its slow climb to two thousand feet.

The view leaves Juanita breathless. There are a few high, scattered cirrus clouds in a clear blue sky, nothing more. Away to the west, the Bighorn Mountains rise, blue, white-capped shadows, rank after rank. Below them are the checkerboards of wheat and beet fields, the long pastures broken here and there by barbed-wire fences, the tiny windmills, long lines of cattle moving toward water tanks. Far below, she sees the shadow of the plane skimming over the buffalo grass. Tom points down and shouts something she doesn't quite hear. They have crossed the Powder River and they're flying over the ranch. The big house, the enormous barn, all the corrals and outbuildings, the bunkhouse, the pastures with their herds of cattle and horses stretching in every direction.

Tom banks the plane to the north. They make a slow pass over the sheepherder's shack. It looks like such a harmless place from the air, a tiny structure marooned on the vast prairie like a boat on the ocean. It is almost impossible to believe that anything terrible might have happened there. They fly on, headed due north, and pass another building four miles north of the cabin. Tom points down and shouts over the roar of the engine.

"What's that?"

She leans forward so he can hear. "It's a hunting lodge. Eli sold this land to a Scotsman a long time ago. He built that lodge, but I don't think he ever used it."

Tom banks to the west, opens the throttle to full power, and eases forward on the stick to get the little Aeronca up near its redline airspeed of a hundred and twenty-five miles per hour. He hauls back on the stick, pulling three times the force of gravity, enough to get Juanita's heart rate up. He decides to do an old trick, one his father learned during the Great War. A little right rudder pressure is needed to compensate for the torque of the propeller. As the plane approaches vertical, the lack of power is obvious to Tom in the cockpit. He's done this before, but only when he was alone. The plane shudders as it loses its airspeed and falls off to the right in an uncontrolled spin. Tom pulls back the power, releases the pressure on the stick, and stomps on the left rudder. After one spin, which is not as violent as it feels to Juanita in the backseat, the rotation stops and the airspeed begins to pick up. He pulls back lightly on the stick to level the plane off. When he does, he's twenty feet off the ground and headed for a line of trees. The plane hops over the trees and begins to gain altitude. He hears Juanita laughing wildly.

Tom shouts back to her, something that sounds like "humble man." She has no idea what he's talking about, but she is terrified and exhilarated all at once and she does not want it to end. When they begin their descent into the airport at Sheridan, Juanita wants to protest, to ask him to turn around and fly them somewhere else. To the Pacific, to the Atlantic, to all the places this magical machine can take them. But Tom eases the plane down onto the runway. There is a slight bump, he throttles down, and the ride is over. He taxis the plane back to the hangar. She presses her hand to her chest, feels her heartbeat. Tom helps her to step down from the plane. She hugs him spontaneously.

"That was . . . that was . . ." She can't find the words.

"I know."

"But you scared me half to death. You should have told me what was coming."

"If I had told you, you wouldn't have let me do it."

"Isn't it awfully dangerous?"

"Somewhat. First time I tried an Immelmann with a passenger. Didn't quite work."

"You mean we might have crashed?"

"We might have. But we didn't."

He grins. She can't tell if he's kidding her or not. She takes his arm. She is breathless, her words tumbling over one another, trying to describe what she has experienced. "It's the most beautiful thing. The sky. You can see forever. I never dreamed . . ."

Juanita understands now why he is hooked on flying. When a man can handle an airplane like that, the sheer, easy competence with which he takes them airborne, why would he do anything else? Why would he leave all this for a woman like Doreen Cody?

"I brought us a picnic lunch," she says. "I thought you might want to eat."

"That's real sweet of you. Where do you want to go?"

"How about right here? Under that cottonwood tree?"

Juanita lifts the picnic basket out of her trunk. She takes Tom's arm and lets him lead her to the tree. When she produces the wine bottle, he laughs.

"I feel like some kind of French king," he says. "Who drinks wine for lunch?"

"The French." She laughs. "I think the Spanish do, too. And the Italians."

He hefts the bottle. "How do you get this open?"

"With a corkscrew, silly." But she has forgotten the corkscrew. Tom takes out his pocketknife and manages to extract the cork. Juanita hasn't forgotten to pack the wineglasses, which are usually hauled out only for Christmas dinner. She pours, a little for herself, more for Tom. They touch glasses. The wine is clean and delicate. The first swallow leaves her light-headed.

When they have finished eating and the wine bottle is half-empty, she leans back in the grass, gazes at the sky. "It's hard to believe. We were just up there."

"Oh, yes. Way up."

"How far? How high did we go?"

"A little more than two thousand feet. I've been a lot higher, but not with that plane."

"It's almost impossible to imagine. That we can do that any time we want."

"Any time you want. As long as Farley isn't using his airplane."

"Will you teach me to fly? Is that possible?"

"You want to be like Amelia Earhart? Of course, I'll teach you."

"I don't want to be like her. I would never take off across the Pacific. I'd really like to be able to fly a plane, but only if you're with me."

He's propped up on one elbow, looking down at her. There are two other planes from the airport soaring high overhead, Sunday folks like her, out for a joyride. She wonders if they can see. Tom leans down, brushes her lips with his lips. Her eyes close. The kiss lingers so long that she feels the whole, whirling day spinning around them, time stopped in their little patch of shade under the cottonwood tree while the world goes on.

Tom pulls back. "Someone might see us out here," he says.

"Can we go to your house?"

"I can't wait that long. Let's go in the hangar."

Tom helps her up. She takes the bag with their picnic things and he leads her by the hand. Farley Parris has a small, windowless office in the back of the hangar. Tom has a key. He opens the door and leads the way and locks the door behind them. There is a cot in the corner where Farley likes to take afternoon naps between flying lessons, but they never make it as far as the cot. Her arms are around his neck. She's the one who can't hold back, her tongue probing his mouth. She wants it all at once, wants to devour him. She is too slender to wear a corset and it is too hot for stockings. There is only her skirt and her underpants. The skirt is up around her waist and her panties are pushed to the side and he is inside her, her right leg crooked around his waist, his long arms wrapped around her hips, pulling her up. It's like falling into that spiral all over again, except that this time she isn't at all afraid.

16.

ON OCTOBER 5, THE DAY OF THE FULL MOON, Two Spuds rides out alone to begin the Choctaw funeral cry ceremony for the dead girl, Mildred Stojko. He is months late, but he has been busy on the ranch, and it is not until after fall roundup that he's able to do what he feels must be done. He's careful to observe the tradition as he remembers it. First he puts out twenty-eight sticks, all around the eaves of the sheepherder's cabin where he found her. Each day he returns shortly before sundown, takes one stick from the eaves, and sets it to burn over a small campfire. As it burns, he stands and faces to the west, toward the mountains and the setting sun. In his tribe, she would be surrounded by her friends and family for the funeral cry, those closest to her sitting nearest the body, more distant relatives and friends farther back. They would rise, one by one, and tell of her, each in turn, day by day until the funeral cry was finished. Two Spuds is without his tribe, so he performs the ritual alone. He chants the Choctaw mourning songs, half-remembered from his youth. He recites everything he knows about the girl, which isn't much. Her body is buried far away, in the cemetery in Gillette, a place he will never go, but he believes that her soul lingers in this place where she died, so it is here that he performs the funeral cry.

When there are ten sticks left, he returns for the final ceremony. It's bitter cold and a stiff wind blows from the north. The weather report says it will snow, but so far there is just the cold and the wind. There is a five-gallon can of kerosene inside the shack. He soaks the bed where she died, still crusted with her blood. He pours the kerosene over the pine floorboards and the rough pine furniture and sloshes it up the walls. When the can is empty, he stands again, hatless in the empty cabin, then steps outside and breathes deeply to clear his lungs. Then he leads his pinto a hundred feet away, ties it to a mesquite brush, and returns to the window of the cabin. He strikes a single match, tosses it through the window, and runs. He's twenty feet away when the cabin explodes in a ball of flame.

The Choctaw mounts his pinto and rides to the high ground, where he turns and watches as the place where Millie Stojko died goes up in smoke and flame and ash. He remains motionless, his face lit by the setting sun, until the last timbers crash and the embers burn out.

He gathers up the reins, turns the pinto to the south and heads for home.

PART 2

Fire on the Water

17.

Pearl Harbor
December 1941

S ATURDAY NIGHT IN OAHU. WAHOO, THE SWABBIES
call it. *Lock up your daughters*, they holler, piling onto the liberty
boats for the run to the dock, *the Navy is coming to town.* Under
a waning moon, a light breeze stirs the Christmas decorations on the
palm trees. It's seventy-five degrees at eight o'clock. Something to write
home about, if you're a Wyoming boy. Gunner's Mate Robert E. Lee
Watson wanders Hotel Street with thousands of other sailors in their
rakish hats and white bell-bottom trousers, meeting and mingling and
occasionally fighting with soldiers and Marines. Swabbies and dogfaces
and jarheads in one long, drunken, boisterous stream, all horny and
hungry and full of hell, needing to let off a little steam. Bobby is with
them and not with them: he doesn't drink much, doesn't fight, doesn't
hurl himself at every female on the street. When his buddies decide
that it's time to go stand in one of the block-long lines outside a three-
dollar whorehouse, he goes his own way. He wants a girl as much as the
next sailor, but the men who leave the bordellos never look happy. They
always come out looking deflated and ashamed. He wants no part of it,
nor of the taxi dancers in the big barnlike halls where liquor is not allowed, where sailors pay a nickel to shuffle along in the arms of a bored
girl with sore feet. He plays pool and Skee-Ball and throws baseballs at
milk cans. He stands in line at a barbershop for a quick haircut from a
pretty Japanese girl, has his limit of three beers in a tavern, and sobers up
with a cup of coffee at a hot-dog joint called Swanky Franky.

Around nine o'clock, Bobby sees his cousin Leo Paint sitting in a
Shore Patrol jeep. Leo is big and polished and a little scary next to a
driver who is even bigger and scarier. Bobby calls out, but Leo doesn't

hear him and he doesn't want to run after the jeep. Sucking up to the Shore Patrol, you'd never live it down, even if the guy is your cousin.

For a payday Saturday night, it's pretty quiet. At midnight in Honolulu, orchestras play the national anthem and the sailors pour out of the saloons along Hotel Street and head east to the YMCA, where they catch buses back to Pearl Harbor. At the docks, there is the usual pushing and shoving. A few fights break out as drunken sailors jockey for places on the last liberty boats that will take them back to their stations. A couple of them fall over the side, laughing, and have to be fished out of the drink. Back on the USS *Tennessee*, the all-night crap games start in the heads for the guys who make it back from Honolulu with payday cash still burning a hole in their pockets. After his first payday in Wahoo, Bobby lost his whole paycheck to a fast-talking seaman deuce from Chicago. He hasn't touched a pair of dice since. By one o'clock, he's asleep in his hammock.

He wakes to the sound of a shot, the last cobwebs of a dream drifting away. He was elk hunting in Wyoming with Leo, a big buck in his sights, then he heard a shot. He sits up and bangs his noggin on the tangle of asbestos piping above his head. The stench leaves him gasping. It wasn't a shot that he heard, it was Logan Przic farting in the hammock below. Przic is rotten inside. The stink rises like gas from a sewer trench. Bobby swings a foot over the edge of the hammock, kicks the fat sailor with a bare toe.

"Przic, you dumb shit! You farted in my face. You're a damned farting machine."

Przic answers with a long snore. Bobby curses again and crawls out of his sweaty hammock in the dark, fumbles for his shoes and dungarees, slips the dungarees on, decides not to bother with his socks, carries the shoes up the ladder so as not to wake the other sailors. All around him the farting, groaning, snoring sailors, most of them barely more than boys, dreaming of home and girls or Honolulu and girls or girls and girls. Asleep in the oily reek of diesel, the stink of spunk and whiskey and the cheap perfume of the three-dollar payday whores. Asleep, they're free of petty officers and warrant officers, surly cooks who spit in the food when they aren't looking, free of the infinite, gnawing tedium of the hurry-up-and-wait peacetime Navy where the watchword is stand by to stand by, of drill and drill again and the boom of the big guns firing at old target ships, the endless inspections, the river of navy shit flowing downhill. *Stow this, sailor. Stow that, square this bunk away, square yourself away, no twenty-four for you this weekend, you squalid shithead, you will sit on this hulk and watch the goddamned paint dry.*

Most of it flows right on by and leaves him smelling like a rose. He's a natural for the military. Not too tall, not too short, not fat, not thin, not too loud, not too quiet, not ugly, not too handsome, neither a Bible pounder nor a hell-raiser. Habitually neat, an excellent shot, fit from years of hard work on farm and ranch, a sailor with an easy smile and a clear tenor voice. Not the guy to tell a joke, maybe, but the man with the best laugh when a joke is told. Not the one to lead, but the fellow who will always have your back. He bitches like everyone else, but in a cheerful way. Down deep, he loves the Navy. He has grown up in drought and dust, howling wind and grit down your neck and livestock half-dead from thirst. Now he can look out over millions of acres of water, watch the big waves roll in, enough water in one of those waves for all the livestock in Wyoming.

It's something, knowing that you're part of the most powerful navy in the world, that you are sitting in the catbird seat surrounded by steel, a row of floating steel fortresses, impenetrable, indestructible, with steel doors, steel hulls, steel of the decks, forged steel of the gun turrets, steel of the men, brass of the great fourteen-inch shells that have to be lifted by elevator and machine to the gun turrets. The *Tennessee* is a great battleship, one of a row of battleships, made vast in foundry and factory, the strength of America hammered into their hulls. Steel ships, steel in the men who sail them: Polacks from Cleveland, Italians from New York and Boston, farm boys like himself from

Indiana or Iowa or Nebraska, coal miners from West Virginia and Kentucky, shrimp fishermen from the Gulf Coast. Lean, hard Okies with narrow, suspicious eyes who behave always as though the Navy might decide to cancel chow, as if everything in life was and always would be as precarious as the life of a migrant fruit picker. Boys who spent the depression working a pick and shovel for the Civilian Conservation Corps so they could get three squares a day, then joined the Navy for the same reason. Men who know what it's like to lie down next to a thin-shanked woman and close your ears to the hungry cries of your children so you can get up and work the next day.

Bobby is still sunburned from the damned Saturday morning parade, his feet blistered from the heat of the asphalt melting under the Honolulu sun, *left-right-left* in dress whites under the palm trees carrying the weight of their rifles, the old .30-caliber Springfield '03s unloaded as they marched, and whose jackass idea was that anyhow? The men marching with empty rifles so the brass can have their parade. Lousy way to spend a Saturday, and what if somebody decided to attack right then? Helpless as kittens the lot of them, far from their ships, with empty weapons. There is no explaining admirals. They go to Annapolis, they spend decades in the Navy, they rise through the ranks, and by the time they have all the stars they can get, they don't know shit from Shinola. There is not an enlisted man in Wahoo who doesn't believe he could run the show better than Admiral Husband E. Kimmel, but if Kimmel says march, they march.

Bobby finishes tying his shoes and goes to see Lucian Quigley IV, his buddy in the galley, the only black man on the *Tennessee*. He is the blackest man Bobby has ever known, black as coal in the hold of a ship. Lucian goes about six foot four and two hundred and forty pounds, and he has just won the ship's heavyweight championship by knocking out three strapping white boys in bouts that lasted less than a minute, total.

"Say, Wat"—Lucian grins—"how come you're the only swabbie who's early for breakfast? Where are your cracker friends?"

"They were all drunk on Hotel Street last night."

"Aint it the way? Get a little money in their pocket, they got to get rid of it, quick as they can. What about you?"

"I behaved myself. Got a haircut, played a little Skee-Ball. That was about it. Did you go ashore?"

"No, sir. I had to start at four o'clock this morning."

"You always have to start at four o'clock."

"That's right. I'm a Negro, or maybe you aint noticed. We generally get the short end. Speakin of short ends, here he comes now."

Bobby looks over his shoulder, sees Paulie Maggio stroll in, swaggering as though the *Tennessee* is his own private yacht. Maggio sports a pair of shiners.

"Whooo, Paulie!" Lucian says. "You look like you lost a fight with the whole doggone Marine Corps."

"You should see the other fella."

Lucian rolls his eyes. "Sure, Paulie. That Marine is telling his buddies how you beat up his knuckles with your face."

"Yeah, you just ask him, Lucie. You find him and ask him. You go to the base hospital, if you wanna look for that Marine. Hey, did you wash them garbage cans like I told you to? I got to watch you Negroes, you never miss a chance to lay down on the job."

"Yassuh, I done washed them cans, massa! I is all done with that job."

"Aw, can it, Lucie. What's your boy Wat doin here? He wants breakfast, right? Two hours before chow, he expects us to feed him."

Bobby shrugs. "Some of us eat early, is all."

"Going to cost you, Wat. Cost you dear. Two tailor-mades, my cowboy friend. Give with the Pall Malls, or no sandwich."

"Lucian was making me a sandwich anyhow. Why should I pay you?"

"Because I'm the best-lookin wop in the Navy, and you love me more'n Lucie, aint that right?"

"No."

"Well, how bout cause I'm stone broke and it's still three more weeks to payday? C'mon, Wat. Two tailor-mades. I know you got 'em. You never spread your money around. I bet you wouldn't spring for fifteen cents for a comic book. You're one of those fellas who could tell his sister every last thing he does in Wahoo and not make her blush."

Bobby grins. "You're right, Maggio. I could and I do, but my sister is tougher than you. All right, then. Two tailor-mades, for one sandwich."

"I don't know. Maybe two tailor-mades aint enough. Maybe I should charge you a whole pack. I don't get you, Wat. Everybody in this man's Navy sleeps when he gets a chance. Everybody except you. Think I'd be here cookin this slop if I wasn't on duty? No way. No. Fucking. Way. I'd be in the sack. But you? You're down here two hours before chow, wanting your breakfast. Every. Fucking. Morning. Why don't you try to sleep, huh? Just once. Sleep till, I dunno, six o'clock."

"I can't. I wake up and there aint no sense tryin to go back to sleep."

"Awright, awright. Two smokes. What kind of sandwich you want?"

"Anything you got. Cup a joe, sandwich, tomatoes, bread, ham, maybe a little butter if you can spare it."

"Butter? Now youse want butter, too? How bout my big old peter between two hamburger buns? That whore down in Mosquito Flats last night didn't half wear it out. It probly smells like her."

"Paulie, you're a pervert, you know that? Navy full of perverts, but you're pervert number one. C'mon, don't jerk my chain. I want to go up to watch the sun rise. Only place in the Navy where a fellow can get a little peace is up in the gun bucket."

"You and that damned gun. I swear, that's the only woman you love. Me, I prefer the real kind. I got a piece last night, her little quim still wet from the last guy but she was tight, woooeee, she never seen anything like Big Paulie, she's whispering in my ear, *Paulie, oh, Paulie, oh-oh, Paulie, gimme more, gimme more, cause I'm a whore . . .*"

Lucian has heard enough. "You know why you got brown eyes, Paulie? Cause they stacked shit all the way to your eyeballs."

"Just for that, you're going to swab this whole kitchen after breakfast, Lucie."

"That's no problem, massa. I'll just turn you upside down and mop the floor with your head. Is everybody in the state of New Jersey an ass-hole, or is it just you?"

"I'm the nicest guy ever came outa the state of New Jersey, Lucie. Don't you ever doubt it."

While Maggio is gabbing, Lucian finishes making Bobby's sandwich and chops it in two with a meat cleaver.

Maggio jumps. "Damn! What are you doin? Tryin to scare a man to death?"

Lucian shrugs. "Aint hard scarin you. You wake up in the morning, you jump at your own shadow."

Maggio begins to dance around again, throwing left jabs. "One of these days, Lucille, I'm gonna to have to teach you a little lesson about boxing."

"Oh, man. If you wasn't white, I'd knock you all the way back to the *Arizona*."

"Right now. C'mon, prove it."

Bobby laughs. "Paulie, why don't you quit while you're ahead? You got a man here that outweighs you by a hundred pounds, he's heavy-weight champ of this boat, and he's holding a meat cleaver. If I was you, I'd just shut up."

Maggio tries his tough-guy glare. "Take. Your. Fuckin. Egg. Fuckin. Sandwich. And get the fuck out of my slop chute. Hey, you know you're still wearing them stinking flowers around your neck?"

Bobby fumbles at his neck. Sure enough. A lei, fragrant as a girl's per-fume, purchased on Hotel Street. An old Hawaiian woman had told him what the flowers were, yellow ilima and sweet mountain maile. The lei is so long that Bobby has wound it around his neck three times to keep from tripping over it. He starts to take it off and shrugs. It's Sunday in Hawaii. A little decoration never hurt anyone.

"Thanks, Lucian," he says on his way out. "You get tired of this arro-gant little pip-squeak, come visit the gun bucket. We can pass the time of day."

Maggio isn't going to let him off that easy. "Where's my tailor-mades?"

"Right in my pocket. I'm going to go topside, smoke 'em for you, okay?"

Lucian waves the meat cleaver by way of saying good-bye. Maggio starts his mouth going again. Bobby takes his coffee and his sandwich and heads for his gun bucket, wondering how it is that Lucian Quigley IV has not yet planted that meat cleaver in Paulie Maggio's skull.

18.

SUNDAY IS THE SWEETEST DAY. SO QUIET YOU CAN hear the Pacific lapping against the hull of the ship. Babysitting his .50-caliber up top gives Bobby what a man accustomed to wide-open spaces needs most on a crowded ship: room to breathe. Alone before dawn, he can imagine himself out on horseback on the 8T8, with the horizon wide as the moon. Grazing cattle in the distance, a sprinkling of antelope, no sound but the horse breathing and its hooves sibilant in the buffalo grass. The nearest you can come to it is the ocean before first light, the cries of seabirds in the semidarkness, the creak of cables as thick as his waist. There is nothing like Pearl Harbor before sunrise on a Sunday, peace like an ocean of grass out there beyond the breakers. He likes to get to his gun bucket in time to watch the superstructures of the big ships swim out of the darkness. It's good practice for his eyesight, sharpens him up to find the shadow of an elk against a gray rock at dawn, the way the animal emerges for an instant, before the light is too strong and the buck spots the gleam of the rifle and hightails it.

An hour later, the sun is all the way up and beginning to scorch. He glances at his watch: it's 7:25, 0725 Navy time. Battleship Row is beginning to stir, sailors coming topside after breakfast, bandsmen getting ready to play the national anthem, tooting their trumpets, loosening their lips. Buddies holler up to him, wanting to know if he has spent the night sleeping with that damned machine gun. Bobby laughs and waves, says he can't help it if he isn't one of those city boys who likes to sleep until noon. He picks up a cloth, starts polishing any surface he can find to polish. His gun bucket is always immaculate, but a little extra polishing never hurt. He's in a fine Sunday morning mood, singing one of the old songs he used to sing in church in his clear, tenor voice:

Keep on the sunny side, always on the sunny side,
Keep on the sunny side of life
It will help us every day, it will brighten all the way
If we'll keep on the sunny side of life . . .

Far in the distance, he hears the drone of airplanes. Sunday morning maneuvers. That will be the Army Air Corps, staging another training exercise on a Sunday morning. Won't let a man have his peace and quiet on the Sabbath. This time they are going all-out. He sees one line of planes approaching from the southeast, another from the northeast, still another coming directly out of the rising sun to the east, another from due south. The fly boys aren't messing around. No one on Oahu is going to sleep in this Sunday morning, not with that many planes buzzing around.

At 0755, he sees the signalman raise the blue-and-white prep flag on the Pearl Harbor tower, the signal to the color guards on all the ships to prepare to raise the Stars and Stripes. Bobby waves to another gunner, sitting with his newspaper on the *West Virginia,* moored alongside the *Tennessee.* The noise of the planes grows louder, like a swarm of angry hornets. As he tosses the dregs of his cold coffee and stands to stretch his limbs, he sees a line of bombers dive toward the hangars and sea-planes on Ford Island, a stick of bombs falling, a hangar exploding in fire and smoke. *Holy Jesus. That pilot was loaded with live bombs. He's going to catch a raft of shit.*

Somewhere in the distance, he hears the sound of more explosions, all of them together now like rolling thunder. *Jesus. When the Air Corps wants to screw up, they don't mess around.* Then he hears a Marine ser-geant screaming. "This aint no drill! This aint no drill! It's the fucking Japs! Battle stations, battle stations, battle stations! Fire! Fire! Fire!"

The gunner on the *West Virginia* is frantically pointing in the op-posite direction. Bobby turns to look, sees the first flight of torpedo bombers skimming the water on their way to Battleship Row. Fighter planes circle above them. He looks up, sees the circle of the rising sun on their wings. *Japs. What are they doing this far from home? Are they lost?*

Falling bombs tumble, gleaming in the sunshine, beautiful silvery fish as they fall before the first concussions rip through the battleships. Choking black smoke rises in one tall column after another. He grabs a web belt of rounds from the ready ammunition box next to the unprotected machine gun and fires a burst through the smoke. Then he is firing in steady bursts as a Japanese pilot wags his wings in triumph and peels away, the bastard, leaving a scene below that looks like the beginning of the end of the world. Bobby is certain he has hit the Jap plane, but the .50-caliber does not fire explosive shells. Unless you hit the pilot or the engine, it's hard to do much damage.

He's so intent that he barely notices that there is someone beside him. It's Lucian, still wearing his apron. He has grabbed an unmanned .50-caliber and is firing it single-handed, as though he had trained his whole life for the job. When there's a brief lull in the fighting, Lucian hollers, "We hit any of them damned Nips yet, Wat?"

Bobby is about to answer when the concussion knocks him down, leaves Lucian standing. He is deafened, trying to figure out what happened, as Lucian gives him a hand and tugs him back to his feet. Lucian points off the stern of the *Tennessee*, where an explosion has torn apart the bow of the *Arizona*, an explosion so powerful that it dwarfs everything else that is going on around them. The ship is still afloat, but the forward half of the *Arizona* is engulfed in flames that shoot hundreds of feet in the air, the heat so intense that he fears they will be burned to a crisp at their stations on the *Tennessee*. He mans the .50-caliber again as another wave of Zeros comes over, bursting through the towering columns of fire and smoke to strafe everything in their path. It's all noise, confusion, smoke, screams, the steady *boomp-boomp boomp-boomp* of the 40-millimeter pom-pom guns, the wail of bombs, the concussion of explosions, the oily smoke so thick they can taste it.

Ten minutes after the explosion on the *Arizona*, the *Tennessee* takes two direct hits from high-level bombs. Each time, Bobby is knocked flat and Lucian has to help him up. Fires are raging, the deck has been sprayed with debris. Everything is covered in oil. He's almost ready to give up hope, but the next lull in the attack is longer, time enough to get the fire under control. The seventeen-year-old boy they call Bedbug vaults into position to do his job, feeding ammo to the .50-caliber while Bobby fires.

"This here's Lucian," Bobby says. "You help keep him in ammo too, hear?"

Bedbug nods, his eyes so wide, it looks like they will swallow his entire face. One of the other gunners gave the kid his name, because he said that any man who would join the Navy before he's old enough to be drafted must be crazy as a bedbug. When another wave of Japanese planes bores in and the bombs begin to fall again, Bedbug curls up in the fetal position on the deck, elbows over his head, shaking and screaming. Bobby prods him in the ribs with his toe.

"What's the matter, kid?" he shouts. "You want to live forever?"

Bedbug scrambles to his knees, tears streaming down his cheeks. He is still trembling like a leaf in a thunderstorm, but he does the job he has been trained to do.

Around nine o'clock, Bobby sees the high-level bombers go over, so high up they are specks in the sky, flying in perfect formation. There is no point even firing at them. He speaks to the boy as calmly as he can. "Ammo, kid. Keep it coming. Don't quit on us now."

All along Battleship Row, black skyscrapers of smoke and fire coil from ships that have been hit. Tons of oil have leaked into the harbor. The oil is burning, the water is on fire. Men who have been ordered to abandon ship are being burned alive. During brief lulls in the firing, Bobby can hear their screams. A handful of the wounded sailors manage to pull themselves out of the burning oil onto the concrete mooring quays, where long, blackened strips of skin peel away from their bodies, exposing the raw, red flesh beneath. He sees a sailor stagger out of the water, blackened like a marshmallow which has been left in a camp-fire. The man looks up at the sky, raises his arms and turns completely around in a slow circle, then falls on his face, dead before he hits the ground. There is nothing Bobby can do except to keep on firing until he runs out of ammo or his gun barrel melts from the heat. He sees sailors do things that no man should be able to do. Like Woodrow Bailey, who chops a ten-inch hawser in half with a single stroke of an ax. He watches another stick of bombs tumble in slow motion, like a school of silvery fish, falling toward the helpless battleships tied at the mooring quays. There are more explosions. Dozens, hundreds, no one could possibly count. Ships erupt around them.

A Jap Zero comes in low, strafing, two lights blinking in front of the nose like flashing headlights, twin strips stitching the deck, coming directly at him. Bobby swings the .50-caliber, gets the plane in his sights. The pilot has his greenhouse pushed back, flying open-canopy at low altitude. Bobby's finger squeezes the trigger. He sees the tracer rounds arc toward the plane, the twin guns in the nose of the Zero still winking as the Jap strafes the deck, raking the ship with parallel lines of fire, like giant sewing needles. Then the plane is almost on top of him. The machine gun has no shield. On the open deck, there is no place to hide. Bobby remains at his post, firing steadily, holding his target until he sees the pilot's head blossom, like an exploding rose.

19

Juanita Paint spends the morning of the first Saturday of December shopping for Christmas gifts in Sheridan. She spends the afternoon in the arms of Tom Call. Eli is away again, visiting his daughter Ruby on her ranch outside Torrington, so Juanita buys a few things for Christmas, treats Emaline and Red to a dime-store lunch of grilled cheese and a cherry Coke, then parks her car in the narrow and rickety garage behind Tom's house and knocks softly on his back door. He pulls her into his arms, into a long kiss, into making love on the linoleum floor of the kitchen even before she has her coat off. All day, a phrase keeps going through her mind. She doesn't know where she heard it or read it, but it plays over and over, like a phonograph record that is stuck in the same groove: *the delirium of love, the delirium of love.* It is the only way to think of what is happening to her. She is delirious with love, they both are, like plague victims in the grip of something over which they have no power.

Lying on his kitchen floor with her coat bunched under her hips, she gasps for breath, laughing.

"Can't you even let a girl get her coat off?"

Tom rolls onto his back. "I didn't hear you complaining. I've been waiting all morning. Couldn't think about anything else."

"I know. But it makes it even better."

"Maybe. All I want to know is what you got me for Christmas while you were out there shopping."

"Not a thing. Why should I? You have me. What more could a man want?"

"I dunno. A new Cadillac? I might swap you for a Cadillac, even up."

She gives him a playful slap and tickles his ribs, but the reference to the Cadillac reminds her uncomfortably of Eli, the night in 1933 when he wrecked his Caddy driving home late and almost died. She changes the subject.

"What do you plan to do for Christmas?"

"Work, probably. That's what I generally do. People spend Christmas with their families and I don't have a family."

"You have me."

"You'll be out at the ranch."

"We could invite you to come out. Eli always has all kinds of people come for Christmas."

"I don't believe I could do that, Juanita. I'd feel awful uneasy and I'd want you all the time. I'd want to sneak off upstairs and lap you up like fresh cream."

"And I would let you."

"That's what worries me."

He helps her up off the floor, takes her coat and hangs it carefully. She goes to the kitchen and puts on a pot of coffee. Tom is tidy as a sailor, but he had almost nothing, not even a coffeepot. She bought inexpensive cups and glasses and dishes, pots and pans, even curtains for his windows. She found a cache of old photographs in a chest, bought some frames, and on a wall over the davenport assembled a series of black-and-white pictures of Tom performing with the Flying Fandangos at various air shows and county fairs. In someways, his little home is more to her taste than the vast house on the 8T8, where she sometimes feels as though she's living in a museum.

They spend a quiet afternoon. They talk, play cards, listen to the radio. There's no question of going out. They can't be seen together, except when he takes her flying. Eli knows about the flying, it doesn't bother him in the least. They usually go Sunday mornings, and it inevitably ends on the cot in Farley's office. Tom has started trying to teach Juanita to fly, but it is maddeningly difficult. Simply to take the stick and keep the Aeronca on a straight, level course is much harder than it looks. She is always banking to the left, or banking to the right, gaining or losing altitude when she doesn't want to. She can't imagine doing the things Tom does with an airplane, the loops and dives, although after that scare the first time out, he refrains from trying such stunts with the Aeronca.

The thought of flying makes her think of what they do after a flight. She wants a bath first, so she slips away to the cozy little bathroom, opens the tap, peels off her clothes, and leaves them neatly folded on a shelf. On her first visit to his house, she was surprised to find that the bathroom had a hot-water heater and a big old claw-foot tub as long as she is tall. She shakes a few drops of shampoo into the tub, waits until it begins to bubble up, then slips into the hot water. She stretches out, enjoying the room she has for her long legs. She closes her eyes, imagines what it would be like to drift in this warmth forever. When she looks up, Tom is watching her from the doorway. She smiles.

"It's a big tub," she says. "Why don't you come in with me?"

"I never took a bath in front of a lady before."

"You wouldn't be in front of me. You'd be with me. Come on. It's a waste, all this hot water for me alone. We can fit."

"All right."

His slender, white body, so pale next to her brown skin. He is all lean muscle: thighs, belly, arms. Much more muscular than he looks with his clothes on. He wedges his long body into a corner of the tub, next to the spout. He winces at the heat of the water.

"Whoa! How can you take it this hot?"

"Relax. You get used to it after a bit. It makes you feel warm all over."

He leans back, admiring her. "That's about the prettiest thing I've ever seen, your breasts with all them soapsuds. God, you are a beautiful woman."

Juanita laughs. "Old as I am?"

"Young or old. Whatever age you are, you put most of them young gals to shame."

She teases him, drawing a fingernail over her brown nipples, making them rise.

"Now you quit that. I came in here to take a bath, not to fool around."

She leans forward to draw her palm across his groin. "Feels to me like you came to fool around, Mr. Call. I guess you didn't get enough before."

Later, as she washes his back, she leans to his ear and whispers, three times over. "I love you, Tom. I love you. I love you."

He strokes her smooth calf. "I love you, too, Juanita. Like nothing else in this world."

After the bath, they get half-dressed, Tom in a tattered robe and Juanita in one of his old shirts. They sit on the davenport, Juanita's head cradled on Tom's shoulder, Tom sipping a cold beer. "What are we going to do, Tom?"

"I don't know, Juanita."

"We must know. We must get to a place where we know."

"It isn't like I haven't thought about it. Some days, I hardly think about anything else. I want to be with you. There's nothing else I really want, except to get back to flying airplanes. But we'd have to leave. Go somewhere like California or Oregon, start over. There aren't that many fellows who know how to fly all kinds of airplanes. Companies are always looking for pilots. Maybe you could work as a nurse again, until we get settled. Could you do that? Would you come with me?"

"I don't know. I think I would, but I owe Eli so much. I owe him the truth. I should tell him. I know this is not right and want to do the right thing. As close to right as we can get, since this has happened."

"So what do you want to do?"

"I want to go with you. Anywhere. California, Louisiana, anywhere you want to go, as long as it's not here. But let's get through Christmas first. Most of Eli's children are coming to spend Christmas with us. When Christmas is over, I'll tell him. I have to. I can't go on like this. Then we can be together. I think you're right. California would be best. That's a place where people go to start over, isn't it?"

"Long as we don't run into Doreen."

"California is a big place. We won't run into Doreen. And even if we do, you have someone better, right?"

"Absolutely."

Tom finishes his beer. It's barely five o'clock, but it's already dark outside. Juanita fixes supper. After supper they sit listening to the radio. It's the first time they have been able to spend a whole night together. She has a nightgown with her, so she puts it on and comes to him, feeling that this is how it will be when they are together.

20

After breakfast every Sunday, Emaline and Red dress in their Sunday best and walk the five blocks to church. The boy runs or skips all the way, skimming rocks at light poles in the summer, throwing snowballs in winter. They sing the old hymns, and she puts a quarter in the collection plate when it comes around. After the service, if the weather is good, she stands outside and talks with the church ladies while Red dashes around with the other children. Then they saunter home. She spends the first part of the afternoon doing her chores, and when the chores are done, she has a cup of tea, listens to the radio, and reads Chekhov or Balzac until it is time for supper.

After a frigid morning, this Sunday is crisp and clear and warm for December, with the temperature already in the mid-thirties and climbing. They linger in the winter sunshine outside the church, chatting with the parson and members of the congregation, then walk home hand in hand, change out of their Sunday clothes, and eat steaming bowls of potato soup before Red runs out to play. The screen door slams as he tears out, forgetting to shut the inner door. She closes it behind him. She starts in on the week's pile of ironing. As she irons, she listens to *Sammy Kaye's Sunday Serenade* on the radio. She tunes in every week, mostly because she loves Tommy Ryan's smooth way with a tune. He isn't Bing Crosby, but he always perks her up. The show ends and the *University of Chicago Round Table* begins. She's ironing a pair of Red's britches when NBC interrupts with a news bulletin: *President Roosevelt said in a statement today that the Japanese have attacked the Pearl Harbor, Hawaii, from the air. I'll repeat that, the president says the Japanese have attacked Pearl Harbor in Hawaii from the air. This bulletin came to you from the NBC newsroom in New York.*

She pauses. She wasn't really listening, so the only part she heard was "attacked Pearl Harbor in Hawaii, from the air." The station returns to the program, a panel discussion of Canada's role in the fight against the Germans in Europe. She returns to her ironing, but now she listens intently. A few minutes later, NBC breaks into the discussion with another bulletin.

The White House also reported today an air attack, er, simultaneous air attacks on army and navy bases in Manila. This report followed the president's declaration that all army and navy bases on the island of Oahu are now under attack . . .

She feels her heart has stopped, that she is about to faint. Had he said all army *and* navy bases on Oahu or only the army bases? Why don't they repeat the bulletin? If all the navy bases have been attacked, then the battleships at Pearl Harbor have surely been attacked, including the *Tennessee*—if the ship is still in Hawaii. If the report is true, then the United States is at war with Japan. Why are they blathering on? Surely an attack on Hawaii is more important than a panel discussion? Fifteen minutes go by with nothing further and she is beginning to believe she imagined the whole thing when the moderator breaks in with more news: *I have just learned that the Japanese are now bombing Burma. This is an act that may lead the United States to war against Japan . . . I merely mention this to show how fast events are moving.*

She puts a kettle of water on the stove for tea, fills the pot and leaves the tea to steep, forgets to pour it. She looks out the window. Red and the Palmer boys are trying to have a snowball fight with the scant and powdery snow. She hears their high-pitched laughter. There's no one else out. People aren't pouring into the streets, screaming hysterically that there is a war on. Finally, an old De Soto crawls up the street headed north, an elderly couple inside. Do they know? Does anyone care?

Emaline has a sudden, terrible image of Bobby, blown to bits as a Japanese bomb scores a direct hit on his machine gun. She knows, for the first time, how mothers feel when they have sons at war. She feels closer to Bobby than anyone in the world, even Juanita. Surely nothing can happen to him? It occurs to her that she is being very selfish, worrying about Bobby and no one else. What about Leo Paint? He's in the Shore Patrol, but he's stationed on Oahu as well. Leo could be in as much in danger as Bobby. She remembers the day, April 1, 1940, when Bobby and Leo enlisted in the Navy. She was furious with them for enlisting, for spoiling the seventieth birthday party for Eli and Ezra with such news. Now they are far out in the Pacific, directly in the path of the Japanese bombers.

She waits for more news. They can't say something like that and then just leave the whole world dangling. Outside, she hears the happy shouts of Red playing with his friends. Let him remain innocent for a few more moments. This war will come down on all their heads soon enough.

At a few minutes past two o'clock, the NBC Red network has a report from Honolulu. This time, there can be no doubt. She listens so intently that her fingernails cut into her palms. There is static on the line, but the news is achingly clear:

Hello, NBC. Hello, NBC. This is KTU in Honolulu, Hawaii. I am speaking from the roof of the Advertiser Publishing Company Building. We have witnessed this morning the distant view of a brief full battle of Pearl Harbor and the severe bombing of Pearl Harbor by enemy planes, undoubtedly Japanese. The city of Honolulu has also been attacked and considerable damage done. This battle has been going on for nearly three hours. One of the bombs dropped within fifty feet of the KTU tower. It is no joke. It is a real war. The public of Honolulu has been advised to keep in their homes and away from the Army and Navy. There has been serious fighting going on in the air and in the sea. The heavy shooting seems to be . . . We cannot estimate just how much damage has been done, but it has been a very severe attack. The Navy and Army appear now to have the air and the sea under control—

A telephone operator interrupts the report to say that she has an emergency call. The reporter tries to explain that he is talking to New York, but he's cut off and the line goes dead. Emaline screams at the radio: "No! You can't do that! You can't cut him off!" But it's done, the reporter is off the air. She's so tense that she has to remind herself to breathe. It's time to tell Red now. There's no point delaying. He idolizes Bobby. Better that he hear it from her than have the Palmers tell him that his uncle might have been killed. She opens the front door and calls him.

"Red, I want you to come in now."

He's about to fling another handful of snow at one of the Palmer boys. "Oh, Ma, it's nowhere near suppertime."

"I need you to come in. Just for a while. Then you can go back out."

Something in the tone of her voice tells him not to argue. He shuffles across the street, sliding along in his overshoes. At the door, she helps him out of his hat, scarf, mittens, coat, and boots.

"Would you like a cup of hot cocoa?"

Red looks at her, puzzled. He can see there is something wrong, as though she might start crying at any moment. He waits quietly on the sofa. She sits beside him and puts a hand on his shoulder.

"Something awful has happened, honey. The Japanese have bombed Pearl Harbor."

"What? You mean Pearl Harbor, where Uncle Bobby is?"

"Yes."

"And Leo?"

"Well, yes. Leo is in the Shore Patrol, but he's there, too."

"Is Bobby hurt?"

"I don't think so. I don't really know. It's possible the *Tennessee* wasn't even at Pearl Harbor. I've been listening to the radio, but they haven't said much, only that there was an attack. Anyway, I wanted to tell you myself. I'm going to need you to be a big boy now and help me listen to the radio so we can see if there's more news. I'm going to try to call Ben to see if he's heard."

The telephone lines are busy. It takes her three attempts to get through to the operator. There is no answer at Ben's house, so she asks the operator to try Eli Paint, but there's no answer at the main house, either. She wonders where Juanita could be at this time on a Sunday afternoon. Finally, she reaches Ben at Ezra's place, where Ben and his wife, Belle, are having Sunday dinner. They haven't been listening to the radio, so Emaline has to give Ben the news. He does his best to reassure her.

"Sis, Bobby's the best shot in the world. If a Jap plane got near him, he'd shoot it down. At least it's the Japs, not the Germans. I'm not even sure the Japs can fly straight."

"Well, they seemed to have been able to find Hawaii just fine. What on earth were those admirals doing? They weren't watching for a surprise attack, that's for sure."

Emaline and Red listen to the radio all the rest of the day and into the evening without learning much more. The boy knows the stations better than she does, so he spins the dial from NBC Blue to NBC Red to CBS and back again. There has been an attack on Pearl Harbor, but beyond that, the details are scarce. Either the reporters don't know what ships have been hit or they aren't saying. Everyone seems to agree that President Roosevelt will go before Congress to ask for a declaration of war, but even that is not official. Before bedtime, Emaline and Red say a prayer for Bobby and Leo and all the sailors and soldiers in Hawaii and the Philippines, which are also under attack. The boy goes right to sleep, but Emaline lies awake until long after midnight.

21

After Juanita leaves for the ranch, Tom Call heads to the office. Strother Leach is always on duty Sundays, but he spends the day in the back room with his buddies, drinking whiskey and playing poker. Tom can hear them laughing from outside the building. He shrugs: that's Strother. He's still the mayor's brother-in-law. Firing him would be more trouble than it's worth. On his desk, he finds a message from a woman named Bessie Hill, a clerk who works in the county records office. He checks the time: Bessie called near six o'clock Friday afternoon, after Tom had left work. He picks up the telephone.

"Operator?"

"Nell, it's Sheriff Call. Can you put me through to Bessie Hill at home, please?"

When Bessie picks up the phone, he can hear noisy kids in the background. She's a heavyset woman with an alcoholic husband and five children to raise.

"It's Tom Call, Bessie. I see you left a message for me."

"Yes, Sheriff. Just a minute. I've got flour all over my hands."

When she returns, she sounds a little less breathless. "Sheriff, you were asking about that ten thousand acres of land that Eli Paint sold to that Scottish fellow some years back?"

"I was."

"Okay, the fellow who purchased it was Sir George Aitken, from Glasgow. Now when he died, in 1939, the land passed to his son, Heath Aitken. I understand he's now an officer with the British troops in North Africa."

"That's right. I was told that Eli has been trying to buy that land back, but he hasn't been able to reach the young man."

"Well, Sheriff, it wouldn't matter if he did."

"Why's that?"

"The land was sold last year. Shortly after Mr. Aitken passed away. Mr. Heath Aitken's son sold it to Montana West."

"Montana West?"

"Yes. It's a land company. A big one. The home office is in Billings."

"Have any idea who's behind it?"

"Of course I do. It took me some time, but I was able to find out for you. Montana West is owned by William C. Bury."

"Big Bill Bury?"

"The very same."

"So Bill Bury owns that land? Where Millie Stojko was killed?"

"That's what I am telling you. He's owned it since the nineteenth day of October, 1940, to be exact."

"So he bought it a couple of months after he had that run-in with Eli Paint over the mustangs."

"I don't know about any run-in with Mr. Paint, but William Bury owns that land."

"And he was the owner when Millie Stojko died."

"If you mean the girl who was killed last May, yes. When they found her in that cabin, Mr. Bury was the owner. Through Montana West, that is. The property is still in their hands."

"Bessie, you're a wonder. I'll let you get back to your dinner, but I won't forget you come Christmastime."

"Oh, pshaw! Just doing my job, Sheriff. It's nice to be helpful."

Tom pulls out the file on the Millie Stojko murder. The fact that Bill Bury has owned the land all along puts a different slant on things. But why had he gone to the trouble to purchase it, unless he was looking to create trouble for Eli Paint? Was it possible he sent someone to frighten Eli by killing calves, shooting up water tanks, cutting barbed wire? What other motive could he possibly have, unless he knew that Eli wanted the land back? Bury owned hundred-thousand-acre ranches in at least four states and a million-acre spread in Texas. Why would he buy such a pic-ayune piece of land, if not to get under Eli's skin? If Bury himself wasn't out there killing calves, it was still possible that someone connected to the old man was responsible. Like Pardo Bury, now serving time in Texas for cutting a Mexican prostitute. Pardo had supposedly been in Texas when Millie was killed—but what if he wasn't? What if his father sent him out of the state to keep him from coming under suspicion?

Tom spreads out the file on his desk, arranges it and rearranges the evidence. The photographs always tear at him. There are three of Millie Stojko. One is her high school yearbook photograph, one was taken at a birthday party when she was thirteen, another shows Millie with her smiling father before his death. A serious, dark-eyed girl, a good student, abused by a brute of a stepfather and murdered by a person or persons unknown.

There are also photographs of two other girls whose murders might or might not be connected to the death of the Stojko girl: Marnie Whitlock, age nineteen, a coed at the University of Wyoming in Laramie, who vanished while walking home after an exam on a cold January night in 1939. She was found three days later, with her throat cut and ligature marks on her wrists and ankles, her body dumped carelessly in a band shell in a park and partially covered by drifting snow. And Grace Stone, seventeen, a high school student in Douglas, strangled after she disappeared during a school outing in March 1940. There were twenty students, two teachers, and a bus driver with that group from Douglas, and not one of them could shed any light on the disappearance of Grace Stone. She went to use the restroom at the bus station in Casper and never returned. A week later, her body was found on the backseat of a wrecked Model T Ford left in a junkyard west of Rawlins. At times, Tom feels as though he is chasing a ghost.

Three young girls found murdered in different parts of the state. The absence of anything resembling real evidence has driven Tom to keep going over what little evidence there is. Now the bits and pieces are coming together. Bill Bury owns the land where Millie was killed. Pardo Bury is in prison for cutting a girl with a knife. It's not a case he can take to court, but he has a whole bunch of questions he would like to ask Pardo, beginning with the date the young man actually left Wyoming.

The highway patrol has taken casts of the boot prints they found around the slaughtered calves, so maybe Tom can send one to the warden down in Huntsville, see if they're a match for Pardo's feet. He remembers the hunting lodge he saw from the air, the first time he took Juanita up in the Aeronca. He'll have to drive out and see what's there. According to what Eli told him, the Scot had the lodge built but never visited there. Was someone else using it? Pardo, for instance? He should also go down to Casper, or maybe get the Natrona County sheriff to ask Bill Bury exactly when his son left for Texas. If Pardo was in Wyoming when Millie was killed, they have a suspect.

Tom thinks of what Bill Brower said, about how these old cases come back to haunt you years later, an itch you can't scratch. He doesn't want that to happen to him. If he can solve this case and bring Millie Stojko's killer to justice, he will be free to go back to flying. Free to go to California with Juanita. Her scent is all over him. Her natural scent, since she wears no perfume. He likes it that way, so that he can inhale her with every breath. He can close his eyes and breathe deeply and it seems that she is right there. He feels his groin begin to tighten, forces himself to go back to the sheaf of notes. It's like stepping into an icy lake, the cold details of this merciless savagery.

He is trying to concentrate on his notes when a bulletin on the radio draws his attention. What was that? Something about attacks on Burma, the Philippines, and Hawaii. What does Burma have to do with Pearl Harbor? Who could be attacking Pearl Harbor? He wonders if Juanita has heard. He tries to go back to his notes. It's hopeless. All he can do is listen to the radio and curse the sketchy bulletins, which raise more questions than they answer.

The telephone rings. Tom picks it up, thinking it might be Juanita. The woman on the phone is almost hysterical. She swears that a Jap plane is circling over Sheridan and that it has dropped a bomb. Tom assures her that, no matter what is happening in Hawaii, it is a very long way from Wyoming. There have been no explosions, no one is dropping bombs on a little mountain town thirteen hundred miles from the coast.

He has barely put down the phone when one of the county

commissioners calls. He wants Tom to help organize the town's able-bodied men to repel a Jap invasion. When Tom points out that, even if the Japs do invade, it will take them a very long time to fight their way over two mountain ranges and a wide desert, the commissioner hangs up, furious that the sheriff doesn't see the immediate danger they're in.

Tom closes the file on the Stojko murder, puts on his hat and coat. The phone is ringing again as he steps out the door.

22

IN SHERIDAN ON MONDAY MORNING, EMALINE AND Red listen to the news broadcast before she walks him to school. Within an hour after she arrives at work, patrons have checked out every book the library has on Japan, Hawaii, battleships, and naval warfare. Even the two books they have on the Spanish Armada are checked out. In the absence of news from Honolulu, people want everything they can get their hands on to explain what happened. Everyone asks if she has any news about Bobby. She has nothing at all, except that she's sure she would know if he was hurt—and that she can't explain.

At 10:15, a dozen patrons and all three librarians gather around the radio to hear what FDR will say to Congress. Emaline expects the president to talk for half an hour at least. Instead, he begins at 10:30 and speaks for only a bit more than six minutes. It's still, in her mind, the greatest speech of all the great speeches he's ever given.

Yesterday, December seventh, 1941—a date which will live in infamy— the United States of America was suddenly and deliberately attacked by naval and air forces of the Empire of Japan. . . .

The president lists the places where the Japanese have attacked American and British forces: Malaya, Hong Kong, Guam, the Philippines, Wake Island, Midway.

I ask that the Congress declare that since the unprovoked and dastardly attack by Japan on Sunday, December seventh, 1941, a state of war has existed between the United States and the Japanese Empire.

When he finishes, the patrons in the Sheridan library give him a spontaneous ovation. Emaline smiles to herself. Most of them, she knows, are isolationist Republicans who were bitterly opposed to any U.S. involvement in the war—until now. She's disappointed in only one way: she had hoped he would give more details about what ships had been hit at Pearl Harbor. In his fireside chat the next day, he still offers no specifics on the damage, other than to say it has been extensive. He mentions the Philippines, Guam, and Wake and Midway Islands before admitting that *the casualty lists of these first few days will undoubtedly be large. I deeply feel the anxiety of all the families of the men in our armed forces and the relatives of people in cities which have been bombed. I can only give them my solemn promise that they will get news just as quickly as possible.*

On December 16, Navy Admiral Husband E. Kimmel, commander of the Pacific Fleet, and Lieutenant General Walter C. Short, commander of the U.S. Army ground and air forces stationed in Hawaii, are relieved of their commands. The same day, Eli receives a short note from Leo, saying that he is alive and well and had been working sixteen-hour watches with the Shore Patrol in Honolulu. Leo also says that the *Tennessee* was hit, but that he wasn't able to learn anything about Bobby. Those paragraphs have been blacked out by the censors.

Juanita can't reach Tom until three days after the attack. As soon as he answers the phone, she catches something strange in his tone.

"What's going on, Tom?"

"I've enlisted in the Army Air Corps. I'm going to see if they won't put me in a Flying Fortress."

"Why didn't you at least tell me first?"

"I couldn't very well call you at the ranch. I've been busy as hell. You can't believe how many people think Jap soldiers are hiding around town."

"You should have waited until you could talk it over with me first."

"Maybe I should have. I was just so damned mad after the attack. I'm a pilot, Juanita, and a damned good one. I never should've left flying. I want to be at the front of the line for a B-17."

"What about us? We were going to California."

"Well, we hadn't exactly decided that just yet."

"I had. I knew I would go with you."

"This doesn't mean we can't be together, Juanita. Only it's going to take a bit longer."

"A bit? Until the war's over. That's what you mean, isn't it? That could be years. Maybe decades."

"It could be over quick, now that America is in the fight. You can't believe what Americans can do, once we make up our minds. Anyway, lots of folks are going to have to wait for things now. It wouldn't be any different if they drafted me."

"Wouldn't you get an exemption? You're an officer of the law."

"I couldn't do that, Juanita. Sit here twiddling my thumbs in Wyoming when there's a war on. I have a skill this country is going to need. That's the way it is in wartime. I love you, Juanita. But this war has got to be fought. Hell, I want to be with you more than anything."

"Anything except flying your precious B-17s, right?"

"Juanita, I don't want to fight with you over the phone. Can you make it into town? I'd rather talk things over."

"We're talking now."

"You know what I mean. Face-to-face. It's better when I can see you."

She hesitates, so angry she's on the verge of telling him she never wants to see him again. "All right. I can come in tomorrow."

From the first hours after the attack, her emotions have been in tumult. She felt enormous relief when Eli made it home the evening of the attack. They listened to the radio with Ezra and Jolene and Ben and Belle. When the others left and she went up to bed with Eli, they made love. She was raw and sore from her time with Tom, but she wanted it as much as Eli did—for comfort and reassurance, if nothing else. In difficult times, she thinks, people turn instinctively to those with whom they are closest. She knows Tom well, but she's been seeing him only a few months. Even then, they usually have only a few precious minutes, stolen from busy days. She has spent years with Eli, seen him in every possible situation. Tom is going off to a hazardous and uncertain future. She and Eli need each other now more than ever. By rushing to enlist before he told her of his plans, Tom made it pretty clear where she stands in his life.

When she sees him at his house, they are awkward with each other. It's as though the shadow of that Flying Fortress hangs over everything they do. Tom is still awaiting his orders, but he's certain that he'll begin training before Christmas. Another sheriff will be appointed to take his place, at least until the next election, and unless a better candidate comes forward, the position will go to Strother Leach. Strother is fat and lazy and corrupt, but Early Porter doesn't want the job and Tom can't think of another likely replacement. The Millie Stojko investigation will have to be put on hold, like so many other things in this country.

Juanita stays less than two hours. It's too painful to linger. It's as though the ground has shifted underneath them, so that she no longer has any idea where they stand. When she is at the door, he asks if he can see her again before he leaves, maybe go up for a last flight in the Aeronca.

Juanita shakes her head. "No. I couldn't stand it. You do what you have to do. Come home safe, then we'll see. I want to say good-bye now and get it over with. I love you. I suppose I always will, but I can't stand this."

"I love you, too. You know that. I'm doing my duty, Juanita. That's all. Same as millions of men all over this country. I'm going to do it, and then I'll come back to you and we'll go to California."

"If you say so."

"I do. I'm not going to let you down. Will you write?"

"Yes. I think so."

"Can I write to you?"

"Yes. I'm the only one who ever gets the mail. Eli never picks it up and he never reads my mail. He doesn't even read *his* mail unless I hand it to him and tell him it's important."

"I wish we were married right now."

"So do I, Tom. But we aren't and it's possible we will never be."

He wants to say more, but she pulls on her coat and leaves without looking back.

Juanita beats Eli home and meets him at the door with a kiss.

"Whoa!" he says. "What brought this on?"

"What? I can't kiss my husband?"

"Well, you can, but . . ."

"I'm just so anxious for everyone," she says. "It's good to have you here."

"It's good to be home."

On December 19, the last Friday before Christmas, Red takes his time sauntering home from school. He's slower than usual, because there's fresh snow on the ground. He and the Palmer boys chuck snowballs at one another all the way home. Today, there's a postcard in the mailbox. He grabs it and runs all the way to the library. Emaline is decorating a small Christmas tree with strings of popcorn and dried cranberries.

"Mom, you've got mail!" he shouts, before she can hush him. She takes the postcard. It shows a view of Waikiki Beach, with a palm tree in the foreground, the dark mass of Diamond Head in the background. It's smudged with oil and it looks as though it had been passed through a hundred pairs of hands. The message is scrawled in pencil:

OK,
Bobby

23

Two weeks after the attack on Pearl Harbor, Bill Bury's secretary comes into his office in Casper to say that his son Lon is waiting to see him.

"What the hell is he doin here?"

"He says it's important."

Bury keeps Lon waiting for twenty minutes, then yells at him to come in. "You know you boys aint allowed to drop in uninvited," he says.

Lon fiddles with his hat, embarrassed. "Sorry, Pop. I come to say good-bye."

"Where are you going? I didn't tell you to go anywhere."

"I'm going to Marine Corps training in San Diego. I enlisted."

Big Bill's fist crashes down on his desk. "You what?"

"I enlisted. I've been swore in already. I'm a U.S. Marine now."

"No, by God. You're a goddamned fool, is what you are. You know how many phone calls it's going to take for me to get you out of this?"

"I don't want you makin no phone calls. I joined up. That's all there is to it. I'm a grown man, I can decide things for myself."

"That's a sorry lie, boy. If you believe that, you're even dumber than I thought. You know how much money there is to be made off this war? I'll call that senator I sent to Washington. It's high time he made himself useful."

"I don't want any favors. Maybe it's time this family did a favor for the country, for a change."

"What are you saying, you damned fool? We *are* this country, people like us. We do plenty. Who the hell do you think drills the oil and gets the copper out of the ground? Who keeps the trains running?"

"Men you hire. Poor fellas who get stuck working for you for a tenth of what they're worth."

"Damn you, boy! I'll cut you off every damned penny. Now I got one son in prison and the other one in the Marines. I don't know which is worse."

"Cut me off, if that's how you feel. The Marines will feed me. I know what you done to Pardo. He wouldn't be in jail if it wasn't for you. He wrote me a letter. A prisoner down in Huntsville heard about it. You fixed it for him to go to jail, you and that damned sneaky Milo Stroud."

"I didn't do a thing except be sure that boy got what he had comin. If you don't like it, that's too bad. You're no better than him, just dumber. Now get the hell out of here and go get shot."

"If I do get shot, at least I won't turn into a sonofabitch like you."

Bill makes like he's going to get up. Lon tenses for a fight, but the old man looks at his big-shouldered, hard-muscled son and thinks better of it. Lon isn't a pip-squeak like Pardo. In a lot of ways, he will make the perfect Marine: dumb and strong.

"To hell with you. Go play soldier. You aint smart enough to be any use around here anyway."

Lon turns on his heel and stalks out. *Look at him,* Big Bill thinks. *The dumb bastard is trying to march already.*

Before he has to report to active duty, Tom Call drives to Casper to question Bill Bury. The old man keeps him waiting more than an hour, then gives him exactly two minutes of his time. Tom has two questions to ask. The first is, exactly when had Lon and Pardo left for Texas?

"The first of April," Bury says. "I remember it clear. I thought it was funny that a pair of damned fools were leaving Wyoming on April Fool's Day. Anything else?"

"You're sure about that date?"

"Are you calling me a liar, son? Because if you are, I don't know how long you'd last as a sheriff in this state."

"No, sir, I just want to be sure."

"I'm sure. That means you're sure. Now we're done. You have a nice drive back to Sheridan."

"Before I go, there's one other thing. A little more than a year ago, you bought a piece of land, about ten thousand acres, off a Scottish lord."

"What's it to you?"

"Well, the land is right next to Eli Paint's spread. There's a hunting lodge at one end, at the other end, there's that sheepherder's shack where Millie Stojko was found."

"Are you accusing me of murder, son? Because if you are, you might be lucky to make it back to Sheridan."

"No, sir, I'm just asking if you own that land."

"There some law against a man owning land in the state of Wyoming?"

"No, sir. It's only that a terrible thing happened there, and I'm trying to determine who owns that place. I've been told that you're the owner, through a company called Montana West."

"That's true. I own the place. And I've never been there. Not even one time. I probably own fifty places, here and there, that I've never set foot on. Now does that scratch your itch?"

The next day, Tom heads out to the piece of land Bury owns adjacent to the 8T8. The building is a half mile from the county road, a rectangular log cabin forty feet long and twenty-five feet wide, with a single large stone chimney, well-crafted and solid. He tries the front door, finds it unlocked, pushes it open. The inside is a mess: empty beer bottles, trash tossed into the corners, dirty plates piled in the kitchen, encrusted with the moldy remnants of old meals. There is an empty icebox, an unmade bed, a rustic couch. On the walls, the heads of a half dozen dead animals: elk, whitetail deer, a black bear. A few old newspapers, the most recent from early May. Around the time Millie Stojko was killed.

He stands in the big empty room with the dead animals, listening to his heartbeat. Maybe it isn't true that the Scot never used this place. Perhaps, somewhere, there is a Scottish lord who wears very small boots. Or maybe someone, knowing the Scot never used the place, was squatting here. But the best explanation is always the simplest. Pardo Bury stayed here. Tom won't have time to prove it, but he can feel it. That won't go far in a court of law, but when the war is over, he'll know where to look.

The last thing Tom does before he leaves is to visit Bill Brower in Gillette. He brings with him his entire file on the Stojko case. Not because he expects Brower to follow it up but because he doesn't want to entrust it to Strother Leach. Strother might lose it, or sell it to the highest bidder if one comes around. Tom tells Brower about his visit to Bill Bury in Casper, about the discovery that Bury owns the land where Millie was killed, about the hunting lodge.

"It don't add up to a case," Brower concludes, "but it gives you a suspect. We still got to find someway to put him in that sheepherder's shack. The lodge is a step in the right direction, but it's a good long ways from the place where the girl was killed. Same with them dead calves. They point to a direction, but they don't get you there."

"Don't I know it."

"But you aint done yet."

"I might be, if I get shot down."

Brower nods. "I know you got to think that way, but you'll come back from the war all right. I got a feeling in my gut tells me it's so. My head's been wrong a thousand times, but my gut? Pretty much never."

Out in the East Texas piney woods, they call the place the Walls Unit. Or, more often, just the Walls, for its red-brick walls. John Wesley Hardin did time here. They claim that it was inside the Walls that Clyde Barrow changed from a schoolboy to a rattlesnake, before he went off and got himself killed, along with Bonnie Parker. They say it's the worst prison in Texas and that Texas has the worst prison system in the entire United States. It's filthy and noisy and dangerous, and the warders, the men they call "bosses," are worse than the prisoners. The men aren't in rooms, they're in cages, open to the other cages. A long row of caged men, most of them at least half-gone in the head. The noise can make you crazy. There's the regimented noise all day long: feet marching in unison, boots on the iron stairs. Iron doors clanging. It's worse at night. They holler and howl, bang metal cups on the bars, sing, scream, pray, cry, roar like lions when they have sex. They never shut up. The bosses

don't want to venture into a dark cellblock at night to tell somebody to
hold it down, so they let it go.

Pardo lies on his bunk with his eyes closed, forcing himself to get
used to the sounds of the place, so that he doesn't jump out of his skin
every time a door clangs. His cellmate is a Mexican from Nogales. Juan
Delgado. They call him Johnny. Plump and smiling, unless he thinks he's
been insulted. Johnny smokes all day long. State tobacco, prison tobacco,
hand-rolled because Johnny can't afford tailor-mades. It smells like pig
shit. It gets into Pardo's clothes and his hair, he can't get it out. He goes
around all day smelling like pig shit, but it's worth it to have a cellmate
who leaves him alone. Johnny gives him some advice the first day and
that's pretty much it. "Keep your eyes down. Don't look at nobody. Don't
ask nobody what they done. Don't watch the queers in the showers, they
get jealous. They'll think you're after their wife. Don't complain about
the food. Don't talk back to the bosses. Don't talk to the bosses period.
And if you got to fart at night, don't fart in your bunk where I can smell
it, cause I'll fuckin kill you."

He's in prison barely a week when Tommie Harris, a twenty-year-old
black man, is executed for rape and murder. In August, they fry a white
man, Arlin Reese. The condemned men are brought to the Death House
in the northeast corner of the Walls on the afternoon they are scheduled
to die. The execution chamber is a nine-by-twelve room. Thinking of
it drives him half-mad. The way a man's life narrows down, to that last
narrow room where he's going to fry. Hell, it would be so much more
merciful if they just crept into a convict's cell in the night and shot him
in the head, so he doesn't have to think about it. But then mercy is not
the point.

Every time there is an execution, Pardo feels the tension rise among
the inmates. Like a pot of water, heated to the boiling point. It doesn't
matter who the dead man is, black or white. Men go crazy. Shout,
scream, weep, drool, bang on the walls, fight, threaten, howl. Piss themselves. Smear shit on the walls.

But he's doing all right. He's going crazy, but he's doing all right.

Then the Japs hit Pearl Harbor and it all goes to hell. When the trustees hear the news on the radio, they pass it on. He howls like a wolf. When a warder stalks down the hall and tells him to put a cork in it, he goes berserk.

"You put a cork in it yourself, you fat fuck. You hear that? The Japs are coming. You're a dead man. They're gonna stick your fat ass on a bayonet. Them little yellow fuckers are comin after you, Ozzie. They'll hand out guns to all us inmates and they'll run you bastards through with bayonets. You better run outside, see if there's any Jap planes about to drop bombs on your sorry ass. They're comin, Ozzie. They're comin after you!"

Ozzie Combs raps his billyclub on the bars, but Pardo keeps howling. The boss waddles off down the cellblock, his gut hanging over his belt. Three cells down, he rattles the club on the bars to wake Earl Toth. Toth, not the warders, runs the cellblock.

"Toth!" Ozzie yells. "Wake up, I got a present for you. I'm bringin you a new wife. I want you to break him in gentle now."

Ozzie calls the bosses from the far end to help. They hold Pardo down, put him in handcuffs, drag him into the cell where Toth waits, grinning to show an uneven row of golden teeth.

"Fasten him to the bars," Toth orders. "And yank down his pants."

The warders do as they're told. Toth runs his hand over Pardo's behind.

"Damn, aint that a sweet little butt? I had a whore in Corpus Christi once, had a ass almost as cute as that. You cut a little girl, didn't you? Now you're the girl, dumb-ass. How does it feel?"

"You touch me, you fuckin ape, and you're the deadest man in this prison."

Toth drives a fist into Pardo's kidneys. "Only dead man I see is this piece of meat hangin here. I got twenty-three men with my bunch, you pretty little fuck. And every last one of us is goin to get our fill before we're done with you."

Down at the end of the cellblock, Ozzie Combs has a good laugh, listening to the screams. *They say that little fuck is rich. Old man owns half this country. Round here, he's just one more piece of meat.*

A week later, seven of Toth's men hold Pardo down and brand his left cheek with a hot poker. The letter *T* for Toth, two inches high. Marking him as prison property, they say. He remembers their names. Every last one.

24.

THE *TENNESSEE* IS TRAPPED AT PEARL HARBOR. When the Japanese strike, the battleship is tied fore and aft on her starboard side to a pair of masonry mooring quays on the southeast side of Ford Island. Astern is the grave of the *Arizona*, with some of her crewmen still alive, trapped in pockets of dwindling oxygen. To her port side is the crippled *West Virginia*, which has settled to the bottom on an even keel. Off her bow is the *Maryland*, with *Oklahoma* outside of her, capsized bottom up. When the order to sortie is given during the battle, the ship's engineers begin to get steam up, but there's nowhere to go. The *West Virginia* has wedged the *Tennessee* against the concrete quays. On her stern and port quarters, the *Tennessee* is engulfed in flames and smoke from the burning oil spilling from the *Arizona* and the *West Virginia*. The fires on the *Tennessee* are extinguished by 10:30 on the morning of the attacks. The fire in the water burns for two more days.

The first night after the attack, jittery sentinels fire at shadows and one another. Bursts of fire light the sky, tracer bullets probe for targets. A flight of friendly planes trying to land is shot down by panicky gunners. The horrors of the morning are temporarily forgotten in the rush to put out fires, clear rubble from the decks, tend to the wounded, rescue those still in the water. Exhausted sailors sleep where they fall, curled up against a bulkhead or sitting in a gun bucket. Shortly after dark, Bobby is ordered to go below and get four hours sack time. He has his shoes off and is about to stretch out on his hammock when he notices that he still has the Saturday night lei wrapped around his neck. He removes it carefully and tucks it into his locker. The flower petals are battered and bruised and streaked with oil, but the lei is still fragrant. Somehow, he's gotten through this day unhurt. The lei is his lucky charm. Before he returns to his gun bucket at midnight, he stuffs a few petals in his pockets for luck. On his way up the steps, he sees a young sailor curled up in the shadows, muttering over and over. *Give us this day our daily bread, on earth as it is in heaven, give us this day our daily bread, on earth as it is in heaven* . . . Everywhere there is the stench of oil and death, fires still burning, the trails of sparks where arc welders work to cut through steel hulls to rescue trapped men, shipyard lights glowing through the night where the repair work has already begun, now and again a sudden burst of fire and tracers crisscrossing the sky. Men seeking targets, anything at all to shoot at, wanting to deal death in return for death suffered. Their faces ache from the strain of peering into the darkness, listening for the drone of massed planes, for the whistling, tumbling bombs, the hiss of torpedoes, and the clatter of machine guns. They are certain there will be another attack. Already there are rumors of invasion, troops landing all over Hawaii. No one believes the Japs would just hit and run. The bombing has to be the prelude to an all-out attack.

Around two o'clock, Lucian Quigley IV comes up from the galley with a sandwich and a cup of coffee.

"Damned Navy," Lucian grumbles. "I almost got my ass shot by a sentry back there."

"The boys are nervous."

"They got a right to be, I guess. How could the Japs sneak up on us like that?"

"I don't know, Lucian. I sure don't know. They won't do it a second time, I know that. They might come back, but we'll be ready."

"Everybody says they'll hit us again first thing in the morning."

"They might. They'll get scalded if they do. I don't believe they will, though. I think they're hightailin it back to Japan right now, fast as their boats can carry them."

"What makes you say that?"

"They were a long way from home. It's always hard to fight that far out. They took a chance and they got away with it. They'll say this was a great victory and leave it at that for now. But they've twisted the tiger's tail. There's going to be hell to pay after this."

"Already been hell. Them boys screamin in the water, all that smoke. Fires of hell, right there, my friend. The very fires of hell."

They sit for a time in silence. Lucian chuckles, a low sound, deep in his chest. "One good thing come of all this."

"What was that?"

"Paulie. He was under a table down in the slop chute the whole time, screamin and hollerin and blubberin like a little girl. He wasn't the only one, but he was the loudest. After all that bragging he does, he aint likely to live this one down."

"I don't think he's all bad. I just don't like the way he treats you. Sometimes I think you're going to snap, bury that meat cleaver in his head."

Lucian chuckles. "Where's that going to get me? Even if I lick the first dozen they send after me, I won't lick the next dozen. Naw, I just got to bide my time. Wait for the world to change."

"What brought you to this man's Navy, anyhow?"

"A mule."

"A mule? What about a mule?"

"Tired of lookin at a mule's ass. Want to save enough money to buy a tractor."

"That why you never go up to Hotel Street?"

"That's part of it. And I'll never go until a black man can get treated same as anyone else up there."

"They ought to know that you were a hero this morning."

"Shoot. I didn't do anything. Somebody yelled it was the Japs after us, I picked up the first thing I could find to shoot back."

"You could have stayed below in the galley."

"Hell, no. Down below, you imagine all kinds of things. If somebody is trying to kill me, I'm going to try to kill him back."

"You did a helluva job of trying."

"I appreciate that. Now I got to get back to work, but I'm going to tell you a secret. Aint nobody going to kill Lucian Quigley the Fourth before I get back to Missouri and get my tractor, hear? You stick with ole

Lucian, Wat. Long as we're on the same boat, we'll both get through this thing alive."

They shake hands, then Lucian is gone. The endless night shivers into the dawn of the eighth day of December and a world not at all like the world the sailors left behind on Saturday night, falling drunkenly into the launches, puking over the side, toting souvenirs from Hotel Street. That's ancient history now, a time long past, never to be known again.

Every piece of the *Tennessee's* hull plating above the waterline is buckled and warped by the heat of the fire. Seams have burst open, rivets worked loose. The seams have to be welded, the rivets reset, the hull and weather decks recaulked. The work goes on day and night, noisier than a shipyard; glowing sparks from the arc welders shower the water on every side. The men on the battleships want only to be able to put out to sea, where they will no longer be sitting ducks for the next wave of Japanese planes. The *Maryland* moves away on December 9, but the forward mooring quay has to be carefully demolished to allow the *Tennessee* to move. With her hull pressed tight to the masonry, it's a delicate job. At last, on December 16, the *Tennessee* begins to move. She creeps past the hull of the sunken *Oklahoma* and remains moored at Pearl Harbor until December 20, when she leaves Hawaii with the *Maryland* and the *Pennsylvania* and heads north, sailing with a screen of four destroyers, bound for the Puget Sound Navy Yard for repairs. It's a spooky voyage, made jittery by repeated sightings, real or imagined, of enemy submarines.

The ships arrive in Puget Sound on December 29. The *Tennessee* remains there for two months while workers repair the hull plating and replace electrical wiring damaged by the heat. The battleship's tall mainmast is replaced by a tower to give the antiaircraft gunners a better field of fire. Air-search radar is installed, fire-control radars are fitted to the main battery and the five-inch antiaircraft gun directors. Her three-inch and .50-caliber antiaircraft guns are replaced by twenty-millimeter and forty-millimeter automatic shell guns, with splinter shields to protect all her antiaircraft gun crews.

In mid-January, Bobby gets a forty-eight-hour leave, which he spends with his aunt Kate. Kate has been married and divorced and lives with her ten-year-old daughter, Dorothy, in a neat little house in Bellingham, north of Seattle. It's strange to sit in Kate's parlor with the pictures on the wall of Emaline and Jake, Eli and Ezra, even his mother, Velma. There is a photo of Emaline and Bobby and Ben with Velma, playing in Little Goose Creek, it must have been around 1924 or 1925. Bobby can remember being a kid there, trying to catch frogs or just wading in the creek with the cold mountain water rushing around his ankles. The war seems a million miles away.

He calls Emaline from Kate's. They talk for ten minutes. He has imagined that he will tell her about the attack and all the rest of it, but once he has her on the phone, they talk about the weather, about Red's schoolwork, about what a nice house Kate has.

"I miss you something awful, Sis," he says.

"I miss you, too." He can hear the worry in her voice. He doesn't want to say anything more. There's no reason for her to know how bad things were at Pearl. She puts Red on for a moment. The boy asks if he's killed any Japs.

"Well, there was one . . . ," he starts to say, and then corrects himself. "I don't think so. It's all kinda crazy, you know, nobody knows what's goin on. Say, Emaline tells me you're doin real good in school. Keep it up, okay?"

It's true that he doesn't know about the Jap pilot. The one whose head exploded. It could be that he shot the man, but it might have been another gunner, guns barking all over the place. *They got too many of ours,* he thinks, *and we didn't get enough of theirs. It don't much matter who did the shooting.*

Before he catches the bus to go back to Puget Sound, Kate loads him up with cookies and cake for himself and for the other sailors, a whole duffel bag full. He feels like a real sailor now, a combat veteran with the duffel over his shoulder, swaggering up the steep gangplank onto the *Tennessee.* Then the duffel catches on an overhanging cable and tumbles into the water. A warrant officer bellows for a grappling hook to catch the bag before it sinks. Bobby is so startled, he swallows the toothpick he has in his teeth and has to be taken to sick bay, where they remove the toothpick from his throat. His duffel bag has been fished from the drink, but the cookies and cake from Aunt Kate are ruined and the sailors aboard are all laughing and joking about Gunner's Mate Robert E. Lee Watson, who almost choked to death on a toothpick after dropping his duffel bag in the water. He has to laugh. The only man on the *Tennessee*, maybe the only man in the whole doggone Navy, who has had to be taken to sick bay for a toothpick wound, suffered while attempting to board ship.

He begins training on the twenty-millimeter guns, now being fitted on the *Tennessee*. He goes over his notes a hundred times, pounding the information into his noggin so that, in combat, he won't have to think. *Misfire faulty ammunition, action to take: (recoil mass forward). Put gun on safe, remove magazine, cock gun, back out live round, throw shell over the side, check broken parts, if none, load and continue fire.* He tries to imagine doing all that in the hell of Pearl Harbor. If you can't do it in combat, the knowledge is useless. He commits whole pages to memory. Then he closes his eyes, performs the operations over and over in his mind until they are as familiar as lifting a knife and fork.

25

O N VALENTINE'S DAY, JUANITA DRIVES INTO town to see Doc Miller. The visit confirms what she already knows: she's pregnant, a little more than two months along. The doctor is not surprised. She is relatively young and healthy, and while it's not common for a man past seventy to father a child, it's not unheard of. He congratulates her. She tries not to look stricken.

Juanita dresses in a hurry, rushes out of the doctor's office, drives aimlessly around the streets. She passes Tom's house, which he has rented to Early Porter's brother for the duration of the war. She drives by the hospital, where Eli was taken after he wrecked his Cadillac in 1933. With no other destination in mind, she parks on East Loucks Street and tiptoes into the Holy Name Church. The sanctuary is empty. She slips into a back pew and sits biting her knuckles, staring at the cross. Taking comfort in the religion of her girlhood, with its incense and Latin and mystery, hoping to find someway out of this morass. She doesn't even know for sure whether Tom or Eli is the father of the child in her womb. They say a woman always knows, but she does not. On the day of the attack on Pearl Harbor, she made love to both men. She has been with Eli for eight years and has never been pregnant, so it seems likely that the child is Tom's, but she doesn't know that. She might know after the baby is born, but she can't be sure. What if the child looks like Tom? With his curly dark blond hair and blue eyes? She and Eli both have straight black hair—or at least Eli's was black, before it began to turn gray. How will she explain it?

She could end her pregnancy, find someone who would end it for her. But she wants the baby. No matter what. Even if Tom is killed in the war. Especially if he is killed. If this is his child, it would be the only trace of him left on this earth.

She needs to talk to someone. There is the pastor at Holy Name, whom she barely knows. Or Reverend Barnwell, who is very sympathetic, but too close to Eli. Emaline would listen without judging and give her a chance to work things out, but she cannot burden Emaline with her infidelity. There are too many blood ties, or perhaps she's too ashamed. She sees the priest slip into the confessional and makes her way into the familiar shadows. *Bless me, father, for I have sinned . . .*

She can go no further. She finds the little booth oppressive as a coffin. She can sense the priest, almost throbbing with anticipation, knowing that she is not one of the habitual penitents. Perhaps he is yearning for the truth she could tell, a lurid tale to stir his celibate dreams. She had known a priest like that when she was a girl, one who would ask for endless details of how and when she touched herself. She is on the verge of telling him about the child growing in her womb, her confusion as to the father, her betrayal. Instead, she tells him of her doubts about her religion, doubts she has felt for thirty years.

When it's over, she crosses herself and rushes from the church. Again she drives aimlessly, trying to think. She's angry with Tom, because in his rush to join the stampede to war, he has diminished himself and diminished their love. She risked everything for him, but she was never his true mistress. His first love is the silver crucifix of the airplane. He wants to fly the biggest and most powerful bomber ever built, a fabulous machine designed to deal out death and destruction while sweeping the shadowy sign of the cross over the earth, from one horizon to the other. Those who make war, she has come to believe, love it as much as they claim to hate it.

In the end, she does go to see Emaline. It's lunchtime when Juanita arrives at the library, so they sit and talk softly while Emaline nibbles a sandwich. Finally, Juanita tells her. "I'm pregnant."

"Oh, that's wonderful news."

"I guess so. I don't know. I didn't expect it. I'm not so young, you know. And I don't know how Eli is going to take it."

"He'll be thrilled. It's not like he can't afford to feed another mouth."

"I know. But he's so busy these days, trying to raise enough beef to keep the War Department happy. I hate this war."

Juanita begins to weep. Emaline hands her a handkerchief and puts her arms around her friend. She understands: pregnancy can make a woman emotional. "I think it will do Eli a world of good," Emaline says. "Take his mind off all his children and grandchildren fighting this war. I hate the war, too. I guess we have to be in it, but I hate every minute of it. All I want is for it to be over and for Bobby to be home safe."

There's no getting around it. The war is likely to go on for a long time. When it's over, nothing will be the same. Juanita stares at the National Geographic map that Emaline has tacked to the wall next to the kitchen table. Red has assembled blue thumbtacks for the Allied Forces, red for the Axis. There is fighting in so many places that it has taken him almost a month to establish the positions of the warring armies. Everyday, it seems, fighting breaks out in a new place. It looks as though the red tacks are swallowing the map, like a virus exploding across the globe.

Emaline tells Juanita about Arliss Gentry, an elderly teacher who spends his days reading in the library. Arliss knows more about the war than anyone. He says that, sooner or later, the Germans will finish with the Soviet Union and Great Britain, and the United States itself will be attacked, with the Germans invading the East Coast and the Japanese attacking the West Coast.

Juanita scrutinizes the map in awe. Before the red tacks are pushed back, so many will die. Hundreds of thousands of young men, all over the world, gone into the maw of the war. Bobby, Tom, Leo. Leo's older brothers, Calvin and Seth, have joined the Army. The list goes on. If the Germans and Japanese invade the United States, it will be far worse. It's possible none of them will survive.

But the one on her mind is Tom Call. She can talk about the others to Emaline, but she can't mention Tom. She leaves her friend a little puzzled. Emaline doesn't understand why Juanita seems so unhappy, when a baby is the happiest thing in the world.

26.

ON FEBRUARY 26, 1942, THE *Tennessee*, THE *Maryland*, and the *Colorado* leave Puget Sound, bound for San Francisco. The first morning out, Bobby eats an early breakfast in the galley with Lucian. Lucian is boiling mad. "My grandpa's in jail," he says. "Eighty-six years old and they hauled him off to jail."

"Why's that?"

"He got into an argument. White man ran his pickup into Granddaddy's old Model A that he shines every morning. Granddad is awful proud of that automobile. He wasn't pleased to see it dented up, so he told the fella he'd have to pay for the damage. Man wouldn't do it. Said he wasn't goin to pay for bustin up some nigger's car."

"What happened?"

"Grandpa knocked him down with his hickory stick. This fella aint more than forty, and he got hisself knocked down by a old man, so he went and complained to the sheriff and the sheriff arrested Grandpa. Says they're going to hold him until he says he's sorry, and he won't do it. Grandma tried to talk to him, but he said he's had a bellyful of that kind of thing his whole damned life, and he won't take it anymore. Not if it means he has to sit in that jail until doomsday. He was born in 1855, my granddaddy. He's old enough to remember when he was a slave."

"That's a helluva note, Lucian."

"Damned right. I'm out here fighting this war, and back home, we get treated the same as always. Like shit on a white man's shoes."

"I'm awful sorry."

"You didn't do a thing to be sorry about, Wat. Right from the first time you come to the galley, you were always real polite. Please and thank you. Never called me boy, never treated me like less than a man. I appreciate that. There's some like you on this ship, but there's plenty who are the other way, fellas who would like to see a branch of the Ku Klux Klan in the Navy. They aint all from the South, either. Anyhow, I just want the old man out of jail."

"I doubt they'll hold your grandpa for long. County jails never have much room, not for a man his age. They get a few drunks Saturday night, they'll kick him out."

"I know. It's the principle of the thing. I'll bet that bastard white man never pays for the damage to the Model A, either."

"Is that why you always call yourself Lucian Quigley the Fourth? Because your grandpa would be Lucian Quigley the Second, right? You never say Lucian Quigley or just plain Lucian?"

"Cause that's what I am. The fourth Lucian Quigley. My great-grand-daddy was born a slave. I'm proud of him and I'm proud of his name. He's the one who taught us all to hold our heads up high. He lived to be a hundred and two, the first Lucian Quigley. Used to sit right there in the middle of our parlor with a big old hickory stick. If one of us kids got to acting up, we'd get it right across the behind with that stick. I'm telling you, it stung. He was a strong man. Had to be. He was whipped when he was a slave, before he was sold to a good man, old Judge Quigley. The judge wrote it in his will, that Great-granddaddy was to be set free on the judge's death. He took the judge's name after the judge passed on, and went to work for a white fella who ran a store boat on the Missis-sippi River. Great-grandpa said they made a real good team, until they were shot at by Johnny Rebs during the Civil War. The white man sold the boat, but he made old Lucian take five hundred dollars from the sale. He walked all across Texas after the Civil War, looking for his wife and children, who had been sold away as slaves. Took him four years, but he found them. That took courage. Texas was a dangerous place for a black man in those days."

"Still is, from what I hear."

"Still is. Anyhow, there's a picture in my grandma's home, right over the fireplace. She calls it the Four Lucians. All of us together,

Great-grandpa down to me. I was about ten years old then, looking proud just to be with them fellas."

"I imagine old Lucian would be proud himself if he could see you now."

"I think he'd say I turned out just about how he meant for all of us to turn out. I'm just ticked off that I'm out here fighting for this country and they put my grandfather in jail because a white man acted like a damned fool. There's too much stupid in this world, Wat. All those dead men at Pearl because of the Navy brass that got caught with their pants down. Now we're in a war because of those dumbshits."

"I thought we were in the war because the Japs bombed us."

"I know that, and I hate the Japs as much as you do. But we're also in it because the generals and the admirals and the politicians were dumber than my mule. If we were ready for the Japs, we would have spanked their butt good. Maybe hit their aircraft carriers, shot down so many planes the war would be over before it got started. But the admirals were stupid, and now we're all going to pay."

"They sure as hell weren't ready."

"No, they weren't. But you don't hardly dare say so, specially if you're a black man. That's the trouble with this country. It's a democracy, but it's only a democracy as long as you go along with the herd. If you got different ideas, say you think a black man ought to be equal to a white man, they slap you in jail. It's liberty and justice for all, unless you're a Negro, or an anarchist, or you say you don't want to go along with this war. Then it's like Russia under the damned czars, and you got no freedom at all. Do you think that's right?"

"I never thought about it."

"That's what I love about you, Wat. Maybe that's why we get along, I can't argue with you. You might be the only guy on this ship who's like that. Twenty-eight hundred men, counting the Marines, and not one of them wants to punch you in the snoot. You're some kind of guy."

"You, too, Lucian. I wish I could help you with your grandfather."

"You can. Shoot down a whole bunch of Japs, get this war over in a hurry, so I can go home."

Two weeks later, Lucian shows Bobby a letter from his grandmother. The old man has been released from jail. He apologized for hitting the white man with his hickory stick, on condition that the fellow pay for the damage to his Model A. Maybe the world is changing after all, a bit at a time, but it would take a hundred years' worth of Lucian Quigleys to see the difference.

27.

IN APRIL, LIEUTENANT TOM CALL LEAVES DOUGLAS Army Air Force Base for Roswell, New Mexico, to begin learning how to fly the B-17. His experience as a pilot speeds the training process, but the effort to absorb all the information keeps him occupied day and night. His head swims with details from the instruction manuals, which emphasize over and over the pilot's responsibilities:

Your assignment to the B-17 airplane means that you are no longer just a pilot. You are now an airplane commander, charged with all the duties and responsibilities of a command post.

You are now flying a 10-man weapon.

Tom is to command a crew of nine. He has to learn to fly a large and bulky airplane in formation and to manage formation takeoffs. At night, he goes over the material until he falls asleep, often with the manual on his chest.

The leader goes into takeoff position and takes off at H hour. No. 2 man starts pulling into position as soon as the leader starts rolling. When the leader's wheel leaves the runway, No. 2 starts taking off. The leader flies straight ahead at 150 mph, 300–500 feet per minute ascent, for one minute plus 30 seconds for each airplane in the formation. He levels off at 1000 feet above the terrain to prevent high rates of climb for succeeding aircraft. (Cruise at 150 mph.)

The prose makes it sound like a manual for typewriter assembly, but the pilots know what they face. Fighter attacks, flak, horrible weather, confusion, damaged airplanes limping home, crashes, crew members killed and wounded, a good chance of ending up in a German POW stockade if they survive a crash. All they can do is master their instructions. Sooner or later, every pilot comes to the section on "How to Ditch the B-17" on water and "How to Bail Out of the B-17."

Tom barely has time to think of Juanita. He writes once a week, but he can't say much about his training because of the censorship and he is afraid to tell her how he feels, for fear that someone else will see the letter. He sticks to talk about the weather, the funny characters he's training with, his desire to see the war through and get back to Wyoming as soon as possible.

Juanita doesn't write for weeks. When she does, she writes a half dozen versions before she is satisfied, carefully tearing the old drafts to shreds and burning them in the coal stove. Then she puts the letter aside for two days, waiting to mail it until she is sure it says what she must say.

April 18, 1942

My dearest Tom,

> *Since the first time you came to the ranch, my thoughts have been with you. I think I have loved you from that first day. Your crooked smile, your lovely eyes, your curly hair, and your sadness. I wanted to wrap my arms around you and hold you, as I wish I could wrap my arms around you now.*
>
> *But I can't. I love you, Tom Call, but I cannot be with you. I cannot be with you now because of the war, I cannot be with you ever for other reasons, beginning with Eli, the husband I still love. I know this is going to hurt you, but I am going to have Eli's baby. It is totally unexpected, of course, especially after all these years, but it is true nevertheless. I am not (quite) too old to have a child, and it will make this big old drafty house a great deal less lonely to have a baby around. I know that you will think perhaps it is yours, but I know that it is not. A woman knows these things. I have been a wife to Eli all along, and if it's not quite as passionate as the days and nights with you, we are still an affectionate couple.*
>
> *I suppose this doesn't mean that we could not make a life together after the war, except that I have decided this is the way it must be, for many reasons. This child needs a stable home, not a mother who is bouncing around from one place to another while waiting for you*

*to come back. In many ways, you and I barely know one another. I
always felt so close to you, but we still had a great deal to learn. It's one
thing for the two of us to go off to California together. It would be quite
another thing to drag a child along.*

*I have other worries. I am older than you, and while I have often
been told (by you) that I have kept my looks and that my age doesn't
matter, I worry that it will. You will be a glamorous Army Air Force
pilot and an inevitable temptation to much younger women wherever
you are stationed, and I fear that one day you will fall for one of
them.*

*I am still disappointed you did not inform me that you intended to
enlist before you went through with it. To me, that indicates that you
were still thinking of yourself as an individual, not as part of a couple.
If you loved me as you say you do, you should have talked it over with
me first. I believe that's an indication of your true feelings and proof
that, for you, I was only a temporary flame.*

*Anyway, my decision is made. I hate to send a "Dear John" letter
to a man in the service, but I must, and our circumstances are different
than most. I am married to someone else, a man for whom I still care,
and with this child I am carrying, I must now dedicate myself to my
husband and my child. I hope you will understand.*

*I send you all my best wishes and prayers for your safety. Unless
you'd rather I didn't, I will continue to write to send you news of
Wyoming and the family, and I hope that you will write to me, too,
but if you prefer to end all contact now, I will understand. God save
and protect you, and I hope that we shall remain friends, because I
love you and I always will.*

Vaya con Dios,
Juanita

She wakes early the morning after she posts the letter. It's not quite five
o'clock, but the bed is empty. Eli is already at his chores. She frees herself

from the tangle of sheets, lights the kerosene lantern. On her feet, she feels out of balance, the weight in her belly pulling against her.

It won't do. She is driving herself mad with hesitation. It' time to tell Eli. She dresses quickly and gets the fire going in the kitchen. It's still chilly, so she goes back upstairs for a sweater, brushes her hair and fusses with herself. She wants to look right for this moment. The kitchen door slams and she hears him, moving around downstairs. She hurries back. He's sitting at the table, reading a newspaper, his graying head bent over the war news, as always. She doesn't want to wait a moment longer. She comes up behind his chair, wraps her arms around him, hugs him tight.

"I have to tell you something, honey. I have some wonderful news. I'm pregnant. We're going to have a baby."

Ezra turns to face her. "Why, that's great, Juanita. Eli must have just about jumped through the roof when you told him."

She blushes and stammers. After all this time, she can still mistake his twin brother for her husband. "Oh, Ezra. I'm so embarrassed. I thought you were Eli. I haven't told him. I meant to tell him just now . . ."

"Well, hell, I won't spoil the surprise. He ought to be back any minute. I rode over on Powdermilk Biscuit this morning and I figured I'd get a jump start on the coffee. Oh, and I got some news, too. Belle had her baby last night in Sheridan. It's a boy. They're goin to name it Ezra Eli Paint, after me and that other old buzzard that you're married to. But I guess he aint all that old, if you're about to have one yourself."

She laughs. Her secret is out, confessed to the wrong man. She pours half a cup of coffee, fills the cup with cream, and sits down next to her brother-in-law, leaning her head on Ezra's shoulder, catching her breath. It's hilarious, when she thinks about it. Now that her secret is out, it weighs less. If Ezra is delighted, Eli will be delighted. It hasn't occurred to Ezra to question how the child came to be, any more than it will occur to Eli. She squeezes Ezra's arm affectionately.

"I think I'll let you tell him for me," she says. "Will you?"

"Me? Hell, I aint the one having the baby."

"I know, Ezra. But somehow I find it hard to tell him. I don't know how he'll react. Will you?"

"Why, sure. If that's what you want. I always knew my brother was quite the rooster, but I didn't expect this. Now Jolene will want us to have one of our own."

"It wouldn't do you any harm, Ezra, but Jolene is past fifty. That would be quite a surprise."

They hear Eli then, bellowing "Sweet Betsy from Pike" as he walks back to the house, trailed by Zeke Ketcham's boar and Rufus the dog.

"When is this blessed event, just so's I know what to say?"

"End of August," she says. "Maybe early September."

Eli comes in and catches the two of them grinning sheepishly.

"Mornin, Ez, mornin, Juanita. What have you two been up to? You look like you got caught with your hands in the cookie jar."

Ezra chuckles. "Well, I was just setting here minding my own business when this little lady came up and gave me a big hug and a bit of news, thinking I was you. I came to bring news myself, so I guess I'll get it all out of the way at once: First, Belle had her baby last night in Sheridan. It's a boy, so they're going to call him Ezra Eli Paint, after a couple of folks we seem to know. But that aint the half of it. Juanita tells me you're going to be a pappy again, so you'll have a child only a few months younger than Belle's. Hell, they can play together."

"Easy now. It aint April Fool's Day, is it?"

"No, it aint. Unless she's fooling me."

Eli turns to Juanita. "Well, I'm real pleased for Ben and Belle, but is this true? Are you going to have a baby? It's raining babies around here, all of a sudden."

"It's true. I'm going to have a baby. Just like Belle."

"End of August," Ezra says.

Eli pulls up a chair, still wary, still thinking they might be stringing him along.

"How did this happen?"

Ezra slaps his thigh. "Hell, I'd think you'd know that much. By my count, this is number fourteen for you."

"I know how it happens, I'm just— I'll be danged." He rests his hand on Juanita's shoulder. "You're sure? It aint just gas or something?"

"No. Doc Miller told me. I waited until I was further along to tell you, just in case something went wrong."

"Well, that's it for you on horseback. We'll have to hire another rider come roundup time."

"There's no reason I can't ride."

"That's not true. The reason is, I won't let you. Dang, this is the best news around here in years. I'll have to write to Leo and Bobby and the whole bunch."

"I'll write the letters, if you want me to. Since you won't let me ride the roundup, what else am I going to do?"

After Ezra leaves, Eli asks again if she's sure about the baby. Then he carries her up the steps and makes love to her so gently that she feels like a dove, cradled in his hands.

Tom's reply arrives three weeks later.

Juanita,

I'm so tired I can't hardly get through writing this, but I've got to say something. I've got to tell you it hurts like hell knowing I've lost you, but I don't blame you a bit. I'm going to be in this war for a while and you've got no idea if I'll be home or not. I suppose there's a bit of extra sting, knowing that you will have Eli's baby, but I can't do a thing about that, either. We had a powerful attraction to each other, still do, but the world don't always sit around and wait for folks. Not in these times, anyhow.

You look after yourself, and you look after that baby. I'll be home one of these days, and I hope you'll still think kindly of old Tom and invite me out to Sunday dinner.

Now I got to get some shut-eye. This old Army Air Force rolls pretty much around the clock.

yours,
Tom

She almost wishes that he had ranted and raved and called her names. But that isn't Tom Call, no matter how he feels. He's not the type to go on about it. Anyway, that's all over now. Her destiny is wrapped up with this hard little foot, poking into the wall of her abdomen. At night, Eli sleeps with his hand on her belly. No matter who the father is, the baby makes her happy. The house will no longer be as lonely. Eli will probably stick around more. Eventually, perhaps, she'll forget all about Tom Call.

Ethan Cristiano Hernando Alberto Paint is born on September 9, 1942, the day the entire West Coast is in a panic after a single Japanese seaplane drops an incendiary bomb, causing a small forest fire in Oregon. They call him Ethan, but he also bears the names of her father and brothers. Eli says it's a whole lot of name for a whippersnapper. He generally refers to the boy as Little Bit. Juanita calls him *chiquito* or *chiquito lindo*.

The baby looks like her. He has walnut brown skin and a shock of straight black hair. For the first few days, she wonders if perhaps the child isn't really Eli's after all. Then one afternoon as she is changing him, she notices something she had missed: a prominent bone at the base of his sternum. She points it out to a nurse at the hospital, who says that in English the bone is called a "sternal notch." The nurse says it isn't uncommon, but Juanita knows only one person who has a similar bone in his chest: Tom Call. It isn't something you'd notice on a fat man, but it's plain as day on a man as lean as Tom, as it is on his son.

28

THE CREW OF THE *TENNESSEE* SPENDS MOST OF the first eighteen months of the war waiting around the Puget Sound Navy Yard for the ship to be repaired. In between repairs, there are exercises off the West Coast, but after Pearl Harbor, their worst enemy is boredom. The old battleship is too slow to keep up with the fast carrier groups fighting a new kind of naval war in the Pacific. After the Battle of Midway begins, in June 1942, Task Force 1 steams to an area twelve hundred miles west of San Francisco to intercept any Japanese attempt at an end-run attack on the West Coast. When word comes that Admiral Yamamoto's fleet has lost four carriers and returned to Japanese waters, the task force goes back to San Francisco. After a week of exercises in August 1942, the *Tennessee* accompanies the carrier *Hornet* as far as Pearl Harbor. The men find it strange and a little frightening to be back at Pearl, so near the submerged hulk of the *Arizona*, but after three days the *Tennessee* returns to Puget Sound.

In April 1943, Bobby enters the naval hospital at Puget Sound to have his appendix out. He suffers complications from the surgery and is still in the hospital three weeks later, when the *Tennessee* leaves for San Pedro. By the time he catches up with his ship, they are about to depart for the Aleutians, where the Japanese have occupied the islands of Attu and Kiska. Attu was recaptured in May, but the Japanese still hold Kiska, so the sunburned sailors who have been on duty in San Pedro find themselves bundled into arctic clothing, enduring intense cold and freezing rain as the radar probes for enemy ships off the Aleutians. On August 1, the *Tennessee* makes a zigzag approach to Kiska with the *Idaho* and three destroyers, closes to within seven thousand yards of the island, and begins the bombardment, hitting a Japanese submarine base and firing sixty rounds before visibility drops to zero. The ship recovers her floatplanes and returns to Adak, then steams to San Francisco.

In October 1943, the *Tennessee* sails to Pearl Harbor, then to New Hebrides to rehearse for the invasion of the Gilbert Islands. The ship crosses the equator on October 26, and Bobby is inducted into the Order of Shellbacks. He's admitted to the Order of the Golden Dragon three days later, when they cross the International Date Line. In his letter to Emaline written the next day, Bobby doesn't mention either event. He has other things on his mind. *Would I love to be home tonight having some cold chicken, some good cold beer, a few sweet tunes on the piano, a nice quiet ride in the old Buick.*

After a week at anchor in New Hebrides, the ship leaves November 13 for Tarawa Atoll. The assault begins on November 20. The Navy shells the island, the Marines go ashore. On November 25, the daily work sheet includes a special note: *Today is Thanksgiving Day and although we are not, due to existing circumstances, observing it with all the tradition and ceremony we would at home we will at least have turkey and each and every officer and man should say a prayer of thanksgiving for the many blessings we have and are enjoying in the TENNESSEE.*

Bobby offers thanks that he's not a Marine, one of the poor devils whose boats stalled on the reef five hundred yards offshore on the first day of the invasion. It seems such a waste: so much death and destruction to grab one tiny Pacific Island.

The *Tennessee* marks the second anniversary of the attack on Pearl Harbor while sailing back to Hawaii from Betio. It beats the first anniversary, which Bobby spent cleaning heads in Puget Sound. By December 11, 1943, the ship is at Pearl Harbor again, then it's back to the West Coast. The sailors spend Christmas in San Francisco while the ship is repainted with a camouflage scheme designed to confuse the enemy. There is more gunnery practice in San Pedro, then on to the Marshall Islands, where the *Tennessee* participates in the bombardment of Kwajalein Atoll, moving in so close at one point that it is firing on Japanese defenses with its forty-millimeter antiaircraft guns. In the summer of 1944 they hit Saipan and Tinian in the Marianas. Off Tinian, the *Tennessee* is damaged by return fire from enemy shore batteries. Japanese 4.7-inch field guns emplaced in a cave score three direct hits on the ship.

One shell knocks out a five-inch twin gun mount, the second strikes the ship's side, and the third tears a hole in the after portion of the main deck and sprays fragments into the wardroom. Eight men are killed by projectile fragments, and twenty-five more are wounded. The damage is considered light. Bobby can't mention the attacks in his letters. When he writes to Emaline, he kids about a sailor's life: *I wonder what it feels like to be on the outside, a civilian I mean, with a job & when your day's work is done come home to your little family & take in the slack, maybe a day off now and then. I imagine it is pretty nice that's what they tell me anyway. I sure wouldn't know myself. Seems like I've been in here all my life & god what a life ha ha I love it.*

On the Fourth of July 1944, the crew of the *Tennessee* dine on soup, salad, roast turkey, cranberry sauce, raisin-apple dressing, candied sweet potatoes, buttered asparagus, hot rolls, citron cake, and ice cream. Bobby sends a copy of the menu home to Emaline, with a note scrawled at the bottom: *Not bad, eh?*

By the end of the month, the *Tennessee* is bombarding Guam.

In late October 1944, the *Tennessee* takes part in the Battle of Surigao Strait. It's the revenge of the ghost ships: the *California*, sunk at Pearl Harbor and raised to rejoin the fleet in May 1944. The *West Virginia*, sunk and raised to rejoin the fleet in July 1944. And the *Pennsylvania*, *Maryland*, and *Tennessee*, damaged at Pearl and repaired. Of the six American battleships in action in the Surigao Strait, only the *Mississippi*, stationed in Iceland when the Japanese attacked, was not damaged at Pearl Harbor. Their target is the massive battleship *Yamashiro*, leading a column of Japanese ships. Operating in darkness in the wee hours of the morning, the American battleships open fire at more than twenty thousand yards and drop hundreds of heavy shells on the *Yamashiro* and the heavy cruiser *Mogami*, both of which are crippled. The *Yamashiro* increases her speed and tries to retreat to the south, but at 0419 she capsizes and sinks. The destroyer *Shigure* turns and flees but loses her steering and stops dead in the water. The *Mogami* catches fire, slows almost to a halt, and is sunk by American aircraft the next morning.

Bobby, manning his antiaircraft gun on turret two of the *Tennessee*, sees distant flashes of gunfire, star shells, and searchlights as PT boats and destroyers engage the Japanese force. A whirling sheet of flame bolts from the battleships, followed by a sound like massive thunder. Red balls rise in majestic arcs across the sky, followed by huge showers of sparks as they strike their targets. Then a dull orange glow appears where a ship has been hit, and slowly fades. The silence after the guns stop firing is more overwhelming than the noise that precedes it. The combat lasts eighteen minutes.

When Bobby heads below for chow, Lucian Quigley IV piles extra potatoes on his plate. "I heard we gave 'em hell last night," he says.

"Hell's about right. I never saw anything like it. Those poor bastards."

"Same poor bastards who came calling at Pearl Harbor."

"I know that. But I know what it feels like to have all that stuff raining down on your head. Like it's you personally they're trying to kill, a whole damned navy aiming everything it has at your particular fanny."

"Uh-huh. As long as it gets us home a little quicker, I'm all for it."

"Amen to that."

It's November before Bobby gets a chance to write Emaline: *Yes, we tangled with some of the friendly Nips this time but it's over now, and we are in safe waters so don't worry about us. It can't last much longer out here so keep your fingers crossed.*

29

IN THE WEE HOURS THE NIGHT BEFORE A MISSION, lying sleepless in his bunk at Grafton Underwood, eighty-five miles northwest of London, Tom finds himself going over the murder of Millie Stojko again and again, hoping to remember some insignificant detail that will confirm his suspicions.

He wonders sometimes why it matters so much, the death of a solitary girl back home. There is so much death here, so many men you see at breakfast who are missing or dead by suppertime. Many more are dying on the ground, some killed by the bombs he drops over Germany. The pilots and navigators and bombardiers do their best, but it's a tricky business. Wind, cloud, flak, mistaken targets. A bomb dropped thirty seconds too late will fall on a civilian neighborhood instead of the armaments factory they meant to hit. For a man with the burdens of a bomber pilot, it's best not to think about it. It's easier to toy with an old murder case that might never be solved. Better than thinking of what happened two days ago and what will happen at dawn, the planes in their ranks taking off, the long flight to the target, the fighters, the ground fire, bombers tumbling in flames, the parachutes that catch fire, the screams when crewmen on his plane are hit. Landing back in England to find that your ball-turret gunner has bled to death or your navigator has lost a leg.

The missions mount up. His nerves hold. Barely. There are times when he sets the B-17 down on the tarmac back in England, with the fire trucks waiting and stricken bombers everywhere, and he steps out on shaky legs knowing that he can never, ever go up again. Then the next mission comes and he is there, in the cockpit of the plane they call Miss Wyoming, bound across the channel, headed straight for a species of hell that will scare the wits out of him before the day is done.

He still writes to Juanita, but not often. He can't say anything about the war that the censors won't black out. That leaves him with little to say. He misses her, but he has a girl named Ginny. A pliable, buxom Welsh girl with red hair, an easy laugh, a fondness for a pint. He drowns himself in her creamy, pink-nippled breasts. Drowning in pale flesh. A way to forget.

Lieutenant Tom Call's B-17 Flying Fortress is shot down on August 17, 1943, over Schweinfurt, Germany. He is flying Mission No. 84 for the Eighth Air Force, on the anniversary of the first daylight raid over Germany. A total of three hundred and seventy-six bombers from sixteen bomb groups take part in the attack on German heavy industry in Regensburg and Schweinfurt. The attack on Regensburg is judged a success, but the attack on Schweinfurt is a failure and the target will have to be attacked again. Sixty of the bombers, Miss Wyoming among them, are lost. They are engaged in a furious battle with German fighters when another pilot sees Tom's B-17 burst into flames and begin a spiraling descent, trailing smoke all the way. Tom Call and his entire crew are listed as missing in action.

It's front-page news back home. Juanita has little Ethan at her breast when Eli points to the headline: WYOMING SHERIFF MISSING IN ACTION. "Did you see this? Tom Call's plane was shot down. Now that's a damned shame. This war is taking the best we've got."

Juanita looks away to hide her reaction. "Does it say what happened?"

"Only that he was shot down. They're sitting ducks, those big bombers. Can't maneuver like those little fighter planes."

She feels as though she herself has been shot down and is plummeting to earth. She switches Ethan from her left breast to her right, strokes his silky black hair. She must be careful not to betray the slightest emotion. Almost every day, there is the name of someone they know in the paper: killed, wounded, missing in action, promoted, decorated for heroism. Now Tom. She has expected it, but she is unprepared when it comes.

When Eli heads out, she reads the story three times. There's very little information. Just a bit of background on Tom Call, from the time he was a stunt flyer with the Flying Fandangos. It doesn't even say where he was flying when he was hit. There are two photographs with the story: one shows Tom when he was sheriff, as he looked when she first met him, with his old leather flight jacket, the hat tilted back on his head, the way he always wore it, that lopsided grin. The other shows the smiling, confident officer in his dress uniform. It makes her dizzy. Almost two years have passed since they were together, but the photos make the time vanish. She is back in the autumn of 1941, flying with Tom in the Aeronca Defender, making love on a cot in the back of an aircraft hangar.

When Ethan is through nursing, she holds him tight. "Tom has been shot down," she whispers. "He's only missing. Don't you worry, honey. He'll be all right. We know he will, don't we?"

Ethan smiles as though he understands, then spits up over her shoulder.

Tom is the last one out of his plane. He sees other chutes open, but he has no way of knowing how many made it down safely. He lands on the edge of a potato field and drags himself to the bank of a stream, where he lies on his belly drinking muddy water until he feels a rifle pressed into the small of his back. He's taken prisoner by three pallid boys, the oldest no more than sixteen, commanded by a drunken sergeant well past fifty. In other circumstances, he might have found the situation almost comic: the three boys arguing about what to do with him, the sergeant so drunk he's staggering and waving his bottle around, all of them shouting at once. They seem to be arguing about whether to shoot him or take him prisoner. He has second-degree burns over his right arm and rib cage and his cheek and neck on the right side, where he was burned as he tried to help evacuate the crew from his burning bomber. His left leg is broken in a half dozen places. He's in so much pain, he almost hopes they'll shoot.

Instead, he's dumped onto a tattered overcoat, which is used as a makeshift stretcher to carry him to an empty corral. The corral once held milk cows. Rusty buckets still hang on a couple of the posts. He and a half dozen other wounded prisoners lie in the dusty manure of the corral until nightfall, when they are taken for an interminable, painful ride in the back of a crowded truck to the interrogation center at Dulag Luft, near Frankfurt am Main. There the prisoners are told at least a dozen times: *Vas du das krieg ist über.* "For you, the war is over."

No, he thinks. *It's just beginning.* After forty-eight hours in intense pain at the interrogation center at Oberursel, he is taken to the hospital at Hohemark. There his broken leg is set. He's still given nothing for the pain, but the dressings on his burns are changed regularly. At intervals, interrogators come in. Good cops, bad cops. He's been a lawman, he understands the routine. The good cops pretend to sympathize with his condition. They whisper of morphine for those who are helpful with details of their units, their crews, their planes, their missions. The bad cops laugh at his pain and swear to let him die unless he cooperates. He repeats his name, rank, and serial number so many times that he becomes confused and can no longer remember the serial number. He passes out. When he comes to, he can't remember what he has said. The interrogation is pointless. He knows little or nothing that could be of use. More planes will come. They will keep dropping bombs until Germany surrenders. He could tell them, but he doesn't think they'll believe it.

After a week in Hohemark, he's moved to another hospital, Lazarett IX-B in Bad Soden. One of the guards was badly wounded in the fighting outside Stalingrad. He has some English, from summers spent in Scotland before the war. When there are no officers or SS men around, he likes to sit next to Tom's bed and smoke and practice his English. He's near forty, and his weariness with the war is of a sort Tom hasn't seen among the Allies. The guard can say *Der Führer* so that the words carry a freight of scorn greater than any insult. He even kids about the constant air raids. He tells a Wehrmacht joke with a rueful laugh. "When we see a silver plane, it's American. A black plane, it's British. When we see no plane, it's German."

Tom spends three weeks in the hospital before the doctors decide he's well enough to be moved to his permanent camp at Stalag Luft III near Sagan, a town near the Polish border known to the Poles as Zagan. The seven-hundred-kilometer trip, in a railroad boxcar carrying fifty prisoners and a single guard, takes nearly a week. Again and again, the train is stopped because of air raids, or because tracks have to be repaired. They're shunted aside to allow troop and supply trains to pass. At times, the train sits in the same place so long, the prisoners think they've been forgotten. Then the train lurches ahead and they travel another twenty, thirty, forty kilometers before the next halt. His burns have begun to heal, but Tom worries about infection: the dressings aren't changed once during trip. They arrive at Sagan at dusk and are loaded into trucks for the ride to the camp. It's the first time they've been off the boxcar since they left Bad Soden.

Most of the American prisoners are held in the South Compound of Stalag Luft III. As they enter, each prisoner is handed a Red Cross package, which includes a diary. Tom borrows a broken pencil, scrawls the date and eight words on the first page, and abandons the effort. There are no words to describe the cramped barracks, the stench of fear, the claustrophobia, the sense that they have been rounded up and forgotten. But at the limits of human endurance, the POWs complain less and show more compassion for one another than barracks soldiers back in England.

The POWs call themselves "kriegies," short for *Kriegsgefangener*, prisoners of war. They are short of everything: food, warmth, medicine. Especially medicine. They are subject to the daily, casual brutality of the German army regulars and the occasional, deliberate horrors inflicted by the SS. Tom struggles with the sense that the world ends at the tree line, with a forest so deep it appears black in all but the brightest sunshine. It's like being trapped in a coffin, the horizon cut off, the world beyond almost unimaginable. At night he dreams of the prairie. Or of the view from his B-17, rising at dawn over the English Channel, with the coast of France looming ahead. When he wakes to that unvarying charcoal smudge of trees, he inevitably feels a dull thud of disappointment, as though somehow the landscape might have changed overnight.

In late March 1944, word reaches the South Compound of the major escape engineered by prisoners in the North Compound, most of whom are British. Eighty POWs made it out, through a hundred-yard tunnel

dug more than thirty feet underground. The escape brings a wave of elation to the camp, which turns into bitter disappointment with the news
that most of the escapees have been caught and at least fifty shot by Ge-
stapo firing squads.

During his months at Stalag Luft III, Tom finds that memory is a
tricky thing. He can barely remember his ex-wife, how she looked before
she ran away to California. He recalls the Welsh girl Ginny, but only as
he first saw her, chatting with a friend in a pub in the Midlands. Juanita
Paint comes to him only in fragments. A shadow across her breast, the
way her hand looked on his thigh, her black hair caught in the wind, a
smile. He can't compose her entire face no matter how hard he tries, but
he can summon the photographs of Millie Stojko in every detail.

In late June 1944, the first prisoners begin to arrive from the invasion
of Normandy. News that American, British, and Canadian troops are
now on French soil causes another wave of elation in the camp, but as
the war drags on, the prisoners fear that it will never end, that the armies
will bog down in something like the trench stalemate of the Great War,
while the kriegies remain forever where they are, constantly hungry and
always at the mercy of their captors.

During the last, cold winter of the war, rumors spread. They say the Red
Army is drawing near and that the prisoners will be moved. Tom has
heard so many rumors that he no longer believes them, but at eleven
o'clock in the evening on January 27, 1945, the POWs of Stalag Luft III
are evacuated and taken on a forced march to Spremberg. The prisoners
make the fifty-five kilometers between Sagan and Muskau in twenty-
seven hours, with only four hours sleep. At Muskau they are given thirty
hours to rest, then marched another twenty-five kilometers to Spremberg, where they are packed into boxcars for the two-day trip to Stalag
13D at Nürnberg. On April 13, the men are told they have to evacuate
again and are taken on a weeklong march southeast to Moosburg.

Halfway to Moosburg, Tom falls out. With his bad leg swollen to
twice its normal size, he collapses into a ditch, tries once to get up, and

rolls onto his back. An eighteen-year-old private falls out a dozen feet farther on. One of the guards, a boy three or four years younger than the fallen POW, saunters over and prods him with a rifle, barking at him in German. When the prisoner fails to get up, the guard fires a burst into his chest. The kid's body bucks a few times, blood spurting from the wounds. His right foot drums the ground and he lies still. Tom waits to be shot. The guard takes a step or two in his direction. A sergeant shouts at him. He shrugs and hurries off to join the others. They leave Tom where he is, along with another American pilot who falls out fifty yards down the road. The two wait until the column of prisoners has marched out of sight, then crawl to an abandoned farmhouse, where they feast that night on a store of half-rotten turnips. The other POW is Lewis Stern, a lieutenant from West Virginia. He was on only his third mission when he was shot down. He has something terribly wrong in his gut. Stern thinks it might be appendicitis.

They fall into an exhausted sleep. When they wake the next morning, Stern is feeling a little better. They set out to find the American troops rumored to be in the vicinity. For Tom, it's the worst part of the war. Lost, starving, foraging for food where there is none. The fleeing German troops took everything they could carry and executed Hitler's scorched-earth policy thoroughly, burning most of the rest. The two Americans find themselves in fields where no spring crop has been planted, digging for potatoes and turnips with their bare hands, sometimes in company with the peasants who own the land, eating the half-frozen lumps raw, often without washing off the dirt. On the third day, they meet up with a Canadian enlisted man from another camp who was taken prisoner during the Dieppe Raid in August 1942. The Canadian comes from Montreal and speaks French, which a few of the local Germans understand. Lieutenant Stern has a smattering of German. Between them, they manage to communicate with the peasants, enough to hear every rumor. The people are terrified of the Red Army. The Soviets are said to be just over the hill, raping five-year-old girls and eighty-year-old grandmothers and shooting every able-bodied German male on sight. The wandering, confused POWs begin to fear the Russian troops almost as much as they fear the Germans.

In mid-May, desperate and half-starved, they blunder into a unit of General Patton's Fourteenth Armored Division. The first soldier to meet them is a buck private from Sundance, Wyoming. He gives Tom two Hershey's bars, which Tom devours and vomits right back up.

30

O N April 12, 1945, Bobby is at his bunk, sort-
ing his laundry. The *Tennessee* is part of the massive flotilla of
fifteen hundred ships off Okinawa. American troops landed
on the island on April 1, but attacks from Japanese kamikazes have kept
the sailors at their posts almost constantly for two weeks. Like the other
antiaircraft gunners, Bobby sleeps when he can. Sometimes in his gun
bucket. Once in a while, for a few merciful hours, in his bunk. This time,
after fourteen hours on duty, he catches a break. He'll square his laundry
away, then hope that he's allowed to sleep until chow.

He's rolling a pair of socks when the call comes to battle stations.
He sighs, slips his shoes back on, grabs his helmet, and pounds up the
steps. He sees them before he reaches his post in Turret 3. Hundreds of
planes on the horizon, flying in a series of Vs, so that from a distance
they resemble waves riding over the Pacific. He hears the buzz of their
engines, a bigger swarm than he's encountered at any point since Pearl
Harbor. As the planes approach, a wall of shell bursts goes up from the
radar picket ships on the perimeter and the Vs begin to break up, as the
pilots pick out targets in the invasion fleet. Bedbug vaults into the gun
bucket right behind him. The kid has grown up in the war. He's about to
celebrate his twenty-first birthday.

It's like fighting a swarm of flies. Jap planes zigzag crazily through
the flak and the smoke. Ships leave white foam in their wake as they
maneuver to throw off the attackers. Everywhere, guns of every caliber
except the big fourteen-inchers are firing steadily. The white arcs of tracers curl toward the targets as they rise, so that the buzzing black speck
of a kamikaze is surrounded by a plume of fireflies. Planes skim over the
water or take long, forty-five-degree arcs to their targets. Others dive
through the shell bursts, almost straight down through puffs of white

smoke, puffs of black smoke. When a kamikaze is hit, there is a sudden midair explosion and blazing hunks of metal float down. Or they tumble over and over, like aerial acrobats, trailing black smoke. Others die in long, wing-dipping arcs into the sea, or impossible dives, engines buzzing, pilots struggling to pull up, then geysers of water a hundred feet high where the planes explode as they crash. Downed planes burn on the water, or slip beneath the surface in a trail of bubbles. Yellow and orange fireballs flare when kamikazes ram ships, followed by the concussions of the explosions and thick, choking veils of black smoke. Fire crews sprint across the decks of the stricken ships. The screams of the wounded and dying are lost in the din.

The destroyer *Zellars* takes a direct hit and bursts into flames. Five suicide planes come on through the dark, billowing smoke off the stricken destroyer. Four are shot down. The last one bears down on the bow of the *Tennessee* at a forty-five-degree angle. It's hit by one of the five-inch guns and plunges down. As it splashes into the sea, lookouts spot a dive bomber coming in at an unconventional angle, flying low off the starboard bow. The gunners open up. Bobby locks in on the target. The tracer follows the bomber as it buzzes toward the ship. The plane is hit, again and again. One of its fixed wheels is torn off. Its engine is smoking. Bobby fires until his hands ache. His tracers slam into the plane's nose cone. Still it comes, headed for the *Tennessee*'s tower foremast. At the last instant, the pilot swerves and crashes into the signal bridge on the starboard side. Sailors dive out of the way as the fiery wreck slides aft along the superstructure. It wipes out a quad forty-millimeter gun and its crew, hits two twenty-millimeter guns and another quad forty before sliding over the side. Part of the wreckage, the bomb still inside, skids to a halt next to Turret 3. There is an awful pause, a count of three, then the bomb crashes through the wooden deck and explodes in a sheet of flame. Bobby and Bedbug, on Turret 2, are knocked flat and deafened by the concussion. They stagger to their feet, coughing and choking. Bobby grabs Bedbug by the collar. *Ammo!* The kid understands. He guides another belt into the twenty-millimeter. Bobby spins, searching for another target. The battle swirls around them, but the remaining kamikazes seek other targets, out of range.

The noise dies away. Smoke drifts low over the water. Lucian Quigley IV appears on deck after helping with the furious struggle to put out the fires below. He finds Bobby slumped over the handles of a gun that is too hot to touch, his face blackened. Bedbug is sprawled at Bobby's feet, his helmet off, an arm shielding his eyes. From below, they hear the screams of the wounded. Lucian puts his hand on Bobby's shoulder. A young ensign struts by. "You splashed two, Wat," he says. "I'm sure it was you. Out of four. You might have got three. Damned fine shooting."

"I don't know how anybody can say who got what. I could see tracers from a dozen guns on every one. We missed one. That's all that matters."

"Hell, you can't get 'em all. Nobody can. They're like flies, buzzin up your ass every which way. Nobody can get 'em all."

"Don't matter. I should have."

The ensign leaves them alone. Lucian strolls to the rail to look out over the carnage, the water strewn with wrecked planes, ships burning, frantic crews still fighting fires in the distance, the sea trailing smoke. He calls Bobby to the rail.

"Wat, come have a look at this."

Bobby stumbles over on shaky legs and looks down to where Lucian is pointing. A dozen yards to starboard, a dead Japanese pilot lies face-down in the water, held on the surface by his flotation jacket. Most of the back of his head has been blown off. Gray smoke still drifts, low over the water. The corpse rotates, head to toe, head to toe, spinning round and round like the hands of a courthouse clock. The body rolls onto its back as it drifts past the stern. They can see where the dead pilot's eye was shot out. The body rotates slowly in the ship's foaming wake, and vanishes down the gullet of the sea.

The dead sailors from the *Tennessee* are wrapped in the canvas bottoms from the bunk beds and laid out next to the rail on deck, in rows of three. One kamikaze. Twenty-two Americans dead. One hundred and seven wounded. The living stand at attention as the bundles slide from the deck, hit the water, and sink, one by one.

The next day, they hear the news. Franklin Delano Roosevelt has died in Warm Springs, Georgia. Harry Truman is president. The war goes on.

31

ASHORE ON OKINAWA, SERGEANT LON BURY shakes out a white pack of Luckies. They never taste quite right. Not like the fags from the green pack before the war. Funny how quick the tobacco company made the switch. Seemed like the fires were still burning at Pearl Harbor when the ads were out. "Lucky Strike green has gone to war." Meaning they shelved the green. Makes no sense to him, a white pack with a red target patch. He always wraps the pack in one big paw. No sense helping a Jap sniper get the range.

Lon has found his way in the Marine Corps. Turns out he is not all that dumb. He's cool under fire, he knows how to handle men, he has an instinctive grasp of cover and terrain, he can read a map at a glance and keep it in his noggin. He has outlived a half dozen lieutenants, from Guadalcanal to Peleliu, and made sergeant in the new Sixth Marine Division. New division, old troops: veteran, raggedy-ass Marines who have been island-hopping so long, they think jungle rot is a normal condition. The Marines are dug in along a six-hundred-yard front facing the Japs on the Shuri Line. The concentration of troops is so dense that it's like living in a sewer. A choking, gagging sewage smell rises day and night, mixed with the sickening sweet of rotting corpses. More than anything, Lon wants to survive long enough to make it to a place that doesn't stink.

His rifle company is down to platoon strength and still fighting. Awake or asleep, they dream of the dead, see guys who were killed yesterday or last month, hear them talking. *Fuck you, Sarge, I aint walkin up that hill for nobody. I told you on Tarawa, I've had it with this shit. Fuckin. Had. It.* That was Platini, who was walking up the hill cursing when a shell turned him into a bloody fizz and he went hissing over the helmets of his crouching comrades. *Fuckin. Had. It.* The last thing he said, but he still talks to Lon every night. *I aint walkin up that hill for nobody, Sarge, not even you.*

Hard to believe this place was green when they came ashore. Now it's brown, a churned, mud-colored, shit-colored brown, every tree and shrub and blade of grass blasted into the mud with the brains and balls and intestines of the Marines who have been beating their heads against the western end of the line while the Army tries the eastern end. The Japs are squirreled away in their caves and tunnels, where the bombs and the big guns of the fleet can't get them. They slip out, do some killing, slip back in. Lon gives the little yellow fuckers credit. They don't have a chance, they're all going to die, but they might take the entire USMC down with them.

If the Japs aren't bad enough, there's always the rain. Driving rain, like somebody turned the Pacific upside down and dumped it on their heads. Even when the rain stops, they are up to their knees in mud. The only way out of the mud is to take Sugar Loaf Hill, a hundred-foot mound they have seized a dozen times and lost as many times. Sugar Loaf is coral and volcanic rock, nowhere to dig. The fighting up there is hand-to-hand, bayonets and boots and teeth. Lon Bury is good at it, lean and hard and quick. There was a time when he had a notion how many Japs he had killed, but he lost count at around a dozen. Maybe a dozen more, just here on Okinawa, not that it makes a difference. He has no illusions. One day his number will be up. They'll get him like they got so many others. He'll join the ranks of the walking, muttering, bitching, rebellious dead. *I don't give a fuck, Sarge. I aint climbing that fuckin hill again.*

They are under shellfire. Japs and Marines both, hit by big artillery, not the small stuff they've seen on other islands. He's seen a piece of metal as long as a bayonet slice a man's head right off. The concussions shake the earth so hard that after a barrage, he always feels like his balls have been torn off. He shakes all the time, they all do. When he looks down the line after a barrage, he sees a row of rifle muzzles, all of them quivering. Men can't stop shaking long enough to aim. Shell-shock cases go back, a new bunch comes up. Within a day some of the replacements are falling apart. Blubbering, sobbing, screaming at the Japs to *please just fucking knock it off because I want to go home in one piece.*

Lon has no idea why he hasn't come undone. No nerves left, maybe. His hands shake all the time, his feet shake, his dick shakes. When he has to take a leak, he pisses all over his hands. To light a single Lucky Strike takes concentration and a half dozen matches.

From Sugar Loaf Hill, what is left of Lon's company shifts west to Half Moon Hill, a muddy lump which supports Sugar Loaf. Ten days of rain, the tanks bog down. In almost every shell hole there's a dead Marine, crawling with maggots. The rain washes the maggots into the foxholes, into the pockets and down the necks of the living. To hold down the smell, they shovel mud over the corpses. At night the Japanese attack, pour into their lines. They kill Japs by the dozen. The enemy dead mingle with the dead Marines, sometimes in the same foxholes. A fresh artillery barrage rips the bodies apart, leaves bits and pieces all over. An elbow here, part of a foot there, who knows if the parts belong to a Marine or a Jap? They call the place Maggot Ridge. Every time a man falls, he comes up with a fresh load of maggots.

For weeks, Lon has been hearing things, seeing things. Usually at night, sometimes during the day. He turns to give a command to a lance corporal who is standing right *there*, except that he knows the man was killed over on Sugar Loaf at the end of April. He gives the command anyway.

There comes a night in May when Maggot Ridge is strangely quiet. Lon is in a foxhole with a dead Marine, but the Marine isn't talking. There are four or five men from his squad still alive, a couple on each side. Hunkered down in the mud and maggots. It's so bad the men don't even bitch anymore, they just stare.

It's a dark, moonless night. Raining, but not hard. He hears a sound out there somewhere, movement in the darkness. Slips the condom off the muzzle of his M1, waits. *Don't shoot until you know where the fuckers are.*

When she speaks, he can't believe it's really her. The little Mexican whore from Galveston, the one he was fucking when Pardo stabbed the other girl and it all went to shit.

"*Gringo*," she says, "you want some, *gringo?* I am so horn-ee, I wan' fuck with you, big man, come on and make fucking with me."

He puts his hands over his ears, tries to block out the sound. He is on his belly in the mud. The sound of her voice makes him hard as a gun barrel. He grinds into the mud. He never got to finish with her in Galveston. Now he wants her every which way. He can't look, he doesn't dare. What if she isn't real? What if it's some Jap trick? The men are taught not to call out to one another by name. Yell *Smittie!* once, and then the Japs yell *Smittie!* and when poor fucking Smittie sticks his head up, they blow it off. Lon bellies down, deeper in the muck, but she keeps at it, taunting him.

"*Gringo*, I wan' that you put it in my ass this time, okay? Thass how I like it, you come and push it in my butt. I waiting for you."

All this time without a woman, he'd fuck a porcupine if he could get it to stand still. When he peeks over the edge of his foxhole, he sees her plain as day. She is standing in the open, thirty feet away. She wears a sheer white dress and she is naked underneath. He can see the patch of silky dark hair, just the way he remembers it, the nipples peeking through the dress. She was the one with real tits, not a flat-chested little girl like the two Pardo chose.

The whore keeps up her taunts. "What's wrong, *gringo?* You no like poo-sie? You queer, *gringo?* Like little boys, maybe? Come on, Marine. *Te quiero mucho.* Right now, big boy, I so wet for you. Come and get little Rosita. I gonna make you feel so good."

He risks another peek and sees her, in sharp relief. Lit by firelight, but from where? She has pulled the white dress up around her waist. How does she keep it clean out here? The light on her thighs, wet from her juices. She writhes, a ghostly pantomime of the sex act. "C'mon, fuck little Rosita with that big dick. I waiting here for you."

Lon stands and walks toward her, bayonet in hand, leaving behind his M1. She waits, smiling, her arms outstretched, her hips still writhing.

He can't remember undoing his fly, but his dick is out, so hard it aches, bobbing in her direction. He follows his pecker, thinking how he wants her. Right here, right now. He'll push her mouth down on it, then lift her up and let her ride him. She's tiny, he can hold her, easy.

Lon is a yard away from the whore when he sees it's not a girl at all. It's the corpse of a dead Jap. Smiling and talking. A talking corpse. *Come on, gringo, come fuck little Rosita* . . . They throw a poncho over his head. A half dozen Japs come at him from all sides, a swarm of them, stabbing with bayonets. They're silent, not wanting to draw fire from his squad. He gags, choking on his own blood. He lashes out with the bayonet in his right hand, feels it plunge into someone's gut, hears the sharp intake of breath—*hunh!*—as the blade goes in. Or maybe it's his own grunt of pain. They weigh him down. Three, four, five on his back. He falls to his knees, one of them underneath him. The warm, bare skin of a neck presses against his cheek. He bites, savagely, teeth seeking the jugular. The Jap writhes, trying to escape, but he's pinned. Lon tastes the hot blood, bites deeper, feels it pump and flow, holds on as they stab him. It feels like he's being punched, like he's in a fistfight, but every punch draws a spurt of blood. His face is awash in blood from the dying Jap. He slashes off to his right, opens up somebody's belly. One of them has a blade against his throat. He feels it tear through to the bone. All the strength goes out of him. He feels warm, as though he's floating away on an ocean wave.

The whore is on his back, grinding herself against him, whispering in his ear. *I want big Yankee dick, Marine. You give me? You give your little Rosita?*

Inside the place they call the Walls, Pardo Bury tests a dozen weapons until he settles on one made of a spring from the bumper of a '32 Dodge, with a rubber handle fashioned from an old tire.

Earl Toth showers alone. It's a rule. No one is allowed near the showers when Toth is there. But Pardo knows how to make himself invisible. He creates a minor distraction with a makeshift smoke bomb, slips past Toth's men to the showers, slips up behind Toth, taps him on the shoulder. He waits until the man turns, then drives the blade under the ribs and twists. Toth makes a grab for his attacker's neck, but his hands are slippery, he can't hold on. Pardo steps back, watches Toth slip to his knees, gouts of blood spurting from his chest. He's back in the machine shop before anyone notices that he's gone. In five minutes, he has turned the shiv into an ashtray.

The warden doesn't pursue it. No witnesses, no murder weapon. Nothing but another dead convict, a man who won't be missed by anyone. Not even his mother.

In the yard and the cafeteria, prisoners edge away, give him room.

32

B Y THE END OF JUNE 1945, TOM CALL IS IN A HOS-
pital in Maryland, where his bad leg is reset. There is talk of
surgery for the burn scars on his face and neck, but others are
in much worse shape and Tom doesn't want more surgery. With the scars
he bears, a few superficial changes won't help. He makes no attempt to
contact Juanita, but he does write to Virginia Barclay in England, to say
that what's left of him wouldn't make much of a husband.

In November 1945, he resumes his duties as sheriff of Sheridan
County. He has offers to go to work as a pilot for three different airlines
where he can earn more money, but he has no desire to fly again. He rents
a different house on the western outskirts of Sheridan, chosen because
it offers a view of the mountains. Each morning, he rises before sunup
and sits at his kitchen table, gazing out over the horizon. With the burn
scars, he'll never again be called a handsome man, but he can do his job.
He learns to cope with the little gasp, the catch of the breath when people
who see his good side first are exposed to the other side of his face, which
resembles a lava flow. He spends his days catching up on his duties as
sheriff and his evenings going over the Millie Stojko case. He writes to
the warden of Huntsville Penitentiary, asking how much longer Pardo
Bury will be a guest of his establishment. The warden says he's scheduled
for release in late June 1946, but the terms of his parole will require him
to remain in the state of Texas for an additional three years. "He'll have
to check in with his probation officer once a week," the warden says, "so if
you get enough evidence to bring charges, he won't be hard to find."

Tom drives over to Gillette to get his files on the case from Bill
Brower. They sit for a couple of hours on Brower's back porch, talking
about this and that, going over the old case. Brower agrees with Tom
that Pardo is their most likely suspect—but with nothing to tie the man
directly to the killing, there's no way to charge him.

"I know it will just about kill you to see the fellow turned loose," Brower says, "but you can't go off half-cocked. Charge him before you can get a conviction and you've made sure he'll never pay for his crime."

"That's about the size of it. This thing is five years old now. It aint like witnesses are going to start popping up all over."

They sit quietly for a time, drinking beer and listening to the wind blow.

"How was it over there?" Brower asks.

"About like you'd think," Tom says. "Maybe a little worse."

"Uh-huh. A whole lot worse, I imagine."

"I've been thinking about it since I got back to this country. There's something about men like Pardo. Down deep, he's like Hitler. They're the same. It's just a matter of degree. I don't quite grasp what's going on in the world, but I expect that a doctor would say it's malignant, like cancer. There have always been bad men, I don't doubt that, but it seems like people used to kill for a reason. Usually because they were poor as hell and they were trying to grab something for themselves. A man like Pardo, though, he had it all. No reason to kill. He's just pure evil. God, I saw enough of that. I wish I could see Pardo hang. Then I could live in peace, more or less."

A week before Christmas, the door of a bank on South Main Street is courteously opened by a gentleman in a gray suit. Juanita Paint steps through, holding Ethan with one hand and tucking deposit slips into her purse with the other. It's a bright winter day and she is blinded by the sunshine. She walks right into a man coming from the other direction. She stumbles back, apologizing, tugging Ethan's hand to steer him out of the way. The man lifts his hat, begging her pardon.

"I'm sorry, Juanita. I should've looked where I was going."

She has to squint to see his face. "Tom. I heard you were back."

"I am. More or less in one piece."

His words hang there. A matter of time and fault lines, the history between them. They look down at the sidewalk, up at the sky, anywhere but at each other. Cars drift by, customers go in and out of the bank. Ethan breaks the spell, tugging on her hand.

"Mom! A malt!"

Tom rests a hand on the boy's dark hair. "This must be your son."

"Yes. This is Ethan. He's three years old. Ethan, this is Mr. Call. Sheriff Call."

Tom bends down and puts out his hand, but the boy ignores it and crowds closer to his mother. He points at Tom's scars. "Hurt your face?"

"That's not polite, honey . . ."

"It's all right, Juanita. It's natural for a kid to ask. I got hurt in the war, son. My plane was shot down over Germany."

"The plane crashed up?"

"Yes, it did. I was able to parachute, but I was burned some before I could get out of the plane."

"Did you get a bandage?"

"Yes, I did. Several of them. It's better now."

"It don't look better."

Tom laughs. "Listen, you said you were going to take him for a malt. Mind if I come along? My treat."

"You can come along, but it's our treat."

They find a booth at the diner. Juanita sits next to Ethan, with him on the inside so she can curb his restlessness.

"He looks like you," Tom says.

"Yes, he does. He's small for his age, but he's wiry. Eli dotes on him, takes him everywhere. He even has his own pony. The only problem is that I'm almost too old to keep up with him."

"You don't look old, Juanita. You look lovely."

She puts a finger to her lips. "I don't know how I look, but I know how I feel."

They order a malted milk and a small hamburger for Ethan, a tuna sandwich for Juanita, two hamburgers for Tom. He waits until Ethan is distracted running his little truck up and down the table. "I think about you," he says.

She nods. "Me, too. I was so relieved when I knew you were still alive."

"I know. I got your letters. Eventually."

"Wouldn't they let you write?"

"Most of the men wrote letters. The Red Cross was supposed to deliver them. I don't know how much of it got out. I wrote eight words in a diary the first day I was in the camp and that was it. I gave up on writing."

"It must have been awful."

He shrugs. "There were others had it a whole lot worse. Like the Jews they rounded up in Europe. Our men who were taken by the Japs in Bataan and Corregidor."

"What a terrible war."

"Yes. But it had to be fought."

The waitress brings their food. Ethan drinks most of his malt, doesn't touch his hamburger. When they finish, Juanita pays the check. They leave together and Tom walks them to the car, thinking how it might be, the three of them going for a stroll. He helps the boy into the passenger seat and then holds the door on the driver's side for Juanita.

"It would be nice if we could do this again."

"I don't think it's a good idea, Tom. Everything is settled, we've gotten used to things the way they are. I have really strong feelings for you, but I have to think about Ethan first. There's no use talking about what might be. The war came and put an end to all that, and this is what we have."

She reaches out to touch his scars, brushes her fingertips lightly from his neck to his face, back to his neck. "It's not the scars, if that's what you're thinking. You're still a very handsome man. That wouldn't matter to me anyway. It's what I said when I wrote you the letter. I had to make a decision for the boy."

Tom tips his hat. "All right, Juanita. I won't argue. I'd best get back to the office."

"Please be careful."

"I'm always careful."

"Don't forget. We lost you once, I couldn't stand to lose you again, even if I can't see you."

She puts her arm around his neck, draws him down to her, and kisses him, once, on the lips. When she lets go, he leans into the car to say good-bye to Ethan.

"It was nice meeting up with you, son. You be a good boy and look after your momma now, hear?"

Ethan smiles, his gleaming teeth white and perfect.

On the drive home, Ethan is his usual self, full of questions. They are halfway home when he mentions Tom. "He's a nice man, Mr. Call."

A few miles later, the boy glances up at his mother. "Why are you crying, Mommy?"

"Because you are such a beautiful boy, honey. It makes me cry sometimes, just to look at you."

He grins, pleased that his mother would say such a thing.

33

THE BOMB PUTS AN END TO THE WAR. TWO bombs: Little Boy, dropped on Hiroshima. Fat Man, which falls on Nagasaki three days later. The world has a kind of peace, and a new horror. The Japanese surrender, the boys come home. Some of them in one piece.

From Okinawa, the *Tennessee* sails to Japan. On September 22, Japanese officers at Wakayama come aboard to sign peace terms with Vice Admiral Jesse B. Oldendorf. The battleship covers the landing of occupation troops the next day. In October, the sailors are allowed their first liberty in Japan—first in Wakayama, then in Tokyo, where Bobby finds time for a letter to Emaline.

Oct. 5, 1945

Emaline,

Well, old Bobby was in the city of Tokyo yesterday, or what is left of it, and had quite a sightseeing tour. I didn't realize that Tokyo was such a modern city. The buildings are like those in Frisco or almost, there are quite a few that have been bombed. There are plenty of dogfaces there and lots of Japanese all sizes and shapes. Went all over the city first on little streetcars like the little trolleys in Frisco, we took in the Imperial Palace which is nothing but fancy, most of it is still standing. I found one jewelry store with some beautiful kimonos and some fine-looking rings and some silver dishes. I asked the Jap man if he had any silver cups and I started into my sign language and talking to myself, come to find out he spoke perfect English ha ha. We tried to eat dinner on the beach, the Army has taken quite a few of the American civilians there at the hotel, one had a Japanese girlfriend

*with him and he said he was waiting for a ship to leave for the States,
I doubt if he can take the bride to be or whatever she was with him.
Tokyo itself stinks and so do its people, some sort of foul odor, it's
beyond me what it smells like.*

    *After seeing all these Japanese, you know how great it is to be an
American, I can tell you for sure. In a way I feel sorry for the Japanese,
especially for the little children, then again there's a hate in my heart for
these people and it will always be there, guess all of us boys feel about
the same way.*

    *It looks like we'll be home soon. Maybe for Christmas, wouldn't that
be sweet?*

*Your little brother,
Bobby*

From Tokyo, the *Tennessee* has to take the long way home. Her wartime
rebuild has increased her beam to one hundred and fourteen feet, too
wide for the Panama Canal. The ship will head for Philadelphia, by way
of Singapore and the Cape of Good Hope. But Robert E. Lee Watson is
not aboard when she leaves Tokyo, because he has been transferred from
the East Coast to the West Coast. With Officer's Cook Third Class Lucian Quigley IV and his pal Bedbug, Bobby leaves the *Tennessee* behind
in Wakayama Harbor. The three sailors are transferred to the USS *Greyhound* for a more direct trip home to Puget Sound. *I'm going to miss the
old Tub,* he writes to Emaline, *but I'm not married to her.*

The *Greyhound* is an old troop transport, once known as the USS
Yale. It's cramped and rusty and offers a far rougher ride than a battleship. Bobby's bunk is so close to the asbestos piping that his nose almost
touches the pipes when he lies on his back. The first night out, he gives
up on sleep and heads for the movie room, where so many restless sailors
are smoking that he can't breathe the air. He heads topside for a peaceful
smoke behind a splash guard. He's been there half an hour when Lucian
appears, toting a big piece of chocolate cake and a fat cigar. He hands

the cake to Bobby, sits down next to him, and lights the cigar. After four bites of cake and as many whiffs of Lucian's cigar, Bobby can stand it no longer. He runs to the rail and donates the cake to the Pacific.

"Five years in the Navy," he says, "and that's the first time I've been seasick."

"What's the matter with you?"

"You can start with that cigar."

"Never bothered you before, a man smoking."

"You never smoked a cigar."

"That's cause I couldn't never afford one. Our last liberty, a fella who was at Pearl recognized me, walked right up and handed me this cigar. Said I was a damned hero."

"You were a hero."

"No, I wasn't. I don't believe I hit a one of those Jap planes."

"But you tried. I let one too many get through at Okinawa and we dropped some good men in the sea."

"It happens. You see how many Nips there were in Tokyo?"

"I did."

"Shit. I couldn't believe it. I thought we killed 'em all."

"Cute kids, though."

"Yep." Lucian takes a long pull on the cigar and blows a few smoke rings. "I don't know, Wat. Maybe you feel sick because you're leavin the Navy. You're gonna miss all us. I bet you even miss the Marines."

"Them jarheads? Not on your life."

"You'll miss the *Tennessee*. Even though you call her a tub."

"I will. She's a good ship. We had good times, in between the bad times. I'll miss you, Lucian. After we muster out, you come see us sometime."

"Aw, hell. I'll be goin back to Missouri. That's a long ways from Washington. And if some big ole black man shows up at your door, you're liable to start shooting."

"You know better. You're the best friend I've had in this man's Navy."

"That's enough, Wat. You keep it up, we're goin to start blubbering like a couple old sisters. I do believe there's a poker game goin on in the latrine. I think I'll go lift a few dollars from some white boys, help make the payment on that tractor."

"You do that, Lucian. And take that chocolate cake along, will you? If I have another bite, I'll upchuck again."

"You're just sick because you're going to miss the Navy."

"Like hell. Get out of here, before you have to put your dukes up and prove you're a heavyweight champ."

When Lucian is gone, Bobby sits for a long while behind the splash guard, watching the stars over the Pacific. Hard to believe, but it's over. They're packing a few nightmares in their seabags, maybe, but they're going home.

34

I N LATE FALL, BOBBY GETS A TWO-WEEK LIBERTY AND
drives to Wyoming in a jalopy bought off a used-car lot in Seattle.
He decides to surprise Emaline, so he arrives in Sheridan in midmorning, when she's at work at the library. He strides through the door
in his dress whites, sees her sitting at her desk, going through a pile of
returned books.

"Howdy, ma'am," he says. "Would you have any books a sailor could
borrow for a year or two?"

She has not seen him since the summer of 1940, but she would
know that voice on the moon. Her delighted shriek startles the elderly
patrons who are always in the library at this hour. Several of them look
up, disapproving, then smile when they see her throw her arms around
his neck.

"Why didn't you tell me you were coming? I would have made a roast
beef dinner. We'll have to call Ben. Maybe I'll take Red out of school.
Oh, Bobby, oh, Bobby. I can't tell you. This is the best day of my life."

He holds on to her, feeling her shoulders quiver. She's crying, and if
she doesn't stop, he's going to open the faucets, too. She takes an early
lunch. They stroll to the diner for hamburgers and malts. She can't stop
looking at him. He's changed, all right. He's thicker in the shoulders,
stronger, older. He's grown from a boy to a man. But he hasn't lost that
twinkle in his eye, the easy smile. All that he's been through, and he's still
cracking jokes, kidding the waitress. She knows there are things he isn't
saying, will never say most likely, but they were raised to believe that a
person makes the best of things, without complaint. *Don't stand in the
corner and bawl for buttermilk.*

When she has to go back to work, she gives him the key and Bobby
drives to her house to wait for Red. He's sitting on the front porch when
Red comes home from school. The boy runs to him, wanting to ask

everything at once, then calms down enough to show off the world map on his wall, with the blue tacks taking over, the red tacks permanently erased from Europe, the Soviet Union, the Pacific. Bobby looks at it for a long time. It's the first time that it has really come home to him, the scale of the enterprise. It was a *world* war, in every sense—the sprawl of the armies and navies locked in battle across the globe, the cost in men and dollars, the importance of the outcome.

That night, Emaline makes a big supper for them. When they've finished eating, she does the washing up while Bobby talks to Red. After the boy goes to bed, they sit on the davenport with cups of hot cocoa, half-listening to the radio while Emaline asks about his plans, his education, what he's going to do with himself now that he's free.

"I dunno. I thought I'd probably reenlist. See a little more of the world."

"You're kidding."

"Yes, I am. I'm done with this old Navy. Now they're talking about how we might have to fight the Russians next. If we do, I'll have to go back, but I'd just as soon not."

"Please don't do that. I couldn't stand to have you in another war."

"Well, if you couldn't stand it, I'll stay home."

They listen to a Vera Lynn tune. Life can be so simple, Bobby thinks. Just folks sitting around, drinking cocoa and listening to the radio. No scrambling for another alert, waiting for the next attack.

"How are you, Sis?" he asks.

"All right. It's great to have Red with me. I like my job at the library."

"I thought by the time I got home, you'd be married up again."

She shrugs. "The men who were around here during the war weren't much. I still get asked out to dances and such, but I generally say no."

"You're only thirty-five and you're still a great-looking gal."

"You're my brother. You're prejudiced."

"Don't mean it isn't true."

"Anyway, Jake is back."

"I don't like the sound of that. What do you mean, he's back?"

"He's working horses on a ranch north of town. His father is in

Scottsbluff now. He's getting too old to run the little farm he has there. Jake wants me to go along. His father is past ninety, and if we help out, Jake would inherit the place someday."

"You're not thinking about it, are you?"

"I don't know. He's settled down some, and his temper isn't as bad as it used to be. I get lonely sometimes, and Red is bound and determined to join the Navy when he's old enough. Then I'll really be alone."

"But Jake McCloskey? I thought you never wanted to see him again."

"We'll see, Bobby. I really don't know what I'm going to do. Let's not talk about it. I have all I want now. The war is over and you're home safe. That's all that matters."

They spend the weekend at the 8T8, Bobby and Emaline and Red, catching up with Ben and Belle, Ezra and Jolene, Eli and Juanita. On Sunday morning, Ben takes Emaline and Bobby, and they head out at dawn, just the three of them, riding Ezra's Appaloosas. Ben wants Bobby to come live on the ranch as soon as he gets out of the Navy, but Bobby plans to settle down in Washington.

"I want to be where I can get to the ocean anytime I want," he says. "I got used to being where I can hear those big old waves rolling in. Too late to change now."

"But you're a prairie boy."

"They're a lot the same, prairie and ocean. You can see forever. But out there, you don't have dust in your teeth all day long. I like rain and things growing. And there's a woman out there. I met her when I was with Aunt Kate. Ruth is her name. A real swell gal. She likes to play the piano and I like to sing. When I go back, I'm going to pop the question."

"So it's more than the Pacific that makes you want to settle on the coast?"

"Yep. But it's the ocean, too."

Leo Paint is also home to show off his new bride, a nurse from Arizona, where her father runs a trading post on a Hopi reservation. As soon as Leo can get out of the Navy, he's going to take over the trading post.

Bobby hasn't seen Leo since the night before the attack on Pearl

Harbor, when his cousin drove past him on Hotel Street, riding shotgun in a Shore Patrol jeep. After a couple of days of big dinners and company, they're both restless. They choose a pair of saddle horses and two packhorses, Leo takes Eli's four-horse trailer, and they head out before dawn to go elk hunting in the Bighorns. They pull the trailer as far as they can go, then unload the horses. By the time they're ready to ride, they are gasping for breath in the thin air. Leo figures they're up around eight thousand feet.

"We spent too much time down at sea level," he says. "We don't have any wind left this high up."

"That's the truth. Makes a fella feel light-headed and weak in the knees." They're both saddle-sore before they've gone two miles, but they ride most of the day. Near dusk, Bobby spots a handful of elk in a meadow more than a mile distant. Leo isn't convinced.

"I can't tell if they're horses or elk or deer."

"Elk," Bobby says. "There's a big old buck with them."

"If you say so."

They camp that night in the shadow of a cliff face. With supper finished and the fire crackling, Leo asks Bobby about the war, how it was for him. Bobby thinks awhile before he answers. "Nobody has a good war. Nobody that fights, anyhow. Mine was better than most, because I didn't get killed and I didn't get wounded and I didn't lose any of my best buddies. I guess that's a good war. We won and we got to go home."

They fall asleep early, under the million stars of the Wyoming sky. Before dawn, they are up and in the saddle. Puffs of steam rise from the nostrils of the horses. Leo is half-asleep, rocking along to the creak of saddle leather. They top a rise and slide down a wide fan of scree onto a meadow, where the grass is knee-high and the sun glares off the early frost. Bobby spots him first, a thousand yards off to the northwest. A ten-point buck, an animal as magnificent as creation. They rein up, paused in the saddle for a long look.

"You take the shot," Leo says. "If I try it, I'll miss."

The elk looks their way, as though sensing something, sniffing the wind.

"We can get a little closer," Bobby says. "Best we stay on horseback. If he sees us move away from the horses, he'll bolt for sure."

They ease along at a slow walk, the reins slack. Fifty yards, a hundred. When they are within eight hundred yards, Bobby eases the rifle from the scabbard. He slips out of the saddle, kneels in the shadow under the horse's neck. It's going to be a tough shot, uphill with a slight crosswind, early-morning shadows playing tricks with the light. He slips the safety off, cocks the rifle, brings it to his shoulder. Leo admires the unhurried way his cousin goes about things, with the elk right there, waiting to be taken. Bobby takes the time to get his spot weld just right, with his cheek snug against the wooden stock. He squints his right eye, gazes down the sight with his left, makes a minor adjustment for the wind blowing right to left, maybe ten miles an hour. He calculates how much the shot will drift over eight hundred yards, and moves the muzzle into the wind to compensate. He takes a deep breath, lets it out, takes another deep breath and holds it. His finger increases the pressure on the trigger by imperceptible degrees. *Easy, easy now. Go slow and easy and squeeze the trigger, don't jerk.* He has a bead on the elk's great heart. Nothing left but the crack of the rifle, the kick as it hits his shoulder, watching the elk as it falls.

He eases his finger off the trigger, sits back on his haunches, points the rifle straight up at the blue sky, and fires a single shot. The elk wheels and gallops over the ridge. Bobby puts the safety on the rifle, slips it into the scabbard, mounts up, and reins the horse around. Leo rides after him. He doesn't ask why Bobby didn't pull the trigger. He doesn't have to.

PART 3

Down the Road a Piece

35

Oklahoma
July 1946

I T TAKES HIM FOUR RIDES AND THREE DAYS TO
travel north from Huntsville, Texas, as far as Muskogee. From
Muskogee, he rides on a truckload of watermelon as far as Tyler
and eats three melons as they bump along, letting the sticky juice pour
down his arms and chest. He waits half a day in Tyler to catch a lift with
three Mexican migrant workers to Sulphur Springs, where he's stuck for
a full day before two oil roughnecks take him on to McAlester, on the
far side of the Oklahoma line. From there he rides north in the back of a
battered and dusty pickup truck with three dogs and five silent, staring
Chickasaws. When they turn east, he bangs on the roof of the cab. The
driver brakes, almost hard enough to throw him out. He hops down,
nods to the Chickasaws, bangs the rear door of the pickup.

Saturday at dusk, he stands at a crossroads, forsaken by God and the
devil in equal measure. "Looks like hell after the fire went out," he says to
no one at all. He raises his arms to the heavens and turns in a complete
circle, taking in the horizon. Flat, treeless, dusty, scorched. Without end.
On the far horizon to the west, a tractor raises a cloud of dust. At the
crossroads, night coming, he looks for a likely place to doss down. The
only structure in sight is a tumbledown farmhouse a half mile off the
road. It looks deserted, but he knocks on the back door anyhow, just in
case there is a crazy farmer inside with a pump shotgun and a snootful
of bootleg liquor. There are creaking noises from within, the sound of
someone coughing, hard. Then the door opens, an old woman peers out.
"Why, Herman Pilbro," she says, "you've come home. They told me you
was kilt in the war."

Her name is Lottie Alice. She wants him to call her that, Lottie Alice,

like she's six years old. Sometimes she calls him Herman and sometimes
she calls him Roy. He sorts it out from the photographs atop the radio.
Roy would be her husband, one of those lean and toothless Okie types
that he knows from Huntsville, hard and mean as a rattlesnake. The son,
that would be Herman. In his army uniform, he looks some better than
the old man, but that's probably because he was getting regular meals
and still had his teeth. Herman died in the war someplace, it doesn't
matter where. Like Lon, one more dead fool. Old Roy flipped a tractor
on himself, trying to plow a grade that was too steep. All that comes out
somehow in the midst of her babble, bits and pieces of this and that, the
slumgullion stew of an old woman's mind.

At suppertime, Lottie Alice feeds him until he groans and calls him
Herman. In the night she calls him Roy and tries to mount him on the
davenport, where he sleeps. He has to punch her in the eye to get her to
quit. She lands on her back on the floor, hard, and crawls on her hands
and knees back to her bed, cursing and praying. In the morning she's still
pissing and moaning. *You've no call to keep hittin me, Roy. When Herman
gets home from the war he's goin to fix your wagon for that. Herman's been
fightin Germans, you aint no more than a skeeter to a man like that.* The
black eye makes her look worse than ever. He scoops up the last of his
hominy and grits, sits back and picks his teeth and stares, trying to decide what to do with her. Trouble is, there are moments when she's lucid.
She watches him with those rheumy old eyes the color of diarrhea and
says, *You aint Roy, who the hell are you? You aint Herman, what did you
do with my Herman? If you kilt Herman, I'll call the law on you.* It's possible that she will miss the twelve dollars and nineteen cents he has taken
from the coffee can in her kitchen, or that she'll collect enough of her
wits to tell the law about the stranger who came calling, how he looks
like a man fresh out of jail someplace.

The old woman is a mess. Stringy gray hair hangs down in her face,
her bathrobe is open so that he has to look at her withered dugs and all
the way down to her wrinkled belly and a thatch of white hair down
there. She takes her false teeth out before she eats, sets them on the
edge of her plate while she gums her eggs. He sits with his feet up on a

kitchen chair and his own chair tilted so far back that if he goes an inch farther he will fall over. He picks his teeth and watches her gum her eggs and wishes to hell she would wipe off that goddamned egg yolk dribbling from her chin. His chair slams to the floor. *Are you at peace with the Lord, Lottie Alice?*

"How's that?"

"You heard me, you goddamned deaf old hag. *Are you at peace with the Lord?*"

"Merciful heaven. How can you ask me that, Roy? I jest got saved all over again last week at the camp meeting. The whole danged world must a heard me a-hollerin and a-prayin, I was that happy to get saved by the Reverend Lester Mooney, that saved me last year and the year before. I was so full of the Lord, I put four bits in the collection plate."

"I want to hear you say it clear, goddamnit. I don't want to hear no gab about no preacher. Say it plain. *I am at peace with the Lord.* Say it, you old crone. I don't want to send nobody to hell, no matter how old and ugly they may be. Say it. *I am Lottie Alice Pilbro, and I am at peace with the Lord.*"

The last words he intones in the voice of a camp-meeting preacher, so that she clasps her hands with their blackened nails and turns her diarrhea-colored eyes to heaven.

"Hallelujah! Praise sweet Jesus! I am at peace with the Lord."

When he is done with her, he is so drenched in her blood that he has to outfit himself all over again. He rummages in the closet and comes up with an old black wool suit that belonged to Herman. The straw hat was Roy's. The hat is too small and the suit is too large, but it can't be helped. He tries two pairs of Roy's shoes. They're smaller than Herman's, but they're still three sizes too large. He washes himself at the well, dresses in the too-hot suit, and dumps his bloody clothes down the well. Then he turns to the shed to see if the Ford will run.

It's a Model T, 1926 or 1927, and it's missing three tires. Probably couldn't get rubber for it during the war, so they let it set where it was. There are automobiles like that all over the country, rusting away in

sheds and barns and garages. They have set there so long the cylinders
have seized up with rust and they can no more run than a steer can sing
on the Grand Ole Opry. He curses and kicks the one remaining tire so
hard he thinks he might have broken a toe, then he curses some more
over his toe. He needs a car and he needs money and he needs something that will shoot. So far, none of it is working out worth a damn.
The Model T rests in the shed in a welter of old harness, behind a rusty
hayrake and a rusty harrow, where an array of old implements dangle
from the ceiling by lengths of baling twine, as odd a system for organiz-
ing tools as a man could invent: a rusty scythe, a rusty ax, a half dozen
rusty hay hooks, three-tined hayforks, a scoop shovel, a sharp-bladed
sickle, an adze that looks to be older than he is, an ancient bayonet that
might have been left from the Civil War, all of it arrayed as though for
some ghastly autopsy. Someone has cared for the bayonet. It's oiled and
sharp. It's eighteen inches long and it comes with a scabbard to fit, and
when he tests it on his forearm, it shaves the hair clean at a single pass.
He hunts around in the shed and finds an old harness buckle with a
length of strap and cuts the strap to fit around his leg, runs it through
the scabbard for the bayonet, and buckles it around his calf, the sheathed
blade protruding all the way down to his anklebone. There is a .22-cali-
ber varmint rifle on pegs over the kitchen door. He takes it down and
hefts it, but it's heavily rusted and there is no ammunition to be found,
so he leaves it behind.

He goes back to the house and steps over the old woman where she
lies like a sack of potatoes with a four-foot puddle of her blood coagulat-
ing on the rough pine floor. Damned old fool, the state she was in. Gum-
ming her eggs with the yolk running down her chin. He has done her
a favor, putting her out of misery. He ought to get a medal, like all the
fools who went off to war so they could get a hunk of ribbon and tin to
hang on their chests.

He finds an old cardboard suitcase that belonged to Roy or Herman, stuffs spare underwear and socks and shirts in it, adjusts the
bayonet in its scabbard so that it isn't poking out where a person might
see it. He fills a canvas water bag at the well and heads back to the

county road with the water bag strapped across his chest. After he's spent three hours standing there watching buzzards in flight, the water bag is empty. He throws it into the bar ditch. This isn't working out a bit like he imagined it.

It's got to be a hundred and ten degrees. The heat from the gravel road bakes the soles of his feet through the thin shoes and he can feel his belt buckle beginning to sear his belly. Even through the straw hat, he feels his scalp starting to burn.

He's thinking that he might have to draw the bayonet and open one of his own veins to get a drink when he sees a cloud of dust up the road and a big, buff-colored Buick emerges from the dust. It's close to brand-new, with a fancy chrome grille on the front and whitewall tires. He sticks out his thumb and waits.

36

Tucker Graff loves windmills. He loves the light glancing off the spinning blades, the height of the towers, the jaunty rake of the vanes, the way they pivot and swivel and pump and do their useful labor without waste. Above all, he loves the clear, cold water that gushes from deep in the earth as a windmill turns. During the drought years of the Dust Bowl, windmills were just about the only beautiful things in the landscape all the way from Texas to the Canadian border. Beautiful and sad, sometimes, the water tanks silted over by blowing dust, fences turned into sand dunes, the windmills stranded like sentinels left behind by a fleeing army. Now most of them are going again, pumping water to fill the stock tanks, to water the crops. The land is green again. Irrigation ditches flow, crops thrive, windbreaks have been planted to keep the land from blowing away. It's a good feeling for a man, knowing that his windmills helped to save this part of the country.

Tucker has a collection of twenty-three windmills on his own little spread back home in Topeka. Some in working order and some not, some old and rusted and near collapse, some brand spanking new, like the windmills he sells for the Currie Windmill Company. He owns six of the Currie windmills himself. He's sold them all over southern Kansas, Oklahoma, and as far south as Texas, because a Currie is the poor man's windmill. During the Great Depression, a farmer could buy an eight-foot Currie windmill for twenty-eight dollars and have a source of water and power for life, because these windmills have hardwood bearings and steel bands encircling the vanes and they are built to last. If a man takes care of his windmill, it will last longer than he will. Tucker remembers every windmill he's ever sold, the name of the buyer, the date, the price, how the payment was made, on time or with cash or a check. When a check bounces, he'll drive a hundred miles to take it back to the farmer

and ask if there isn't someway he can write it again so that it will clear
the bank. Or maybe he'd rather pay it off on time, take three years or five
years or ten years, it makes no difference to Tucker. He'll drive a dozen
miles out of his way to see a machine he has sold, to watch it pump,
watch the reserve tank fill, see the cattle gather at sunset to drink their
fill. Nothing makes him happier than to kill the engine of his big Buick
in some backcountry cow pasture, stand and stretch his legs, and hear no
sound except the wind, the meadowlarks, and the creak of the windmill.
He'll stroll over to the stock tank, sweep the green algae away with his
hands, cup the cool water in his palms, and drink deep, splash a little
under his hat and down the back of his neck, and step back into the car,
dripping wet and happy as a clam.

Tucker has spent the night in Muskogee. He's headed north to Topeka. Between Collinsville and Nowata, he decides to drive a dozen
miles west to pay a call on a fellow named Ennis Ankeny, who runs a big
outfit and owns fifteen Currie windmills, each one sold to him by Tucker
Graff. It's out of his way, but Tucker is a man who believes in keeping up
with his customers. Ennis lost a boy in the war and he's adrift. He'll start
to say something and lose the thread halfway and stare off across the
fields, like a man who has come loose from his moorings.

After Tucker finishes his coffee and a slice of Mrs. Ankeny's home-
baked bread slathered with fresh butter and chokecherry jam, he and
Ennis head out to check the windmills. Tucker finds every part greased
and running smooth. It's the way Ennis does things. He was able to hang
on when this part of the country was blowing off to New Mexico, when
the dust poured over the barbed-wire fences and the stock tanks and
silted window-high on the wind-blasted houses. After they've had a look
around, the men sit on the porch, poking at their teeth with blades of
grass. Tucker fills his water bags. Ennis's wife fixes a sandwich for him to
eat on the way. He thanks her and promises to stop in next time he's in
the neighborhood. He drives back to the county road, thinking that he
hopes things will be better the next time, knowing they will not.

From the Ankeny place, Tucker heads west on the gravel road as
far as Ramona, where he picks up Highway 75 headed due north to

the Kansas line. He has just finished the sandwich when he sees the hitchhiker standing on the edge of the bar ditch with his thumb out. It crosses his mind to wonder what the fellow is doing out here, but Tucker does not possess a suspicious cast of mind. He eases off the gas pedal enough to see a very young man wearing a straw hat a size too small and a dark wool suit that is about three sizes too big for him, made for North Dakota in January. He brakes a little too hard. The car slews sideways on loose gravel, and it looks as though the Buick will knock the hitchhiker down into the slimy water of the bar ditch, but the car stops a foot short of the man's shins. Tucker reaches over to open the passenger door, squints to see the face hidden in shadows under the straw hat.

"Where you headed, son?"

"Down the road a piece."

"Well, get in before you fry. I'm goin all the way to Topeka, if that suits you."

The hitchhiker slides his cardboard suitcase onto the backseat, removes the jacket of his suit and a dirty white shirt, folds them precisely and lays them on top of the suitcase. He slides onto the passenger seat, wearing the pants that are too big and shoes that are too big and a white undershirt that fits snugly on his small, wiry frame.

"It's hot," he says, and he takes off his straw hat and wipes the sweatband with a dirty handkerchief and puts it on the seat between them. He has a stem of wheatgrass stuck between his teeth. He takes it out to speak and shoves it back in after, as though closing a gate he doesn't intend to open again.

Dirty blond hair, blue eyes, as pretty a young man as you will ever see, except for the expression he wears, his lip curled like he is about to say something unpleasant. He wears a two-day growth of wispy blond beard and a vivid purple scar such as a hot poker might leave just below his left cheekbone. Tucker tries not to stare, but the thing looks like a brand, something you would slap on a calf's hind end. The letter *T*, if he's not mistaken. Tucker thinks the hitchhiker might be as young as seventeen or eighteen, but up close, he looks more like twenty-five. He has a prison haircut perpetrated with dull clippers in clumsy hands, and there is prison in the way he tenses against the passenger door, like a coiled diamondback, ready to strike.

Tucker is not troubled. He has picked them up by the dozen, over the years. The 1930s were hard times and a whole lot of good men ended up doing time in one place or another. He takes his foot off the brake and releases the clutch and the car spins through the loose gravel until the tires catch. Between second and third gear, he sticks out a hand. "Name's Tucker Graff, windmill salesman outa Topeka."

The hitchhiker ignores the proffered hand. Tucker lets it dangle a minute, then reels it in like a fisherman with an empty hook.

"I didn't catch your name."

"I didn't say."

Tucker waits, but the fellow shows no inclination to give his name. "Where you from?"

"Around."

"You see a lot of that these days." Tucker rambles on, unable to stop himself. "The depression and the war and all. Folks aint really from a particular place. They been all over. What brings you to this part of the country, son?"

"I aint your son."

"Well, no. You aint. It's just a manner of speakin, you being considerable younger than I am and all."

"I aint your son."

"How old are you, anyhow?"

"Old enough."

"Did I ask where you was headed?"

"You did and I told you. Down the road a piece."

The wheatgrass bobs between the man's teeth. Straight and white, those teeth, like a fellow who has taken care of himself at one time.

"You aint the talkative sort, I guess?"

"Nope."

Tucker figures he'll talk anyway. The way he sees it, it's cheap at the price. A hitchhiker gets a ride and sometimes a free meal and all that's required of him is to listen to Tucker's stories about Currie windmills and

his years on the road and his yarns about the folks who bought his windmills, like old Mizzus Portman west of Tulsa, who ran her own spread
after her husband died, raised eight kids and bought eight windmills,
one for each child. They ride on, with Tucker talking and the hitchhiker
working that stalk of wheatgrass until he has just about chewed it up.

Ten miles on, Tucker stops by the side of the road to pee. When he
stands with his pecker in his hand, it throbs and stiffens until it is thick
and hot and his pee arcs like it did when he was a ten-year-old boy. He
glances back over his shoulder to see if the hitchhiker has noticed. The
man stares straight ahead. Tucker shakes himself off and has to grunt to
tuck his hard pecker back in his pants and work the zipper up.

It's a weakness. Tucker knows it. A weakness and a sin. It started
with a big, handsome Swede from a threshing crew and him a fourteen-
year-old boy. He watched the Swede for three days, and at suppertime
after the third day he was seated across from the man when he felt the
Swede's toe on his calf. After supper, the Swede winked at him and said
he wanted to see Tucker's pony. The man followed him into the dark
behind the barn and pushed him down onto his knees in the shadows. It
was thick as his wrist and it made him gag. Then he was lifted up by the
straps of his overalls and the Swede yanked the straps off his shoulders
and bent him over, and after the pain it was so good Tucker bit his lip.
After the Swede, there was no chance he would be any way other than
what he is and likely was all along, Swede or no Swede, sitting at the
wheel of the Buick on empty country roads, hoping to find a likely fellow
with his thumb out, waiting around the next bend.

He tried to pray it away. It didn't work. He tried to marry it away,
and that didn't work either. She stuck for three years, then took off with
a man whose inclinations didn't run against the grain. Tucker didn't
blame her one damned bit. He would step out on himself, if he could.
He has tried to screw it away, to plain wear it out. He's still trying, with
saddle tramps and gandy dancers, oil roughnecks and hitchhiking soldiers. Now and then, he reads a fellow wrong. Not often. His observa-
tion is that a man alone on the road is not too particular as to where

he parks his pecker. But until this moment on a gravel country road in Oklahoma, he has never met a man who could make him want it so bad he shakes like a leaf. Well, maybe the Swede. He licks his lips, thinking of the Swede, and gets back behind the wheel. If he reads it right and the hitchhiker is fresh out of prison, then he knows the drill. If he doesn't, it won't matter much. Tucker is six foot three and near three hundred pounds. In his younger days, he played football and rassled at county fairs for easy money. He can handle this pip-squeak with one hand.

Before he climbs back behind the wheel, he offers the hitchhiker a drink from the water bag. The man takes it and drinks long and deep, water trickling down his beard onto his chest. The thin white cotton undershirt sticks to his chest. Tucker squints up and down the road. There isn't a vehicle in sight, but you never know when someone might come along and spoil things. Ten miles farther on, there is a farm that was abandoned during the Dust Bowl and never occupied again. He knows the place because he sold the farmer a windmill back in 1930, before the worst of it. The old farmhouse is down in a grove of cottonwood trees, out of sight of the road. It will just about do.

When Tucker stops to pee and stands there watching him drink from the water bag, Pardo sees it all, plain as day. The man tucking that bulge into his pants. Queer as a three-dollar bill.

A mile up the road, Tucker has to swerve to dodge a buzzard pecking at a rabbit carcass. He turns the wheel so hard that Pardo is thrown into him just long enough to find out what he wants to know for sure. He braces his hand on the man's thigh and leaves it there a moment too long and hears the sharp intake of breath. He settles back in his seat, looking out the window, feeling the bayonet against his calf, knowing how it will go.

Tucker says he has to pay a visit to a farm where he once sold a windmill to a fellow. They bump along half a mile of road where the dust has never been bulldozed away, the fences filled with tumbleweeds and then covered with dust that has been watered and baked and blown and watered again until it has taken on the consistency of pottery baked in a

kiln. They pull over a rise and see the house, the southern half of it col-
lapsed under the weight of the dust, the façade and the parlor still standing, beneath the cottonwoods a shady and sheltered grove for the rabbits
and the crows and the rats. The blade of the old windmill still turns, but
the shaft is broken, connected to nothing at all.

The stock tank is silted over. Pardo decides that Tucker ought to have
a good look, understand how useless his life has been. Might as well
have pumped dirt, that goddamned windmill, all the good it did. Cost
poor folks a fortune and there it stands, four panes short of a flush, as
sad-looking a goddamned thing as you will see on this sorry earth, and
money still owed by some poor bastard farmer, feeding the worms six
feet underground and still up to his eye sockets in debt.

Tucker kills the engine and listens to the sudden quiet, feeling the
sweat trickle down his back as he pulls away from the seat. He lays a paw
on Pardo's leg. When he speaks, his voice is thick with lust.

"Gets awful lonely out on the road sometimes," he says.

"I expect it does."

"A young fella like you, good-looking like you are . . ."

"Uh-huh."

"Well, a man can't help but have thoughts."

"Is that a fact? What sort of thoughts?"

"Do I got to draw you a picture? You just got outa prison, unless
I miss my guess. You know how it goes. Can't nobody see us from the
county road. We could do most anything right here."

"Anything, like what?"

"All right, then. You got to have it laid out plain. I'll pay three dollars
to see you unzip them pants and take out your pecker," he says.

"Gimme the three dollars first."

"And I'll pay you five dollars to let me gap it."

"Is that three dollars to unzip and five dollars to let you suck it, or is
it eight dollars total?"

"Let's say ten dollars, but you got to do mine, too."

He doesn't say yes and he doesn't say no. Tucker reaches out his billfold and hands the man ten dollars. Pardo tucks the sawbuck in his pants pocket.

"I got a better notion," he says. "You ever get tied up? You get a fellow like me that knows what he's doin, he can get you to where you think you're about to blow a gasket. I've put some study into it. Man or woman, don't matter to me. I can do it real fine. Take my time, make it real sweet. Like nothing you ever felt, except that will cost you another sawbuck."

"I dunno. I never done nothing like that."

"Then today's your lucky day. Time I get done with you, you won't want it no other way. You'll thank me all the way to wherever in hell you're going. Topeka, I believe you said. Maybe we'll do it again a time or two."

He reaches over and kneads Tucker's privates through his pants. Just enough to take away any sense the man might have left, not enough so that he blows his load before he's good and tied up. Tucker's eyes roll back in his head. He moans, a low, gargling moan deep in his chest.

"Okay. Okay. Let's do it. Goddamn, yes. You're about the best-looking human bein I ever seen. It will be a treat."

He grabs Pardo's hair and tries to pull him forward into a wet-lipped kiss, but Pardo shoves him away, hard. "Nothin until my say-so, pops. That's the way it works. First off, you owe me another sawbuck."

Tucker fumbles in his billfold and hands over another ten. "Where did you have in mind for this tying business?"

"How bout over against that windmill yonder? You're a windmill man. You ought to feel right at home. There's baling wire hangin all over it. That ought to do. We could use bobwire, but that might scrape you up some."

"I'd druther some soft rope I got in the back. I don't want to get all cut up."

"Soft rope it is. You dig it out, pops, I'll put it to good use."

"You'll turn me loose when you're done?"

"Hell, yes. You got to have your turn on your knees, too, don't you? You aint gettin away that easy."

Tucker leads the way to the windmill, undoing his pants as he walks. He kicks his shoes off and yanks his pants down, and he is fat and throbbing, bobbing up and down as Pardo helps him out of his shirt. He winds the rope around Tucker's chest and thighs, and then uses baling wire to bind the man's wrists and ankles to the windmill. Tucker protests that they haven't agreed nothing about baling wire, but Pardo stuffs the man's handkerchief in his mouth and tells him to shut up. When the work is done to his satisfaction and Tucker is so worked up he is grinding his hips against the rope, Pardo reaches down to his ankle and undoes the strap that holds the bayonet. He looks into Tucker's eyes. They have gone all cloudy, half-closed, waiting for Pardo to give him some relief. He nudges the man's balls with the sharp edge of the bayonet, watches the eyes widen. Cuts a little, hears the scream die in the hankie wedged in the man's mouth. Terror now. That's a look of real terror. Little girls or grown men, at a certain point they get the same look. He steps up to grin in Tucker's face. *Are you at peace with the Lord?*

The dogs find Tucker Graff two days later. They belong to Clyde Llewellyn. He's out hunting jackrabbits just after sunup when he hears the hounds baying as though they have treed a coon. He catches up to the dogs and finds what is left of a big, beefy carcass, tied to a windmill stark naked and burned to a lobster red in the sun. The poor devil's throat has been cut and he has either bled to death or died of thirst, or maybe a little of both. He's been tied with rope and baling wire, and someone has taken rusty barbed wire from an old spool in a shed next to the windmill and wrapped about ten yards of it around his torso, so that the spikes have stuck into the skin and drawn blood in a hundred places. Where his private parts ought to be, it looks like he's been butchered with an ax. The man's clothes are on the ground next to his shoes, but his billfold is gone. There are tire tracks on the ground, but no car. Clyde kicks one of the dogs to stop it howling.

"Goddamnit, you dogs shut up. We got to go back and call the law."

Ennis Ankeny hears about the dead man on the radio and reckons from the description that it could be Tucker Graff. He calls the county sheriff and drives to the morgue himself to identify the body. Hoping all the way it won't be Tucker that he finds on that slab, knowing somehow that's exactly who it is. It's the least he can do, all the times Tucker has come by to check on the windmills. Ennis is able to give a fair description of the buff-colored 1946 Buick with the whitewall tires that Tucker is driving. He doesn't know the license number, but the Buick bears Kansas plates. The sheriff says that's real helpful.

37

PARDO DRIVES TEN MILES BEFORE HE PULLS OVER next to a cow pasture and goes through the man's billfold. He takes the driver's license and counts the cash, three hundred and forty-seven dollars. That's three hundred and sixty-seven with the double sawbuck paid to him for services rendered. Any damned fool that would travel with that kind of dough in his billfold deserves what he gets. He tosses the empty billfold into a muddy irrigation ditch. After that, he keeps to the back roads, working his way north. He spends the night at a dingy, five-lodge motel outside Tulsa, sleeps like a baby, wakes at dawn feeling like the prince of the world. He drives through Pryor Creek and Big Cabin before turning west at Vinita, passing just north of Oologah Lake through Nowata and Bartlesville before turning north again at Ponca City. He crosses the Kansas state line south of Arkansas City and turns west to avoid Wichita, driving through Medicine Lodge and Coldwater and stopping for a bite to eat in Dodge City near noon. Around the time the dogs find Tucker Graff, Pardo is passing the time with a good-looking gal who works the soda fountain at a Dodge City dime store. She looks about fifteen, but she's cute as a button and she has the tightest little can when she bends over. After five years in Huntsville, he could eat her with a spoon.

He grins at her. "What's your name?"

"I aint going to tell you mine unless you tell me yours."

"Why, it's Tucker," he says. "Tucker Graff."

The girl smiles and puts out her hand. "I'm Arleen Swain, but they call me Arlie. Say, I don't suppose you'd let a little gal go for a ride in that big old car of yours, would you?"

"Well, aint you a forward little gal?"

"What if I am?"

"I don't mean nothing by it. Tell you what. First, you bring me a tuna-fish sandwich with lettuce and mayo and pickles, no ketchup. I hate ketchup. And a cherry Coke. Then we'll see about that ride. A man can't drive on a empty stomach, can he? Especially if we're going a long ways."

"Who says we're going a long ways? You aint even showed me that you know how to drive that thing."

"Oh, darlin. I can drive it. I can drive it so hard, your eyes roll back in your head and you scream for mercy."

"Uh-huh. We'll see about that. That was a virgin Coke and a swimmer with greens and mayo, am I right?"

"You're the rightest thing I've seen since I left Texas."

He likes Arlie Swain. She's his first girl since the whores in Galveston in 1941, and she has spunk. She's known Pardo exactly one hour when she asks him to drive her home so she can get some things, because wherever he is headed, she is bound to come along. Just that quick, no hemming and hawing. He likes her and she likes him. She lives with her mother in a tiny yellow frame house on the south side of Dodge City. She doesn't mention a father and Pardo doesn't ask. He parks in the shade of the three big elm trees in front and waits with his windows rolled down, listening to the hiss of a water sprinkler in the next lawn.

Arlie runs into the house. He watches the flash of her legs, lean and white, the bounce of her skirt as she runs. Dark red hair cut short, green eyes and a sprinkling of freckles across her nose, the widest mouth he's ever seen. Like she can smile all the way to her ears. Five years in prison, dreaming of something like her, a girl with creamy skin and a round bottom and a hairless chest and breath that doesn't stink of jailhouse tobacco. He hears the screen door slam and she's through into the darkness of the sitting room in the front of her house, where her mother sits on the davenport, with a migraine and a wet cloth on her forehead. Pardo hears kids yelling down the street, a dog barking. A mother somewhere, calling the kids in for cookies. It's a nice, shady street with big trees and neat little houses. A place to sit on the front porch and eat watermelon on summer evenings and play with sparklers on the Fourth of July. A good place to be, if you are poor and dumb and don't know no better.

After five minutes, Arlie is back. She has changed her blouse, but she wears the same skirt, which is good. He likes the skirt. It's short, almost up to her knee, and she has slim brown calves. Pardo hears the woman call in a whining, weary voice from inside the house. "Where you goin, Arlie?"

"Out."

A flash of white panties as she tosses a plaid suitcase into the back-seat and scoots over next to him, sitting with her legs wide apart, her hip pressed tight to his even before he drops the Buick into first gear.

"Let's go, mister. I want out of this town."

"How old are you?"

"Almost sixteen."

"Uh-huh. When's your birthday?"

"May."

"So you just turned fifteen."

"Well, yeah."

"Great. So I'm riding with jailbait."

She gives him a steady, green-eyed gaze.

"Best jailbait you'll ever have," she says.

Once they clear the town limits, she bends down and sucks his pecker all the way to Cimarron, near twenty miles. He drives as slow as he can. After he finishes once, tightening his thigh muscles and pushing her head down with the heel of his right hand, she sits up and kisses him on the neck. A minute later, she is back at it, as though she can't get enough, letting him loll around on her tongue, and pretty soon he is hard and pushing into her mouth again. Finally, he has to tell her to stop it and just about drag her off, they are coming to a town.

"Cimarron aint a town," she says.

"Well, stop it anyhow."

She digs a handkerchief out of her pocket and wipes her mouth. "I'll stop for now, mister. But you aint seen nothing yet."

"I believe you," he says. "Where'd you learn all that?"

"Truckers, mostly. A sailor or two. They come through. They take care of me, I take care of them. Fair is fair. But aint none of them fellas half as pretty as you, even with that scar. How'd you get that thing? Looks like somebody laid a brand on your face."

She sees his face cloud over for a moment, like a thunderhead sliding unnoticed into the blue calm of a summer afternoon, when everything goes dark and then the lightning flashes and the thunder rolls. She likes a man like that. It's like a carnival ride, where you're going up one second and then it drops and your stomach is back there somewhere, waiting to catch up. "Well, you don't have to tell me about it, if you don't want to," she says.

"I don't want to."

Pardo is looking for a town of some size, where he can lay off the Buick. They turn north at Cimarron and drive for over an hour, stop at a gas station outside Grainfield and buy a map of Kansas and Nebraska. He squats in the shade to study the map while the girl uses the ladies' room. The only town he's heard of within driving range is McCook, on the far side of the Nebraska line. He folds the map and sticks it in his hip pocket, heads back into the station, and pays a nickel each for a root beer for himself and a cream soda for the girl. While he waits for his change, he asks the old boy at the cash register how far it is to McCook.

"A little better than eighty miles, as the crow flies."

"I aint a crow, or maybe you aint noticed."

"I didn't say you was. Only out here, the roads run straight as a string and flat as a pancake. Might be eighty-five miles, but taint more than that."

"Thank you, kindly." Pardo starts for the door, a soda pop in each hand.

"Say, your daughter is a real swell-lookin little gal."

He turns. The old man chews tobacco. A chaw is stuffed in his right cheek, his lips are flecked with the stuff, and his teeth are brown. It turns Pardo's stomach, a man who chews tobacco. It's a hundred and seven degrees outside, but the old man feels like he's been dropped into a bucket of ice water.

"I don't recollect telling you that it was okay to look at her."

The old man swallows his chaw. He gags. His face turns purple, his eyes bulge. Pardo leaves him be.

Arlie is waiting by the Buick. As he starts the engine, he can hear the old bastard puking inside the station, like he's going to heave his bowels right onto the floor. He laughs so hard that he has to pull over a hundred yards down the road. He pounds the steering wheel, laughing until his belly hurts.

"What's so darned funny?"

"Old-timer back there. He called you my daughter, said something about what a good-looking gal you are. I scared him so bad, he swallowed his chewin tobacco. He'll be green for a month."

He stomps on the gas pedal and they laugh together, barreling north through a cloud of dust, doing near eighty miles an hour on a dirt road, laughing until their faces are red and their noses run and tears pour down their cheeks. Laughing makes Arlie want something else. He watches for a place where they can stop, pulls into a grove of cottonwoods a quarter mile from the side of the road, and parks the Buick. He wants to move to the backseat, but she straddles him right where he is, sticks her tongue in his ear and rides him hard. He is just about to pop when he sees a police car go by, its siren wailing. He wonders if the old man called the law on them. He's tempted to go back and kill the old fart, but he finishes with Arlie and waits until he can't hear the siren anymore. Then he pulls back onto the highway.

In McCook, Pardo drives around until he finds a joint called the Republican River Cabins, where it doesn't look like they'll want a marriage license. He pays five dollars for a cabin, signs "Tucker Graff" on the register with a flourish, and takes the girl to cabin number thirteen. He wants to find a used-car lot where he can get rid of the Buick, but the girl isn't having it.

"I rode all this way with wet panties, honey. I been stuck to the seat since way back in Kansas, and that little ride in the cottonwoods didn't half do it. You shut that door and come over here and let Arlie Swain take care of what ails you."

She is lithe and muscular, hungry and pantherish. She's fifteen years old and she knows tricks that would embarrass a whore. Girls her age, he decides, must have changed a whole lot between 1941 and 1946. Maybe it's the war that did it. She has already let slip that in July 1945 she spent an entire week shacked up in a motel in Salina with a forty-year-old war-rant officer just mustered out of the Navy. Arlie knows what she's up to, and she knows what she wants. By the time Pardo heads out to scare up some supper for them, he's weak in the knees. He takes his time, need-ing to get a second wind before he goes back to the cabins. Wondering what he'll do with her. When she got into the car in Dodge City, he knew. Now he's not so sure. Arlie Swain is not a bit like the others. She's more like him. Like a big bad wolf in a world full of little pigs. Back at the cabin, she's waiting on the bed. She has put her clothes back on but left her panties off. He likes that. They sit cross-legged on the bed eating thick hamburgers and drinking bottles of pop.

There's a shower in a corner of the room next to the toilet. When they are through eating, she turns the knobs until the faucet produces a thin spray of water, and she stands under it and washes with the sliver of soap that is left, making a show of it, turning this way and that so he can watch, spreading her cheeks so he can look right into her rump. She crooks a finger to him and stands leaning her face to the wall with her rear tipped out, glancing over her shoulder to see, can he take a hint. He strips down and comes to her then, stands under the shower until the hot water runs cold, and lets it pour over both of them as his groin slaps into her bottom. Remembering the showers in the prison and things that happened there. Earl Toth, the way he slipped to the floor, trying to reach Pardo's throat. Blood bubbling from his mouth. He drives into her hard enough that he knows it hurts. She pushes back into him. He grabs a handful of hair, pulls her head back. She tilts her face to him, sucks his tongue. His hands close around her throat. She's slick with soap. He gets enough purchase to yank her back, and she gives him some tongue and he takes it and thrusts until his legs go weak. They fall down, wet and laughing, onto the sheets, drying each other with the one threadbare towel in the room.

"Damn," he says.

"Yeah. Damn. That's it, all right. Damn."

38

ARLY MORNING, FIRST LIGHT. HE SITS ON THE only chair in the room, watching Arlie sleep. Her white throat, enough sunshine seeping through the curtains so that he can watch her pulse beat, count the seconds of her life flowing by, take the measure of the beating heart. He's jaybird naked, and he holds the bayonet by the blade and wonders what he will do. He likes the girl. He really does. She has spunk and she makes up her mind. She doesn't hem and haw or wait to be coaxed, doesn't ask stupid questions, doesn't pry. He can usually grab on to a thing about a girl he doesn't like: the way she chews gum, how her teeth rake his penis, the smell down there, the way she keeps asking too goddamn many questions. With Arlie Swain, he can't find a solitary thing he doesn't like. Not that it matters. Liking her doesn't matter. He might kill her anyway, if it happens like that. He's done that before, a girl back in Wyoming. The more time he spent with her, the better he liked her. So he killed her, before he got to liking her too much. It isn't liking or not liking. It's chance, it's always down to chance. Like a girl walking out of the bus station to have a cigarette in the evening dark. A thing so simple, a simple act that decides, life or death. He watches Arlie's throat. So white, so bare. The beating pulse. If he does it, he will do it quick. She's a good girl, he doesn't want her to suffer. There will be a neat, pale slice where the white skin opens, like a second mouth, then the blood will leap and pulse as the slice turns a brilliant crimson, the girl gargling blood as she dies.

He flips the bayonet, catches it by the blade, flips it again. Heads or tails. Handle or sword. If he misses, sharp as it is, flipping it naked like this, it might slice his pecker right off. He giggles, enjoying the game, trying to flip it so that the blade flashes nearer and nearer before he catches it. The danger makes him hard. The harder he is, the more it stands up where the blade might cut him. Twice he almost misses and he grabs the bayonet sideways. The second time, it cuts his palm and blood trickles down his thighs. He licks it off his hand. Waits for the sign. She lives, she dies. Which will it be? It isn't something you can think through. It will come to him and then it will be done.

When he glances up, the girl is awake, watching him, as though she has opened her eyes every day of her life to the sight of a naked man juggling a bayonet within an inch of his privates. He giggles.

"Mornin," he says.

She smiles a sleepy smile. "Mornin. What are you doin with that thing?"

"Settin here, tryin to decide whether to cut your throat."

She doesn't flinch. Just looks at him with that same steady expression, her green eyes like a woman much older than she is.

"All right then," she says. "So why don't you come down here between Arlie's legs and do that sweet thing you do with your tongue one more time? Then if you still got to cut my throat, you got to cut."

Later he dresses and heads down the road a piece, finds a short-order house where he gets the cook to make up a couple of bacon-and-egg sandwiches to go. On the way back, he passes a used-car lot. He turns in, finds the proprietor just unlocking the door. He browses the lot for ten minutes and cuts a deal: the 1946 Buick for a 1940 Ford Coupe. The Coupe is a royal blue, and it has a good eighty-five-horsepower engine, but what matters is that it doesn't belong to a dead man. Tucker Graff, fool that he was, left the bill of sale for the Buick in the cubbyhole, which makes it easy. Pardo has the bill of sale, the registration, Tucker's driver's license, everything the salesman wants. If the man looked close, he'd see that the license says Tucker Graff is six foot three and two hundred and eighty pounds, but he's about to make a killing on this swap, he's not going to look at anything too close. Pardo takes the Ford and two hundred dollars cash and the salesman parks the Buick on the lot and watches for more suckers coming down the highway, waiting to make another killing.

On the way back to the Republican River Cabins in the Ford, Pardo thinks about Arlie again. Why hadn't he killed her while she was lying there, the pulse beating in her neck, sweet and pale and innocent? Not killing her felt almost as good as killing her. Once you know that you can do it, then you kill or don't kill. Either way, you get almost the same thrill. You still have the power. By not killing her, it's like he's created her, as though Arlie Swain is on this earth because Pardo Bury made her. Whether she lives another day or a hundred years, this is Pardo's time, a gift he has given her whether she knows it or not, a gift he can snatch away whenever he pleases. He remembers the others at the end, the way the light went out, so that they were with you and then they were in another place and you had put them there. It was like that even with Tucker Graff and Lottie Alice Pilbro and Earl Toth down in Huntsville. Something was there and then it vanished, but it's less thrilling when they're old, because you haven't taken much away. It's still good when the light goes out. He has learned to watch for it, because that's the moment he craves. With Arlie Swain, he may strike or he may not. Until he does, she is his. People like to say they belong to each other, but it's bullshit. It's only true until something better comes along. They belong until they get pissed off because a pie was burned, or because the mother-in-law wants to stay for a week, or because a man loses his job, or because another man smells better or he has a bigger pecker. Then they don't belong anymore, so they never really belonged at all. With Arlie, it's for real. She belongs to him now, because he let her live. He might yet change his mind, or he might not. That feels good, knowing that he can, not knowing whether he will or not. There is always a moment when he knows, and then he just does it while the moment is on him, neither too soon nor too late.

He'll feel bad if it ends up that he kills Arlie. He'll miss her. She doesn't blab. She hasn't asked him a single question about his past, where he came from or where he is headed. She hasn't offered to tell him one thing about herself. She's not one of those girls that keep at him with the questions until he admits his father is one of the richest bastards in the country. Then they go all fuzzy and out of focus, like they're having a magic-carpet daydream, the poor girl meets the handsome prince and becomes princess of the castle. Arlie isn't like that. She's a good kid. But she belongs to him now. It might be that her time is already up and she doesn't know it. He might do it right now, before he leaves town, or tomorrow or next week. Or never. That's the beauty of it. It's all so damned beautiful, it's enough to make a grown man weep.

By the time he gets back to the Republican River Cabins, she's packed and ready to go. "What happened to the Buick?" she asks.

He giggles. "If I aint going to cut your throat, you can't ask no questions, all right?"

"Why ain't you going to cut my throat?"

"Now that's a question, see?"

She laughs. She's a good kid, to see the humor in the situation. Two minutes later they are on the road, headed west. Pardo isn't hungry, so Arlie eats both the sandwiches and drinks from the water bag, letting it run down her chin onto her hard little breasts. The cool water makes her nipples stand up. He reaches over and rubs the back of his hand over them. She puts the cap back on and reaches out to hang the bag from the mirror just as Pardo makes a hard left turn. Her door flies open, and she is hanging over the road with her hands clinging to the open window and her toes on the seat, and then he brings the Ford out of the turn and she tumbles back in, slamming the door as she sprawls into his lap, banging her head on the steering wheel. She laughs wildly and kisses him as he drives, so hard she draws blood from his bottom lip. The blood has a metallic taste on her tongue, and the taste of blood makes her wild. They find a place to pull over, behind a row of trees by a small lake, and she sprawls in the backseat with her legs open, one calf hooked over the front seat, watching his eyes as he enters her.

"God, you're a beautiful man. You're like a damned angel."

"That's me, all right. I aint nothin but a goddamned angel."

39

IN OGALLALA, THEY STOP SO PARDO CAN SHOP FOR
clothes. He buys two pairs of blue jeans and two cowboy shirts
and a pair of cowboy boots and a belt and some underwear and
socks. Once he is dressed in clothes that fit him, he feels better and he
walks with a swagger, liking the way the salesgirls peek at him. He buys
two pairs of tight-fitting pants for Arlie Swain, because he likes to watch
her rump when she walks, and a new pair of shoes and a blouse that
she likes and sunglasses for both of them. She asks him to buy a pretty
Indian blanket because the nights are cold under the thin motel blan-
kets, even though it is hotter than blazes during the day. They stop at a
grocery store and buy lunch meat, white bread and mustard, and a few
other things that strike their fancy. Arlie makes sandwiches as he drives.
When they are back in the car, he mentions that she hasn't asked where
they are going.

"Do you want me to ask?"

"No. I like that you don't ask. That's why I'll tell you where we're
goin. Because you didn't ask, see? We're goin to Casper. That's up in
Wyoming. We're goin there, so's I can kill my old man."

"Okay," the girl says.

She doesn't even ask why he's going to kill his old man. This is a swell
gal, Arlie Swain. A real peach. He's glad he didn't happen to kill her, back
in the Republican River Cabins.

East of Ogallala, they pick up a woman, hitchhiking on the Lincoln
Highway. Her name is Hilda Zogg. She's not much over twenty, but
she's hefty and that makes her look older than she is. She comes from
Minnesota and she's on her way to California, she says, because she
wants to get into the movie business. Hilda is sprawled in the backseat
when she says it, the part about wanting to be a movie star, and he looks

in the rearview and tilts it down so he can see Arlie. She is biting her lip, trying not to laugh, and he takes a notion right then to set up a little experiment, to see if Arlie is like him. Really like him. If she can do the things he does, if she can be creator and destroyer.

"So you want to be in pictures?" he says to Hilda.

"Yep. All my life. I'm a big girl, but I got a good face for pictures. The camera likes me."

"Does it, now? What part are you going to play? King Kong?"

Hilda looks like she's going to cry. "You don't have to be mean. Every gal has a dream."

"Sure, honey. I was only funning you. I knew a little girl once, she wanted to be Veronica Lake."

"What happened to her?"

"She asked too many questions. Ended up with her throat cut." Arlie smiles at him in the mirror. He giggles.

"It's not funny. A crack like that."

"Sure it is. When you're with friends, that's funny. You got to be able to kid. You're with friends, aint you?"

She looks at them doubtfully. "I guess. I dunno. I mean, you just picked me up and all."

"Tell ya what. Arlie, you climb over the seat and set with Hilda there. I want you to show her how we can be friends. Real good friends. I seen how you was lookin at Arlie, Hilda. I know what you're thinking, see, even if you don't know it yourself. I got a gift that way. Now Arlie is goin to show you how friendly she can be."

He catches Arlie's eye again in the rearview and winks at her. She understands. She catches his drift right away. You don't have to draw pictures for this gal.

Arlie is young and lithe and agile. She slithers over the seat like a snake and lands in Hilda's lap. The woman giggles but she holds on, her arms around the young girl's back, her legs open, the slip of a girl that is Arlie Swain parked between the fat woman's thighs. Hilda tangles her fingers in Arlie's curly hair and pulls her face down and kisses her. She is wearing lipstick the color of dried blood, and it smears Arlie's face. As

Pardo watches in the mirror, Arlie pokes her tongue between Hilda's thick lips, and the woman sucks it into her mouth with a slurping noise. He watches her pudgy hands go down to Arlie's rump. She tugs the girl toward her, and Arlie responds, thrusting into Hilda's crotch like a man screwing a woman. He congratulates himself for buying the girl those pants. The way they cling to her butt, he can see the muscles clench with every thrust. He watches too intently; the Ford slides off the shoulder and skids sideways before he can yank it back onto the asphalt. Arlie, intent on what she is doing to the woman, doesn't even look up. This is the way to drive, he thinks, sailing along, seventy miles an hour, watching the gals go at it in the backseat. Hell, he could drive all the way across America like this.

At Kimball, he turns off Highway 30 to head north to Scottsbluff. When they pass a liquor store along the main drag in Kimball, he pulls over and pops inside and buys four bottles of bourbon. He wants to buy mescal, but the store doesn't stock any. The store clerk is a skinny kid who has never heard of mescal. He gives Pardo a look, like he's crazy for asking, and Pardo lingers after the kid counts out his change, staring at him. He sees the fear start then, the way the kid's eyes get big when he sees that he has put a foot down in the wrong place, and he's hoping to get out of the trap before the jaws close on him. *Creator and destroyer.*

"What's the matter, son? You look a little peaked."

"Nothin, sir. I'm just real sorry. I oughtn't to laughed when you mentioned that drink, what is it? Mescalita?"

"Mescal. You're getting two things mixed up there, see? Mescal and tequila. Not the same drink. You remember that, next time. And tell the fella who owns this place, the next time I come through here, I want to see mescal on the shelves, you got that?"

"Yessir. Mescal. Do you know when that might be?"

"Do I know when what might be?"

"The next time you come through, uh, sir."

"Now you're askin too many goddamned questions. You just get the fuckin mescal, okay? I'll be by."

"Yessir."

It feels wrong. Nothing clear, one way or the other. He is waiting for a signal, waiting to know. When he doesn't know, it leaves him confused and angry.

"Shut up," he says. "Just shut the fuck up."

But that feels wrong, too, and he storms out of the liquor store, slams the door behind him. He feels a fierce need for liquor, pulls a bottle of bourbon out of the paper bag and takes the cap off, pours it down his throat, standing there in plain sight next to the Ford. Almost hoping a cop will pull over. *Son, we got laws around here against drinkin in public.* He is in the mood to kill a cop, but there is no one around except a square-built woman in square, sensible shoes and a square, sensible dress. She glares at him. He pauses to lick the bourbon off his lips.

"Keep your eyes to yourself, you old bitch, or I'll cut your tits off and feed 'em to my dog."

The old woman covers her mouth in horror and scuttles away. Pardo jerks the door of the Ford open. The women are sitting straight up in the backseat, as though nothing is going on, but the button of Arlie's pants is undone and the zipper is down and the fat one has two fingers inside the girl, stirring her up. Arlie looks at him then, her mouth open, panting a little, her eyes the color of smoke. *Creator and destroyer*, he thinks, *creator and destroyer.*

"Take your fingers out of there," he says to Hilda. She pulls her fingers out, a little scared.

"Hold them up. Show me."

She holds them up, wet and glistening.

He sniffs. "Ah, that's sweet. Aint that sweet? Lick 'em off, Hilda. Lick 'em nice and clean." She does as she's told, making a show out of it. "Now slip them back in there. I want you to make Arlie feel real good, hear? That's your job with our little crew here. You make Arlie feel good and we'll be nice to you."

Before they pull out of Kimball, he passes the bottle around, and they all take long pulls of the bourbon. The booze sets Arlie's throat on fire, makes her eyes water. The fat woman gulps it down like a glass of chocolate milk and shows no reaction. By the time they are ten miles out of town, they have polished off one bottle. He tosses it out the window, hears it smash on the pavement, opens another bottle. In the rearview, he sees the woman leaning toward Arlie, her lips on the girl's neck, her smeared lipstick there, a trail across Arlie's throat like the slash of a clumsy knife. Oh, yes. *Creator and destroyer.* Even as she is fingering the girl, the woman keeps jawing. She has a lot to say. Her lipsticked mouth flaps like a wound. She talks pretty much solid, until Pardo sees a gravel road that leads up into the Wildcat Hills. He brakes hard and takes it on two wheels, skidding onto the gravel. Hilda Zogg asks where they are going.

"For a picnic," he says.

"Oh, I like picnics. I could eat a steer."

"I bet you could. First, we want to find someplace where we can be alone, have a little fun."

Hilda perks up. "Oh, I like fun. I like fun almost as much as I like to eat. Boys or girls, I'm game, long as it's fun." She wiggles her tongue at him, takes another long pull of bourbon.

He stops the car where the road has turned into twin dirt tracks. There is nothing but prickly pear cactus and yucca and mesquite and buffalo grass and the strange clay bluffs left from thousands of years of erosion in the sedimentary rock, Scotch pine growing right out of the side of the bluffs. Hilda spreads the Indian blanket on the ground for a picnic and Arlie sets out the things from the grocery store. He lifts Arlie and carries her over to a yucca plant and sets her down on the sharp spikes, her round little butt in the thin tight pants punctured in a dozen places as she yelps and giggles. He carries her back to the blanket and lays her down on her stomach and rubs her bottom to make the pain go away. He tells Hilda to do the same.

"Only take her pants down. Take 'em down and lick her, every place she got stuck by them yucca spines." Hilda does as she's told, grinning at him, pulling Arlie's pants down and sticking her face in the girl's white bottom, each little bloody pinprick getting its share of her raw, pink tongue, the girl's butt smeared with blood-red lipstick.

* * *

They are well out of sight of the highway. They sit drinking bourbon, feeling the warmth spread through them, eating some of the lunch meat and bread and watching the sun go down, until he says that he wants to see the girls kiss. They peck each other on the lips two or three times, then Hilda pulls the girl to her. Her hand is already down between Arlie's legs. He watches, curious. They are slow, women, the way they go about it. Too damned slow, sometimes. He drinks more bourbon. Hilda has her clothes off. Great creamy breasts, swaying back and forth, pulling Arlie's head into them. A great creamy bottom. Funny how her butt and her tits are alike, one mimics the other. Arlie takes the bottle, spilling a little of the bourbon, licks it off the woman's breasts. Then Arlie is on her back and the woman is on her knees between the girl's legs, her big mouth shut for once as she licks, the big white rump almost in his face. He shrugs. What the hell. He might as well, she's right there in front of him, wide open. He takes her, hard, driving into that cushiony, wobbly behind. He watches Arlie watching him, her eyes like smoke. He sees her shudder, lifting her hips to the woman's mouth. She likes it, the little bitch. He finishes then and pulls back and watches. Hilda makes greedy sounds like she's eating ice cream.

"You better get ready again quick, Tucker," Arlie says. "I didn't get mine and I want it. Jesus, do I want it."

"You guys are fun," Hilda says. "Geez, I like people who are fun. They say there are a bunch like us in California."

He gives her a hard look then, eyes like slate. "What do you mean, a bunch like us?"

She giggles. "People who like to have fun. Not a bunch of old church ladies who are afraid to lick a little pussy cause they might go to hell."

"You aint like us."

"Not in someways, maybe. I like to have fun. I aint particular, man or woman. Not everybody is made that way."

"You aint like us."

"Geez, who pissed in your beer? Can't a gal talk?"

"You don't do nothing but talk. You got to learn to shut up." He grabs

Hilda by the hair and pulls her face close to him. *Are you at peace with the Lord?*

"Ouch! You're hurting me. You want to hurt me, take your belt off and smack my butt. I like that."

"I don't want to smack your fat ass. I asked you a question. *Are you at peace with the Lord?*"

"What? Are you some kind of religious nut?"

He pulls the bayonet out of the scabbard on his ankle. He slips it to Arlie and she takes the handle, awkwardly at first. The big woman sees the flash of the blade and squeals. He pulls her hair back hard, exposing her throat. She struggles to get up. She's strong and she weighs more than he does, strong enough to lift him. Pardo hangs on to her, riding her back, yanking at her hair with both hands. She staggers under his weight, falls to her knees. Arlie rolls, quick as a snake, and sticks the woman in the ribs with the bayonet, just enough to break the skin. Arlie sticks her two or three more times, not deep enough, and the woman screams and takes off downhill, running naked, her great breasts swaying. She leaps over a little hummock of grass and comes down with both bare feet on a prickly pear cactus. She screams again and tries to run with her feet stuck full of spines, screaming at every step. Arlie is after her like a leopard, lean and muscular, her slim white body knifing through the dusk as she catches up and takes the big girl down, gouging at her throat as they fall.

When Hilda is dead, he reaches for Arlie and drags her away from the smell of blood and shit. The girl is laughing wildly, her naked body streaked with blood. He falls onto his back and drags her on top of him and lets her ride him until she has all she wants.

He's suddenly cold, his chest heaving, gasping for breath. Arlie stretches out on top of him. He holds her tight. He sees the evening star then, barely visible, points it out to her. She looks over her shoulder. "It's beautiful. Everything is beautiful as long as I'm with you."

"You can't never *not* be with me," he says. "You are me. Do you understand that? You are me."

"You mean I'm just like you?"

"No. That's not it at all. You *are* me, see, and I am you. We are creator and destroyer. One and the same."

She thinks it over. "Yes. I understand. I am you. And you are me."

"Creator and destroyer."

"Yes. Creator and destroyer. You and me."

40

T HEY LIE STILL UNTIL THEY ARE SHIVERING WITH cold, then get up and fumble around in the dark until Arlie finds the bayonet next to Hilda's body. He tucks it in its scabbard, and they walk back up the hill holding hands, looking for their clothes. They dress, fumbling and laughing, and climb in the Ford. Pardo presses the starter and pops the clutch, and the car slews in the gravel as the wheels spin. He remembers the hitchhiker's gear in the backseat and slams on the brakes and tells Arlie to toss it out. She flings the big woman's duffel bag down the embankment and gets back in and slams the door and he drives much too fast, back onto the highway and north again. When a car passes, he glances at Arlie's face in the light.

"Jesus Christ. You got blood all over you, girl. We got to go someplace and get you cleaned up. Somebody sees you like that, they'll call the law on us for sure."

They stop at a gas station in a town called Gering. Arlie takes her bag of clothes and goes to the ladies' to clean up while Pardo gets gas. The pump jockey is a tall, cadaverous gent with a narrow, suspicious face. Pardo sees him looking at the girl's rump, too far away to see the blood on her but staring anyhow. When he goes to pay, he sees the shotgun in the rack over the cash register, put there to deter outlaws. He leans close as the man counts out his change.

Are you at peace with the Lord?

"More at peace than you are, sonny boy. At least I go to church. I bet you aint been in a month of Sundays. You and that little twist you're with. I bet she aint even of age."

Sonny boy. He hates being called "sonny boy." It's like folks don't take him seriously. There is a greasy crescent wrench on the counter, left there by one of the mechanics during the day. He grabs it with his left hand and swings from his heels, bringing it straight across the bridge of the man's skinny nose. The pump jockey drops, his nose spurting blood. Pardo vaults the counter and grabs the shotgun. He presses it to the man's chest and trips the triggers, one after the other.

The roar of the shotgun in the cubbyhole office deafens him. The man is driven back, into a shelf of thirty-weight oil. The cans tumble down on his head as Pardo reaches up to grab two boxes of twelve-gauge shotgun shells. He reloads the gun, yanks the bills from the cash register and leaves the change, runs from the station carrying the shotgun down low, and slides behind the wheel just as Arlie comes out, wiping her hands dry on her pants because there's no towel in the ladies' room. He starts the engine and waves to her. A trucker has pulled up at another pump and headed in to see what's keeping the pump jockey. Now he's coming back, sprinting toward the car, a big man running hard and low, like a football player. Pardo slides out of the Ford with the car in first gear already moving, trailing the shotgun in his right hand and bringing it up to fire. He catches the sprinting trucker from a dozen feet away. The trucker squeals and drops to the pavement.

Arlie runs to the car and jumps in on the passenger side while it's still moving, jams her left foot on the brake and kills the engine because she couldn't reach the clutch.

He tosses the empty shotgun into the backseat. "Don't do that, god-damnit. I woulda caught up." He grinds the starter, but the Ford doesn't catch. He debates whether to give it a little choke, afraid of flooding the engine. In the rearview, he can see the trucker has rolled onto his knees and is trying to crawl toward them. He hits the starter again. This time the engine turns over and the Ford jerks forward. He hits the clutch just in time to keep the engine running, guns it once or twice to be sure as the trucker's bloody fist punches the window on Arlie's side, showering glass into her lap. He pops the clutch and floors it, the rear tires lay-ing two smoky streaks as he squeals toward the road. The back fender catches the trucker on the leg, and he falls and rolls on the asphalt. They pull back onto the highway just as a farm pickup turns off to the gas station, the faces of an elderly farmer and his wife staring right at them as Pardo guns it onto the bridge that crosses the North Platte River to Scottsbluff.

"They saw us," he says to the girl. "Maybe I ought to go back and kill them old folks. And put that trucker down for good, the sonofabitch."

But he doesn't. He wants to get away quick. He doesn't like it one bit. The pump jockey was okay, what happened to him, because Pardo played the game of chance and it came out snake eyes, with the man looking at Arlie's rump and calling him "sonny boy." Anyway, they needed the shotgun. But the trucker, coming up like that, he wasn't supposed to be part of it. Pardo hadn't decided a thing where he was concerned, there was no time, there was just the running man and the shotgun and then the trucker down on his knees. Now the old couple would see him and call for an ambulance and if the trucker lived he could give a good description. Even if he couldn't, the old folks had seen him with the girl and the blue Ford Coupe. He's come from Huntsville, Texas, all the way north, as far as the western edge of Nebraska, better than a thousand miles without the law on his tail. It's all changed now. They'll be looking for him, and he hasn't even begun to do what he came all this way to do.

He wants to race through this little burg, Scottsbluff or Scottsdale or what the hell ever it's called, but he doesn't dare. He tells Arlie to roll the window down so folks won't notice that it's smashed. He hopes there isn't more blood, but if there is, a dark red streak on a royal blue car won't show much. There are stoplights and stop signs and slow-moving hay trucks, and they have to crawl along as far as Highway 26, where Pardo turns west to Wyoming. He watches the town vanish in his rearview and takes a long swig of bourbon. He jams the gas pedal to the floor. The speedometer needle leaps up, almost to a hundred. He's taking crazy chances, passing on uphill grades and going around curves, Arlie beside him laughing wildly each time they pass another car.

Once they are across the Wyoming state line, Pardo rolls his window down and howls like a wolf. In Torrington, he drives up and down side streets until he spots a '38 Chevy Master that shouldn't attract too much attention. He finds the key in the ignition, starts it and transfers their things to the Chevy, and tells Arlie to get behind the wheel and follow him. He doesn't even think to ask if she can drive, but when he looks in the rearview, she's right behind him. She follows him back east, to a big irrigation ditch he had seen on the way into town. Pardo turns and follows the ditch road for half a mile, then leaves the Ford running, points it toward the ditch and jumps out. It bumps downhill and sinks in a trail of bubbles.

Hilda Zogg's body is found early the next morning. The big Swede from the Nebraska Safety Patrol who does murder investigations is still at the gas station, working the murder of the pump jockey, when he gets the call from a park ranger in the Wildcat Hills. The ranger says it sounds like the same two, a man and a girl, he can see their footprints. It's the damnedest thing, the girl has bigger feet than the man.

"Smallest doggone feet you ever saw," the ranger says. "You'd think it was a kid about eight years old that done this. Anyhow, we got to have a good look around, make sure he didn't kill the other girl and leave her out here, too. If he didn't, then he's got a hostage."

41

Big Bill Bury glares at the world from his wheelchair, fixing all visitors with his one good eye. He is unable to open his right eye, or to move the muscles on the right side of his face, or the right side of his body. His legs don't work. He has some use of his left hand. When he tries to talk, he sounds like a man gargling with kerosene. His tongue lolls. He drools. His big, scarred head rolls around on his thick neck, like a bowling ball in a circular gutter. Milo Stroud claims to understand him. His business associates don't know whether that's true, or whether Stroud claims it's true so he can run things.

Bury has been like this since August 6, 1945. The day they dropped the bomb on Hiroshima. The day the richest man in Wyoming had a stroke. He was standing over Lindy Banks at the time. A girl from the typing pool. They had a long-established routine. At ten each morning, Lindy sashayed past Bill's personal secretary, carrying a steno pad and a pencil. She locked the door behind her, put down the pencil and pad, stripped to the waist, and stood in front of him, squeezing her nipples. He never asked to see anything else. When he was ready, he came out from behind his desk and she dropped to her knees in front of the boss, who liked to look out over the refinery while she worked on him. The first time, she removed her glasses. He slapped her hard. *Keep the glasses,* he said. Lindy Banks was paid twice as much as any other secretary on the payroll, good pay for a typist who could not type. Bury also made a down payment on a little house in Casper where Lindy lived with her three-year-old son.

When he had the stroke, he didn't make a sound. There was no warning at all. He simply fell over, all his weight on top of her. As she tumbled onto her back, his knee drove into her rib cage. She had an awful, panicky moment, thinking she would be crushed by a man who outweighed her by two hundred pounds. She managed to crawl out from under him and do up his pants and make herself decent before she called for help, but she had three cracked ribs. When he was taken away, Lindy thought he was dead. She wondered how she would make a living without him. But the big man took a lot of killing. He had suffered a massive stroke, but he lived.

A month later, a man knocked on the door of her little house at ten o'clock in the evening, when she was already in her nightgown. She had seen him around the office a few times, an accountant or something. He said his name was Milo Stroud, and he was an assistant to Mr. Bury. He had a check for ten thousand dollars written out in her name and signed with a terrible scrawl by William C. Bury, who was learning to write with his left hand. Stroud also had some legal papers for her to sign. She started to read them over, but Stroud stopped her.

"All it says is that you got no more claim on Mr. Bury, legal or otherwise. By accepting this check, you and him are quits. You are also through at the refinery, so you will have to seek employment elsewhere. Understood?"

She understood. She wanted to argue, to say that maybe she should consult a lawyer herself. After all, she was still hurting from those cracked ribs. Not to mention the indignity of it all, having this enormous man collapse on top of her with his pecker spurting in her mouth. But Stroud scared her out of her wits. He was quiet and polite and he talked like an Englishman, but he left the impression that if she didn't do what he asked, he could introduce her to a world of pain. She signed the documents, in triplicate, and when Stroud left she locked the door behind him and took a long, hot bath.

The atomic bomb didn't cause the stroke. Bury didn't hear about it until three days later, because Harry Truman waited until August 9 to announce it. *The world will note that the first atomic bomb was dropped on Hiroshima, a military base. That was because we wished in this first attack to avoid, insofar as possible, the killing of civilians. But that attack is only a warning of things to come . . .*

Big Bill, listening from his hospital bed, filed it away, because information is money. On the advice of some well-placed connections in Washington, he had started buying into uranium mines back in 1943. The bomb, like pretty much everything else connected with the war, was going to make him richer.

Since the stroke, Bury has rarely left his mansion on South Wolcott Street in Casper. His spends his days in a wheelchair, gazing out the big picture window at the lake and the Bighorn Mountains beyond. A nurse and a physical therapist come by five days a week, along with a Chinese couple who do the cooking and cleaning. The Chinese woman speaks no English, her husband only enough to understand what is wanted and translate for his wife. They are paid almost nothing, and Milo Stroud makes sure they grasp that if he is unhappy, they will be bundled back to China. Bury won't have anyone but Milo Stroud living in the house, so they stay in a two-room apartment over a greasy spoon and arrive for work at six sharp every day.

After months of laborious practice, Bury is able to write well enough with his left hand to run his empire through short notes, all of them passed to Stroud and relayed to various managers. It's an awkward, tedious way of doing business, and it costs him much of the fluid speed that made it possible for him to outdo his rivals by getting there first. He blames his sons for the stroke. Lon for getting himself killed on Okinawa, Pardo because even prison was too good for him. Bury tells himself that if he had better sons, he wouldn't have driven himself so hard that he had a stroke. He wouldn't be confined to this wheelchair, and he wouldn't have to trust every detail of his life to Milo Stroud.

Pardo knows all about Stroud. Some of the boys in the Walls had dealings with him. Not one of them came out ahead. Stroud was not a man to jaw, they warned. When you were still sizing him up, trying to figure out your play, Stroud would come up shooting. Or he'd knife you in the back, or dispose of your carcass in any of a dozen other ways. "People don't take him serious, that's his secret," said one old boy, who was missing three fingers from an encounter with Milo Stroud. "He looks like a goddamned banker. You think, *This fella can't hurt me*, and then you're down and bleeding."

Most of what Pardo knows about his father comes from Jeannie Moore, a switchboard operator at X-Bury who was his girl for a few weeks in the fall of 1940. Pardo treated her well, because he wanted someone who could tell him what was going on in his father's company, and switchboard operators knew more than anyone. Jeannie wrote once a week while he was in Huntsville. From her, he learned of Lon's death, his father's stroke, the odd living arrangements at the Bury mansion in Casper, where Milo Stroud ruled on the ground floor and Big Bill was pretty much trapped in his wheelchair upstairs. They were installing an elevator, Jeannie said, to help the old man get up and down, but there was some problem with the design of the house and the work wasn't complete.

To get to Bill, Pardo will have to go through Stroud. Jeannie says the man doesn't drink or smoke or run after whores or have any known weaknesses. But Pardo's ace in the hole is Arlie Swain. She looks so sweet and innocent, like she wouldn't hurt a fly. Pardo tells her the plan as they are about to leave the motel.

"We're going to visit my old man," he says. "There's a fella there name of Stroud, might try to keep a son from visiting his own father. So here's what I want you to do."

She smiles. She ought to be going to high school, trying again to get through ninth grade, but she's out here in the world, earning her keep. Pardo starts the Chevy and heads for the mansion on South Wolcott Street. He cruises past once, turns around, and cruises by again. He sees the light on in the downstairs parlor, another in an upstairs window.

Milo Stroud sits by the radio with his feet up. When the doorbell rings, Stroud moves like a snake uncoiling, slides the .38 from its shoulder holster. He turns off the lamp, peers through the keyhole. He sees a girl who might conceivably be sixteen, but probably isn't. She looks scared and nervous. Behind her, Stroud sees an old Chevy in the middle of the street with its hood up. He curses under his breath. Don't people tell these kids not to let their cars break down in front of the Bury mansion? He looks the girl over. Freckles, a wide smile, a clean white blouse and a plain green skirt. Like a young miss from a finishing school.

He slides the bolt back and opens the door a crack, but keeps the chain in place. The girl can't see the pistol aimed at her heart.

"What is it?"

She jumps a little, steadies herself. "Mister? My car broke down. My daddy is going to whale me if I don't get it home. He said sometimes it's the distributor cap, but I don't know how to find the distributor cap."

Stroud hesitates. He does have a weakness. He likes innocent young girls. He would like to put her over his knee and spank her bare bottom. "You're alone?"

"Sure, I'm alone, mister. I wouldn't need help if I wasn't, would I?"

"You shouldn't come around here, bothering people."

"I'm real sorry. I was just driving along the street and the engine went dead. There aren't many houses on this street. This is the only one where the lights are on."

Stroud takes the chain off the door. "What's your name, girlie?"

"Arlie, sir. Miss Arlie Swain."

He holsters the .38. "All right, Miss Arlie Swain. Why don't you show me what the trouble is?"

She leads him back to the Chevy. Pardo, crouched in the shadows of the thick hedge that surround the property, sees Stroud bend over to look at the engine.

"Here's your problem right here, miss. Your distributor cap is disconnected."

Before he can connect it, Arlie throws all her weight onto the hood, slamming it down on his back, hard enough to take his breath away. Pardo rushes from the shadows, presses the tip of the bayonet in the small of Stroud's back, and yanks the .38 from its holster with his free hand. Stroud ignores the bayonet and straightens up, throwing Arlie from the hood. Pardo rips at Stroud's spine with the bayonet. The man goes limp, falls face first onto the bumper of the Chevy, and rolls onto the pavement. Pardo kicks him in the face.

"That's an old trick I learned from a shiv artist in the joint," Pardo says. "How to get at a man's spinal cord to paralyze him. It's damned hard to cut, but if you do enough damage, you bruise the spinal cord, see. It swells up, so's he'll never walk again. That's what happened to you, Stroud. I might let you live, so you can set in a wheelchair just like the old man."

Stroud groans. "You're a fucking savage, Pardo."

"You're damned right I'm a savage. I've got a good mind to boil your guts while you watch. Get his feet, Arlie."

Pardo lifts under Stroud's armpits and drags him toward the house, with Arlie tugging at his feet. They bump his torso up the steps and through the open door.

"I'll stay with him," Pardo says to Arlie. "Start the car and move it into the driveway, then get back in here quick." He glances up and down the street. Nothing but a few big, dark houses, no sign of life.

Arlie dashes out to the Chevy, connects the distributor cap, grinds the starter when it catches, pulls into the driveway, and comes bouncing back into the house like she's there to sell Girl Scout cookies. They drag Stroud into the parlor and dump him on the floor. A pool of blood spreads across the rug. He seems to have lost the use of his legs, but his arms are working fine. As they're dragging him, he punches Pardo in the solar plexus hard enough to wind him. Pardo steps back and kicks him in the throat.

"You do that one more time and I'll kill you. Only reason you're alive, we got a score to settle."

"Like hell we do."

"Like hell we don't. That judge down in Galveston. You handed him an envelope of cash to give me ten years in Huntsville. It was hard time. You see what they done to me? I was *branded*, Milo. I was made to wear a brand to show that I was a whore and that the boss of our wing was my pimp. I was a fucking *slave*. You and my goddamned father let them turn me into a slave. You are a pitiful sight, Milo. You lay real still, y'hear? We got to take care of your boss."

Pardo takes Arlie by the hand and leads her upstairs. They check three rooms before they find Big Bill, seated in a wheelchair next to his old rolltop desk. When he sees them, he hits a buzzer attached to the wheelchair and leans on it frantically. Pardo can hear it buzzing downstairs. He laughs.

"You trying to get Stroud up here, you old sonofabitch? You don't even say hello to your own son, you just ring for the cavalry, is that it? Well, hello to you. Aint life grand? Here I am, free as a bird, and you're stuck in a jail you made for yourself."

He giggles and pulls Arlie into the cone of light from the lamp on his father's desk. "See this little lady here, Bill? Aint she sweet? This is Arlie Swain. We're thinking to get married, except that she aint yet sixteen. In good time, I guess. She's the sweetest little piece of ass I've ever had, and she's smart to boot. Honey, why don't you take your shirt off and drop your drawers. I want to show this old fart what he's missing, being in a wheelchair and all."

Arlie grins at Pardo and peels her shirt over her head. She doesn't wear a brassiere. Small hard breasts, the nipples erect. She unbuttons the skirt and slides it down over her slender hips, stands in her white cotton panties, looking to Pardo for instructions. He nods. She pulls them down. He has her turn around, awkwardly, with her underpants around her ankles. He runs his hand over her nipples and her belly, the cleft in her buttocks, the fuzz of hair between her legs. Big Bill glares with his single eye. His head is tilted to one side, a steady stream of drool runs down his neck.

Pardo smacks her bottom. "Okay, honey. You can dress yourself now."

He leans toward his father until they're almost nose to nose. "How'd you enjoy the show?"

Bury says something that sounds like *ugh-oo*. Pardo frowns. "Fuck you? Did you just say fuck you?" He backhands the old man across the face.

"Remember when you busted my nose, that time in your office in front of Lon? Right before we went to Texas? That's when I knew I was going to kill you one day. Jail kind of delayed things."

Bury says something. Pardo can't make out what it is.

"You're probably wondering what's going to happen, aint you, Bill? Remember when you taught us how to gut a trout? Make one cut up at the gills, you said. Then put two fingers up inside his mouth. Start cutting at his asshole and don't stop until you reach the gills. That's what I'm going to do now, y'see. I'm going to gut you like a trout. Belly to throat. That's all. I aint going to do nothing else. I got no idea how long it will take you to die, but I expect it will be a while."

Bury struggles to form a word. *My-o.*

"Milo? Milo Stroud? He's in pretty bad shape. He's right downstairs. But I got a blade into his spinal cord. He can't move his legs to speak of. I aint gutted him yet, although I expect I will. A pretty pair you two will make when they find you."

Pardo reaches for the bayonet. He holds it up to the light, then shaves a patch of Big Bill's right cheek to show how sharp it is. He sees something in the old man's eye that looks like a glimmer of terror.

"Now that's something I never thought I'd see. You're afraid, aint you, Bill? Scared plumb to death."

In the enclosed room, the shots sound like grenades exploding. Rounds tear into the ceiling over their heads, touching off a shower of plaster. A splinter off a ricochet hits Pardo in the calf. He screams and grabs his leg. The chandelier breaks loose and falls to the floor in the center of the room in a shower of sparks. Arlie dives, scrambling to get behind the desk. Pardo whirls to see who it is. Someone firing from the stairs. Cops, he thinks, or maybe another guard, somebody he didn't know about. He slithers on his belly to the edge of the staircase and comes up with the .38. Milo Stroud has managed to drag himself up the lower flight of stairs and two or three steps of the second flight with a military M1 rifle. He has fired off one clip and reloaded, and he's searching for a target when Pardo gets off two shots with the .38. The first shot misses. The second catches Stroud in the mouth and seems to tear away his entire lower jaw. Stroud falls back onto the landing. The rifle clatters down the steps. Stroud makes an odd, gurgling sound, blood gushing from the place where his jaw used to be. Pardo stalks down the stairs, slow and deliberate. He stands over the man and aims carefully. *Are you at peace with the Lord?*

Stroud makes some sort of unidentifiable noise. Pardo shakes his head. "I can't understand a fucking word, but I'm going to take that as a yes." He pulls the trigger and shoots the man between the eyes.

Pardo turns his attention back to his father. There is real terror there now. He wants to linger over the job, make it last half the night, but the shots might attract the law.

Are you at peace with the Lord?

Ugh-oo!

The bayonet flashes. Pardo reaches for Arlie and pushes her toward the stairs. When he looks back, the old man is trying to spread his single useful hand wide enough to hold in his guts.

42

T HE NEWS OF THE MURDERS OF HILDA ZOGG AND the pump jockey Alvin Neubach over in Nebraska doesn't reach Sheriff Tom Call for three days. The murders occurred on a Friday evening, but he doesn't hear about them until Monday morning. He's taken up fishing, because it calms his nerves. He spends the weekend fishing alone at Romeo Lake, west of Buffalo, makes the drive back to Sheridan after dark Sunday evening, goes straight to bed, and turns up at the office, as always, on the dot at seven o'clock in the morning. He pours himself a cup of coffee from the pot perking in the corner and reads the advisory from the Nebraska Safety Patrol. The trucker at the gas station, it seems, had a pretty good look before he took a shotgun blast in the hip. Tom perks up when he reads the description: the trucker says the shooter was short, five foot five the most, a good-looking young fellow with blond hair and a scar on his left cheek. The trucker is able to identify the getaway car as a Ford Coupe. The car has Nebraska plates, beginning with "48," the plate number for Red Willow County. By Monday morning, the Safety Patrol has traced the Ford back to a used-car lot in McCook, where a man named Tucker Graff had swapped an almost new Buick with Kansas plates for the old Ford. Two hours later, they establish that Graff, a traveling windmill salesman, was murdered in Oklahoma and that he had been dead for at least two days when his Buick ended up in McCook.

An item in the report on the murder of Hilda Zogg catches Tom's eye. The killer wore a size-four boot. Tom nods, as though he had been expecting that detail all along. "Baby Foot. Pardo Bury."

The secretary peeks in the door. "Did you call me?"

"No. Just that Pardo Bury is on the loose."

He also has a message to call the warden of the Texas State Penitentiary in Huntsville. He knows what the man will have to say even before he picks up the phone: Pardo missed the first meeting with his parole officer and is wanted for violating parole. They also have a stoolie who says the young man had a grudge to settle with his father, Big Bill Bury.

"Seems the old man didn't lift a finger to keep Pardo out of prison," the warden says. "That aint common with rich folk. They generally hire enough lawyers to keep their own out of here. Do you know where the old man lives?"

"Casper."

"Maybe you ought to let him know."

Tom asks the operator to put him through to the Bury house in Casper. There's no answer, so he tries the X-Bury Refinery. He's told that Mr. Bury does not come in to work anymore, but that his assistant, a man named Milo Stroud, usually phones in early Monday morning with a long list of instructions from the boss. They haven't heard from Stroud yet today.

The Natrona County sheriff is Nate Goodrow, a former army sergeant who was shot up in the hedgerow country in Normandy. Goodrow has heard about the murders in Nebraska, but he hasn't made the connection to Pardo.

"You might want to keep an eye peeled," Tom says. "Warden down in Huntsville says he has a grudge against the old man. He could be headed your way like the wrath of God."

Goodrow chuckles. "If he is, he's dead. Big Bill keeps this fella Milo Stroud around. Man totes more weapons than a infantry platoon. He don't look like much, but I wouldn't fool with him."

"I tried to call the Bury place this morning and there was no answer. I tried the refinery and they said Stroud usually calls first thing Mondays, but they haven't heard from him today."

"I'll send a deputy over," Goodrow says. "Bill's apt to be mad as hell, cause he don't like visitors, but I'll take the chance."

"Good. Can you let me know if everything is all right over there?"

"Will do."

Tom fidgets for nearly an hour before Goodrow calls back. "My deputies had to break the door down," he says. "They found Stroud downstairs. Cut up some and shot. The old man was upstairs, in his wheelchair. Split open from his pecker to his throat, like somebody took a can opener to him."

"Jesus."

"You're a lucky man, Tom. Lucky it didn't happen in your county. Bill Bury was the worst sonofabitch I ever met, but when a man with that much money gets himself murdered, the shit has hit the fan. We're calling everybody in, the Highway Patrol, FBI, I wouldn't be surprised if they call out the National Guard. That little peckerwood has stirred up the hornets' nest. You hear anything about a girl with him?"

"One of the witnesses in Nebraska mentioned a young woman."

"Shit. That makes it complicated. If we track him down, we can't just go in shooting. We might hit the girl."

"That's about the size of it."

"By the time this is over, I'll wish I was back in Normandy."

"I don't believe so, Nate. Nothing could make you wish that."

"You'd be surprised."

With lawmen in eight states hunting for him, Pardo vanishes. It's like he's fallen into a hole and pulled the earth over him. His picture is everywhere, on wanted posters in post offices and on the front pages of newspapers. Handsome, blond, a scar in the shape of the letter T on his left cheek. Less than normal height. It isn't like he would be hard to spot, especially not if he's traveling with a female hostage. But a week goes by, and another week, and they're no closer to catching him than they were the evening he killed Big Bill and Milo Stroud in Casper. There are phantom sightings everywhere, but the man is nowhere to be found. Nor is the female who was seen with him in Nebraska. Nate Goodrow thinks he probably killed her somewhere and dumped the body.

Tom Call watches the whole manhunt unfold from his office. After the war, the Sheridan County sheriff's department purchased a military surplus Model 15 Teletype, a solid, reliable machine that chatters away most of the day and half the night. It's the best link the department has with other law enforcement agencies, but the furious clattering of the

Teletype brings little information that is useful. Pardo has been spotted everywhere from Texas to Montana, but the phantom suspects turn out to be everything from a thirteen-year-old farm kid driving his daddy's blue Ford to a sixty-year-old black man traveling with his granddaughter.

The papers have turned Pardo into a cross between John Dillinger and Clyde Barrow. He's on the front pages of papers from Dallas to Denver day after day. The only thing that is missing is for the FBI to declare him Public Enemy Number 1, but J. Edgar Hoover has been strangely silent. The FBI director never misses a shot at the limelight, but there are rumors that he once clashed with Big Bill Bury and that he doesn't give a damn if Pardo is ever caught.

Once the sensational reports of Pardo's wealthy background and the killings in which he was the prime suspect are exhausted, the papers begin to write editorials wondering why, with so many lawmen looking for him, it's so hard to find a man with a brand on his face. The directors of the X-Bury Refinery offer a ten-thousand-dollar reward for Pardo, dead or alive, meaning that every duck hunter from Canada to the Mexican border will be out looking for him with a shotgun. With a little bad luck, one of them might find him—which would be a good way to end up dead. Someone notices that a beige Chevy Master was stolen in Torrington the same night Hilda Zogg and Alvin Neubach were murdered in Nebraska, so lawmen start pulling over Chevys, with as much luck as they had stopping Fords.

Tom assumes that it's only a matter of time before Pardo is caught. The manhunt is too large, there are too many people looking for him. Sooner or later, he'll be brought in or shot dead. But as the phantom sightings begin to dry up, Pardo is still at large and even the newspapers have lost interest.

A month after the murders of Bill Bury and Milo Stroud, Tom Call wakes in the middle of the night. He cranes his neck to see the time. Two o'clock. He doesn't know if the knowledge came to him in a dream or if he was half-awake all along, thinking, but the revelation is as clear as a red apple on a white plate: Pardo Bury is at Romeo Lake. Tom's fishing

ground. It's a place he knows well, a little less than twenty miles south-
west of Buffalo, maybe sixty or seventy miles from Sheridan. During the
depression, Bill Bury had a large stone house built in the foothills above
the lake, accessible only on horseback or by foot. During the war, there
were rumors that Bury had stocked the place with a year's supply of
provisions, turning it into a bunker where he could hole up if the Japanese invaded. Only a few of the locals even know it exists. Tom himself
wouldn't know if he didn't fish the lake. He's sure that Bury stopped
using the bunker after his stroke, but if Pardo knows about it, it would
be a perfect place for him to hide. Hide in plain sight, in one of the old
man's houses. The last place anyone would look for him.

Tom has an urge to jump out of bed and drive out to investigate,
but he decides that the more sensible course is to wait for daylight.
It's a Sunday morning, the eighteenth day of August. At six o'clock, he
phones Strother Leach, who is supposed to be working the overnight
shift. Strother answers on the tenth ring. He sounds at least half-drunk.
Strother usually hosts a poker game when he works Saturday nights.
This time, from the sound of it, the game is still going on. When he
hears Tom's voice, he makes an effort to sound alert, but he isn't too successful.

"Yeah, boss?"

"Strother, I'm about to head out to Romeo Lake."

"Uh-huh."

"The reason I'm going out there, I think that may be where Pardo
Bury is holed up."

"Uh-huh."

"Well, I'm not dumb enough to go in there by my lonesome. I want
you to wrangle all our deputies and call in Natrona County and the
Highway Patrol, too. I'll wait for the cavalry at the Buffalo turnout.
That's the only way out of there, so if my hunch is right, he can't leave
without going past me. Put on some speed, and make sure all the boys
have their shotguns."

"Uh-huh. You say you're goin right now, boss?"

"Yes. Right now. Are you sober enough to drive, Strother?"

"Hell, yes. What kind of deputy sheriff do you think I am?"

"I know exactly what you are, Strother. That's why I'm asking. Now get moving. I don't want to play the Lone Ranger up there, hear?"

"Loud and clear. We'll be movin out soon as I can call the boys."

Tom grabs his shotgun on the way out the door. He drives as far as Buffalo with his siren on, makes it in forty-five minutes, turns onto the gravel road at exactly seven o'clock, pulls off to the side, kills the engine, and settles down to wait. It's the only road out of Romeo Lake unless you're part mountain goat. He has something of the same feeling in the pit of his stomach that he used to get on the morning of a bombing run—eager, anxious, a little queasy. He wishes he had taken time to eat breakfast.

Strother Leach goes back to his poker game. He's down seventy-seven dollars and sitting on the best hand he's had all night. This is no time to fold. He pours himself a healthy bourbon and drains half of it. The others look at him, questioning.

"That was the boss on the phone," he says. "He's got some damned fool notion that this Pardo character is holed up down by Romeo Lake."

Vic Ruplinger glances up, over a pair of aces. "He wants you down there?"

"Hell, yes. Me and all the rest of the law in Wyoming."

"Maybe you ought to get along, Strother."

"Not while you're holding pretty much my entire paycheck."

"What if he's right? That little bastard Pardo is dangerous. You can't leave the sheriff alone."

"I aint going to. But I tell you, the only reason to go down there is to humor the boss. He aint been right since the war. It don't do a man no good upstairs, settin in a prisoner of war camp wondering if you're going to get shot or what. But just as soon as we're done here, I'll skedaddle. Way I see it, only two things can happen, and they're both bad. Either this Pardo fella is there, in which case he comes out shooting and some-body gets plugged. Or he aint, and I drive all the way down there and bust up a perfectly good poker game for no damned reason at all. Now, Vic, I'll see your ten and raise you five."

An hour later, Tom Call is still waiting for Strother Leach. He tries the radio a half dozen times. No response. No other law on the road. Tom rarely loses his temper, but he has had about all he can stand. He should have fired Strother years ago, before the war. Bad enough that he's lazy, he's stupid, and he's on the take. Now he's stranded Tom without a backup. As soon as he gets back to Sheridan, Tom's going to fire Strother Leach. Let his brother-in-law the mayor give him a job.

43

BEFORE THEY LEAVE THE BURY MANSION IN Casper, Pardo takes a thousand dollars in cash from the drawer in his father's rolltop desk and grabs a ring of keys and a flashlight off a shelf on a wall near the entrance. He has a notion where he's headed, and he figures the keys might come in handy.

By the time they reach Buffalo and turn west to Romeo Lake, it's past midnight. They take the two-lane dirt track as far as they can go and roll the Chevy into a stand of pines. It's too dark to climb the rest of the way, so they spend a chilly night sleeping in the car and hike up to the house at daybreak.

Unless you know where it is, it's almost impossible to find the lodge his father built. It's surrounded by birch trees and lodgepole pine and set well back from the trail, behind a rocky outcrop that hides the structure from the view of any casual hiker or hunter passing by. It's twice the size of the place Pardo remembers, built of concrete and stone and timber. It must have been an awful job to cart all that stuff up here, but when you have money, you can do most anything. He tries two dozen keys in the front door before he finds one that fits. The massive oak door swings open and they step into a living room that is at least forty feet square, with a huge picture window opening on a view to the west.

Arlie whistles. "Aint this the place, though? I hope you don't think I'm going to clean it for you."

Pardo smacks her rear. "All we're gonna do," he says, "is drink the old man's wine and fuck a lot."

They spend most of the day exploring the house. It really is a bunker, with a deep cellar stocked with almost everything a man could want. Canned goods, dried beef and pork, beer, cases of French wine and champagne, an array of weapons and ammunition of every caliber. There is even an entire woman's wardrobe here, including three drawers of fancy underthings. They drink a bottle of the wine and eat a couple of cans of tuna fish, and Pardo watches while Arlie tries on one lingerie outfit after another. It's all a bit too large for her, but that makes it sexier, as far as he is concerned. He wonders again if he's going to kill her or not. She would make a pretty corpse in one of these getups, but she's so doggoned much fun to be around, he's not sure he could do it anymore.

They lose track of the days. They eat, sleep, screw, go for walks. Fish in the lake, where he catches fresh trout and cleans them and Arlie fries a mess for their supper. They listen to the radio, laugh at the wild speculation as to his whereabouts. In a single day, he's sighted in Bozeman, Montana; Pocatello, Idaho; and Stillwater, Oklahoma. Despite the scope of the manhunt, they feel safe. Very few people know about this place, fewer come out this way, even in summer. From what they hear on the radio, the search is concentrating farther west, toward Jackson Hole and Idaho. The woman who worked the desk at the motel in Casper says that Pardo has a pretty girl with him, and that she's sure the girl is a hostage. That makes Arlie laugh.

"How do they know *you're* not the hostage?" she asks. "Could be I'm the one holding you, forcing you to pleasure me."

"I wouldn't put it past you. You're a handful of girl. The way you took down that fat lady over in Nebraska. I wouldn't want to tangle with you."

When Arlie first hears that his real name is Pardo, she makes a face. "I like Tucker better," she says. "I got used to you as Tucker. I can't get used to Pardo."

"Don't make no nevermind what you call me," he says, "long as you keep using that pretty little mouth all the ways that you use it."

Come fall, Pardo says, the heat should be off and they can make a clean getaway somewhere. Maybe California. Maybe Canada. Maybe get down to Mexico. He has grown a beard and let his hair grow, but none of it covers the brand on his face. Arlie cuts her hair short. From some angles, she looks just like a boy, but she's growing up, getting prettier every day. Even her tits are growing. If he was an ordinary kind of guy, Pardo thinks, he'd probably be in love with her by now. He wonders if he might marry her, if they get away. Find a *padre* down in Mexico or someplace, get hitched. He tries to summon the image, the two of them with a little white house somewhere, going about their business, eating supper with the neighbors, folks not knowing where they come from or what they are. He can never quite imagine it, which makes him think that it probably won't happen. When he can imagine a thing, like cutting his father's belly open and watching his guts spill out, it usually happens. If he can't imagine it, then it's somehow outside the world that he can make. He doesn't give up trying. He has Arlie put on some of the clothes in the wardrobe, things a woman of forty would wear. He tries to imagine her dressed like that, him in a suit, the two of them going to church on Easter. Tipping his hat to folks as they pass. He still can't get the picture to come into focus. Still, this gal Arlie Swain, if he knew her, say, ten years ago, before it all started, maybe things would have gone a different way. Maybe he would not have done any of what he's done. But if he had known her then, she would have been five years old.

"We're goin to California, girl," he tells her late one Saturday night. "Before we leave, I got one last little job I got to do."

"You going to tell me what it is?"

"Because it's you, I'll tell. It's an old buzzard named Eli Paint. Rancher, has a big spread out by the Powder River. We're goin to pay a call on him and his wife, a Mexican bitch he picked up somewhere."

"What did he do?"

"He said I was so mean, I was probably raised by boll weevils. Said it in front of a bunch of people. We'll have a little fun with them, then we'll head for the ocean."

"I can't wait."

"For what? The fun or the ocean?"

"Both."

"I'll bet. You can play with this Mexican lady first. She's a looker. You can do what you done with that fat one back in Nebraska. I'll watch. I like that."

"Mmmmm . . ."

She licks his ear, they start up again.

* * *

Early Sunday morning, Pardo is out chopping wood for the fireplace. The days are still hot, but the nights are turning colder. Without a fire, they shiver until dawn. It's the kind of work he likes, destructive but useful, the clean smell of the pine, the bite of the ax, something you can do in a good rhythm until you start to sweat. Arlie sits and watches him, her freckled face turned to the morning sunshine, with the shotgun leaning against the wall beside her. He has taken a hacksaw to the barrel, turned it into a sawed-off so it will be useful at close quarters. It's a rule he has: they're never more than five feet from a loaded gun, even when they're screwing. He's not going to be taken by surprise.

When he stops to peel off his shirt, he sees the tourist couple struggling up the trail. They are both wearing Bermuda shorts with knee-length socks and sensible shoes. The man has a box Brownie on a strap around his neck, and she totes a hefty pair of binoculars. He waves from a hundred feet downhill and marches right on up, without waiting for an invitation. Pardo leans on the ax, amazed. *There are people on this earth that are too damned dumb to live.*

By the time he reaches the woodpile, the man is so winded he can barely speak. "Say there, young fella," he says. "We was out doing a little bird-watching and we heard the ax, so I says to Madge here, 'Madge, we got company, we ought to be friendly and pay these folks a visit. Us and some other folks from back home, see, we're all camped down by the lake. The rest of them, they got into the wine last night and they won't be up for a while, so we come up here to have a look-see. Shoot, this place is hid real good. If it wasn't for the sound of that ax, we wouldn't never have found you."

He bends over, resting his pudgy hands on his fat thighs, trying to catch his breath. The one he calls Madge catches up then, gives them a brassy smile.

"How do?" she says. "Doggone, the air is thin up here."

The man recovers enough to make the introductions. "Name's Lester," he says. "Lester Eikelberry. This here's the little woman, Madge. We hail from Kokomo, Indiana. Dragged an Airstream trailer all this way. Thirteen hundred miles, give or take. Don't know if you've ever been to

Kokomo, but you ought to make it a point to visit sometime. It's a real swell town. Friendly people, like out here in Wyoming. Why, I says to Madge just the other day, now that I took my retirement, aint nothing stopping us, we could move right out here to Wyoming. Sell up back in Indiana, buy a little place out here where we can breathe this clear mountain air night and day. Nothing like this here house, understand, we couldn't begin to afford a spread like this. You must have a real good job to buy this house, being as young as you are and all. Say, I didn't catch your name."

Pardo grins. "Name's Tucker. Tucker Graff. Young lady there, she's Barbara Ann."

"Well, Tucker and Barbara Ann, we're just as pleased as punch to make your acquaintance. Way off up here, we aint seen a living soul in three days."

"That so?"

Pardo takes off his baseball cap then, to wipe the sweat off his brow. Eikelberry gives him an odd stare.

"Say, you look like that young fella, picture was in the paper the other day. Don't he, Madge? Don't he look like that fella, what was his name? Wanted for something or other. What was that about, Madge?"

"His name is Pardo, I remember that, because it's an unusual name. Something about a killing, wasn't it? Isn't he the one with the rich father?"

"By gosh, I think you're right. Your name aint Tucker, it's Pardo. Say, could we get a picture with you? You just stand in between us here and maybe the little gal there can take a photograph that we can show folks back in Indiana. They're not going to believe we ran into a real-life western outlaw."

Pardo plays along. Arlie takes the camera, Madge bundles in next to him, shoving an armored tit into his elbow. Lester steps up on the other side. He's bathed in sweat from the climb and the reek up close would drive a wolf away. He shows Arlie how to click the camera, and she takes a couple of shots of the two of them. Then Lester wants a picture of Pardo holding the shotgun.

"Look like a real desperado," he says. Pardo grins, tries a half dozen different poses, including one where he's pointing the gun right into the camera.

"Say, I hope that thing isn't loaded."

"Course it's loaded," Pardo says. "Never saw the use of holding a gun, if it aint loaded."

"You've got a point there, son, you really do."

Eikelberry lowers the camera. The shotgun is still pointing at him. Pardo says something, so quiet the man barely hears. *Are you at peace with the Lord?*

"What's that you say?"

Eikelberry steps closer, one hand cupped behind his ear. He's no more than four feet away when Pardo trips both triggers of the shotgun. The man's head explodes in a shower of blood and bone and brains. He stands for a moment before the legs give way and he topples, gouts of blood pumping from his open skull.

Madge Eikelberry is on her knees, screaming something that sounds like *Gaaaaaa! Gaaaaaa! Gaaaaaa!*

Pardo hands the ax to Arlie. "Shut her up, will you?"

The Eikelberry woman understands then and tries to run, but Arlie is much too quick. She's ahead of the woman in a flash of slim brown legs and she swings the ax like a woodsman, getting her hips into it. The first blow takes Madge in the abdomen and doubles her over. Arlie hacks at her back, her spine, finally manages to cut her head about half off. The woman is making an awful noise still, but Arlie drives the ax into the side of her skull and she's silent.

Pardo reloads the smoking shotgun. "Damn, girl. It's like I said. I wouldn't want to tangle with you."

Eikelberry said they were with a bunch of people down by the lake. Pardo is afraid someone will come looking for the couple. They drag the bodies off into the brush at the side of the house. Pardo rubs down the ax handle because he doesn't want Arlie's fingerprints on a murder weapon, then tosses it far back into the trees behind the house. In ten minutes, they're hiking down to where he has hidden the Chevy. When they pass the lake, he weights the case for the box Brownie camera with a couple of rocks and flings it into deep water.

The Chevy is where he left it, covered with pine boughs to disguise it from the air. They load the supplies they have carried out, including a half dozen bottles of wine, into the trunk. The Chevy starts right off.

"Damn, that was fun," he says. "Shall we go get that old buzzard Eli, girl?"

"Uh-huh. I want to get that pretty Mexican lady you told me about to do what Hilda done."

"Then you going to do her the same way after?"

"Nope. I want to use that shotgun. It's my turn."

44

FTER ANOTHER HALF HOUR WAITING BY THE side of the road, Tom Call decides he's had enough. He's going to head on up to Romeo Lake and have a look for himself. If he sees any sign of life around the house, he'll wait for backup. Otherwise, he'll give it up as a poor notion and head back to town to deal with Strother Leach.

He's no more than three miles west of Buffalo when he sees the dust cloud a mile off, a car headed his way, moving way too fast on the gravel. To drive that way on these roads, you'd have to be crazy, drunk, or too young to know better. Crazy seems the most likely. Crazy like Pardo Bury. By the time the car is boiling through the dust a half mile away, Tom can see it's a beige Chevy Master. He flips on his siren and brakes to a halt, slewing the patrol car sideways to block the narrow road. He climbs out, aims the shotgun over the roof of the patrol car, and stands his ground. He doesn't have long to wait. The Chevy is a quarter mile away and coming like a bat out of hell, close enough that he can see clearly that there is a female in the passenger seat. At the last minute, Tom realizes the driver is not going to stop. He rolls down into the barrow pit. The Chevy has nowhere to go: there's a steep hill on one side, the barrow pit on the other.

Pardo spots the patrol car, sees a man with a shotgun, and curses a blue streak. What the hell is a lawman doing out here at this hour on a Sunday morning? When he sees the patrol car blocking the road, he decides to go right through it. If he hits it hard enough, the car should spin out of the way, maybe kill the bastard at the same time. He's no more than a hundred feet away when Arlie screams. He hits the brakes, a reflex action, but the tires are on loose gravel. The brakes slow the hurtling car, but he doesn't have time to stop.

"Jump!" he yells to Arlie. The girl doesn't have to be told twice. She flings the door open and rolls out, skinning her knees and elbows as she falls.

Tom crouches in the barrow pit like a soldier in a foxhole, his arms wrapped over his head. He hears a collision that sounds like a bomb going off, keeps his head down as broken glass and debris shower down on him. The collision is followed by an explosion as one of the gas tanks goes up. He raises his head to see a yellow ball of flame from the rear of the Chevy, then the entire automobile is ablaze. He starts to run to the passenger door to see if he can pry the girl out, sees that the door is wide open. Maybe she was thrown clear. Then the gas tank on the patrol car blows and the two automobiles are fused in a death pyre. Too damned late for anything. He comes up out of the ditch, still holding the shotgun. It doesn't seem possible that anyone could survive that impact, but he isn't taking chances. He circles behind the burning patrol car, keeping it between him and the Chevy. The heat is so intense that he has to back off a dozen feet and take a wider circle, along the edge of the hill that rises almost straight up from the road. He's still thirty feet away from the coupe when he sees something moving behind a pall of smoke. Pardo staggers out, his face blackened and his hair scorched, trailing a sawed-off shotgun in his left hand. He's hatless, wearing nothing but a bloody white undershirt and blue jeans and a pair of old boots.

Tom starts to say something, but before he can speak, Pardo jerks the shotgun up and trips both barrels. With the long-barreled Remington pointed at the ground, Tom has no chance. The blast catches him in the left shoulder and spins him around. He falls heavily. His shotgun goes spinning out of reach. He rolls and gets to his knees. Pardo hits him in the jaw with the butt of the sawed-off, knocking him onto his back. He stands straddling the sheriff, calmly reloading the shotgun.

"Sheriff Tom Call. What the fuck are you doing down here?"

"Playing a hunch."

"Romeo Lake, right? How'd you figure that?"

"It hit me last night, that's where you would be. The whole damned state is out looking for you, but nobody thought that you might hole up in a place your daddy owns."

"Owned. He's dead."

"That's why so many folks are looking for you."

"Don't I know it. I heard all about it, on the radio. I had to keep the Chevy hid. I was thinking maybe we ought to get a different car. Now we got to get a different car."

"It doesn't have to be this way, Pardo. You could come in. You kill a lawman and it's going to go worse for you."

"How? They're going to hang me twice, that what you mean?"

"You don't know they're going to hang you."

"Hell I don't."

"If you give yourself up, you'll get a chance to explain. About your father and all."

"All anybody knows about him, he was the biggest bastard in the country. He taught me everything I know."

"I believe you're a self-made man, Pardo. You're a murderous little coward. But if you're going to kill me, I want to know. You killed Millie Stojko, didn't you?"

"Why the fuck should I tell you?"

"Who's going to know? Anyway, how many others were there altogether? Five? Six?"

Pardo grins. He can't resist the chance to brag. "Closer to twelve. Girl in Laramie, girl I grabbed outside Casper before the one from the station. You got two more now, up at the house. Dumb goddamned tourists came by at the wrong time, wanted to get their picture took with a real desperado, you believe that? I think they make it an even dozen."

"But Millie was one of them, right?"

"Is she the girl I took at the Sheridan bus station? That the one you're talking about?"

"You know it is."

"She could have made it. She just wouldn't stop talking, about her goddamned stepfather who liked to screw her and all."

"And the calves on the Paint ranch? You kill them, too?"

"Hell, yes. Just trying to put a scare in old Eli. Y'know, my old man broke my nose for that. It was when he done that to me that I knew I

was goin to have to kill him, sooner or later. Now I'm goin to take care of
Eli Paint. Him and that Mexican bitch. Then I'm done, unless somebody
gets in my way. Course that's not counting you. You and Eli Paint and
his wife, that would make fifteen. I'm a goddamned all-American killer,
y'know that?"

Pardo has a gash on his forehead, probably from where he hit the
steering wheel. His face is a bloody mask. "Remember that time you
ran me in for drunk and disorderly?" he says. "I ought to have killed you
then."

"You've killed enough. Surely to God there's been enough killing in
this world, the past ten years. Leave Juanita alone."

"Who's Juanita?"

"Eli's wife."

"The Mexican bitch? What are you, sweet on her or something? Hell
no, I aint going to leave her alone."

Tom feels a sudden rage in his gut. Pardo's going to go after Juanita.
Probably end up killing Ethan, too. This murderous little bastard, holding a shotgun on him. After all he went through in the POW camp and
after, to get killed by a rich punk. His left arm is useless, but his right is
still working and his .38 is still in the holster. He slips his hand down
toward the butt of his pistol, feels its solid weight right where he needs
it. He gathers himself. His chances are slim and none, but a man has to
try. Pardo leans so that the shotgun is almost in Tom's eyes. Tom can see
the jagged edges where Pardo did a piss-poor job sawing it off.

Are you at peace with the Lord?

"What?"

The sound is an unearthly screech, like some kind of wild creature
being eaten alive. Pardo swivels the shotgun toward the girl, who is staggering out of the barrow pit a dozen yards back up the road. She screams
again. *Be careful! He's got a gun!*

Pardo grins. "Don't worry, honey. I'm going to kill this sonofabitch
right now."

The .38 clears the holster. Tom raises it and fires straight up into
Pardo's crotch. Once, twice, three times. Pardo's body jumps like a

marionette on a string. He falls back, staggering, clutching at himself, blood gushing from where his privates used to be. Tom sits up and keeps firing into the man's heart. Four. Five. Six. A tight cluster, just to the left of the sternum. The shots drive Pardo back, as though he's being hit with a baseball bat. An ugly mushroom of blood wells out of his chest. He tries to grip the sawed-off, to bring it up to fire, but his hand won't grip the stock. His fingers go slack, the gun tumbles into the dust. Tom can see his eyes beginning to cloud. Pardo opens his mouth to speak. Nothing comes out but a thick bubble of blood. Tom sees the light go out of his eyes. Pardo is dead.

The girl comes after Tom then, her nails flashing, aiming for his eyes. He beats her to the sawed-off and jams the butt of it into her belly with his good hand, catching her on the run. She sinks to her knees, gasping for breath. She sobs as she crawls to Pardo and cradles his head. "No baby no baby no," she says, over and over. "No, baby! No!" Then she turns on Tom. "You're a murderer! You're a fucking murderer! You'll burn in hell! You killed Tucker, you bastard!"

"His name aint Tucker. Tucker Graff is a fella he killed, back in Oklahoma. This nasty little piece of coyote shit is Pardo Bury."

"Fuck you. You're the killer, mister."

"And you aint no hostage. That's pretty plain. At least I got one of you to stand trial."

Tom drops the sawed-off next to Pardo's body, picks up his own shotgun and reloads the .38. The blast from the shotgun caught him in the shoulder and chest. The pain is nearly as bad as the pain the day they shot down his Flying Fortress. He's losing blood, but the range was too much for a sawed-off and the shot scattered. If Pardo had left the barrel alone, Tom would be a dead man and Pardo would still be alive. Still, he feels weak as a kitten. Shock or loss of blood, he isn't sure which. He has to get help.

"Now, miss," he says. "We're going to walk on down that road into Buffalo and get to a telephone, so's I can call for an ambulance. That murdering sonofabitch is dead and you're wasting your time crying over him. I don't want to have to put handcuffs on a girl, but if you don't come along peaceful, I'll do just that."

The black smoke from the burning cars rises in a tall column. He can hear a siren coming from somewhere. Help is on the way. He turns his back on the girl, feels his legs beginning to go.

Arlie Swain sees the sheriff turn away from her. She's a panther and like a panther she strikes. She grabs the bayonet from the scabbard strapped to Pardo's ankle and leaps, driving it into Tom Call's heart as she jumps on his back and rides him down onto the road. He is dead before his face hits the gravel.

The town of Buffalo has in its employ a single constable, Orin Sears. He is near seventy years old and has taken the job only because he is the biggest fellow in town and he's looking for something to do. After he retired from his job as a surveyor for the railroad, Sears chose to settle down in Buffalo because it's quiet and it's close to the mountains. His experience with law enforcement is minimal and his knowledge less, but it doesn't matter in a place where the worst crime he has ever dealt with is the theft of a milk cow.

Orin was sound asleep when someone heard a terrific collision on the Romeo Lake Road and woke him out of bed, too damned early on a Sunday morning. He took his time pulling on his boots and headed out. Probably just some damned kid that run his car into a tree.

From about half a mile away, he can see there are two automobiles on fire and one of them is a sheriff's department patrol car from Sheridan. He brakes to a halt a dozen feet before he would have run over Sheriff Tom Call, with a bayonet blade sticking out of his back.

Ten yards farther on, Orin sees the man who killed him. Has to be Pardo Bury, he figures. Pictures of the man all over the place, you couldn't help but recognize him, even with six bullets in him. Judging from where the bullets went, Tom Call must have blown his pecker and balls clean off and put three rounds in his heart. *My goodness gracious,* Orin Sears says to himself, over and over. *My goodness gracious.* He checks Tom's pulse first, then Pardo's. Both are dead as roadkill. It's a damned shame. Tom, anyway. Not Pardo. Orin knows Tom's story, what he went through in the war and all. He walks around the scene, trying to piece together how it happened. Tom was also hit in the shoulder by the sawed-off shotgun, probably before he was stabbed. Must have been trying to make the arrest with the .38 when Pardo got the drop on him somehow and got that long toad stabber into his back. The way it went in, looks as though Pardo hit him right in the heart. Still, Tom somehow managed to fire six shots after he was stuck and kill the sonofabitch before he died. Helluva man, right to the end.

Orin circles for a time, his size-thirteen boots scuffing out all traces of anyone else. He sits down on the hood of his patrol car, tries to think. It's hot enough to melt a jackrabbit's ears, which doesn't help. The thing doesn't fit together real well, but hell, it couldn't be any other way. There's no one else around. He braces himself and tugs the bayonet out of Tom's back, wipes the blood on the dead man's shirt, gathers up the .38 pistol and the sawed-off shotgun and Tom's long Remington, wondering if he could get away with keeping the Remington for himself. He's still thinking it over when he hears another siren coming. He can smell the booze as soon as Strother Leach gets out of the car. Strother takes one look at Tom Call lying dead in the road, says *Oh, Jesus,* and reaches into his cubbyhole for a flask. He takes a long pull and offers the flask to Orin Sears. The two men pass it back and forth until it's half-empty. They walk around the scene again, Orin telling Strother what must have happened.

"Jesus mothering Christ," Strother says. "I told the damned fool not to go after this sonofabitch alone."

Strother goes to his radio and starts calling for backup, anybody and everybody. They are still on the scene half an hour later when the thunderstorm hits, a real gullywasher. They wait it out in Strother's cruiser. He reaches under the seat, pulls out another bottle of bourbon. "This here storm is going to pay hell with the evidence, if we had any," he says. "I guess it don't matter. It's plain enough what happened. The sheriff killed Pardo, and Pardo killed him."

Orin hiccups. "Only way it could be."

Strother thinks awhile. "Say, aint there a reward for Pardo? Ten thousand, alive or dead?"

"By God, I believe there is."

"Well, hell. Tom Call can't collect it. I'd say it belongs to us."

Arlie Swain flattens herself in the ditch as the patrol car blows past in a cloud of dust. When it's safely by, she scrambles to her feet and runs, keeping to a low crouch. She's sure the cop will look in the rearview and spot her, but once she's around the curve of the road, she sees there's a chance she might get clean away. She slips through a barbed-wire fence into a pasture and washes her hands in a stock tank, scrubs until she has gotten rid of all the blood. She washes the dust from her arms and legs, examines the tender spots where her knees and elbows are skinned, brushes a little water through her hair with her fingers. She has nothing but the clothes on her back, but she has more than a hundred dollars in cash stuffed in her pockets, plenty to get her all the way home. She strolls through the little town, acting casual. A couple of dogs bark, but it seems that most folks are still asleep. At the highway she begins walking south, wanting to get out of sight of the town as quickly as she can. She hasn't gone half a mile when she hears the roar of a big truck, coming fast. She slicks her hair again and stands with her pelvis thrust out, wiggling her thumb. The trucker hits the air brakes, and she runs along beside until he's able to stop so she can climb in. He says his name is Pete Driver, which she thinks is pretty funny. He's hauling a load of hogs to Cheyenne. He looks her up and down.

"Looks like you had a fall there, girl."

"Uh-huh."

"Where were you headed?"

"Nowhere special."

"I didn't catch your name."

"Madge. Madge Eikelberry."

"Pleased to meet you. I'm headed to Denver, if that suits you."

"It suits me."

The way he looks at her, Arlie knows that he will take her all the way to Dodge City, if that's what she wants. She spends that night in Pete's trailer house north of Denver. He wants things, but Arlie puts him off. It's that time of the month, she says, so he'll just have to wait. When he heads off to scare up some breakfast early the next morning, she sneaks out the back way, circles around to the road, and sticks her thumb out.

Two weeks and a half dozen truckers later, Arlie Swain is back in Dodge City after a detour that takes her west all the way to Salt Lake City, south to Santa Fe and back to Kansas. When she walks through the door, her mother is sitting in the darkened living room with a cold cloth over her eyes, nursing a migraine. Arlie ignores her, darts up the stairs. Her mother hears the footsteps, lifts the cloth from her face.

"Where the hell have you been?"

Arlie pauses on the landing.

"Out!"

PART 4

A Winter's Tale

45.

Wyoming,
1949

FOLKS FROM THE NEW YEAR'S EVE WINGDING THE night before are still sleeping all over the house, strewn about like old clothing left in heaps. Young Ethan, who got to stay up until midnight because he's now a big boy of six, is still on the davenport, where he fell asleep one minute into the new year. Others are on chairs, on the floor, under the dining room table. It was quite the party. Fiddles and a piano, dancing until dawn.

Eli tiptoes over and around the sleeping bodies. While the coffee perks, he steps outside and sniffs the crisp winter air. It is bone-chilling cold, but it feels like one of those days when a man cutting wood will strip down to a flannel shirt by noon. Back indoors, he watches Ethan asleep. He has always been a man in a hurry, places to go and things to do. His greatest pleasure now is to linger with the boy, do things at his pace. Shake out oats for the horses, help a cow give birth, scan the sweep of stars at night, trying to pick out the constellations. He's approaching his seventy-ninth birthday, and in the time that is left to him, he wants to give the boy all the learning he has to give. Ethan has taught him much as well: his lively curiosity, a fresh way of looking at the world, the willingness to ask questions that his elders have forgotten how to ask.

Eli finishes his coffee and biscuits and heads out to do the chores. The sun is up, the thin winter light shimmers in the strings of velvet mist that hang low over the prairie, like milk strained through cotton. Maybe he'll rouse the boy later, take him out for a ride before breakfast. Juanita will put on a big feed once her guests are up, bacon and waffles and biscuits, fried eggs, scrambled eggs, oatmeal. A boy needs some fresh air and exercise if he's to get on the outside of any part of that. Eli has fed the horses, slopped the hogs, and milked the cows. He's halfway back to the house with a two-gallon bucket of fresh milk in each hand when he notices the sky beginning to thicken. It takes on a viscous texture, like mercury, and the color shifts from cornflower blue to a dull gray and then to lead. It happens quickly, in the time it takes him to walk back to the house. The scent of the morning air has a tang to it now. A light, icy drizzle begins to fall. He hurries a little, slopping the milk, sets it down next to the cream separator on the back porch and hurries inside to find the downstairs bedroom where Two Spuds and Jenny Hoot Owl are sleeping after the party. He raps sharply on the door.

"Go away, goddamnit. It's New Year's morning."

"Tell Jenny to get dressed quick and come outside. She can go right back to bed."

"You tell her. We only been asleep three hours. She's liable to shoot me."

"I hate to bother you, Miss Jenny," Eli sings out, in his sweetest voice, "but I need you to come out and sniff the air for me."

"Go straight to hell."

"Now, Jenny, that's no way to talk to a man. I need you for two minutes and you can go right back to sleep."

"Jesus H. Christ. White men."

Jenny curses as she pulls on her clothes in darkness, but five minutes later, she and Two Spuds are standing with Eli on the porch. Jenny is the only person Eli knows who can tell the weather better than he can. He knows better than to rush her. She takes her time, turns in a slow circle, looking at the sky in all directions. She lifts her head and sniffs the damp air and shakes her head.

"Blizzard," she says and heads back to bed.

Within half an hour, a dozen men are ready to ride out. Two Spuds takes half with him and heads north, the rest follow Eli to the south pasture. Eli has devised an elaborate system to keep his livestock alive in harsh weather: in each section of land, there is a low-slung, hundred-and-fifty-foot shed for shelter, with hay mangers and water tanks carefully sited so that each shed is open in front, with the back to the northwest, facing the storms that blow in. Protein cakes have replaced the cheap cotton-seed cakes of the depression, and in a corner of each shed, there is a stack of protein cakes under a tarp. Behind the shelters are windbreaks of willow trees and cottonwoods, with snow fences on exposed ridges. There are haystacks at close intervals and along each barbed-wire fence there are ten-foot poles every hundred feet, with a single wire strung along the tops of the tall posts to guide a man on horseback if the snow has drifted over the fence lines. The men kid about it, call the system Eli's Telegraph, but in a blizzard, they know the line might mean the difference between a man finding his way home and freezing to death.

Some of the cattle have begun to drift toward the sheds. Some are already there, but the men labor to gather up the rest, riding into gullies after strays. There is far too much ground to cover. Within an hour, the wind has picked up and they can ride no more than a minute before they have to turn their backs to the wind in order to breathe. If they don't, the breath will be snatched from their mouths. Their beards and mustaches are frozen solid, their blue jeans under the stiff leather chaps are hard as iron, their fingers frozen on the reins of the horses, which are steaming and lathered despite the cold.

By one o'clock they have done what they can and they're fighting their way back to the house. The snow has already drifted four and five feet high, and they pick their way through the drifts, giving the horses their head until they sight the ranch buildings. They curry the horses down and feed them buckets of oats, then file into the house, peel off their cold, wet clothes and dip their frostbitten fingers in lukewarm water, put on dry things, and sit at the big table eating breakfast in midafternoon, as the snow falls parallel to the ground and the wind howls. Most of them have water blisters on their faces and wrists, where the skin has frozen because their jackets don't quite meet their gloves. As they eat, the blisters turn to black spots, so that you can tell where each man has been frostbitten.

From the first day of January until the twentieth of February, the storms come with a yelp and a holler, one after another. The temperature drops to ten below and then to twenty below, the wind blows in gales up to sixty miles an hour. Trains are stopped from Salt Lake City as far east as Omaha. Snowplow locomotives are sent out in pairs and grind to a halt, smothered by mountains of snow. A mother and father and their children freeze to death in their car near Hillsdale, Wyoming, less than a mile from home. Two weeks into the storm, they say that twenty-two people have died on the plains and that it might get worse. When it's possible to fly, army planes drop supplies to isolated ranchers and scour the fields for those trapped in automobiles or flying distress signals from the roofs of homes all but buried in snow.

There is nothing to be done. They ride out when they can, battling to make it as far as half a mile from the house. Ezra and Ben aren't worried about their prize Appaloosas, which are in well-insulated stalls. So are a dozen of Eli's bulls and all his best horses, but that leaves fifteen thousand cattle and four hundred horses where they cannot be reached. Tractors can't get through, so they haul hay to isolated bunches of cattle, using four bulky draft horses to drag hay sleds over the snow. The men who accompany the sleds are roped together, horse to horse, so they won't get lost. Lanterns are hung along the way to guide them back. The cattle left exposed to the elements are found in terrible condition, coated in two inches or more of ice, their eyes frozen shut. Ice balls have formed over their mouths and nostrils, and some have already suffocated. On the coldest days, when the temperature is ten below or worse and the wind tears across the open plains, Eli orders the men to stay indoors, as close to the fire as they can get. As much as he wants to save the livestock, he doesn't want to lose one cowhand doing it. They follow his orders, but in the bunkhouse, a bucket of water ten feet from a glowing stove will freeze solid.

The blizzard of '87 put an end to the open range. Eli fears that the blizzard of '49 will put an end to ranching, period. Late at night, listening to the house groan and shudder as the blizzards wail on, he worries also about the band of mustangs they freed from a federal holding pen in 1940: the stallion they called the black and about four hundred others made it as far as the western edge of Bighorn Canyon in Wyoming, where they were thriving. Eli, Two Spuds, and Joe Plenty Doors rode to Montana after the fall roundup in 1948 and found the black looking fat and healthy, surrounded by two dozen young horses who were clearly his progeny. But the stallion is getting old, and in a winter like this, the predators get hungry, the wolves come down from the high country, and a horse trapped in a snowdrift is helpless prey.

Eight days into January, there is a brief, sunny break in the morning. The wind dies down and Eli decides to put in a full day checking on as many cattle as they can get to, hauling feed, breaking down snow barriers outside the sheds, doing whatever can be done. By eleven o'clock, another blizzard is bearing down and there is nothing to be done except to retreat to the house. When Eli gets there, he finds Juanita frantic with worry, wearing a pair of old overalls and a heavy coat and scarf and heavy boots and walking in circles from the house, calling Ethan. She let him go outside to play in the sunshine. When it started to snow again, he was nowhere to be found.

Eli and Two Spuds join the search, Eli working south of the house, the Choctaw taking the north side. Eli drives himself to the brink of exhaustion battling the drifts, trying to call the boy, having the wind tear the breath out of his mouth before he can make a sound. He was tired and wet through when the search began, stumbling with fatigue fifteen minutes later, afraid he'll freeze to death himself. He fights his way around one big drift southeast of the house, slides down the far side, and comes to a halt with his boots on the rump of six-year-old Ethan, curled up in the snow.

Eli drapes the boy over his shoulders in a fireman's carry and begins fighting his way back. He is blinded by the wind, but he meets Two Spuds heading in the opposite direction, and together they fight their way to the porch, where Juanita has left three kerosene lanterns hanging. She takes the sobbing boy and spends the next three hours gradually warming his hands and feet in lukewarm water. He is frostbitten and exhausted, but he'll be all right.

* * *

Two days after fishing Ethan out of the snowdrift, Eli comes down with a heavy cold. Juanita gets out her stethoscope and listens to his chest.

"I think you have pneumonia," she says. "I'm going to give you a shot of penicillin."

"I don't need no shot."

"I'm the nurse and you'll do as you're told. Ethan needs you."

Juanita keeps antibiotics in her old medical bag for such emergencies. She gives Eli a shot, but he goes through one course of antibiotics and still his lungs refuse to clear. She orders him to stay in bed, but most mornings, he fights his way out to do the chores himself.

In mid-March, the old boar Eli inherited from Zeke Ketcham dies. His big dog, Rufus, expires two days after the hog, as though the dog didn't want to go on without its buddy.

When the Paint twins celebrate their seventy-ninth birthday, on April Fool's Day, the snowdrifts in some places on the range are still a dozen feet deep. The birthday party amounts to a slice of angel food cake and a couple of jokes from Ezra, who points out that they're two of the luckiest fellows he knows. They still have most of their teeth and all their hair, even if it's gone the same color as the prairie snow.

When they're able to take stock, they find three hundred and twenty-four cattle and eighteen horses either dead or in such bad shape they have to be shot. It's almost a miracle, a fraction of what it might have been if not for Eli's system of sheds and shelters, snow fences and windbreaks. You can't beat nature out here, but sometimes you can battle her to a draw.

When May begins with three warm days in succession, Eli decides it's time to head up to Montana to check on the mustangs. He plans to go alone, but Juanita has a quiet word with Ben, and soon there are ten riders in all, including Ezra, Ben, Two Spuds, Joe Plenty Doors and his son Little Joe, Farron Blue (who once nearly lost his life in a tangle with the black), Ignacio Salazar, Squirrel Nutt, and Elroy Titus, whose grandfather Roy Titus had been along with the Paint brothers on that horse-stealing escapade in the spring of 1887.

They load up their horses, including packhorses and spare saddle horses, in four-horse trailers. They also bring along four flatbed trucks, each loaded with two hundred bales of hay for the mustangs. They drive to a spot a half dozen miles south of Bighorn Canyon and park the trucks, unload and saddle the horses, and set out on a brilliant spring morning. The weather could not be better, but it's still rough going through thick mud where the snow has melted and slick patches of ice where it hasn't. Anywhere there is shade even part of the day, the thick drifts remain, some higher than the head of a rider on a horseback.

It's midafternoon before they come on the first signs of the battle that raged all winter. They find the carcass of a very young foal, torn apart by wolves. There are two more dead foals in the next half mile, then what's left of yearlings and older mares. Within two miles are the remains of nearly twenty mustangs and pieces of some of the wolves, casualties of their attempts to take down the horses, the starving attacking the famished. The prairie reeks with the smell of carrion, the men ride with their bandannas pulled over their faces. Buzzards and magpies peck at the carcasses. All the merriment and high spirits of the morning have vanished.

On the western edge of the canyon, it takes nearly an hour to find a way through a stand of small pines where the snowdrifts are still ten feet high. They come out onto a long, narrow clearing five hundred yards long, and at the north end of the clearing, the tableau that haunted Eli through the winter: the black standing alone, surrounded by a dozen wolves, so intent on their prey they didn't notice the approaching riders. Little Joe Plenty Doors, riding up front, is the first to see the horse. He thunders down on the wolves, firing with his carbine as he rides, dropping two of the animals. The others scatter, those which are able. Seven wolves were down and maimed, two crawling along and whimpering, their backs plainly broken by the hooves of the black.

The big horse stands, his flanks dripping blood, his eyes wild with fury, his teeth bloody where he has caught wolves and shaken them as a cat would shake a mouse. There were too many. His powerful chest is gouged in a dozen places, his left rear leg dangles, useless. The wolves have hamstrung the stallion. Little Joe dismounts and starts to approach the horse, but his father warns him away. The black is still dangerous, even on three legs.

Eli and Ezra are the last to catch up. By the time they arrive, the other riders have shot the wounded wolves to put them out of their misery. Most were so badly maimed that they would not have lasted the day. At the edge of the next wooded area, they see thirty or forty head of what remains of the black's band. There are mares and two or three young stallions, but not a single foal in sight. The winter and the wolves have killed them all. They ride a wide circle around the stallion. The hamstrung leg is so torn there's no chance he will walk again. His long, shaggy winter coat drips blood. Another hour and the wolves would have had their meal.

Farron Blue rides within five feet of the black and sights down the barrel of his carbine. There have been times when he wanted to shoot this horse. This is not one of them. His hands shake and his aim wobbles back and forth.

Eli raises a hand. "Let him be, Farron," he says. "This is my job. Why don't you boys start on back? Head west once you get past that stand of pines, ride on up into the first of the foothills, away from all these dead horses, where a man can breathe. There are good campsites up there with fresh water and the ground ought to be drier up high. I'll follow your tracks. We'll make camp tonight and break out the hay tomorrow."

When the last of the riders are out of sight, Eli rides up close and draws his Winchester out of the scabbard. The black looks at him, as though he's pleading for an end. As though he knows what's to come.

"I'm real sorry about this, old horse," Eli says. "If we could have got up here earlier, maybe we could have done something about them wolves. You're about the most remarkable animal I've seen in near eighty years, but we all got to go sometime. If it helps any, they'll be telling stories about you as long as there are cowboys in Wyoming."

The black tries to move, staggers and almost goes down. Eli thumbs off the safety and raises the Winchester to his shoulder, sights on the wide, shaggy head, and squeezes the trigger.

Far off in the timber, the men hear the shot and cringe. By the time Eli catches up, they're making camp next to a clear mountain stream on a sunny slope, the winter's carnage far down below, out of sight and smell.

That evening, they're all subdued after the business of the black. Ben and Eli never say much anyway, the younger cowpokes are too much in awe, they're all too tired for chatter. They hunker down around the campfire, watch the big yellow moon sail over the mountains, gaze at the sweep of stars in the Montana sky and wonder how it is that in a universe so immense, a dozen men could come to a place where they are all a little blue over the death of a wild horse that had never been ridden.

Ezra can't abide silence. Never could. To him, it's a void that needs to be filled. He has a tale to tell at times like these, and he never tires of telling it. He chews a blade of buffalo grass and stares into the burning coals, as though peering into another world, a time when a man couldn't pull a Dodge truck out onto the range and back it up to a stock chute, when there wasn't a solitary strand of barbed wire from Texas to the Canadian border. He takes a deep breath, gazes around at the sprawled cowhands.

"We've always been like this, me and Eli," he says, twisting one gnarled finger over another to illustrate his point. "Close as two peas in a pod. Have been since the day we was born. Twin brothers, see, are just one soul split into two bodies. Don't one of them go to take a leak that the other one don't know about it. So when them vigilantes caught up to Eli back in eighteen and eighty-seven, I knew it right off. I was a hundred miles away with old Teeter Spawn and a fellow we called Honest Abe, but I didn't need no special-delivery telegram to tell me what happened."

The cowhands pull up in a tighter circle. Some close to the fire, some back in the shadows sipping coffee thick as paint. Some miss their women, wives, or girlfriends, some miss their mamas. Ezra spits into the fire, pauses to let them settle in.

"We were an hour's ride into Montana at the time. Trailing three hundred head of saddle horses through Blackfoot Country on the way to

Fort Benton, looking for a spot to lay up along the Crazy Woman fork of the Powder River."

Elroy Titus, a jug-eared, red-haired boy with buck teeth and no manners, interrupts. "Last time, you said you was trailin two hundred head to Fort Whoop-up, which was supposed to be way t'other side of the Canadian border, and you said you was layin up on the Clear Fork."

The boy, Ezra thinks, is just like his grandfather Roy, who as it happened, had come along on that expedition to Fort Benton: more gumption than brains.

"I said three hundred to Fort Benton and you thought two hundred to Fort Whoop-up, Elroy, because you got buffalo chips where your noggin ought to be. Now drink your coffee and let a man tell his story, why don't you?"

Elroy sips from his cup, which like most of their cups is laced with more whiskey than coffee, poured when Eli wasn't looking. "Anyhow, I don't believe there was ever such a place as Fort Whoop-up," he says. "That's a danged dime-novel name for a fort if I ever heard one. You made it up, didn't you?"

"No, Elroy. I didn't make it up at all. You think it aint true, because you aint never cracked a book, which is why you are still a ignorant little pissant. There was a Fort Whoop-up, right enough, and they sold enough whiskey and Blackfoot rum out of there to just about kill off four different Indian tribes. I know, because one of the men that built the place was Joe Kipp himself. There was also a Fort Kipp, a few miles from Fort Whoop-up, because Joe had a disagreement with his partners and decided to build his own fort and name it after himself. If you ever got close enough to old Joe to shake his hand, he might of took a notion to lift your hair, just to stay in practice. Not that you drugstore cowboys will ever come across the likes of Joe Kipp."

Elroy Titus lifts his hat and runs his fingers through his hair. "I aint no drugstore cowboy," he says.

"Hush and let me tell this thing, Elroy. Like I said, we was maybe a hour's ride into Montana, Teeter Spawn and me and Honest Abe. Your grandpa Roy was supposed to be riding with us, but he had gone off somewhere. We figured he had turned tail and run. I was too bone-tired and scared of dying to worry about Roy. I had come down with a fever so bad, I felt like my hind end was going to light that saddle afire, and I was dry as a alkali creek. I'd drain my water bottle and fill her again in the Powder, but I couldn't beat that thirst if I was to drink the whole river dry. I was hoping that if Dermott Cull and his vigilantes caught up, they'd hang me high, so's my neck broke clean. We'd been on horseback more than twelve hours straight, wore down three mounts trying to keep all those horses headed north. I had the saddle wolf so bad, it felt like I'd been all day long astride a armadillo bareback."

"I aint never seen no armadillo, let alone rid one," Elroy says.

"Nor ever will if you don't shut up and let a man tell his tale. I might be old, son, but like my brother there, I can still manage a bullwhip if I have to."

Elroy lowers his head. Some of the cowhands glance at Eli to see how he's taking all this, but Eli has his hat down over his eyes. They shift a little to get comfortable, waiting for the old man to find his way back to the trail.

"We was damned fool kids, barely seventeen years old, thinking we could get away with a thing like stealin three hundred head of saddle horses from the O-Bar, one of the biggest cow outfits in Wyoming. Now you might ask why a couple of young fellas still wet behind the ears would take a notion to do such a thing, but these was perilous times, with banks going bust left and right and the whole country from Texas right up to Canada drier than a preacher's breakfast. This was right after the winter of 'eighty-seven, a winter so bad it just about killed the whole cattle business. The ranch we call the 8T8 was the O-Bar back then, and it was run by a misbegotten rattlesnake name of Dermott Cull, as mean a slab of Texas killer as you will ever come across. Dermott, he come and told us that the O-Bar wasn't goin to pay our wages for the winter. This after we lost a half dozen good hands dragging O-Bar cows out of snowdrifts. We were desperate men, and we were mad, and we done a desperate thing. That's how we come to be out on the prairie, pushing them horses for all we was worth. That's why it don't matter how many horses it was, Roy, because in them days, stealing one lame old cull was enough to get a man hung. One horse or a thousand, the result was the same. I was just about ready to lay down and die, except I knew if I did, Eli would come along and wake me up and kill me all over again. I was more afraid of him than anything else on God's green earth, man or beast, and that's the truth.

"We laid up at a coulee next to Baking Powder Creek. Teeter and Honest Abe set pickets for a dozen of the best horses. We were going to wait there and move out after dark. I was somewhere between dead and alive when I heard a crack of lightning and looked up and there they were, thunderheads as tall as mountains. I heard it then, before I saw it, a *whuff-whuff-whuff* comin fast across the prairie. *Whuff! Whuff! Whuff!* A dark thing it was, with wings of fire. *Whuff! Whuff! Whuff!* Wide as a hundred bald eagles flying wingtip to wingtip, black as midnight in Hades. It flew so low, the blaze from them fiery wings almost touched the prairie. *Whuff! Whuff! Whuff!* There was a screeching noise, like a tornado ripping a tin roof or a man's soul pulled right out of its socket. I felt my heart gum up right then, clogged like there was sand in the pump. I thought at first it was Eli's soul, you see."

Elroy butts in. "You mean a soul is a big black bird with fiery wings? That aint what the preacher says."

"And when has a preacher ever been out on the prairie in a lightning storm? When it comes to the things of this world, you can put all a preacher knows in a thimble, son. Now, Roy, if you'll kindly let me finish ..."

"Name's Elroy."

"Beg your pardon, Elroy. Now I finally figured out that wasn't a soul at all. It was death itself, and we was in the shadow of its black wings, all of us, but especially Eli, wherever he was. You get close to that great black shadow, boys, it can be a scary thing. The air went cold and the sun went black and the horses spooked. Two of them tore loose from their pickets. Then that great, dark, fiery thing just disappeared. A little smoke, and it was gone. I looked around careful, scared half to death. Wasn't nothing out there but the Crazy Woman fork of the Powder, and them horses and a pair of hawks way up high. My whole body was shaking and trembling like I fell into a river in January. And me not knowing if Eli was dead or alive, only that the thing had touched me with them fiery wings."

One of the cowpokes scoops the coffeepot out of the fire with a hand gloved against the heat and pours another cup. Ezra stays quiet so long they figure maybe he forgot the rest of the yarn. The old boy has so many miles on him, he's apt to drift on you, like a cottonwood bough on a spring flood river.

"This would be sixty-two years ago," Ezra says. "We weren't but seventeen years old at the time. That's younger than you, Elroy. Eli was tougher than anybody thought. Tougher than whalebone. Tougher than Dermott Cull, and Cull was mean as a wolverine with the toothache."

Ezra seems to lose the thread of it then. His watery eyes stare into the campfire.

Elroy fidgets. Finally, he can't stand it anymore. "What happened? What happened to Eli?"

"Why, they hung him by the neck, son. They hung him until he was dead."

Joe Plenty Doors laughs at that and pokes Elroy in the ribs. The hands toss a few more sticks on the fire and reach for their bedrolls. Morning comes early and cold at fall roundup time, and the young ones need their sleep. The wind picks up, the horses shift on their picket lines. Ezra sniffs the air. There's more snow coming, no mistake. A spring blizzard will catch a man by surprise in the high country, leave him frozen stiff as a bull's pizzle, waiting for a thaw so the magpies can come peck out his eyes. He gazes round at the cowpokes and winds up his tale.

"Then a bolt of lightning split the tree where he was hung, and Elroy's grandpa Roy found Eli lying there still alive, and brought him back to us. He was just fine, except for a sore neck. That, boys, is the God's truth as I know it."

Eli laughs and tosses the dregs of his cup in the fire. "I swear, he gets you fellas with that yarn every year. There aint a particle of truth in it. I never stole a horse in my life and I never got hung for it neither. Now we'd best turn in. I need you boys with some bottom in you tomorrow if we're going to drag that hay to them mustangs."

He crawls into his sleeping roll and pulls his hat down over his eyes again and falls asleep without another word. Ezra has always envied his brother that, the ability to sleep at any time and to wake, whether he's been asleep ten minutes or eight hours, fresh and ready to go.

Ezra sits up alone, staring into the embers of the fire. The black is gone. It makes a man think. The stallion was the toughest horse he had ever known. Cowpokes gave up trying to break him, because they knew the horse would die before he would give up. He was like Eli that way, always battling. Ezra himself is different and he knows it. He wasn't one to shy from a fight if there was no other way, but he would try to find a way around trouble if it could be found. Eli would go right at a thing and try to beat it down, Ezra would look for a way to avoid the conflict in the first place. You didn't want to walk right into it, like poor Tom Call did with Pardo Bury. Life is too short. Even a long life, a life like his own. The longest life is no more than a sliver of light between two boundless ribbons of dark, like the light you see through the chinks of a log cabin at sunrise. And that last ribbon of dark, the one that comes after you are gone, that one goes on until the end of time.

Ezra throws more wood onto the fire and sleeps fitfully, waking a dozen times. It starts to snow in the night and it turns colder. By the time it's light enough to make out the shapes of the horses, there is a foot of powdery snow on the ground. The men come up laughing, shaking wet snow out of their necks. Young Elroy throws a snowball at Ben. Ben throws one back, hard, catches Elroy in the jaw and the battle is on. Ezra gets the fire roaring, surprised that he's up before Eli, with all this racket going on. The snowball fight gets the horses in the rope corral stirred up, and Ezra hollers for the boys to cut it out.

Ezra and Two Spuds start bacon and eggs going in two big frying pans, and Ben sets the coffee on. When breakfast is ready, Ezra hollers at Eli, asks if he plans to sleep until noon. Eli doesn't stir. When Ezra hollers again and there is still no answer, he prods Eli with his toe. The hat falls away from his face. Eli stares up at the falling snow, his eyes wide open, seeing nothing at all.

The men stand around, beating their hands together and stomping their feet, stunned into silence, waiting while Ezra, Ben, and Two Spuds decide what to do. They can't just tie Eli's body over a packhorse.

"I had to carry him home once on a pony drag, after he wrecked his Cadillac," the Choctaw says. "I expect I can do it again."

They cut down two slender lodgepole pines, lop the branches off, take the long, narrow canvas tarp from under Ben's sleeping roll and punch holes in it every three or four inches along each side, then wind it around each pole until the slack has been taken up and the poles are about three feet apart. They run a thin lariat back and forth through the holes and pull the rope taut and tie it at both ends and do the same on the other side. When they're done, they have a passable travois.

When the pony drag is ready, they lash it to the straps of a pack-saddle on a gentle albino gelding and lift Eli's body onto the drag, still wrapped in his bedroll. They belt his body to the drag with three spare saddle cinches. Ezra goes to cover Eli's face with the blanket and decides not to. *If this is his last ride, let him see where we're headed.*

Ezra mounts his Appaloosa, winds the rope around his saddle horn, and sets out through the thickly falling snow, the great heavy flakes that drift between the tall pine trees, down the slope that leads around the drifts, skirting stands of pine trees and down along the Bighorn River past the great slash in the earth that is Bighorn Canyon. Ezra rides up front, trailing the packhorse on a slack line. Ben rides behind, and the rest follow along single file.

Two Spuds lets the others ride ahead. He crouches in the snow next to the dying embers of the campfire and rocks back and forth on his heels, chanting the Choctaw funeral cry.

When he is through, he listens to the last echo of the cry down the hills, kicks snow over the campfire to smother it, mounts his pinto, and rides under the pines through the falling snow, seeing plainly the tracks of the two long poles and the shod horses following the trail. Overhead, he hears a bird call, the *chrrrrt! chrrrrt! chrrrt!* of a magpie. Snow is shaken loose from a low-hanging branch. It cascades down his neck. He looks up and sees a lone white magpie. The wings beat heavily and the bird calls again, *chrrrrt! chrrrrt! chrrrt!* Two Spuds tips his hat and nods. The magpie sails off through the falling snow, flying west.

AUTHOR'S NOTE

When I was very young, we played a game called "bombs over Tokyo." Arms thrust out like wings, we ran in tight circles shrieking *"Bombs over Tokyo!"* I don't know why, but it was always Tokyo, never Hiroshima or Nagasaki, Dresden or Berlin.

I played all our war games with a fierce pride. My uncle Lemoine was a Marine who lost fifty pounds on Guadalcanal. His brothers, George and Thaine, island-hopped across the Pacific with the U.S. Army. Cousin Jimmy parachuted into Normandy on D-Day. Cousin Edwin was killed by a kamikaze that hit the destroyer USS *Hazelwood* off Okinawa in April 1945.

My hero was Uncle Jimmy, an antiaircraft gunner on the battleship USS *Tennessee*, from Pearl Harbor to Japan. When I wasn't playing bombs over Tokyo, I was shooting at Jap planes from the deck of the *Tennessee*. If I didn't have a popgun or a squirt gun, a stick would do.

Boys grow up, the games change. In January 1958, I waited in the cold and dark with my friend Sonny Walter. We had real guns by then, and we were waiting for Charlie Starkweather. He was in jail in our hometown with his fourteen-year-old girlfriend, Caril Ann Fugate, after a killing spree that had left eleven people dead in Nebraska and Wyoming. We were convinced the jail would never hold a desperado like Starkweather, so we waited with loaded guns until we were too cold and tired to stay out any longer.

As a journalist working for the Lincoln *Journal* ten years later, I covered a probation hearing for Caril Ann Fugate. She was denied probation, but she had always claimed that she was a hostage, not an accomplice. I was intrigued. She seemed so innocent. Which was she, hostage or accomplice?

Two decades after the Fugate probation hearing, I covered a mass murder, the attack on the engineering faculty at the University of

Montreal in which fourteen young women were killed. I stood for hours in the snow, watching the fourteen people who had been wounded carried on stretchers from the building before we learned the awful truth: that a killer had methodically made his way through the building, singling out the women for slaughter.

This is a work of fiction, but it flows from these events. I have written, in passing, of the heroes I worshiped and the impact Starkweather and Fugate had on our lives in a memoir called *Desertion*. The twin themes, the savagery and heroism of war, the savagery confronting those who attempt to keep the peace, remained in the recesses of my mind, in the mysterious backwaters where writers invent their tales. Pardo Bury is not Starkweather, nor is he even based on Starkweather, but the essence of what he is can be found in the history of the Nebraska killer, who at the time was something new on the landscape: the killer who kills for no reason at all. With absurd gun laws which both enable and invite more mass killers to wreak havoc on the innocent, the Starkweather breed is likely to remain with us for a long, long time.

If Starkweather put an end to the innocence of my generation, the previous generation had undergone a different trial by fire. Every family has its narratives, stories that are told over and over, until they have been burnished like fine marble. The most unforgettable for me was the tale of the attack on Pearl Harbor and its aftermath: my mother's long, agonizing wait to learn the fate of her adored younger brother Jimmy, the single postcard that arrived weeks later. When Pearl Harbor was duplicated by the attacks on the World Trade Center sixty years later, I went back to that earlier time, to a more innocent America enduring a national trauma and to the first jittery days after the beginning of a war that absolutely had to be fought, trying to imagine the impact on those whose lives would be changed forever, even if they were never called to serve.

This is the third volume of the Paint Trilogy, based on the story of my mother's family through a period of exactly one hundred years of American history, between the Gold Rush of 1849 and the great blizzard of the winter of 1949. I have been aided throughout by my sisters, Linda Dittmar and Jeanne Dennison, and by my cousin Nancy Crabtree. It was Nancy's exhaustive compilation of the wartime letters from her father, Jimmy Wilson, which made the central section of this book possible.

I don't wish to conceal my background. I have always been simultaneously fascinated and repelled by the wars men fight, in part because I am a deserter from the U.S. Army. I came to Canada early in 1970, because of my profound opposition to the war in Vietnam, a war which was as immoral and unnecessary as World War II was moral and necessary. During my flight from Mexico to Vancouver at the end of 1969, I left my dog tags behind in Seattle. When I returned to Seattle while researching this book in 2008, Nancy Crabtree had a surprise for me. After her father's death, they found my dog tags in a box with his medals from the war. No one knows how Jimmy came to have them or why he hung on to them, but nothing I have ever received has touched me like those long-forgotten dog tags.

I would also like to thank Trish Todd, Elaine Pfefferblit, Mick Lowe, Lina Basile, Sue Hayward, Caroline Mustard, Judy Riggs, Arnold Marcowitz, Catherine Wallace, Raymond Brassard, my friend and mentor Dr. John X. Cooper; my infinitely patient wife, Irene Marc; and last but not least, my old friend Dr. Jon Vanderhoof, now a lecturer in pediatrics at the Harvard Medical School, who once scared me half to death doing aerial stunts as I rode in the backseat of his Aeronca Defender and who provided, nearly fifty years later, a precise description of how one such stunt would be performed.

ABOUT THE AUTHOR

JACK TODD grew up in Nebraska and Wyoming, the son of a boxer and horseman. His passion for Nebraska, Wyoming, and the American West has survived four decades of self-imposed exile. A track and field athlete and editor of the student newspaper at the University of Nebraska, Todd has worked as a reporter and columnist for the Lincoln *Journal*, the Akron *Beacon-Journal*, the *Detroit Free Press*, *The Miami Herald*, *The Vancouver Sun*, the CBC, and the Montreal *Gazette*. He is the author of the novels *Sun Going Down* and *Come Again No More* and the memoir *Desertion*, which won the Quebec Writers' Federation First Book Prize and the Mavis Gallant Prize for Non-Fiction. Todd is the father of three sons. He lives in Montreal.

To my Weight Watchers Family!

Thank you so much for picking up my book. I really hope you find some inspiration on these pages. I wrote it from my heart and I know that you, as a Weight Watchers member, will understand how much this weight loss has impacted my life. I never imagined that the decision to lose weight would change me forever or that it would inspire so many people. It has been one of the biggest surprises of my life and a huge honor. I take the responsibility seriously and knowing that I am inspiring people keeps me inspired every day. I want to make my Weight Watchers family proud and I want to be a positive role model for anyone who feels they can't do this. If I can do this I know you can too, but you have to stick with the program, even when you feel like it's not going well. And if you stick with the program, it will change your life for the better. My advice is to do something every day. It doesn't have to be everything, just something. Trust the plan and take advantage of all the tools available to you, especially the support. I love my meetings and I get to as many as I can. Hope to see you in one soon!

All my love,
Jennifer

I GOT THIS

JENNIFER HUDSON

I GOT THIS

How I Changed My Ways and
Lost What Weighed Me Down

DUTTON

DUTTON

Published by Penguin Group (USA) Inc.

375 Hudson Street, New York, New York 10014, U.S.A.

Penguin Group (Canada), 90 Eglinton Avenue East, Suite 700, Toronto, Ontario M4P 2Y3,
Canada (a division of Pearson Penguin Canada Inc.); Penguin Books Ltd, 80 Strand, London
WC2R 0RL, England; Penguin Ireland, 25 St Stephen's Green, Dublin 2, Ireland (a division
of Penguin Books Ltd); Penguin Group (Australia), 250 Camberwell Road, Camberwell,
Victoria 3124, Australia (a division of Pearson Australia Group Pty Ltd); Penguin Books India
Pvt Ltd, 11 Community Centre, Panchsheel Park, New Delhi–110 017, India; Penguin
Group (NZ), 67 Apollo Drive, Rosedale, Auckland 0632, New Zealand (a division of
Pearson New Zealand Ltd); Penguin Books (South Africa) (Pty) Ltd, 24 Sturdee Avenue,
Rosebank, Johannesburg 2196, South Africa

Penguin Books Ltd, Registered Offices: 80 Strand, London WC2R 0RL, England

Published by Dutton, a member of Penguin Group (USA) Inc.

First printing, January 2012
10 9 8 7 6 5 4 3 2 1

 REGISTERED TRADEMARK—MARCA REGISTRADA

LIBRARY OF CONGRESS CATALOGING-IN-PUBLICATION DATA

Hudson, Jennifer, 1981–
   I got this : how I changed my ways and lost what weighed me down / Jennifer Hudson.
      p.   cm.
   ISBN 978-0-525-95277-0
   SPECIAL MARKETS ISBN 978-0-525-42567-0 NOT FOR RESALE.
   1. Hudson, Jennifer, 1981–   2. Singers—United States—Biography.   3. Motion picture actors
and actresses—United States—Biography.   4. Overweight persons—United States—Biography.
I. Title.
   ML420.H835A3 2012
   782.42164092—dc23
   [B]

                                                                              2011043578

Printed in the United States of America
Set in Walbaum MT Std
Designed by Alissa Amell

While the author has made every effort to provide accurate telephone numbers and Internet
addresses at the time of publication, neither the publisher nor the author assumes any
responsibility for errors, or for changes that occur after publication. Further, the
publisher does not have any control over and does not assume any responsibility for author
or third-party websites or their content.

*Penguin is committed to publishing works of quality and integrity.
In that spirit, we are proud to offer this book to our readers;
however, the story, the experiences, and the words
are the author's alone.*

To my cousin Angela White—who is the ultimate health fanatic, my workout buddy, and a huge part of my inspiration.

CONTENTS

CONTENTS

I GOT THIS

INTRODUCTION

"Jennifer! Over here!"

"Jennifer, look this way."

"Jennifer, Jennifer."

"Over here!"

"No, over here!"

"Jennifer, turn to the right!"

I always dreamed of someday walking the red carpet in Hollywood. Let's be real. It's fun. Everyone there is shouting out your name just to get a glimpse of what you're wearing. The press asks you to pose, wave, and smile as they snap photo after photo, with flashes popping so bright you can hardly see. It's a moment in time a girl feels truly beautiful. And on this particular night, I thought I was looking fierce.

It was one of my first red-carpet events. I was a contestant on *American Idol*, and was living my dream of singing for millions of people on the highest-rated show on television. I was a long way from singing in church and talent shows on the South Side of

Chicago. I was excited, taking in the red-carpet finery for the first time. I felt on top of the world.

"Jennifer, are you insecure about being a 'big girl' in Holly-wood?"

That is, until *that* question.

Oh, *hell* no. She didn't just ask me that.

But she did.

It took me a minute to figure out who the reporter was actually talking to.

Who, me? I thought. Insecure?

Surely, she wasn't addressing *me* that way. I had the height of a supermodel, breasts that were naturally big *and* real, and a God-given shape. Why would I feel insecure about that? I looked around hoping to spot another Jennifer—an insecure "big" girl, but there wasn't anyone else there.

Nope.

Just me.

Like Randy Jackson said to me after my *American Idol* audition: "Welcome to Hollywood, girl!"

CHAPTER ONE

BELIEVE

I was born on September 12, 1981, in the Englewood area of Chicago. I am the third child of my parents, Darnell Hudson Donnerson and Samuel Simpson. My mama raised me, my sister Julia, and my brother Jason on her own as a single parent. We were a close family, surrounded by lots of aunts, uncles, cousins, and our grandparents.

I come from the South Side of Chicago, where a lot of the girls have curves. Most of the men there don't want their ladies too skinny. Oh, no. They want a little meat on the bones, and a little something to hold on to. Most of the girls in my neighborhood were built just like me—and that's what we wanted. Now, I don't know about you, but I'd much rather have my share of nice curves than no shape at all. That's not to say that I didn't know I was bigger than some girls—I just never really felt all that insecure about it.

My sister, Julia, has been a big girl for her entire life. My brother, Jason, was built exactly the same.

As for me?

Comparatively speaking, I was the skinny one in my family! In fact, I was so thin as a little girl that you could see my ribs beneath my shirts. My mama took me, not Julia and Jason—the heavy kids in our family—to the doctor. She thought something had to be wrong.

"My child must be very sick! I can see her ribs!" Mama spoke desperately to the doctor as if I was dying. I wasn't sick and I surely wasn't dying—I was just *thin*.

In my family, if you were too skinny, something *had* to be wrong. My family likes to see some shape, too, and if you don't have that, they'll feed you until you do. And trust me—when it comes to food, the Hudsons don't play around.

Like a lot of families in my neighborhood, food was a central focus for all types of gatherings, from family reunions to Sunday-night dinners. There were, of course, the exceptions, and I grew up knowing kids from school who were rarely served home-cooked meals—they ate TV dinners and frozen vegetables—but that wasn't our family. My mama would never allow that kind of food in our house. She loved to cook. I never knew times were tough or that money was short in our home because Mama always had a hot meal on the table. And if she cooked it, we ate it. My grandma and mama were the best cooks, and later, Jason became a good cook, too. Not me—I didn't start cooking much until I got older and had a family of my own.

It gave my mama a lot of joy to make meals for her kids. She especially loved making hot breakfasts so we could start our days off right and nourished. Before school, we filled our plates with bacon, ham or sausage, pancakes, waffles, eggs, and biscuits. I said *nourished* . . . not healthy! But oh, that food was so good.

When it came time for dinner, meals were always prepared fresh and from scratch, too. We were a family of tradition and creatures of habit, so Wednesday was spaghetti night, Friday was always our fried fish night, and Sunday was strictly about praising God, spending time with family, and eating really good food. We'd all go to church in the morning and then stop someplace after service for a bite to eat for lunch. Sundays were the only day of the week that we ate out. It was a special treat I looked forward to every week. My grandma and mama loved to stop at Kentucky Fried Chicken, but we kids always wanted to eat at McDonald's. I usually ordered a cheeseburger with *no* onions—I hated onions as a kid and still do. If my burger came with onions, I'd sit there, cry, and refuse to eat it until my mama picked the onions off—or my brother ate my burger for me.

Whenever we ate out, I nitpicked my meal so I could make it last longer, and I was a slow eater, anyway. Eating out was that much of a treat. We weren't allowed to order a drink because it cost too much money. Mind you, this was before the days of value meals, so everything on the menu was à la carte. Jason told my mama that if he didn't have a drink he'd throw up his food. That was his way of being slick to get himself a drink. It worked every time, too.

Sunday nights were full-on family-style dinners with all the fixings. Those meals were like a traditional Christmas dinner at my mama's house every week, with most of my favorite foods being served—collard greens, creamy mashed potatoes, pork chops with heavy gravy, macaroni and cheese, fried chicken with biscuits, and more. Just talking about those meals takes me back to the days of mindless eating without a care. And when it came to dessert, Mama made the best peanut butter cookies and pound cake on the planet. Everyone loved her pound cake. It tasted like she used at least two pounds of butter. For that reason alone, we should have called it "two pound cake." All that butter made it taste so much better.

One thing is for sure: We ate very well seven days a week. It wasn't just at my mama's house that we ate this way. It was at Grandma's house and our aunts' houses, too. I always ate my fill, but I hardly ever finished all of the food I piled on my plate back then. My brother didn't mind, though, because he got to eat all of my leftovers.

When we weren't eating those delicious meals, my granddaddy used to spoil us with goodies from the gas station where he worked.

He frequently brought home chips, candy, and other special treats. On payday, he gave each of us some money to walk to the store and pick out all of the junk food we wanted. We loved when Granddaddy got paid because Mama only gave us a quarter when we wanted to buy something special. If I asked for fifty cents, it was as if I was trying to rob a bank.

"Mama, it's only fifty cents!" I'd plead.

"Jenny, money doesn't grow on trees!" And then she'd send me off to ask my granddaddy for the money.

Now, *he'd* give us three dollars—each! It felt like I could buy up the whole store with that money. I have always had more of a taste for salty treats than sugary ones, so as a kid I preferred eating pickles and potato chips over candy and cakes. The saltier the better for me.

As I got older, all of those big meals and all that junk food began to catch up with me. I went from being a skinny chicken to a round and robust young woman. I wasn't fat, but people were no longer seeing my ribs. I was starting to look like the rest of my family.

As I gradually gained weight, I started to develop my own way of dressing. I liked to call it "free style." I chose clothes I liked, not things that were trendy or name brands, which is what my brother and sister always went for. I chose to accentuate my curves, or to just show my personal flair. Some might have thought my outfits were a little weird—but I liked to think of them as unique. I didn't care what size I wore, I just wore what I liked. One of my favorite outfits included a pair of overalls, which I wore to high school at least once a week. I was establishing a personal style . . . and flair, in lots of different ways, something my mama started to notice.

For example, I have always signed my name with great flourish. Even as a child, I made big swoops and grand letters.

"Jenny, you have an artistic signature. I think you can draw!" my mother said with great enthusiasm.

"Whatever," I said.

At the time, I had no interest in drawing. But then, one day, I gave it a try and I've not put my pencil down since. My whole bedroom was covered in my sketches. I have an uncanny ability to draw whatever I see. I always tell people that I got my grandma's voice and my mother's artistic talent.

Then my mother came to me and said, "Jenny, you're such a prankster, I think you might be able to act. I really believe you will be an actress someday."

It's true that as a kid, I was a real practical joker. I loved (and still love) to play tricks on my family and did so whenever I had the chance.

"Whatever," I said.

Do you see a pattern? My usual response of "whatever" turned out to be quite appropriate because *whatever* my mama spoke of *inevitably* came true.

My family always says my voice is a gift—a precious jewel I

inherited from my maternal grandmother. My grandma's name was Julia Kate Hudson. My sister and I used to joke that the Kates in our family got all the talent. (My middle name is Kate, and one of my names in my family is Jenny Kate—which I call myself when I'm just being me, hanging out and doing ordinary things.)

People often spoke about how beautifully my grandmother could sing. She was also the sweetest, kindest, most loving, and giving woman. I absolutely loved spending time with her, and especially listening to her sing. She loved to sing hymns and praise God with her voice.

Grandma's house had high ceilings and hardwood floors, which resulted in amazing acoustics. The openness created a sound as if I was singing into a microphone. I would sit on her stairs and just sing my heart out. We have a lot of great singers in our family, so my voice wasn't all that unusual, but some of my older family members told me I had "the gift." They also often said I reminded them of my grandma. I loved to sing and perform. People responded to my voice when I started singing in church or at local talent shows. People would come from all over Chicago just to hear me sing. I became aware that I could move them with my music and I liked the way that felt. There was a certain sense of power that came with capturing my audience that left me wanting more. They say that most performers live for the applause. Even as a little girl I understood what that meant, and the more I got, the more I wanted.

Even though Grandma had a beautiful voice, she used to tell me that she never wanted to become famous because she'd have to move and perform on demand even if she didn't feel like it—what we would call being "on" today. There are plenty of days performers need to be lifted up and are expected to have the energy to do the lifting. Grandma was perfectly content singing for the Lord. As long as she was reading her Bible or singing in church, she was happy. I remember being mesmerized watching her sing in our church choir. She did more than one hundred solos in that church. Grandma taught me her favorite gospel songs, which I loved to sing. They were powerful and emotional, and everything I thought a song should be to evoke those same reactions from the audience. Grandma's love for gospel is the reason I make sure to have at least one inspirational song on my albums. It is my way of keeping her close, even now.

Around my thirteenth birthday, Grandma had her first stroke and then started having seizures. I never wanted her to be alone so I spent most of my free time keeping her company. I was always quick to volunteer to spend the day at her house so she wouldn't get lonely. There were some good days when Grandma would be up and well, shuffling her feet, singing her hymns; but then there were days when she couldn't get out of bed. Those days were my inspiration to write my first song called "To Love Somebody," so Grandma would know how much she meant to me. I sat on the side of her bed and sang it to her.

I GOT THIS

"It feels good to love somebody, but it hurts to let them go.
And it hurts to love somebody when you know
you have to let them go."

Grandma passed away when I was sixteen years old. Since then, I've carried a heart-shaped stone with me wherever I go, as a way to connect to my grandma. I inherited her gift, and I try to keep her memory close.

After Grandma died, instead of wallowing in my sadness, I vowed that I would go on with my life, follow my dream, and make good decisions along the way so I would make her proud. My grandma and mama were the two most important women in my life because they showed me that with the faith of a mustard seed, anything was possible.

In high school, I wasn't what you'd call a typical teenager. I didn't hang out much with girlfriends, other than my friends from choir. I spent most of my free time with my family. I did have a boyfriend, but he went to a different high school and we only saw each other in the neighborhood. My life wasn't full of the typical teenager things like movies and parties and dances and things like that. I was focused, even then, on my music.

I still love spending time with my family and old friends from home. Being with these familiar touchstones helps me to stay grounded. I am still the same person I've always been, which I think surprises people. I remind them that my career doesn't define me. Sure, it's a part of who I am but it doesn't determine how I act.

I do.

I've never forgotten where I came from, so when it comes to family and good friends, bring it on. The more the merrier. That is why my cousin helps me with my son and one of my brothers works security for me. Even my best friend from middle school, Walter Williams III, works for me as my executive assistant. He's my gatekeeper, and my best friend in the whole world.

Walter and I met in the sixth grade and have been best friends ever since. Even though Walter is slightly older than me, he is still the same height as he was on the day we met—meaning short. I was unusually tall for my age back then. We were quite a pair. We still are.

I will never forget when Walter and I truly connected. There was a new music teacher at our school who wanted to hear each kid sing. I guess she wanted to know what she had to work with. All of the kids in the class pointed toward me, saying, "Jennifer should sing first!" I really had no choice but to do my thing when the teacher asked me to get up to sing.

Up to this point, Walter had never heard my voice. But when I finished, I could tell that he had fallen in love with what he heard. He became my number one fan that day and we've been insepa-rable ever since. He decided that he would make it his business to make me a star, and I am being honest when I say that I wouldn't be where I am today without his help and support.

Although I had a desire to perform in those early years, I *was* sometimes shy. It was Walter who eventually helped me to come out of my shell. He encouraged me to sing wherever and as often as I could. When we graduated eighth grade, I was asked to sing a solo during the ceremony. I did my own rendition of "Wind Beneath My Wings," and cried through the entire song. Walter and my mama were mad at me for blowing that big moment. In fact, Walter got so upset that he decided he was done with trying to promote my career right then and there. This would mark the first of many times to come that Walter would fire himself out of my life.

After that, Walter and I ended up attending different high schools, but we still saw each other almost every day. We'd go shopping after school, work on music, talk about whom we had crushes on, and just hang out like typical kids our age. We even went to my high school prom together. Walter was my date—he had a car and could drive to the dance. My boyfriend at the time didn't have a car, so he was out and Walter was in. I wore a long cream-colored gown. Every year I have a favorite color, and that year I was in love with anything cream or brown. (This year I'm all about purple, by the way.)

During high school, I took my first job. At the time, my sister was the queen of our local Burger King. Although she wasn't the manager, it was as if she worked that whole place by herself. My sister suggested I come to work with her as a way to make some extra money to support my retail habit—it took money to develop my "free style." I gave it my best shot, but I wasn't cut out for it. The grill was too hot for me! Plus, the manager was not very nice and talked to everyone with disrespect. She may have intimidated the other employees, but not me (or my sister, for that matter). Shortly after I started, I looked at the manager square in the eyes and said, "Honey, I am only sixteen years old. I don't need this job! I quit!" My sister gave me a hard time about giving up so quickly, but I knew it was the moment to get serious about what I really wanted to do.

Walter was happy that I quit—and started to work even harder to help me launch my career.

Somewhere around the end of my freshman year of high school, Walter phoned me up and said that he wanted to be my official manager. My first response was a gut-busting laugh, and one of my classic "Whatever"s. But then I said, "All right. You wanna be my manager? Fine!" I figured he would last about a hot minute. Much to my surprise, Walter took his new position very seriously. He started booking shows for me almost right away and escorted me to all of my events. Neither of us could afford to buy the fancy dresses I needed to wear for my gigs. He used his credit card to buy them, and I would wear them once. Walter would then return the outfits for a full refund. Oh, some of those outfits were something else. Walter did the shopping, and because of my curves we were limited in where we could shop. One outfit that I may never forgive Walter for was an orange suit consisting of a jacket and capri pants. I believe there was some gold trim involved. It was definitely more of something a grandmother would wear. A very stylish grandma, but a grandma nonetheless.

Walter even had business cards printed up that read, "Weddings, funerals, and church functions." It also listed my rate of $25 per song in the upper-left corner. Walter's name and number were on the bottom right as my booking contact.

I'd do my events, get paid, and promptly give Walter his 10 percent. Then we'd return whatever dress we had chosen for the event. We were making money! For a couple of kids, we thought we had a pretty good idea of how show business worked. Boy, we had a lot to learn.

Although I did lots of private parties, my real moneymakers were competing in talent competitions. There were many talent shows around Chicago that I could enter. I sometimes wish I could go back and watch myself onstage. I was pretty confident by this point. Both Walter and I knew that if I entered, I'd win them all. We'd look at the prize money and base our decision on which shows to do on how much money we could make.

I will admit, however, that winning wasn't always easy. You see, talent shows are a lot like beauty pageants. I felt like I was under a microscope sometimes, and the atmosphere could be intense and really competitive. There was so much backstabbing, politics and dirty tricks going on behind the scenes of those things that I learned to anticipate the *worst* every time we went to a show. I once sang in a competition where another contestant hid my music so I wouldn't be able to perform. This type of sabotage went on all the time. I learned to brush it off and remembered to carry a spare tape.

When I was seventeen, I entered a gospel singing contest at the mall in Evergreen, Chicago. This was like a local gospel version of *American Idol*. It was one of the biggest competitions in the area. The organizers of the contest had made hair and makeup people available, but Walter had arranged for my own personal glam squad to be with me that day, including a wardrobe stylist, a hairstylist, and a makeup artist. Walter thought it would be better if I showed up with my own team. It wasn't that we were pulling a diva act. He wanted me to have my own glam squad so I would look the part of a star. My dress that day had been made especially for me by one of Walter's friends. It was a dramatic, black velvet gown, complete with a train and long-fitted sleeves lined with silver fabric.

In an ironic twist of fate, one of the makeup artists provided by the contest organizers is now one of my personal makeup artists.

"I remember you back when you thought you were too good and had your own stylist and hairdresser." She still teases me to this day every chance she gets!

Round one was held at the Evergreen Plaza Shopping Center, and I won. I also won the second round. Like I said, I usually won whatever talent show I entered, and this time I was hoping for the same result.

Round three was held at Salem Baptist Church led by the Reverend James T. Meeks, in Chicago. The church was massive and was by far the largest venue I had ever played. In addition to coming down with a terrible cold, for whatever reason, I switched my song for this round. In the end I don't think I sang the right song to win that contest. I ended up placing third. No matter how big the glam squad, or how dramatic the dress, sometimes things just don't work out.

Walter was always incredibly passionate about ways to move my career in a forward motion. He had the highest expectations for me and would stop at nothing to help me get to the top. One thing I know he wasn't expecting was that I would ever go back to work at Burger King, something I could do only because it was, as they say, "under new management."

This time, I worked the drive-through window. You didn't hear, "Welcome to Burger King, may I take your order" when you drove up to my window. Oh, no. You heard my big ol' mouth singing whatever came to mind. That window had a microphone and I couldn't resist. I have never met a microphone I didn't like—even if it was at a Burger King. I especially loved singing songs from commercials like ". . . Always, Coca-Cola . . ." and even jingles from competitors like McDonald's. That drive-through was my stage and I made sure to entertain our customers as they came by to pick up their Whoppers and fries.

It turned out the new manager of that Burger King was a club promoter on the weekends at a local nightclub called Mr. G's Supperclub & Entertainment Center. Mr. G's was a big deal in Chicago back then. My Burger King manager asked me if I wanted to come down to the club and sing a set or two. He said he could only pay me a hundred and fifty dollars.

Say what?

That was a lot more money than I was making working the drive-through or singing at weddings.

I was all over his offer like white on rice.

At the time, I loved listening to Whitney Houston and Destiny's Child, so I figured I could sing a few of their songs and just do my thing. Much to my surprise, the club turned into a regular gig. And just like that, I was done working at Burger King, much to Walter's satisfaction. I made up my mind then and there to make a living by carving out my career using my talents and doing the one thing I love. Working at Burger King was the first and last nine-to-five job I've ever had. I was nineteen years old and have never looked back.

I took general courses while attending college, and naturally, music was one of them. My teacher there was a gentleman named Rufus Hill. On the first day of class, he made each of the students get up and sing for him. I felt like it was grade school all over again! When it was my turn, I sang "His Eye Is on the Sparrow," which was a traditional gospel song I knew I could handle. By the time I finished singing, Mr. Hill was practically on the phone to his friend, a well-known theater coach. He called to have her come hear me sing.

The following week, she came to our classroom so I could sing for her. At the time, I had no idea why, but if someone asked me to perform, I was always happy to oblige. Turns out that she was looking for people to audition for the musical *Big River.* It was being staged at Marriott Theatre in Lincolnshire, about an hour and a half outside of Chicago. I was going to try out.

Mr. Hill and his friend spent the next several weeks helping me prepare for my audition. They worked with me and helped me learn the music and lines. I practiced "How Blest We Are," the most important song from *Big River,* until I knew it cold. I got the part and finally had my first real *professional* singing job.

From that point forward, Walter and I knew we'd ultimately take this journey together. I have always called Walter my life partner because we have been through everything together from the start. He knows me better than I know myself, and he's always believed in me. I personally think every girl ought to have herself at least one gay man in her life because he will always tell you if your shoes are so last season, your outfit is not working for you, your hair is a total wreck, or to get rid of that man you are dating if he isn't treating you right! I always tell people that if they don't like Walter, there isn't something wrong with him—there's something wrong with them!

CHAPTER TWO

INVISIBLE

By the time I was in my teens I was aware that I had become a plus-size girl. C'mon, I wasn't blind. I may never have called myself "fat" but I still knew that I couldn't shop where other girls shopped. I just felt confident that I could work with the body God gave me. I wasn't insecure—I had all the great curves that a lot of women have to pay for!

When I was fourteen years old, I was in a group called Final Notice. The other two girls were a little older than me and comparatively speaking, they were petite. I was younger and, well, not as delicate. I wasn't overweight, and because of my five-foot-nine frame, I was able to carry a few extra pounds—and carry them well. Even though I didn't fit the look they were going for, they kept me around because I had the most talent. Image was always the bigger issue with the girls in that group. The other girls didn't want what I wanted—which was to sing. They wanted to wear skimpy little outfits so they would look hot. I wanted to choose costumes we could all wear to *entertain*.

The girls from Final Notice and I would go to pick our outfits together, and this was often a frustrating experience. We'd go shopping and I'd try on matching jeans that were supposed to be in my size. While they always fit the other girls perfectly, mine were never quite right. Since I am so tall, I'd usually end up with jeans that were tight in the waist and far too short. If I went up a size, they were baggy all over and made me look even bigger than I was.

Many studies claim that approximately 60 percent of the population is considered overweight. If half of the population is women, then roughly ninety-three million are female shoppers in the double-digit size range. That is a lot of women. Those women are the average, not the exception. I've been one of those women, and I've had many times in my life when I felt like I was not going to find the right things to wear. That's why I got the idea of opening up a clothing store of my own and calling it Average Sizes, because the average woman in America wears a size 14. If the average American woman is a size 14, wouldn't it stand to reason that a size 14 would be the most common size sold? It's not. It seems like sizes 12 and 14 are in fashion hell because manufacturers can't figure out how to make clothes that really appeal to women who are that size. I always hated that most stores carried clothes in small, medium, and large or sizes 0 to 14. If you didn't fit into those sizes there was a separation that suddenly made you "plus" size and forced you into shopping at places like Fashion Bug and Lane Bryant. I had nothing against these stores. In fact, I was grateful for their existence. I just didn't want to feel different for having to shop there. There was a store near us called 5-7-9, and my sister, Julia, and I used to joke that if you combined those sizes, *that* was a size that would fit us!

There are more options now than there used to be, but there is still some stigma attached to shopping in the plus department or at plus-size stores. And don't get me started on some of the things that designers think plus-size women want to wear. It seems as if they think that the bigger you are, the more sparkles or prints you want on your body. I'm sorry, but why would that be true? Why can't plus-size women just have a nice pair of jeans that fit well, and a great black top that hugs in all the right ways? (This is my note to designers out there—do right by the average woman!)

Why is it so hard for an average-size woman to find clothes that fit? According to Women's Wear Daily, *women who used to be a size 8 or 10 and have gained weight often don't want to shop for a size 14 or 16. They end up making do with the clothes they have. Interestingly, women sizes 20 and up, many of whom have likely been plus size their entire lives, seem to be more likely to have accepted themselves physically, and shop as frequently as single-digit-size women.*

Julia once came to a Final Notice show and overheard people talking in the audience, saying, "She can sing but her clothes are too small!" Now, Julia has always been a big girl herself, so she didn't understand why these girls in the audience were commenting on the size of *my* outfits. I was only wearing what the group put me in. The bigger dilemma for me was that I had to conform to their image or I'd be out of the group. We were definitely at a crossroads. Even though I couldn't fit into the clothes they wore most of the time, I was still expected to do all the work in pants that were too tight, too short, and, truthfully, really uncomfortable. The other girls had the look but couldn't sing. This didn't make a lot of sense to me. I moved on.

The next group I was in was called Fate's Cousins, a group I was in with two of my cousins. We picked the name as our way of paying homage to our favorite group at the time, Destiny's Child. Ironically, I was the *smallest* girl in that group. We didn't last very long, but after my experiences with Final Notice, I made sure Fate's Cousins were about one thing and one thing only. *Singing.*

There were plenty of times I auditioned for other groups and didn't get the job because I didn't fit the image. I didn't see this at the time. Then I was just confused, and hurt. I honestly thought that my talent was the thing that should, or should not secure jobs for me. I didn't fully grasp how important image was in show business. One such experience really sticks out in my memory—when I auditioned to be a backup singer for Barry Manilow. I was nineteen years old and probably at my peak weight of around 236 pounds.

I had never been on an audition where I would have to sing *and* dance. I'll dance if I have to and sometimes when I perform, but I don't necessarily think of myself as a dancer. Still, I'm a professional, and I'll do what is required when it is called for.

The audition went amazingly.

I performed a gospel song called "Silver and Gold." All of the casting people there, including Barry Manilow himself, absolutely loved what they heard. They were crazy excited when I finished. Where I come from, people will throw things at you when they think you did a great job. And when I finished singing that day, everyone in the room was throwing things my way. They picked up whatever they had nearby and tossed it at me so I would know they thought it was great. People in the hallway still waiting to audition were saying they didn't want to follow me. "What's the point?" I heard one girl say.

Oh yeah. I killed it.

I waited in the hallway for someone to come tell me a start date.

"I'm so sorry, Jennifer. We don't have anything for you."

You read that right.

That's exactly what they said.

"Are you kidding me?" I asked.

You could have knocked me over with a feather. Turns out, I didn't have the look so I didn't get the part. I was extremely disappointed. I was dismayed. I thought I had nailed it and the job was mine. It took me years to realize that I didn't get the job because of my size. At the time, I was just upset that I wasn't going to get a chance to share my talents with a larger audience.

The thing I got from these experiences was that not everyone has the same values and focus. My focus has always been on talent over looks. This theme of people putting an emphasis on looks first has been a constant reminder throughout my life that most people don't see things in the same way that I do. Looking back, I realize that it has always been my appearance that I have been judged on first. It made a difference whether I was fat or skinny. This is something I never totally accepted but was learning that I had to deal with.

Coming off of the Barry Manilow disappointment, I was given a challenge. At the time, I was signed to a record deal with a Chicago-based independent label called Righteous Records, headed by a man named David Johnson. He created a contest for me to be inspired to lose the weight, pitting me against another girl on the label who was much smaller than I was. David said we both needed to lose weight and whoever lost the most would win money. I am the type of person who doesn't like being told what she can and cannot do. And if you challenge me, I will accept. And don't expect to win, because I will crush you.

Let me say that I've always been a real girl. If I can't do something naturally, I won't do it at all. Period. So I knew that if I wanted to win this contest, I'd be doing it the old-fashioned way—by working for it.

So I started exercising every day. I'd get up in the morning and do my DVD workouts, first with Billy Blanks's Tae Bo and then aerobics with Denise Austin. Next, I'd go jogging around my neighborhood. I heard that people used to look out their window and ask, "Who's that girl running around out there?" It didn't take long for everyone to figure out it was just me. Next I'd then run up and down some local stairs for fifteen minutes and then jog back home. When I wasn't working out around my house, I'd head to the gym.

I started watching what I ate for the first time in my life. I stopped eating fried foods, red meat, pizza, carbonated sodas, and ice cream (all foods I would avoid, as a rule until I started Weight Watchers). I went on a total meat-tox, cheese-tox, and sugar-tox. I ate grilled chicken, brown rice, and broccoli—straight-up diet foods. All the time. And nothing else. I did this same exercise routine for the first half of my day—every day—until I lost sixty pounds and got down to a size 10.

To me, being a size 10 was perfect. I thought, surely I could become a star looking like this. Who would have ever believed that size 10 is still considered plus size in Hollywood? Really, I just didn't get it.

Shortly after this first weight loss, Walter came to me and said, "The world needs to hear you, Jen, and I'm going to make sure they do!" God bless Walter because he would go around finding anything I could sing for or be a part of. Walter found out that Disney was holding auditions for cruise-ship singers at a theater school on the northwest side of Chicago. I hadn't sung for anyone in a while. I had been so focused on losing weight and getting myself in shape. To be honest, I wasn't very excited about the audition but I reluctantly agreed to go. Really, I didn't love the idea of taking a job on a cruise ship and traveling so far from home.

But the audition was two days after my birthday, and I had just gotten a new dress I looked fab in. Since Walter was so insistent, I agreed.

Disney hired me on the spot. Interestingly, the casting director told me they would have hired me regardless of how much I weighed. Disney didn't seem to have the same hang-ups about weight and appearances as other entertainment companies I'd auditioned for in the past. They believed in my talent above everything else. I guess I finally fit the bill for that.

It was around this time that *American Idol* was holding its auditions for its second season. Walter and my mama kept telling me I should try out this time. In the summer of 2002, *American Idol* made its television debut. It wasn't yet the phenomenon it is today, so I didn't pay much attention to it that first year. But my mama watched the show all the time. One day she came to me and said, "Jenny, I think you ought to go and audition for this show."

"Whatever," I said . . . again.

I'd already had my fill of talent shows, and truth be told, I wasn't the least bit interested in this one. But by the time Kelly Clarkson was named the first American Idol, I was stunned that something like that could actually happen on television. I was suddenly embarrassed that I had been so cavalier about this show, and started asking myself, "Why didn't I go?" over and over again. I was completely hooked from that point on.

Unsurprisingly, Walter was on me pretty hard about missing that shot at fame.

Even so, I wasn't so sure about auditioning for *American Idol* now. Since I had already been offered the Disney position, I knew that was a sure thing. If I gave that up to audition for *American Idol*, I'd be taking a risk even I wasn't willing to bet on. I figured that I better go with the sure thing. So, I skipped the second year of *American Idol* to work on the cruise ship.

Disney moved me down to Orlando, Florida, for two months of training before I spent the next six months performing on the ship. I was cast as one of the Muses in a production of *Hercules the Musical*, and I also had a solo in *Disney Dreams*, which was a show made up of songs and clips from Disney classics. My song was "The Circle of Life" from *The Lion King*.

The shows were a lot of fun but definitely rigorous and grueling. I had to dance and sing all throughout the productions. Thankfully my weight was in a good place, which made it easier for me to keep up the pace than if I had been heavier.

Doing those shows was so energizing, and the audiences were amazing week after week. There's something wonderful about entertaining people on vacation. Everyone is there to have a good time. Even though I loved performing each night, being on the ship, was a little boring, because we'd go to the same places over and over again. I never knew what day it was, because they were all pretty much the same.

I've always been a homebody and a mama's girl, so being away from my family, stuck on a cruise ship, wasn't easy. I'm going to be honest and tell you that two days into my contract I began counting down the days until I could get off the ship and go home. I genuinely missed my family. I lasted the eight months working for Disney, and then I went home. That was enough for me.

In the end, I was extremely grateful for the time I spent on the ship, especially because it gave me the opportunity to save up my pay. I have always been a saver, but living on the ship meant all my meals and living expenses were covered and I could save a lot.

As soon as I got back to Chicago, Walter surprised me with the news that he had arranged for us to go audition for season three of

American Idol. He had already bought the plane tickets. There was no way I could back out. Just two days after my return from the cruise ship, he and I headed down to Atlanta, where I would audition among thousands of other hopefuls. And as fate would have it, this is really where it all began.

CHAPTER THREE

SPOTLIGHT

Walter and I arrived in Atlanta and headed straight to the Georgia Dome, where the first round of auditions for the 2004 season of *American Idol* were taking place. When we arrived, the show staff gave me a bracelet with a number on it to hold my place. The staff told auditioning hopefuls from the start that if we left or missed our number being called, we would miss our chance to audition.

I didn't have a job to get back to. I could afford to wait for my shot to audition. As the day went on, I could see the line trickle down as one by one people gave up before they even tried.

Basically, the producers wanted us to sleep inside of that dome and wait it out until it was our turn to sing. People had sleeping bags, full camping gear with them. Walter and I only had the tiny blanket and leftover bags of peanuts and pretzels that we took from the airplane. The blanket was hardly big enough to keep either of us warm for the night. We were just not prepared for camping out anywhere, much less on the floor of the Georgia Dome. I also knew I needed some sleep so my voice would be at its best. Thankfully, I had enough money saved to get Walter and myself a hotel room for the night. I also figured my audition number was high enough that I could slip away. I could get a good night's sleep and come back fresh early the next morning for my audition, and that's just what we did. We quietly snuck off-site and slept in a nearby hotel on that first night. Luckily, when we came back the next morning, they hadn't called my number yet.

The second day, while waiting my turn, I sat back and took in everything that was happening around me. Being at the dome was like a dream come true because it was a room full of amazing singers from all over the world. Eleven thousand of them! Even though it's called *American Idol*, I met hopefuls from South America, Canada, and Europe. What was absolutely thrilling was that every person was there for the same reason—to sing. Some of the kids formed choirs and sang off in a corner. Others were running around showing off their skills to one another. While I had an appreciation for all of the talent, I didn't do either. I wanted to wait for my moment. I was going to sing when it counted and that meant for the talent judges. So Walter and I pretty much stayed to ourselves until it was time for me to sing.

The actual audition took place inside the dome, where there were eleven tables spread across the span of the football field. There were people everywhere. It looked like those tables were handing out cheese samples or something like that because of the way organizers quickly moved people in and out. Randy, Paula, and Simon were not a part of this round. They didn't actually come into the process until your final audition—if you made it that far.

When you're called to the field, you are directed to one of the eleven tables where you are asked to sing at the same time as the other ten contestants down the row. It is a little distracting to have eleven people concurrently singing. If you don't have a great ear, you will likely get distracted by the others. And if that happens, you'll get a "Don't call us, we'll call you. Thank you very much, good-bye."

My audition took place very early that morning. I was a little worried that my voice wouldn't be ready as I hadn't warmed up yet the way I usually did before I sang. But now was my time to show what I could do.

For my audition, I chose an outfit that I thought looked great on me. I was wearing black corduroy fitted pants, a white halter top that was too short so my stomach hung out, a black bra that showed, always a great look, and really big hair. I mean *big* hair. I had done my eyeliner in thick black Cleopatra swoops up to the outer brim of my eyes. I thought I looked fierce and no one could tell me otherwise. Oh, don't get me wrong. Walter tried to talk me out of this look, but I didn't want to hear it. And trust me, there were some *amazing* getups going on in the dome that day. Looking back now, though, I would have definitely changed my hair.

"Hello. My name is Jennifer Hudson."

"And what are you going to sing for us today?" one of the producers asked.

" 'This Empty Place,' by Cissy Houston."

"All right. Go ahead and begin."

I opened up my big mouth and did my thing—belted out that tune. Everyone in the venue heard my audition. When it was over, they all started clapping. I was so flattered, but also shocked that so many people seemed to know the song I had chosen. We're talking about Whitney's mama so I guess I shouldn't have been that surprised. Even so, they asked me if I could sing one more song for them, something more current and familiar. I chose Celine Dion's "The Power of Love," which I thought would show them a big leap in range and a total switch in genre. When I finished that song, I thought I had done really well—but the producers asked me to sing still one more song. This time I chose "Survivor" by Destiny's Child, a song I'd been singing for years and felt very comfortable with.

In the end, I had gone through three eras, genres, and artists. Thank God I did, because it got me through to the next audition phase. When I finished my last song, I was sent to the right, while those who weren't being asked to stay were sent to the left. As I was leaving, I overheard two boys say, "We can't sing after her!" But they did and they made it, too. I met them afterward and shared a good laugh together about their comment.

The second audition meant going back to Atlanta a few weeks later and singing for the executive producers of the show, Nigel Lythgoe, Ken Warwick, and Cecile Frot-Coutaz. That audition took place in a much smaller venue than the dome. The producers told me to do the exact same thing as I had done in my first audition. Meeting the executive producers was significantly more intense than the prior audition. To be honest, at the time I found their presence to be a little intimidating.

But when I sang "The Power of Love," I could see it in their eyes that I would be going on to the next round in the audition process.

The third round of auditions took place in Pasadena, California, which is where I first actually met Randy Jackson, Paula Abdul, and Simon Cowell. I walked into the room wearing a black Versace dress that I had found while shopping in Atlanta during the second audition. It had a hole cut out between my breasts and the belly button, exposing my midriff. Truth be told, I thought it was a good look. I always joked that my *present gut* was simply my *future abs*. I used to walk around patting my stomach telling everyone I had a six-pack. Of course, they couldn't see it, but it was there, just waiting to come out! Funnily, when my audition aired on television, network censors insisted that the cutout in my dress be filled in; this made it look like it was a simple black dress.

Rest assured that I was still rocking my big hair and swoopy eyes. I introduced myself to the judges and told Randy, Paula, and Simon that I had just finished a job singing on a Disney cruise ship.

"We're expecting something more than a cruise-ship performance," Randy said.

I knew just what he meant.

I sang Aretha Franklin's "Share Your Love with Me" for the judges. When I finished, Randy said I was "brilliant. Absolutely brilliant. The best singer I've heard so far."

Paula seconded him, saying, "No doubt about it—you can sing your . . . behind off! You've got an excellent voice."

Simon didn't actually comment at that time. He simply told the judges to vote, and then said, "Jennifer, see you in Hollywood!"

"Yes!" I said as I pumped my fist in the air.

Oh, yeah, I was going to Hollywood.

My mama, my sister, and Walter were waiting for me in the hallway. They were screaming at the top of their lungs when I came out of the room. I was amazed and excited because I had made it. I overheard Ryan Seacrest say, "Now *that* is how you celebrate."

I was beyond happy. I couldn't believe that I had a chance to be part of this show that had turned Kelly Clarkson and Ruben Studdard into stars overnight. I couldn't believe that Jennifer Hudson, from the South Side of Chicago, was going to get to sing on what was now the most-watched television show in America. I couldn't believe that my voice was going to be heard by millions of people.

I arrived in Los Angeles in early 2004 to start filming season three of *American Idol*. My main goal going into the auditions was to make it far enough to hear Simon tell me I was the best singer he'd seen. I wouldn't stop giving my all in that competition until I could hear him say that. And before all was said and done, I hoped he would. I always set goals for myself so I have something to work toward. This was my goal for *American Idol*.

I ended up in the final twelve by a stroke of luck. I was picked as one of the judges' wild-card contestants. That was the start of what was a very strange experience for me. I went into *American Idol* thinking it was just another talent show, and quickly learned that this was in no way the case. People reacted to my voice, but they also reacted to me and my look and my stage presence. I was starting to realize what an integral part image was to success in Hollywood.

I was grateful when I made it to the final twelve because I was being given a third chance in a single-chance business. I had made it past the executive producers, I had been sent to Hollywood, and now I was in the final round. I had to make the most of it, and put my best foot forward.

The final twelve contestants on *American Idol* have a tremendous opportunity, one unlike any that you can really imagine unless you've done it. The exposure it provides for someone who has a dream to be a performer is unparalleled. But along with the opportunity comes a very packed schedule. We had a lot of long days, so the 9 P.M. curfew was not only important, but necessary. By the end of every day, I was very tired.

The final twelve lived together in a large house in the Hollywood Hills. The bedroom for the female contestants was sort of set up like a slumber party. We were all in the same room. I shared a room with Fantasia Barrino, La Toya London, Camile Velasco, and Amy Adams. There was a cook in the house who prepared meals for us, and we ate what was prepared, together. We were together all the time. Sometimes things were tense.

Early on, I remember one of the musical directors from *American Idol* telling me that everything about me was too big. She said my voice was too big, my size was too big, and my personality was too big.

"Isn't that what being a star is?" I asked. "Stars are larger than life!"

I didn't understand her motivation in telling me that. Perhaps she was trying to break me down. Who knows? Clearly, she wasn't a fan. And clearly, this was not another talent show. This was reality.

Once you make the final twelve, the show provides you with a stylist and makeup artist who are there to help you create your signature look. Before that, however, you are completely on your own. Needless to say, some of my choices got some attention. In those early rounds I wore some outfits that probably put the focus on everything but my voice. I was still thinking that my talent should be the thing people concentrated on, but I was now learning that part of "making it" was cultivating a whole package. Obviously my look didn't fit into the right package at this point.

I'll never forget Simon telling me that my conservative white skirt suit reminded him of a "leather nurse look." When I chose to wear a metallic silver jumpsuit, he said I reminded him of "something a Thanksgiving turkey should be wrapped in." I took it in stride, though. I told him not to knock it until he checked it out and then proceeded to model it for him like I was working the runway in a Paris fashion show. Simon also said that I looked "hideous" in my custom-made pink taffeta dress. This was a dress that I had designed myself, and had made for me by a friend. I liked it. But even my sister called to say I looked like I should be on an Easter egg hunt. So, maybe that outfit wasn't my best, but at least the judges said they liked my song that night, and to me, that was the reason I was there.

Look, I'd been through years of cheeky comments about my fashion choices. I endured them from my siblings; I heard them during the Final Notice days. That said, I did sometimes wonder if I would have heard these sorts of things if I was rail thin. I didn't always have the best things to choose from when it came to my outfits—the options weren't there in the way they were for the ladies who wore "normal" sizes. Everyone told me to hide my curves, the very things I loved about my body. Once I had a stylist, it was all about suit jackets and things that covered me up. I found it all so confusing.

Luckily, there was a fan base building for me out there. Their support helped me keep my confidence high. There wasn't much of anything the judges could say that would have made me fold and give up my dream. Believe me; I'd heard much worse than what those judges were dishing out.

When it comes time to pick our songs, each contestant has a certain amount of leeway. We received our category for the week on the Sunday before the show. "This week is country week" or "This week is Motown week." The producers then give you a catalog of music and let you pick your song from that particular selection. Sometimes the producers would direct you toward a specific song, but *mostly* they let you decide on whatever you want to sing.

We'd go into the studio and record our song on Monday so the band could hear the arrangements, which were often different than the original recording, and then they would break it down to fit the allotted time for our performance on the broadcast. A typical *American Idol* performance comes in a little under the four-minute mark. Once the timing has been worked out, we were given until 5 P.M. the next day, Tuesday, to nail it down. The show aired live Tuesday night. All in all, we really only got two days to learn and perfect our selections before going in front of the cameras and singing for the judges. In that time we also had to pick our "look" for the show and work on our stage presence.

My first night of performing, I sang John Lennon's "Imagine." The world was finally getting to hear me sing. That night was an unbelievable blessing for me because it meant that I had reached that goal. I was overjoyed and overcome with so much emotion that I got very teary standing with Ryan Seacrest afterward. I was living my dream.

Season three was the first season *American Idol* brought in celebrity guest judges to coach us for particular episodes. I had the honor and privilege to work with some of the greatest talents in the music business, such as Sir Elton John, and from the film world, Quentin Tarantino. Elton John was a guest judge during week four. I absolutely loved working with him—we connected from the very start. From the moment we met, he became my mentor, and as it would turn out, after my time on the show he was my biggest advocate.

When Elton came to rehearsals that week, he said he thought I was destined to become the next *American Idol*. He loved my voice and supported me in a kind and loving way. Of course, I chose "The Circle of Life" as my song that week. I'd sung it many times before while working on the Disney cruise ship, but I had never sung it like I did that week—and that was all due to the guidance I received from its composer, Sir Elton John.

Quentin Tarantino was the celebrity guest judge during week

five on the show producers called "Movie Night." He was apparently a big fan of the show. To be totally honest, I didn't really know who Quentin Tarantino was at that point. I had never seen any of his movies before the producers of *American Idol* said we'd be attending a screening of his latest film, *Kill Bill: Vol. 2*. Believe it or not, I actually fell asleep at the screening. Now, for those of you who have seen *Kill Bill: Vol. 2*, you know it is hardly a movie to put you to sleep. But I was so tired from our nonstop schedule and being on the go, go, go that a dark movie theater became the perfect nap spot.

After the screening, all of the contestants and crew had a reception for Quentin. I still hadn't met him, so I didn't realize that the guy who had asked me what I thought of the movie was actually the director.

"I fell asleep!" I said, completely oblivious to whom I was speaking. Thank goodness Quentin has a great sense of humor because his reaction was simply to laugh. I am hoping he thought I was kidding. Later, when I realized who he was, I figured I blew any chance I had of ever being in a Quentin Tarantino movie. Funny enough, at his request, I auditioned for him several years later. I was told to show up at his house wearing cutoff blue jean shorts and flip-flops. I didn't get the part, but I hope I'll get another chance to work with him one day!

In the end, Quentin loved my performance on the show that week, for which I sang Whitney Houston's "I Have Nothing," later commenting, "Hudson takes on Houston and wins!" That was the highest compliment I could ever imagine because I *love* Whitney Houston. She is one of my greatest musical inspirations and has been for as long as I have been singing. Thanks, Quentin, but Ms. Houston will always be the gold standard. I am just flattered to be compared to her.

My last week on the show, none other than Barry Manilow was the special guest. I was wondering if Barry would remember me. It would be the first time I saw him since my audition to become his backup singer. The audition that I thought I had nailed, only to be disappointed.

Sure enough, when we met again, Barry said, "Don't I know you from somewhere?" When I reminded him, he remembered me and my audition right away, which was really flattering. He said he was glad to finally be working together. That acknowledgment made me better. The fact that he remembered me meant so much. It's experiences like that that keep me from dwelling on the jobs I didn't get or what didn't work out as planned, because I am a true believer that what is supposed to happen will.

My original song choice that week was "All the Time," a song Barry Manilow wrote for Dionne Warwick. I had already made up my mind about my song choice when someone told me that La Toya had decided to do that song, too. So in the end, I ended up singing Barry's "Weekend in New England." We worked hard to create a performance that would wow America and the judges.

Barry wanted to structure the arrangement of the song in the same way he had done for Jennifer Holliday, a singer he said I reminded him of. It was an ironic comparison, given what would happen next, but I had no idea how connected I was to her at that moment. Barry knew that the arrangement he had done for her on this song would work for me, and it was a truly brilliant arrangement. In the end, it was perfect. I sang my heart out; I thought I brought the house down. It turned out that America didn't agree.

On elimination night, as usual, the safe contestants were separated from the bottom three. George Huff was the odd man standing, awaiting his group assignment. Ryan told him to "join the top group" because he was, in fact, also safe. He hesitated as he slowly made his way toward Fantasia, La Toya, and me.

"George, I said step into the *top* group," Ryan said. "You're in the wrong group because tonight, this is our bottom three— Fantasia, Jennifer Hudson, and La Toya London, America!"

The look of total shock came over everyone's faces, including my own, as the crowd booed and screamed in total disapproval. George, obviously confused, slowly walked toward the other group, which was made up of John Stevens, Diana DeGarmo, and Jasmine Trias, leaving us on our own.

Ryan asked each of the judges what they thought had happened.

When it came time for Simon's comments, he started off by saying, "Tongue . . . floor." I knew what he was feeling. But then he pointed out that the others who were safe had earned it. And again, he was right.

In a rare effort not to draw out the final results, Ryan quickly sent La Toya to the couch, where she was safe and would be back to fight for the title the following week, leaving Fantasia and me on the stage anxiously awaiting our fate. We stood there together, holding hands, like we were lifelong best friends. The whole moment was surreal. One of us was definitely going home. We were told that it was the smallest margin ever that separated two contestants in the bottom two, yet enough of a distance to end the journey for one of us, too.

Secretly, I was praying to God, "Let it be me." I was ready. I knew that *American Idol* was a fantastic launching pad. I didn't care if I won or not. As far as I was concerned, my dream had already come true when I was allowed to sing for millions of Americans for those six incredible weeks.

And then it was time for the moment of truth.

Ryan walked over with the results in his hand and said, "The person going home tonight, in a previous show had the highest number of votes but tonight has the lowest. And that person is . . . Jennifer Hudson."

On April 21, 2004, I was the sixth contestant voted off of *American Idol* season three. I wasn't upset. I wasn't disappointed. To be totally honest, I was relieved. I endured so much to be on that show. I was proud of the struggles I went through because I was, and continue to be, a survivor. But it was time for me to take another step.

As I stood watching my farewell video, I realized that there was so much to be grateful for, too. Going in to *American Idol*, your mind is blown, thinking that you are going to be part of this massive television show. But once you are on the inside, you see it is something so much more than just a show. It is like a boot camp for the music business. It gives you tough skin and a realistic opportunity to see what it is like to live that way. It is an amazing chance to live the life of a famous musician, at least for a little while. To the average person on the street, you're a celebrity, because they see you on TV every week. But to the music executives and Hollywood, you are on the bottom, with a lot of work to do to keep rising to the top. I can't imagine being in a place that could have prepared me any better for my career than *American Idol*. I got to meet people like Elton John and I reconnected with Barry Manilow, both of whom became big fans of mine because of the show. And even Simon Cowell inspired me to follow my dreams, despite the fact that he was a pretty tough critic at times.

I knew in my gut that winning *American Idol* wasn't what God had planned for me. I knew I was going to get to sing again, and that I just had to wait for the right opportunity.

When all was said and done, I wasn't expecting to feel so emotional after leaving the studio that night. I actually cried for a few minutes in the limousine on the way back to the *Idol* house after the show, and again the day after my elimination. I wasn't sad to be leaving the show so much as I was disappointed, and more so, I felt like I was disappointing others, like Walter and my family. Plus, there were so many fans who wanted to see me get to the finals. And for their love and support, I will always be eternally grateful because I know in the deepest part of my heart and soul, those fans are the reason I was able to take my leap off the *Idol* stage.

I wiped away those final tears as the limousine swept me off to the airport so I could fly to New York City and do a myriad of press. Since my elimination had caused such an uproar, there were several extra interviews added to my already full schedule. I stayed in New York for about a week answering as many questions as I could about what I thought went wrong. But inside, I was okay with what had happened. It was hard for a lot of people to understand that sentiment, but I was just at peace with it. And when the storm finally died down, I flew back to Chicago and my family.

We started rehearsals for the *American Idol* Tour a couple of days after Fantasia was named the new American Idol. I was really excited to be a part of that experience because I had never even been to a concert and now, here I was—part of one! I had always vowed that the first concert I wanted to go to would be my own. I felt so lucky.

The tour was a real treat. I loved being onstage, singing and giving everything I had to the audiences each night—especially with so many other talented people. Being on that tour was like a dream come true because we could finally be successful, *together.* Listening to George Huff sing gospel, and warmly embracing music with Fantasia and La Toya was something I will never forget. If I could bring them all back together, I would. Once the tension of the competition had gone away, it was just pure fun.

I'm so lucky to have been able to maintain my relationship with George—he's now one of the backup singers for me on tour! He is such a dear friend. There will always be an inexplicable bond among all of us from season three, which I hope they all feel as much as I do.

After *American Idol,* life was never the same again. I suddenly saw that I was a familiar face to so many strangers. They saw me as famous even though I had barely started my journey. I had, for the first time in my life, real *fans* from outside of Chicago. It was so cool!

At the time, Walter was still acting as my manager. Sharing my voice with others is what I knew I needed to do, so I hit the road on my own, doing club work and other appearances. God bless the gay community, who embraced my act from the very start. For a while there, it seemed like I was always in Atlanta performing at a gay club.

I was only twenty-two years old and I had been on one of the biggest shows on television, on a coast-to-coast tour that I loved, and was now making a pretty good living singing in clubs on the weekends. But I was just getting started.

CHAPTER FOUR

WHERE YOU AT

Six months after I finished *American Idol*, I was approached by Ed Whitlow, one of the directors I had worked with on the Disney cruise ship, to record an album. Ed said he knew a producer who had previously worked with *NSYNC in the past and who could work with me on a couple of songs. Ed reminded me of Walter in a lot of ways. He was willing to do whatever it took to get people to hear my voice. So, I left Chicago and moved to Orlando, Florida, to begin work on an album. Ed allowed me to stay at his home while we worked on putting a record deal together for me and then I went to work in the studio. I had no idea if anyone would ever hear the music we were working on, but I was simply happy to get into the studio.

For several months, the only thing I did was go to the studio and record. I did a few performances whenever they came up. I took a quick trip to Los Angeles to audition for a part in the movie version of *Rent*—which I didn't get. It seemed God had something else in store for me. In the meantime, I kept working.

In Florida, I was a bit off the radar. I also didn't really focus on my weight at all. I ate what I wanted, relaxed when I could. It was like I needed to hit pause after the hectic but great year I had. I just focused on my music and making my first album.

It was around early spring when I began hearing about a buzz in Hollywood that Jennifer Hudson was being considered to play the role of Effie White in the upcoming film adaptation of the highly popular and successful musical *Dreamgirls*. I kept seeing articles and reading blogs that mentioned me for the part, but I hadn't heard from anyone connected to the film. I had no idea why or how the rumor got started. I had never even seen the stage version. I was completely clueless about the story, music, or its history. I didn't know anything about the character of Effie White. I only knew of Jennifer Holliday, the originator of the role, because Barry Manilow had spoken of her on *American Idol*. I had never even heard her sing, and I certainly hadn't heard Effie's signature song from the show.

As the rumors began to swirl, I needed to find out who Effie White was and why people were saying I was perfect to play her.

Set in the turbulent early 1960s to mid-1970s, the story of *Dreamgirls* follows the rise of three women—Effie, Deena, and

Lorrell, best friends from Chicago (in the movie they're from Detroit), who form a singing group called the Dreamettes. The group goes to New York City to perform in a talent show at the Apollo Theater in Harlem. They don't win the competition, but backstage they meet an ambitious young manager by the name of Curtis Taylor Jr. Curtis gets the group a spot as the backup singers for James "Thunder" Early, though he makes moves for them to eventually break out on their own. Curtis reshapes the group to "cross over" from the R&B genre to the more lucrative and emerging pop music scene. Effie White, who had been the lead singer of the group due to her amazing voice, is sidelined because as a full-figured woman, she doesn't fit the group's image as Curtis sees it. Effie's journey is at the emotional center of the film and the show, as she resents the change in the group and is eventually replaced, only then to have her life spiral downward as her career stalls. But Effie hangs on and eventually finds success, and more important, peace.

Okay, so this was a role I could completely sink my teeth into. I knew exactly how it felt to be judged for your look. I knew what it was like to not get jobs because you didn't fit an "image." I knew what it was like to deal with people who thought there were things more important than talent. This was practically *my* life. This was a role I had to play.

It turns out that the producers of the film were in fact trying to reach me, but since I didn't really have a manager at this point

(Walter had taken a job abroad during this time), no one associated with the film knew how to find me.

At the time, my cousin Marita Hudson was a publicist for *Ebony* magazine. We called ourselves J-Hud and M-Hud. She is well-known in the entertainment industry and everyone knows we are related. Luckily, one of the casting agents made the connection, too, and figured Marita could contact me. They finally put a call in to Marita and asked if she would relay the message that the producers of *Dreamgirls* would like to meet me.

Her phone call to me went something like this:

"Hello?"

"Girl, it's Marita. Some casting people phoned and said they want to fly you to New York to audition for *Dreamgirls*!"

That was all I needed to hear.

"I waited, Jesus—you said it was going to happen and now it is here!" I screamed.

All I had to do now was pick a song to audition with and study the script that the studio sent to me ahead of time. After giving it a lot of thought, I decided to sing "Easy to Be Hard" from *Hair* because it was similar to the music from *Dreamgirls* and it was also from a musical that made it on Broadway. Plus, I thought the song really showcased my vocal ability.

Marita met me in New York so she could accompany me to the audition. A lot about that first audition is a blur, but I went into it thinking that I had to fully encompass the character of Effie. I felt so connected to her—another big girl with a big voice. I wondered if all the women auditioning were full figured. I wondered if the producers were looking for someone with a different look than mine, even though I knew I could fill that role perfectly. I wore a simple black dress and readied my voice.

I'm almost certain that the film's director, Bill Condon, an Oscar winner for his screenplay for *Gods and Monsters* and a nominee for the screenplay adaptation of *Chicago*, and casting director Jay Binder were both there the day I auditioned. Besides that, there isn't much I can recall, except feeling like I had done a really good job.

"If we don't call you by July, you probably didn't get the part," someone said to me before I left.

It was only April. I had to wait three months to see what happened next? That was going to be hard—much harder than results night on *American Idol*. Luckily I could go back to Florida and continue working on my album. And wait for news.

It turned out that 782 other women had auditioned for the role of Effie. The producers were intent on casting a relative unknown actress and searched the country, from Hollywood to Harlem, to find their Effie. All kinds of women, in all shapes and sizes, tried out for that part. Would you believe that the script called for Effie to be much taller and heavier than I was at the time? I guess I didn't have to worry too much about not getting the role because I was too heavy. The irony of that became much clearer to me later.

May came and went, then June and then July—and I received no call. My heart sank with the thought that someone else had gotten the role. I couldn't get Effie out of my head, and I hated thinking that another actress would play her. Had the audition not gone as well as I had thought?

But the producers hadn't cast someone else. On the last day of July I received a call in Florida, telling me that I needed to go to Los Angeles for a second audition. This time they said they wanted me to sing *the* song.

Oh yeah.

That song.

The casting department sent me the sheet music so I could prepare for my next audition. I only received part of the song, not the whole thing. I prepared that portion as best as I could. When I got to the audition, much to my surprise, the woman who went just before I did sang the *entire* song. I was panicking because I didn't know the *whole* song. There was no way I could go into that room pretending I knew the entire song without failing. I certainly didn't want to go in making excuses, as that is not my style. So I slowly walked through the doors and into the room, and proceeded to sing the part I knew. Needless to say, this wasn't my finest hour. I was sure they would cross my name off their potential Effie list. I was devastated.

But they didn't.

Bill Condon got word about what had happened with my sheet

music. About a month after that audition, someone called to sign me to a two-week-hold contract. This meant that I could be given the role sometime in the next two weeks, but that they weren't obligated in any way to hire me. Also, for those two weeks, I couldn't agree to do anything else. Of course, I quickly signed. Once again, I had been given another chance in a one-chance business. I couldn't believe how blessed I was.

Those two weeks were pure torture. I was on pins and needles the whole time. I was so close . . . and yet I still felt so far. Nearly six months had lapsed since I first received the call to audition. They literally waited until the very last second to call. But they called.

I was once again asked to come out to Los Angeles, this time for a screen test. In fact, they asked me to drop everything and hop on a flight that same day.

"And Jennifer, this time, bring enough stuff with you in case you're asked to stay."

"How much stuff is that?" I asked.

"Everything you own."

I ran out of the recording studio, drove home as fast as I could so I could quickly pack and make my flight. Somewhere in the middle of that hurricane moment, I got a fax of the full sheet music for "And I Am Telling You I'm Not Going" so I could learn the entire song. By the time those wheels touched down in La-La Land, I needed to know that baby inside and out.

I spent the entire six-hour flight singing to myself. I didn't care who heard me or what they thought. I'd occasionally apologize for disrupting the other passengers, but knew what I had to do. I had to focus on my goal. I had to keep the faith and not let anything get in the way of the job in front to me. I am sure there were a few people on board who recognized me from *American Idol*, but there were many more praying to God I'd shut my big mouth!

By the time we landed, it was very late at night. I went straight to bed so I would be well rested for my big day ahead. I woke up extra early the next morning, so excited to get to the audition that I was nearly jumping out of my skin.

I called my mama before heading to the studio. Being the good mama that she was, she said, "If some things don't work out and you don't get it, then that is okay because something else, something bigger will come."

I heard her and understood why she was saying that to me, so on the ride over, I kept telling myself, "If it's meant for me, it will be." Those words are my mantra in life, and it has never let me down.

It soon became painfully obvious to me that my purpose for being in L.A. was not just another audition. This was a screen test—the last stop, the final step to getting the coveted part. I knew all the other big roles had been cast at this point. If I was cast as Effie, I'd be working alongside a roster of incredible talents—Jamie Foxx, Danny Glover, Beyoncé Knowles, and Eddie Murphy—just to name a few.

I was completely green at this point in my career. I had never had a screen test before. It was like being under a microscope, and I'd be lying if I told you that I didn't feel self-conscious. The screen test took almost six hours. First, they dressed me as Effie, did my hair and makeup so I would look like Effie, and then checked every bit of my appearance. And I mean every bit. They shot my profile from every possible angle, looking at my body from head to toe. I felt scrutinized in a way that I never had before. This was like *American Idol* times a million. I felt like every inch of my body was on display.

When they finished shooting my screen test, the producers brought me into a room and asked me to do the pivotal scene where Effie sings her big song. I did this over and over and over again.

After several hours, I heard someone in the room whisper, "Her voice is the only one that has sustained the entire time."

I did the best I could and gave it my very best effort. And before I left the studio, I was told I would be going home.

I got on a plane and went back to Orlando.

I wasn't sure what to make of this. I didn't have the part yet. But no one else did, either. So, when I walked through my front door, I placed my suitcase in the middle of the floor on the landing as a show of faith. I didn't unpack a thing. I would just wait for them to call me back. I really hoped they would.

By the following morning, I was already back in the studio recording my album. It was a weekend, so our regular crew wasn't there. I was in the booth recording when I heard that I had a phone call. I instinctively knew it was about the movie. I stepped outside to take the call. I stood still, waiting to hear my fate.

"Jennifer Hudson . . ." It was Bill Condon calling. He spoke slowly and methodically, as if he was about to deliver a verdict in a courtroom.

I was barely breathing, waiting with fantastic anticipation as my heart lay on the ground.

"Jennifer Hudson, I called to tell you that you are Effie White!"

"WOOOOOOOO!" I let out a scream of relief that turned to tears of sheer joy.

I did it! I made it!

I fell to my knees and cried. I was so relieved and overwhelmed and thrilled and thankful.

Bill asked me to get on a flight that same day. Of course, I said I would.

I've been gone ever since.

CHAPTER FIVE

I'M YOUR *DREAMGIRL* . . .

When I got the role as Effie in *Dreamgirls*, I had never done any professional acting. On the flight to Los Angeles, I kept reminding myself of this blessing God had given me. My grandma used to praise the Lord and say, "How great thou art!" She was talking about the wonders of God's love and His glory. Looking out the window of my plane I realized that, perhaps for the first time in my life, I truly understood what she meant. She was talking about the wonders of this world, wonders that I was now going to see. I cried tears of joy for most of that flight.

One of the first things I found out when I got to Los Angeles to start shooting was that in order to take this role, I was going to have to *gain* weight. You read that right. Gain weight! The script called for Effie to be heavier than I was at the time, and I needed to put on some pounds. Needless to say, I was pretty surprised. So many times I had felt judged for being too big, had lost jobs because I didn't fit the image required. And now, for the first time ever, I was told I was *too small*! Who gets a job in Hollywood and has to *gain* weight?

Me!

I was told to put on an extra twenty pounds before shooting started so I could really look like Effie as the director wanted her to appear. By gaining the weight, I wouldn't have to wear padded costumes or anything. I could be more "natural." Okay, I thought. I know how to do this—I can put on pounds if that is what was required. I launched into a diet of cookies, cakes, and pies all day, every day.

In addition to my new eating regimen, I started rehearsals right away, too. Every day I would walk around the studios like a high school student going to class, with my backpack slung over my shoulder, full of all the different clothes I would need. I went from dance class to vocal class to acting class. I was constantly on the go. In fact, there was so much physical activity during rehearsals that despite my carb-heavy, sugar-laden diet, I started losing weight. The producers quickly noticed my weight loss and told me I needed to focus on gaining. I kicked up my intake a notch and continued to load up on calories, so I could keep on the pounds despite my very active schedule. It wasn't easy, but I knew I couldn't disappoint the producers.

The film officially started shooting on January 9, 2006. Being on the set of *Dreamgirls* was nothing short of—well, a dream come true. First, I actually got to be in this film, and second, I was set to work with some of the biggest stars on the planet. Eddie Murphy, Danny Glover—these were actors I grew up watching. I had been a big Destiny's Child fan, so it was a thrill to work with Beyoncé. And none other than Jamie Foxx, who had just won an Oscar for his amazing performance as Ray Charles, was going to be my love interest. The first time I met Jamie was on the set. We had never said so much as a hello to each other before that first scene together. After doing *American Idol*, I had made a personal promise that I would never let anyone ever intimidate me again. But Lord help me, the first time I met Jamie, I was scared. He walked onto the set and the director said, "Action. . . . Okay, kiss!"

Huh? I thought. I was shocked. I was hoping Jamie and I would at least be introduced before we launched into a kissing scene! Oh well, I had a job to do. And luckily, Jamie had done this all a few times before, so he did his best to make me feel comfortable. Here I was, an actress playing her first scene, and I had to kiss Jamie Foxx square on the mouth.

As filming continued, I remember thinking my grandma would have loved seeing all that was happening to me.

"Look, Grandma. Look at what I am doing." I had conversations with her in my head, especially while listening to the music from *Dreamgirls*.

Whenever I wasn't singing or dancing, I wore my headphones, learning the songs for the movie. I would listen closely to those songs, and ask myself the question that I always ask when I'm learning new music: "What is the message I am trying to get across? What does this song mean?" I need to feel the meaning of the song to be able to perform it with emotion. Music always means something. Music is powerful. It can be both spiritual and emotional. My grandmother taught me that all great singers sing with purpose. For this movie, every song had a purpose in that it propelled the story forward. The songs were almost as important as the dialogue—especially for Effie, who was the girl known for her amazing voice. Effie shared her heartache, her joys through singing. If I was going to play Effie with all my heart, I had to do the same. I certainly used that approach when it came time to do my big scene.

Whenever "And I Am Telling You I'm Not Going" came on my headphones, it felt as if the ghost of my grandma was singing in my ears. I could hear her shouting praise and singing gospel like I was seven years old again watching her in church. Once I started singing the song, it was as if she could see me. Feeling her presence helped me find my emotion to power through that very challenging scene.

I have a cousin who once told me not to sing *at* a song, but to just sing the song—and there is a difference. I sink my teeth into a song and attack it like Jaws. If I can't feel the song when I'm singing it, how can I expect the listener to? Every song tells a story. My job is to be the storyteller. I knew that was exactly what I needed to do going into my big scene—I had to own it and make it mine.

My mama used to tell me that she thought I usually worked best under pressure. I never noticed that about myself, but she sure did. When I was a little girl, I used to run around our family church begging for my first solo. When the pastor finally gave me that chance, I was terrified. It was like I was on the edge of a nervous breakdown. But, I also remember feeling a certain exhilarating electricity about it, too. Those feelings are what gave me the presence of mind I needed when it came time to sing in front of a crowd. I became addicted to the anxiety of performing every bit as much as the thrill of it. Now, when I don't have that sense of panic before performing, I worry about being too calm.

I was anything but calm when it came time to film "And I Am Telling You I'm Not Going." That song is part of one of the most important scenes in the movie. I am not sure I really understood just how big it actually was until after we finished filming. It didn't register until after I completed the scene that I, an unknown actress, had been given the role of a lifetime. The lyrics "And you're gonna love me . . ." were especially poignant because for me, they marked my return to the world stage after my time on *American Idol.* I felt like I was being given a huge chance to send a message out to the world about what I could really do. Truly, I was overwhelmed.

Not knowing the impact of that scene at the time is probably what helped get me through it. What I did know all too well was how Effie felt in that moment after being told she had to leave the group because she didn't fit the image. Lord knows I had been there too many times myself. This was my story every bit as much as it was Effie's. For things to be real, they have to come from a real place. I had lived these moments myself, more than once, and now I could bring all of my past rejection, pain, anger, confusion, and frustration to life through Effie White.

The day we shot my big scene, the set was full of lots of people I didn't recognize—from drivers to crew. Spike Lee and Jamie Foxx came to watch me. When I did my first take, I felt a little self-conscious with so many eyes watching. It was a little like singing in the shower, and turning around to find a bathroom full of people. Luckily, that feeling didn't last very long. By the time I got through that first take, it didn't matter who was there—as far as I was concerned, it was just Grandma and me. I was Effie, and I was feeling her pain.

People gathered all day long to watch. One by one, I could see tears in most everyone's eyes as I sang straight from my gut take after take after take. By the end of the first day, my head was pounding, I was emotionally exhausted and I wanted to rest. Surely, I thought, they had captured the footage they needed. But Bill Condon, being the brilliant filmmaker that he is, knew I could give more. So we continued with the same hard push the entire next day until we got exactly what was needed.

The scene took two whole days to shoot. It felt like the people I saw going into the studio were coming back for their next shift, just as I was leaving. It was an emotional roller-coaster ride for those two days, to say the least. We did the scene over and over again. At times, I felt I had no more to give. I'd start to cry, asking the director what more he wanted from me. I felt tapped out. I was tired. At one point, Bill actually had to tell me to pull back the emotion because I was crying too much for the scene to feel real. At the end of my final take, Bill announced, "Ladies and gentlemen, the star of tomorrow, Ms. Jennifer Hudson." I had to wipe the tears from my tired and weary eyes as the entire studio burst into applause for me. I was overcome.

Without knowing it then, what happened that day created a path for me that I could never have imagined. This day marked a transition in my life, from struggling singer and performer to film actress. I don't think anyone in that studio really understood what had happened that day, and certainly not me. Bill Condon may have. Looking back on that moment now with clear eyes, I know that my life changed forever that day.

I had never acted before this movie, so no one knew what to expect. I was an unknown actress who had been given the role of a lifetime. I felt a real shift in the way I was perceived on the set, a shift that was a nod of approval from my colleagues that I felt happy to receive.

Jamie Foxx was the first person to actually say something about what had happened to me.

"Jennifer, you could get an Oscar nod for this," he said.

Those were big words coming from Jamie Foxx, an Oscar winner himself. The thought of winning awards for my first acting role certainly had not crossed my mind at all.

"Whatever!" I said to Jamie, just like I was talking to my mama. Me and my "whatever"s.

I remember getting a call one day asking me to come to the offices of the studio making the film, DreamWorks, the production company founded by Jeffrey Katzenberg, Steven Spielberg, and David Geffen. David Geffen owned the film rights to *Dreamgirls*, and was one of the producers on the film.

What do they want to talk to *me* about? I wondered. I worried that the producers were concerned about my performance. I felt a little like I was being called to the principal's office. It turned out to be just the opposite. I was told that the buzz on the film was very good, and that Beyoncé, Jamie Foxx, Anika Noni Rose, and I would be attending the 2006 Cannes International Film Festival in May to promote the movie. Cannes? France? I had heard of the festival before, but I never dreamed I'd actually be going there. I was thrilled but nervous, too. I had no idea what kind of appearance I was expected to make. There were going to be numerous grand red-carpet moments, where I would be photographed with some of the most famous people in the world. This was the big time, not like the events that I had attended with *American Idol*, but a huge industry gathering.

The press attending the film festival was going to be given an opportunity to see twenty minutes of never-before-seen footage from *Dreamgirls*. In addition, the press was invited to go "behind the scenes" and meet some of the talent involved in the making of the movie. It was all fantastic.

After Cannes, I started to realize that things were really going to change in my life once this film was released. When I was in the studio recording the sound track for *Dreamgirls*, Beyoncé offered me some advice I've never forgotten. She said, "The way you are starting your acting career is an amazing opportunity for you. Don't hop at just anything. You will have a lot coming at you. Take your time and make the right decisions." These were important words of wisdom coming from a woman I very much admired and respected. At the time, I didn't realize just how amazing the opportunity to play Effie was for me. But I do now, and I have lived by Beyoncé's advice ever since.

The biggest moment for me before *Dreamgirls* was released was one day when I received a phone call from none other than Oprah. You know, Winfrey. I was in a hotel room in New York City when someone from her staff called ahead to let me know she would be calling me later that day. I guess they didn't want me to be taken off guard. Instead, I just didn't believe them.

Whatever, I thought.

I mean, why would Oprah be calling me? I actually thought it was a practical joke someone was playing.

Me and my "whatever"s strike again.

But Oprah did call me the next day. My makeup artist answered the phone.

"Oprah's on the phone," she said.

Now, I was *sure* this was a joke, so I decided to play along.

"Hello?" I said in a disbelieving tone.

"Hi, this is Oprah," the voice on the other end of the phone said.

I didn't believe it was her. "This isn't Oprah," I said, and then I hung up the phone.

I have to believe this happens to her a lot because she called right back and laughingly said, "It is Oprah, like, for real!"

"Girl, I don't know who you are but stop playing with me!" I said. Before I could slam down the phone again, Oprah repeated that it was really her. She was calling to congratulate me on the movie. She had seen an advanced screening and said she was blown away by my performance, calling it "a religious experience."

Wow!

That's about all you can really say after hearing something like that from Ms. Oprah Winfrey. That phone call was the beginning of a much-cherished relationship I now have with "Mama O." I always tease her and say that she is the queen and I am a princess. Oprah is one of the few people I've come to know through my career who will take the time to talk to me and tell it to me like it is.

Whether I want to hear it or not, Oprah tells the truth. And if you're smart, you'll listen. I say a lot of "Yes, ma'am"s when we get together. Oprah will say what she has to say *one* time. She's not out to convince me of anything other than that her heart is always in the right place. It is up to me to accept what she says or not. And let me say that when Oprah talks, I listen, because she has a lifetime of insights and experience ahead of me that would be foolish to ignore. Oprah reminds me so much of my own mother, because that is exactly the way Mama was with me, too.

So, I had played my first role in a feature film, the role of a lifetime. I had been to Cannes. I had been told I could get an Oscar nod for the work I did. I had received a call of congratulations from Ms. Oprah Winfrey. What more could a girl ask for? I was already blessed beyond my wildest dreams. But more was coming, more than I could imagine.

CHAPTER SIX

AND I AM TELLING YOU I'M NOT GOING

After Cannes, the buzz on *Dreamgirls* really got going. I was feeling so much love from Hollywood, something I was completely not prepared for. It was all really flattering, but also a little confusing and overwhelming at the same time. The big girl with the big voice was getting congratulated on her success, and not told that she had to lose weight to fit the right image for a celebrity. I thought that sentiment would last, but just in case, I tried to enjoy it for as long as I could.

After the movie wrapped production I went back home to Chicago for the summer and tried to get back to life as I once knew it. I lost the twenty pounds I had gained for the film doing what I had always done—eating brown rice, chicken, and broccoli, and getting up every day at 5 A.M. to run. I was back on the same cycle that had worked for me before. I spent that entire summer working out on my own in the morning, and then again at a local gym in the afternoon. I was doing what basketball players refer to as "two-a-days." I thought I was doing everything right, eating the right things, exercising the right way. My system was effective, because by the end of the summer, I got right back to where I always landed—a comfortable size 10.

I continued working on my album, spending most of my spare time recording in the studio. Sometime toward the end of the summer, the producers of *Dreamgirls* called to say they wanted me to come back to Los Angeles to do some pickup shots they needed to finish the film. Pickups are small or minor shots that are filmed after a movie is wrapped to augment existing footage. This sometimes is needed when the right shot isn't available during the editing process or when the studio wants to tweak a scene because it doesn't play well once they've put the pieces together. I was happy to do whatever they needed me to do, of course. In fact, I was happy to step back into the role of Effie.

And then they dropped a real bomb.

"You have to gain back all of the weight you've lost," the producers said.

I didn't even have to think about it. "No way," was my response.

I had worked hard to lose those twenty pounds. Too hard to pack them back on again. I was feeling good, back in my size-10 clothes. I thought I looked good, too. Plus, gaining that much weight in such a short amount of time couldn't possibly be healthy. They only needed me to do one or two quick shots. Surely they would be able to work something out without me having to gain back all of the weight I had just dropped! I stood my ground, and though it was a bit of a struggle, the studio finally let it go. They solved the problem by shooting close-ups of me, so the audience could not see the difference in my body.

Back in Cannes, I had been introduced to a Hollywood agent at the special screening for the film set up by the studio. After the movie ended, she came over to talk to me.

"Has Clive Davis ever heard you sing?" she asked.

As far as I knew, the answer was no. Clive Davis is the legendary music producer and musical genius behind the careers of so many talented singers, including Whitney Houston, Alicia Keys, and Kelly Clarkson, just to name a few. The agent assured me that as soon as she got back to the United States, she would go straight to his office and tell him all about me. I figured I'd wait and see if that really happened. I thought that I was in the right place to meet the kind of person who could make such a fantastic connection for me, so I felt cautiously optimistic.

By November 2006, Clive Davis had bought out my existing recording contract with another label and signed me to Arista Records. Clive took me under his wing and has treated me like a daughter from day one. In his own way, Clive let me know that I didn't stand a chance of becoming a superstar performer if I stayed "fat." It was actually Walter who shared this with me. I think he dreaded saying it to me, but as my best friend, he knew he had to. My response was, "When was someone going to tell me?" But as tough as it was to hear, I knew it was tough love coming from Clive Davis. I also knew that Clive Davis understood the music business far better than I did. I also knew that he had an understanding that image sets the standard in the record industry. If Clive doesn't like your image, he isn't signing you. So the fact that he believed in me enough to say what he said made me take it to heart.

I announced my record deal on *The Oprah Winfrey Show,* where I shared my plans to get into the studio to record my *official* "first" album in early 2007. It was during that same show that I received a videotaped apology from none other than Mr. Simon Cowell for being so tough on me on *American Idol.* "Don't forget to thank me in your Oscar acceptance speech!" he joked. To be honest, though, I had never harbored one moment of anger or disrespect for Simon or any of the other judges from that show. They did exactly what they were supposed to do. They offered advice, which was mine to accept or reject. I was eternally grateful for the chance to be on *American Idol,* now more than ever, because I know I got to stand before the world as Effie White because of the chance that show gave me to sing in front of millions of people.

was so excited to start work on my first real record, but before I could do that *Dreamgirls* was going to open, and I would see myself on the big screen for the first time. Just before the worldwide premiere of *Dreamgirls*, the reality of what had happened suddenly hit me. It was early December 2006. I was sitting in a parking lot one night just thinking, *Oh my God.* I just did a major motion picture. I got the part of Effie White and the world is about to see what I can really do. I have a record deal with Arista and Clive Davis. I am beyond fortunate. What else could be in store for me?

Dreamgirls had a limited opening in theaters on December 22, 2006, and its national release on January 12, 2007. Studios will sometimes release a film early in a small number of theaters so it can be considered for the upcoming awards season, and Dream-Works had high hopes for *Dreamgirls*.

In the fall, I attended premieres for the film in New York, Los Angeles, and London. These evenings were amazing, like a dream. I wore gorgeous gowns, walked the red carpet, and tried to live in these once-in-a-lifetime moments. Not once during any of the premieres did I hear a single comment about my look. I hoped those days were behind me.

I wanted to watch the film with regular moviegoers, not with just my family or other industry professionals, to see what it was like. The first time I watched the film with strangers was around Christmas. Julia, Jason, and I went to a theater in my old neighborhood in Chicago and snuck in after the film started so no one would know I was there. We stood off to the side and watched the audience's reactions. I was dying inside, waiting for that moment when I sing "And I Am Telling You I'm Not Going." I knew what that scene meant to me because of the way I had connected to the emotions to create that moment, but I had no idea how regular folks would react. It was like being naked and exposed up there with hundreds of eyes watching and judging me. When the time finally came for that scene, I wanted to crawl under a chair and hide. Thank God my brother and sister were there.

On the heels of my last note, everyone in the audience stood from their chairs and clapped. I got a standing ovation—in a movie theater!

I was stunned by their response. Absolutely, positively taken aback.

It was so honest, so real. It was a completely different type of applause than I had ever received. It was tender, moving, and fulfilling in every way. I was emotional but very happy.

I will never forget that experience because it opened my eyes to the journey I was taking in a way I couldn't otherwise understand or see until that moment. If it weren't for the fans' reaction and their support, I am not sure I would be where I am today. And for that, I will be forever appreciative and grateful.

Dreamgirls was an instant smash hit with both audiences and the press. I was being called the breakout star of the film for my role as Effie White. The studio called to tell me they were going to put a big push behind me for the Academy Awards category of Best Supporting Actress. I could hardly believe what I was hearing.

Were they really talking about me?

Jennifer Hudson . . . Academy Award–nominated *actress*?

Singer I could wrap my head around. But this was difficult to comprehend.

By mid-January, I attended my first press event in New York City to kick off awards season. I was back to my regular low point of size 10, and feeling really good. I stood in the middle of a large room filled with members of the press, all there to see the breakout star from *Dreamgirls*. Suddenly, someone turned to me and said, "Wait a minute. Who is this? This is not Effie!" I was stunned. Was I *that* unrecognizable? I had lost only twenty pounds!

As I was leaving the event, my publicist turned to me and said, "The producers really want you to gain back the weight. You no longer look like Effie. The press and media feels connected to Effie. If you want their support, you have to get into character."

I was shocked. First of all, the irony of the situation was almost too much to take. I remembered the comments about my weight during

American Idol. I remembered not getting the Barry Manilow job. I remembered the comments from the audience during my Final Notice days about my outfits not fitting. Now here I was in Hollywood, in a town where a size 10 is considered plus size, and I was being told to put *on* weight! I had been lauded for my role as Effie. Why couldn't my performance speak for itself? Why did what the scale said when I stepped on it *always* come into play, either one way or the other? I was at my comfortable size. I couldn't win for losing. Literally.

"They want me to do what?" I asked. My publicist could see that I wasn't at all happy with the request. She explained the process of the awards season—Golden Globes to Oscars. She explained that everyone wanted to see Effie. Not Jennifer.

"It's not going to happen," I said to my publicist.

"You are the leading contender, Jennifer. You have the potential to win every award you're nominated for. You don't want to do anything to affect your chances, do you?"

I told her, "It is what it is." And even though I knew it was a risk, I stuck to my guns. Oh, yes. Jenny Kate had made a decision. I was so tired of losing and gaining weight to please other people. I was going to let my work speak for itself.

I had learned a lot of lessons over the years, but especially since my time on *American Idol.* They are the two notions I cling to always—and you've heard me refer to them before in this book.

They are:

1. If it is meant for me, it will be.

2. The talent should speak for itself.

I was done being judged for my appearance. It shouldn't matter if I weighed the same, fifty pounds more, or a hundred pounds less. Effie was a *character* I *played*. When I look back at pictures of me as Effie, I see a heavier version of me, but she wasn't me. I thought the difference in my appearance only helped to show off my range and commitment as an actress. I wanted people to understand that Effie isn't Jennifer and Jennifer isn't Effie. I certainly didn't want to get pigeonholed as a plus-size actress. I wanted to demonstrate that I did what I had to do to play Effie, but now I was moving forward with other plans. And my gamble paid off because despite my weight at the time, I was nominated for an Oscar after all.

I transformed my look all throughout awards season. For the Golden Globes, I left my hair down in soft waves and wore a navy blue Vera Wang gown with a deep V-neck that twisted at my waist. I was going for old Hollywood glamour that night, and I felt truly glamorous when I received my award for Best Supporting Actress.

Then came the Grammys, which I attended for the first time in February 2007. I was asked that night to present an award with

Justin Timberlake. I chose a tight red dress that I knew really showed off my curves. This was Jennifer's big night out. That night I was J-Hud! I loved that look and felt like I was showing off who I really was outside of Effie White.

And finally, on February 25, 2007, after a whirlwind of accolades, I won the Academy Award for Best Supporting Actress.

When George Clooney announced, "And the Oscar goes to Jennifer Hudson!" I was frozen in my seat. I was positive that I was the only one who heard my name. But then everyone was looking at me in a strange way, clapping and waiting for me to do something. Bill Condon, who escorted me to the awards ceremony that evening and who was sitting next to me, hit me to get up.

"Huh? I just won?" It was the most surreal experience of my life.

When I got to the stage, I had to pause, take a step back, and soak up that moment.

As I began my acceptance speech, thoughts of my grandma came to my mind. That's when I exclaimed her poignant words I'd heard so many times as a child, "Look at what God can do!"

Grandma would have been shouting God's glory across the stage and into the theater. Everything she said to me growing up was suddenly so very real. I really didn't think I was going to win that night, so I did my very best to thank everyone who had helped me keep the faith even when I didn't.

So here it was, almost three years after being voted off *Ameri-*

can Idol, and I was now an Academy Award–winning actress. It was almost too much to take.

In an unfortunate twist, I made many "worst dressed at the Oscars" lists. To be truthful, I wasn't very happy with the dress that I wore that night, a brown high-waisted gown paired with a python bolero jacket with a prominent collar. It was not something I ever would have chosen for myself. But I was still pretty new to the Hollywood game. I wore what I had been committed to wear, by someone else and without my knowledge. Let me tell you—that was the last time that happened! I would never again wear something I didn't love 100 percent.

Winning the Oscar opened up the floodgates for more acting opportunities in Hollywood. Movie offers came pouring in. Some were interesting, while others weren't right for me at all. I remembered back to what Beyoncé had told me and carefully considered each before saying yes or no. When the producers of the movie *Precious* asked me to play the title role, I knew it was an amazing role. But I also knew that I would have to again gain a lot of weight to play her. I had done that with Effie, and as much as I was moved by this film, I wanted to try a role that had nothing at all to do with my weight. I turned down *Precious,* and the role went to Gabourey Sidibe. She gave an unforgettable performance in the film, was nominated for an Oscar herself, and the career of another unknown actress was launched.

One movie I did say yes to was *Sex and the City.* I played Carrie Bradshaw's assistant, Louise. This fantastic ensemble cast had been doing their show together for years, so it was a real honor to be asked to become a part of their tight-knit family. It was also a little like being the new kid at school. The cast members of *Sex and the City* are fashion icons, each known for a distinctive, often trendsetting look. I was a little intimidated about how I was going to fit into all of that. I quickly found my stride, and ended up really enjoying playing Louise alongside SJP, as Sarah Jessica Parker is often called.

Doing *Sex and the City* was a really great experience and very different from doing *Dreamgirls.* This set was very fast-paced. The cast members of *Sex and the City* had a long-established groove after years of doing the television show, and they moved each scene right along. While *Dreamgirls* was shot primarily on a soundstage in Los Angeles, *Sex and the City* took place on the streets of New York City. I spent three months living and working in Manhattan, and loved every minute of it. I even got to record "All Dressed in Love," an original song for the movie sound track.

During the time I was filming *Sex and the City,* I began taking notice of a very handsome actor named David Otunga. I told Walter, "Oh, I would love to meet that guy." But I knew that if it is meant to be, it would happen, so I wasn't going to pursue him.

Luckily, things fell into place, and David and I met. I couldn't have been more surprised when I realized he was the *one*.

I had certainly been bitten by the acting bug, but my heart still belonged to making music. As much as I enjoyed acting, I thought it was time to put my focus back on my first true love—singing, and my new love—David.

CHAPTER SEVEN

GIVING MYSELF

S eptember 2008 was a very special time in my life. There were two unforgettable moments that altered the course of my life forever. The first was the impending release of my debut album. But before we get to the actual release, let me take you back to how it all came about.

A week after winning my Oscar, I was in the recording studio working on the album. It was almost as if I had to be reintroduced to myself because the last year or so of my life had been such a whirlwind: singer to actress and back again. I knew there had been a shift in my persona to the world. To almost everyone, I was now thought of as an actress first. I had always been a singer first and foremost.

Clive Davis had taken a very active role in my album and in my career, and this was a great feeling. I also knew that I was going to have to listen closely to what he had to say. I don't always take it well when someone tries to tell me what to do, especially when it comes to my music. However, when that "someone" happens to be Clive Davis, I listen. He's the pro. I was lucky that I got to have a little more freedom than most first-time recording artists, something I didn't take lightly at all. I spoke up when I felt I needed to, and listened to Clive and others when that felt right.

It took me two years to complete my first album, due in part to the fact that out of the gate we had no idea which direction to go in. Coming from singing on *American Idol* and then to *Dreamgirls*, my audience was vast and varied. The musical landscape I was entering was very much in flux. I had a hard time choosing the right songs that would appeal to my audience, but also remain true to my voice and what I think I do best. I like to do big, sweeping ballads, full of emotion and feeling. When you turned on the radio in 2007 and 2008, you didn't really hear songs like that. It was strange to hear Akon's "Smack That" or Amy Winehouse sing "Rehab" followed up by "And I Am Telling You . . ." on the radio. I knew my audience was out there. It was just going to take some time to make the right music for them.

I recorded somewhere around sixty songs over the course of the next two years to pick the final thirteen that ultimately made the album. I took my time recording because I wanted it to be great, for my fans and for me. I thought the fans deserved to have the very best, and you never get a second chance to make your first album. I worked with several different producers and songwriters, including

Ne-Yo, Missy Elliott, Robin Thicke, T-Pain, Tank, Timbaland, and the Underdogs—Harvey Mason Jr. and Damon Thomas. The Underdogs had produced all of my tracks from the *Dreamgirls* album, so I was extremely comfortable working with them. They knew me really well, so it helped to have that rapport in the studio. And since I was signed with Clive, no one in the music business was out of reach. I even had the chance to work with the legendary Jimmy Jam and Terry Lewis, who became teachers to me. Terry became a father figure, too. He always had a life lesson to share, and I was always willing to listen. I practically lived in their Los Angeles studio while we worked on our songs together. Unfortunately, none of those songs ended up on the final album, but I will never forget the relationships that were formed as a result.

I had been traveling around the country with David that summer, promoting the upcoming release of my album. Since I had booked a show in Boston, David was excited to take me on a tour of Harvard, where he attended law school. I loved seeing college through his eyes and sharing in his history prior to meeting me. Our relationship was growing.

I was floored and honored that I was asked to sing the national anthem for the opening of the Democratic National Convention, held in Denver on August 25, 2008. I knew it was going to be a defining moment in our country's history, but I had no idea how impactful that experience would be for me. I sang for all of the constituents and politicians in attendance, including the new Democratic presidential nominee, Barack Obama. Being from the same hometown, it was truly a thrill to sing for him. As with so many events I am privileged to be a part of, I could hardly believe that I had been given the opportunity to be a part of this historic occasion. Although my brother and sister weren't able to be with me, they kept calling to see how I was doing. My sister kept asking if I was nervous—which I wasn't. I was so excited to get out there and represent Chicago that I could hardly wait for my moment. My brother kept reminding me that the altitude in Denver might make me woozy or parched before I sang. Thank God he warned me because just before I was set to walk out onto the stage, I got so light-headed, I almost passed out. Thankfully, it was just the altitude, so I gave myself a minute or two to pull it together and was able to go out and sing with no problem.

David, my mama, and my aunt were also with me on this trip. Mama never liked being in the spotlight, but she sure loved to be with me at all of my important events. And I was so happy having her by my side. Unbeknownst to me, David used that opportunity to spend a few minutes alone with my mama to ask for her blessing in marriage. Thank God my mama said yes! According to David, he let out a big sigh of relief.

———

A couple of weeks later, David and I were in Los Angeles—our last stop of the many appearances I'd done to promote the upcoming album release. It was my twenty-seventh birthday.

David took me on a drive up the Pacific Coast Highway . . . and when he parked the car, he asked me to marry him. I was truly shocked. David had picked out the perfect ring for me! I was going to get married . . . someday. Of course, I started thinking about all the things girls think about when they get engaged. The date. The venue. The dress. Looking like a princess in the dress. But those wedding plans were going to have to wait. I had an album coming out, and David had big plans for his career that he wanted to pursue.

Shortly after David and I became engaged, David made a decision to pursue a passion of his that would ultimately change the course of his life and his career. David wanted to become a professional wrestler for the WWE. This was his dream, and when he was given the opportunity to turn that dream into a reality, he took it. The one glitch was that David would have to move to Tampa, Florida, to train for several months, which meant we were suddenly going to be in a long-distance relationship. But I wanted David to live his dream just like I was living mine. We figured out that I could come to Tampa on weekends, or whenever there was an opportunity, so we wouldn't go long periods without seeing each other. A week after being asked to join the WWE, David packed up and left for Tampa. My life was changing so fast.

My album finally dropped on September 27, 2008. I remember that day like it was yesterday. I was so excited but incredibly frightened, too. A lot was riding on the success of this record. As I said, you never get a second chance to make your first record. I always get nervous right before I go onstage. I am putting myself out there and trusting the audience will embrace whatever I have to give. Releasing an album is that same feeling—only on steroids. Even though I was a nervous wreck, I went down to my local record store the day the album came out so I could see it on the shelves for myself.

This was the moment I had waited for my entire life.

The album was simply called *Jennifer Hudson*. I figured the world that knew me as the actress who played Effie White needed to know me as the singer Jennifer Hudson. The cover was a simple black-and-white photo of me. I had recently cut my hair short and wore a dress the stylist picked out for me, with a wide belt at the waist.

Imagine my surprise when I saw the album cover. I had clearly been Photoshopped to look thinner for the cover of my record. I had not been told this was going to happen, and I was pretty shocked. So were my fans, and many of them voiced their disappointment since a lot of them had identified with me as a plus-size gal. It was another case of needing to fit an image. But I was able to put that disappointment aside for the excitement that came with finally having an album of my own, for the world to hear.

There were three singles from the album, including the first, "Spotlight," which was released as a single before the record dropped in June 2008. The other two singles were "If This Isn't Love" and "Giving Myself," which were later released in 2009.

"Spotlight" was my first top-30 hit, peaking at number twenty-four on the Billboard Hot 100 and becoming a top-20 hit in the United Kingdom. The song peaked at number one on the Billboard Hot R&B/Hip-Hop Songs, spending two consecutive weeks in the top spot.

When I was a little girl, I used to dream about the day when I would make my own music video. Thank God I spent so much time rehearsing in the mirror as a kid because when it came time to actually do the video for "Spotlight," I was ready. Even though there was a music video for "And I Am Telling You I'm Not Going," it was just the scene from the movie. This was different because that video belonged to Effie—and "Spotlight" was all mine. The choreographer was shocked at how natural I appeared. He said I didn't look like an amateur. Of course not! I had prepared my whole life for this moment.

When I read the various treatments for the video, I wasn't really sure what to think. They wanted to put me in tight, sexy clothes and spiky high heels for a scene that had me "at home on the couch."

I remember thinking, Now, why would I have on heels? I hate wearing high heels! In fact, someday I want to find a way to create a sexy heel girls can walk in all day long without their feet getting sore. Can I please get an Amen on that?

We shot the video in a Los Angeles studio. I decided to bring my own clothes to the shoot. The process of shooting this video took a really long time. We ended up shooting until 4 A.M. the next day, and I had to stand in those high heels the whole time. By the last shot, my feet were killing me! Luckily, the video turned out well, and I was very happy with the final product and liked working with the director, Chris Robinson. Sore feet were a small price to pay.

The album did better than the label expected. The album made its debut on the Billboard 200 and the Top R&B/Hip-Hop Albums chart with first week's sales of 217,000 copies. It was eventually certified gold for selling more than a half million copies.

In the fall of 2008, I had started a new weight-loss regimen in preparation for a film adaptation of Winnie Mandela's life called *Winnie*. I had been cast to play the amazing Winnie Mandela under the assumption that I would lose a significant amount of weight to look more like her. I noticed I was feeling unusually tired. I know my body, and something felt very different. I wasn't sure if the way I was feeling was due in part to my new dieting habits, stress, or perhaps some combination of both.

I didn't think I was pregnant because I had no obvious symptoms. Even so, I decided to take a home pregnancy test just to rule it out. I stood in the bathroom and waited for my results. I couldn't help but let my mind wander and think about the possibility . . . and the irony.

I looked down.

Positive.

I was pregnant.

The only person we decided to tell right away was my manager so that he could let the producers of *Winnie* know I wouldn't be able to do the movie anytime soon. We didn't give them an exact reason. We just told them it was personal. Thankfully, they agreed to wait it out because they didn't want to recast the lead. They wanted me to play Winnie and were willing to wait. The producers told me to do whatever I needed to do and that they would be ready whenever I was. I couldn't have asked for anything more. I thanked them for their gracious patience and understanding.

David and I loved to take weekend trips to amusement parks like Disney World and Universal Studios. I had always loved going on rides. One day we approached a ride that had a sign posted that read, "Do not ride this if you are pregnant." Funny, I had ridden this roller coaster many times before I was pregnant, but had never noticed that sign until that day. I stood there for a moment trying to figure out what to do. I couldn't make up my mind. The people behind us in line were getting annoyed for sure. Of course, no one knew I was pregnant so they couldn't understand my hesitation. These types of decisions were all so new and unfamiliar to me.

I suddenly went from thinking for myself to thinking like a mama in thirty seconds flat and have never looked back since. Going forward, everything I did, every decision I made, and every road traveled would be considered with my baby's welfare in mind first. It was exciting to approach life from this brand-new perspective, and even better, without anyone knowing why—at least for a little while.

I had been keeping a pretty low profile, but I couldn't stay out of the spotlight forever. I was asked to sing the national anthem at the 2009 Super Bowl, scheduled in Tampa on February 2. It was an easy decision since I didn't even have to fly anywhere. Thankfully, I wasn't showing yet, so I wasn't worried about anyone finding out that I was pregnant. Although I had been on one of the most-watched television shows on the planet, *American Idol*, I don't think there is a larger audience and platform than the Super Bowl. God gave me the nerves of steel that I needed that night. This was the first time I was stepping out since the tragedy that struck my family. It was a very strange evening because I had never been hounded or stalked by the media like I was that night. It was overwhelming. When I stood on the field facing the crowd, there was a roar in the stadium unlike anything I had ever heard. Luckily, once I started to sing, the tension faded away, as it always does. Singing is always my saving grace. I sang from my heart and soul that night—and I think it showed.

Even though we had been given a skybox to watch the game, as soon as I hit that last note, I was eager to leave. David stayed and watched the game with my brothers and a few other relatives while I headed straight from the stadium to the nearest Chipotle, in full hair and makeup. A pregnant woman wants what she wants!

The next time I would sing in public was at the 2009 Grammy Awards. I wore a black-and-white dress that strategically hid my ever-growing baby bump. I simply wasn't ready to let the world know I was expecting, much less answer questions from the press. That night, I worked with a new stylist who kept trying to put me into undergarments that were way too tight across my belly. I had to tell her I wouldn't wear them. I also had to tell her not to push on my stomach, but I never told her why. Hopefully she only thought I was just strangely obsessed with my abs. At my record label, no one ever suggested that I might be pregnant, though I wonder if they suspected. No one ever asked me. And really, when you think about it, who asks a grown woman if she's pregnant, anyway? What if she isn't? Boy, that's awkward.

The Grammys that year were pretty special to me, wardrobe

issues or not. My album received three nominations, including Best Female R&B Vocal Performance for "Spotlight," Best R&B Performance by a Duo or a Group with Vocal for "I'm His Only Woman," a duet I recorded with Fantasia Barrino, and Best R&B Album, for which I ended up winning the award.

Winning a Grammy was a dream come true for two very special reasons. To begin with, it was my first, and a great vote of confidence in my music career from my peers. And while that *was* truly exciting, receiving that award from Whitney Houston, my idol and greatest musical influence, was the icing on the cake. I couldn't believe I was standing right next to her on the same stage, much less receiving an award from her. I was in complete awe, but not for the first time when it came to Ms. Whitney Houston.

I actually met Whitney Houston for the first time at a charity event in October 2006. It was one of the first times in my life that I can honestly say I was starstruck. I was scheduled to sing during the event and was sitting in a hallway inside the Beverly Hilton hotel, where the fund-raiser was taking place. I was waiting to go into the ballroom to perform. My publicist and choreographer were sitting with me when I noticed a herd of men rushing down the hallway looking like secret service. They were surrounding a woman and walking very fast. When I looked up, I realized it was Whitney. As she passed by us, she held up her index finger and said, "Stop."

Her entourage stopped cold in their tracks.

Whitney walked over to me and stood about three inches from my face.

"You. You're the one." She practically whispered when she spoke.

I had no idea what she was talking about. I was mesmerized and frozen by her presence. It was such a surprise that Whitney Houston came over . . . to me!

"You're the one. It is you. I know you."

My publicist elbowed me to get up out of my seat, but I couldn't move. Before I could say anything, she was gone.

I didn't see Whitney Houston again until the night of the Grammys. If there was anything that could have lifted my spirits at this time, it was receiving my first Grammy Award from her. As a way of showing my appreciation and respect for everyone who had reached out to me over the months since the family tragedy I had just endured, for my Grammy performance I chose to sing a song from my album called "You Pulled Me Through." When I recorded the song, I had no idea why I was singing it, but I knew it had a purpose. Singing it that night helped me discover that purpose. That song suddenly made perfect sense because I felt as if I had seen the highest of the highs and the lowest of the lows in my life. Rickey Minor, my musical director at the time, told me that I am a storyteller and I could paint the picture for an audience through my music. I knew that song had the potential to reach people on a deeply spiritual level—and in the end, I believe it did.

If it's true that God never gives us anything more than we can handle, he sure knew I would be able to handle things that night. I was able to go out there and still have a sweet taste in my mouth after all of the bitterness I had suffered. I've always been emotional when I sing, but on this particular night I was extremely so. As I've said, my crying through a song used to irritate my mama. She'd say, "Jenny, why do you have to be crying when you're up there to sing. What are you crying for, baby girl?" On that night, I was thinking of my family and just wanted to make them proud. I didn't care if I cried or not. I don't think anyone did.

I don't think there was a dry eye in the house.

After the Grammys, I agreed to perform on *American Idol* for the first time since I was voted off. I have to admit, it felt good to be back on that stage. It was like going home. For sure I thought someone there would notice my belly—but they didn't! I even appeared on *The Oprah Winfrey Show* and *The Ellen DeGeneres Show* around this time, and even though I was now several months pregnant, no one ever said a word.

I tried maintaining my regular diet and exercise routine for the first four months of the pregnancy. My first trimester was easy. I had no signs or symptoms that I was carrying a baby and therefore often forgot that I was. David was terrified as I'd race up flights of stairs, go for a run, or do anything physical. I felt great and kept living my life as I normally did. Funny things started to happen though, like not being able to stand the smell of David's cologne and an occasional unexplained meltdown over the smallest things. I never wore maternity clothes throughout my pregnancy. I just wore my regular clothes, though I went for the looser stretchy ones as my belly grew. This was a big realization for me . . . maybe I did need to think about losing some weight after this baby was born. If I could wear my regular clothes during pregnancy, maybe they were a little . . . big.

By my fifth month, my hormones really took over and my body wanted me to eat whatever it wanted to eat. I like spicy food and was craving it morning, noon, and night. I remember going to a Mexican restaurant to order up some nachos (without onions, of course) to go. I was very specific about what I did and did not want on my nachos. The waitress took my order just as I had given it— *no* onions! Unfortunately, when I opened the box in the car, those nachos were covered in everything I had asked them to skip. I was so mad that I threw them out the window! Now, maybe it was the hormones that caused me to act that way—but everyone knows you don't play with a pregnant woman's food!

As he always did, David acted nonchalant about the scene I had just caused. Looking back, I hope it wasn't because I had been acting that way so often he was no longer fazed by that behavior. Oh well. You *can* get away with more when you're pregnant, right, ladies?

Not long after this, my sister sent me a text that said, "If one more person asks me if you're pregnant, I'm going to give them a due date. Jenny—what's the deal?" she asked.

I texted her back with my due date, and that's how I told Julia I was pregnant.

I then wanted to make sure my whole family knew the good news now, before the press started talking. So in the spring of 2009, I decided it was time to make an official announcement to my big family. It had been a while since I had seen them. As I said, I was still wearing my regular clothes, so even after I shared the good news, everyone thought I was playing a trick on them. My aunts were all there that day, and in my family, all I really needed to do was tell my aunts. Sure enough, shortly afterward, everyone else in the extended family was finally in the know.

The rest of the world found out I was pregnant when I sang at Michael Jackson's memorial on July 7, 2009. The service was held at the Staples Center and was covered by the media worldwide. By this time I was eight months pregnant and really only wanted to be at home resting. I was getting uncomfortable and just wanted my baby out and my body back. Of course, Michael's death was so sudden and unexpected. So I was happy to be part of the celebration of his life and to have my chance to honor Michael. It was a sad but amazing day, and I was glad that I was included, despite feeling very tired at this point.

Even though my sister has special feelings about these things and had predicted that we were going to have a boy, David and I never knew the sex of our baby until he was born. We shopped for a boy and a girl and had outfits for both in my suitcase that I took to the hospital. We had names picked out for both, too. We had resigned ourselves that whatever it was going to be, it would be.

When the baby came, David said, "It's a boy, Jenny!"

I could hear my son yelling and screaming. He definitely inherited my strong voice!

And there he was—my little munchkin. David placed our baby atop my chest so I could feel his little heart beat against mine. He looked just like a mini version of David. We named him David Daniel Otunga Jr.

It was love at first sight.

As I held him close, I cried more than my newborn son.

My circle of life was now complete. I had a man I loved and, together, we brought a new life into the world. After everything we had been through, we were both so happy. I couldn't think of a better way to honor my mother than becoming a mother myself. From the very moment my son was born, I have felt my mama's presence guiding me. She was such a great role model in so many ways. I want to be that same kind of inspiration to my son, too. And now, I had the rest of my life to do just that.

I loved being a mom from the very start. Little David is the light of my life. Whenever I had to travel for work in those first few months, I did what I had to do and hurried back home to be with my son. I had someone waiting for me, someone who unconditionally loved me with all his heart, and someone I couldn't wait to hold in my arms. I cherish every moment we have together.

Munchkin quickly developed his own unique personality. The older he got, the more of me I saw in him. My son never met an audience he didn't like. He loves the sound of a cheering crowd. Maybe it is because I performed so much during my pregnancy, the sound of a clapping audience is familiar to him.

About a year or so after David Jr. was born, I was doing a show in Barbados. The crowd began to cheer in the middle of one of my songs. I thought it was odd, but chalked it up to the audience just feeling the music. I looked to my right and noticed Munchkin standing off in the corner of the stage with his own microphone in his hands. They were cheering for *him*—not me.

I asked my engineer to turn up the house lights so David could see the audience. He loved it. He had no fear whatsoever. As long as he is happy, I am, too. I guess we will all have to wait and see what happens!

CHAPTER EIGHT

I AM CHANGING

Within days of bringing David home from the hospital, I made a decision that ultimately altered my health for life. Becoming a mother brought on tremendous responsibilities, but none greater than the obligation I felt to get healthy to be there for my son.

I gained thirty-five pounds during my pregnancy. Like most women, I was shocked that even after giving birth, I still weighed around 237 pounds. I felt that surely I would drop at least some of the weight once that baby came out. This was the biggest number I had seen on the scale in many years. It was time to think about how I was going to lose the excess baby weight and then put that plan into action.

Since I had given birth via C-section, I was unable to do much of anything for the first ten days or so. I could barely get off the sofa and couldn't walk fully upright without pain for some time. For six weeks after giving birth, going to the gym or working out was definitely out of the question. What I could do during that time was try to break my body's cravings for the unhealthy foods I freely ate during the last few months of my pregnancy. While I didn't completely go crazy, I didn't deprive myself of anything while I was pregnant, either. If I wanted cupcakes—I ate them. If I wanted Mexican food—and I did—often, I ate it. So when the time came to gain control over my eating again and hopefully once and for all, I fell back into my old diet mentality that had worked for me so many times before having my baby.

It was an all-too-familiar routine. I had grown comfortable with eating skinless baked chicken, brown rice, and steamed broccoli—morning, noon, and night. My staple diet foods. My big treat was two apple slices with peanut butter slathered on top. I only drank water and occasionally treated myself to Crystal Light. That way of eating is effective for quick weight loss, but it isn't very interesting. And like anything, if we get bored we change things up, and usually not in our favor. It's a total setup for failure because eating that way forever just isn't realistic.

Once I was finally able to get active, I started walking a loop around my neighborhood that took close to thirty minutes to complete. To be honest, when I first began taking these walks, this same route took me closer to an hour because I had to take it slow.

After a few weeks I was able to cut that time in half. I relished these walks by myself because those precious moments were my "thinking" time. I enjoy being outdoors, especially when it's really hot and humid. I put my headphones on and away I go. I do most everything with music playing in my ears. It gives me motivation to get up off that sofa and inspiration to take those extra laps. But sometimes, the motivation was hard to come by. If the baby had been up a lot or he was napping and I could get a few quiet moments at home, sometimes I just wanted to stay on the couch.

Whenever I'd try to talk myself out of going for a walk, and there were a few days like that, I'd take myself through a series of simple tasks so I would get up and go.

1. **Get up.**
2. **Find your house keys.**
3. **Put on some shoes.**
4. **Grab your iPod.**
5. **Walk out the front door.**

Like I said, I like to set goals for myself, and these small goals got me out the door more than a few times.

And if after all that I still didn't move from the chair, as a sure-fire way of talking myself into just doing it, I'd trick myself by saying, "It is okay to walk for just ten minutes—because that would be better than doing nothing." And once I got up, ten minutes turned into thirty and eventually an hour. It got to the point where I would begin to miss how good I felt from working out that I'd actually get inspired by that, too.

According to the Organization for Economic Cooperation and Development (OECD), the number of obese people in the United States will increase from 99 million in 2008 to 164 million by 2030. The U.S. obesity rate will rise from 32 percent to about 50 percent for men and from 35 percent to between 45 percent and 52 percent for women.

Later in the year, when I was well on my way to losing the baby weight I had gained, I met with a team of people from Weight Watchers. They sat with me and explained the principles of their program. The best way to think about the program is as a plan that gives its members a personalized budget of Points values per day. Your available Points are calculated based on your weight, age, and activity level. Every food has a Points value and you use those values to fill your day up with food. You keep track of your Points by writing down everything you eat. There is flexibility in the program in this regard, but many members cite tracking what they eat and the values associated with their food as the key to their success.

To be frank, I thought it all sounded lame and I wasn't all that interested. All I could think of was, Who wants to eat and then have to write all of that down? I was polite, but I felt like this program was in no way right for me.

The representative said that the way the numbers work is that they quantify food for you. They show you that one food choice is better than another based on the Points assigned to that food. For example, a processed nutrition bar, which is something most people think of as a good choice when trying to lose weight, might have a seven *PointsPlus*® value and may carry as many as two hundred and fifty calories. On the other hand, a banana has a zero *PointsPlus*® value and will actually keep you fuller for longer than a protein bar. It has more fiber and more water and vitamins, too. So the program quantifies food in a way that teaches you to navigate the environment that we all live in. As I listened, one of the more promising aspects of the program for me was learning that the program builds in some extra flexibility for you because they know that if you don't get in some of the things you love—the sweets you crave and such, you won't stick with the plan. They actually give you an added allowance of an extra forty-nine Points every week so you can have those things along the way.

What this means is, if you're going to a wedding over the weekend and you don't want to sit it out because you're afraid of breaking the plan, you can still go. You can even have a cocktail or a piece of the wedding cake without worrying about your Points allowance for the day. If a friend calls you to go to dinner and you've already had twenty-five of your daily twenty-nine Points, you can pull from the extra forty-nine allowed for the week. It gives a kind of real-life flexibility I had never seen in any other plan. When I first talked to Weight Watchers, they hadn't yet launched their current program, *PointsPlus*®, but did so soon after. It is now in full swing and has been used by millions to great results.

About the Weight Watchers®
PointsPlus® Program

The biggest innovation from Weight Watchers in more than a decade, *PointsPlus*® uses the latest scientific research to create a program that goes far beyond traditional calorie counting to give people the edge they need to lose weight and keep it off in a fundamentally healthier way.

The program is designed to educate and encourage people to make choices that:

- Favor foods the body works harder to convert into energy, resulting in fewer net calories absorbed.

- Focus on foods that create a sense of fullness and satisfaction and are more healthful.

- Nudge toward natural foods rather than foods with excess added sugars and fats.

- Still allow flexibility for indulgences, special occasions, and eating out.

HOW IT WORKS

While calorie counting has been the foundation of many weight-loss programs, including the Weight Watchers former *Points*® system, the *PointsPlus*® program goes beyond just calories to help people make healthful and satisfying choices.

The formula takes into account the energy contained in each of the components that make up calories—protein, carbohydrates, fat, and fiber—and it also factors in how hard the body works to process them (conversion cost) as well as their respective eating satisfaction (satiety). As a result, the *PointsPlus*® formula guides people beyond reducing overall calorie intake toward foods that enhance feelings of satisfaction and fullness.

In addition to the new formula, foods that are low in energy density, and therefore more highly satisfying, are emphasized within the program. Specifically, all fresh fruits and most vegetables now have zero *PointsPlus*® values. Furthermore, power foods, an important element of the new *PointsPlus®* program, provide an easy way to identify the best food choices among similar foods; for example, those foods with higher eating satisfaction, lower sugar, lower sodium, healthier fat, and more fiber, and it also factors how hard the body works to process them (conversion cost) as well as their respective eating satisfaction (satiety). As a result, the *PointsPlus®* formula guides people beyond reducing overall calorie intake toward foods that enhance feelings of satisfaction and fullness.

The program features, combined with the fundamentals of the Weight Watchers approach—that is, weight loss built on healthy eating, physical activity, behavior modification, and a supportive environment—make the *Points-Plus®* program revolutionary and innovative.

PROGRAM HIGHLIGHTS

PointsPlus® values reflect the energy that's available after the body has processed a food.

Power foods are an easy way to identify the best food choices among similar foods; for example, those foods with higher eating satisfaction, lower sugar, lower sodium, healthier fat, and more fiber.

Zero *PointsPlus®* values are assigned to fresh fruit and most vegetables, which are nutrient dense and are highly satisfying.

Weekly *PointsPlus®* gives an allowance of 49 extra *PointsPlus®* values per week, in addition to the daily *PointsPlus®* target. This allows for flexibility so members and online subscribers can avoid feeling deprived and are therefore motivated to stick with the program since real life often means unplanned eating opportunities.

Activity *PointsPlus®* values are used to reward activity because it is important for good health and is a critical component of weight loss. Members and online subscribers can track activity *PointsPlus®* values for motivation or they can swap them for extra food *PointsPlus®* values.

INDUSTRY-LEADING RESEARCH AND PROVEN EFFECTIVENESS

The *PointsPlus®* program has been tested in a rigorous, independent clinical trial, and the results demonstrate that it delivers significant weight loss as well as improvements in decreasing cardiovascular risk factors and eating behaviors linked with long-term weight loss and hedonistic hunger.

The testing applied to this new program is a reflection of Weight Watchers' commitment to clinical testing with more than sixty-five original scientific publications over the past fifteen years that demonstrate the efficacy of the Weight Watchers approach to weight loss and long-term health.

Thousands of people across the United States were involved in beta testing the *PointsPlus®* program. In addition to being thrilled with their weight loss, these individuals reported they felt healthier and more satisfied. People shifted their choices away from energy-dense, processed foods toward fruit, vegetables, whole grains, and lean proteins, changing their life in a meaningful and natural way and demonstrating the effectiveness of the *PointsPlus®* program.

A global study recently published in *The Lancet* indicated that overweight and obese adults referred to Weight Watchers lost more than twice as much weight when compared with those who received standard care. This study provides significant evidence to the value of a primary care and Weight Watchers partnership for an effective weight-loss approach.

I listened carefully as the folks from Weight Watchers explained the program, but I still didn't believe most of what they were saying. I nodded in agreement, but they lost me at "You can eat whatever you want."

I thought, There is no way I can eat those types of foods and lose weight, because it was against everything I knew about weight loss and healthy eating. My mind was programmed to think deprivation, not freedom of choice. No one can sustain a diet of grilled skinless chicken, brown rice, and steamed broccoli forever. Eventually you have to nourish your body with something else and when you do, the weight comes right back. I would stop myself from having the foods I loved until the cravings got so bad I couldn't take it for one more second. I'd inevitably break down and give in by heading to my favorite chicken wing place, ordering a huge box of wings, and eating the entire thing. Afterward, I'd feel so bad about making that choice, the next day I'd go right back on my extreme deprivation diet until I'd repeat the same pattern over and over again.

I had been so brainwashed into believing that dieting meant excruciating limitations that I had rejected the principles of the Weight Watchers program. I simply didn't believe I could eat chips, cookies, or pizza and lose weight. My mind was made up. There was no way their plan would work. But out of courtesy, I reluctantly agreed to try the program for one week.

Weight Watchers assigned a woman named Liz Josefsberg to be

my Weight Watchers leader. Liz was there to help me understand and then navigate my plan on the program. The first thing Liz and I spoke about was the ways I'd lost weight before and what I had done to take off the excess baby weight. She recognized that I had what she called "a lot of diet baggage" left over from my past.

By the time I met Liz, I had lost a fair amount of weight on my own, but as it usually did, my weight hit the familiar plateau around 193 pounds. It seemed that no matter what I tried, I couldn't break through. Liz spent a great deal of time talking to me about small healthy changes I could make that would get me there.

Although I was already a pretty healthy eater for the most part, and had a lot of firsthand knowledge about losing weight, Liz helped me see that I was making tiny mistakes that were throwing me off and keeping my weight loss stagnant. For example, I knew I was eating good snack choices, such as trail mix with nuts and dried fruit. What I didn't realize was the amount I was eating was actually detrimental. Liz asked me how much trail mix I'd eat in a sitting and the truth is, I didn't know. I ate my snack without paying any attention to the amount. I was aware that I was eating several handfuls at a time—if not more—but I had no idea how much that really added up to. Liz suggested trying a quarter cup at a sitting instead of eating as much as I wanted. That seemed reasonable enough, although at the time, I wasn't sure what a quarter of a cup actually looked like. I shared with Liz that I also loved eating Greek yogurt with peanut butter. Once again, Liz asked me how much peanut butter I was eating with that serving of yogurt.

Again, I didn't know.

She explained that one tablespoon of peanut butter is a great choice for a snack, but adding a giant dollop into the yogurt can throw me out of my weight-loss zone. When Liz pointed out that the food choice was right but the amount was the problem, I realized that *portion control* and *lack of awareness* were my two biggest challenges to weight loss.

Liz gave me a visual demonstration on what amounts of food were doable in the Weight Watchers program and what amounts would set me back. Next, she reintroduced me to all the foods I could eat—as long as they were measured in the right amounts. It was interesting to see, but the fact remained that I was still in my "diet" mentality, so I thought she was crazy as she told me that I could have ice cream, chocolate, popcorn, pizza, and sushi. Sushi! It's one of my most favorite meals on the planet and I hadn't eaten it for two years because of the high carbohydrates in the rice and because I was avoiding it while pregnant. The promise was enticing, but the reality seemed a little suspect.

"What do I do when I get a craving for chicken wings?" I asked, knowing damn well those would never be a choice on a healthy weight-loss program.

"You can eat wings, but eat six instead of twelve. Have a green salad first so you're not as hungry by the time you get to the wings," Liz said. "If you don't branch outside of what you know, you will break down, which means you will fall away from the program, and we don't want that to happen."

Hold on.

She was insistent that I could eat whatever I wanted and all I had to do was track the Points and I would lose weight?

Was she serious?

She was. For the first time ever, that is exactly what someone was telling me. I could not believe it, so I did what I always do when I can't wrap my brain around an idea.

I said, "Whatever."

Uh huh. I did. I said it. I said, "Whatever," and by now we all know how that movie ends.

Sensing my doubt, Liz insisted that as long as I stayed within my allotted-Points-per-day budget, I would definitely lose weight. At the end of the day, the Weight Watchers program is an education in sidestepping the misinformation out there about dieting, and breaking the negative diet mentality that predominates the world we all live in. Weight Watchers hands you the tools to make the right choices. But you still have to make those choices or the program, like any program, won't work.

I found that out the hard way.

I still had my doubts, but as I said, out of courtesy I agreed to give Weight Watchers a try. I figured I would give it a week to see what happened. Honestly, I had nothing to lose—except a few pounds. But of course, I wasn't expecting that to happen. If I wasn't satisfied with the results, then I could just as easily go back to my old way of dieting. Nothing ventured, nothing gained.

The first week on the program I created my own version of the Weight Watchers program. I mostly stuck to what I had already been doing and combined it with some of the food choices Liz said I could have. Nice try, but I didn't lose a pound. It turned out that Jenny Kate's way didn't quite meet the criteria set for me by Weight Watchers. When I saw Liz a week later, she wasn't shocked by my lack of results, because she immediately knew I hadn't stuck with the program. Then Liz shared that I was like a lot of her other members. I didn't *trust* the program. She was absolutely right about that.

By the second week, I had actually gained weight. I think I tried that first week five different times before I realized I had two roads I could walk down on this journey. I could keep doing things my way and keep getting the same dismal results, or I could finally give in and try Weight Watchers for real, and see what happened.

I decided to give the plan a try. I fully committed. Here's what I discovered: Weight Watchers is not a painful program. I was like most people, believing that weight loss has to be a struggle and a painful experience. It *can* be that, but it doesn't have to be. Through Weight Watchers, you can learn to take weight off in a healthy manner without giving up all the foods that make you feel good. After my first real week, I lost five pounds. With that result, I actually wanted to stick to their program.

"Walter! I don't know what they did, but this plan works!" I was excited by my progress. I thought I had found the weight-loss miracle. "This is it. This is all I need." From that moment on, I was hooked. "You got me," I said to Liz. And they did. I even agreed to sign on as a spokeswoman for the company—an ambassador of sorts, and I haven't looked back since.

My contract to be an ambassador for Weight Watchers only called for me to lose 10 percent of my body weight. That's it. No more, no less. Needless to say, that goal was met pretty early on. After that, I didn't stick with the plan out of some contractual obligation. No way. It became a healthy lifestyle choice for me—one that helped me discover a program that was not only doable but also realistic for sustained weight loss.

My relationship with Liz became one of the most important in my journey to regain my health. I connected with her from the start. She was easy to talk to and understood me from the beginning. When we first met, Liz explained that all Weight Watchers leaders were once members, and to become a leader, she had to have been on the program. Knowing that helped me because she could relate to everything I was going through. Liz told me that before joining the company, she had lost and gained the same thirty pounds several times over the years. Frustrated after many failed diets, she decided to join Weight Watchers as her last hope. She eventually lost fifty pounds and has kept it off, which gave me a tremendous amount of comfort and confidence in her. She knew what it was like to lose that much weight, so I could really open up to her along the way. Liz knew where I was coming from and was able to answer all my questions, and address my concerns and challenges as we forged ahead.

I was lucky to have the relationship I developed with Liz, but it's important to know that my experience was very much like anyone who is a member of the program. Every Weight Watchers meeting has a leader there to support you through your own journey. And while your schedule and challenges may not be the same as mine, we are all busy just living our lives—doing the best we can. I can promise you that if you trust in the program and trust your leader, you will see positive results. In doing my own research, there was no other plan out there that offered the healthy Weight Watchers message or support and, more so, delivered with the results.

CHAPTER NINE

FEELING GOOD

t's important to me that you all know that the hard work I've done to take control of my health, I have done completely on my own. I don't live in a mansion with a private chef or personal trainer at my beck and call. Oh no. I get so frustrated when people make that imaginary leap that I live like a princess in a castle with all of my needs met by others. I cook my own meals, and when I can't because I'm on a movie set all day or in the recording studio, Walter takes care of making sure my meals are fixed as if I made them myself.

Whenever people ask me how they can lose weight, too, the first thing I tell them is that they have to make up their mind that they really want to do it and do it for themselves. I suppose that way of thinking is true for breaking any addiction, but for me, that was the difference in losing the weight and keeping it off. *If you can't take responsibility for your own well-being, you will never take control over it.* That is the truth.

Look, change is scary. If you aren't completely ready to make adjustments that will ultimately alter the course of your life, you are not ready to embrace change. My fiancé is the type of man who likes things to be the way they've always been. He doesn't like change, but he's been very supportive. He understands I did this for me and for me alone. You can't make a life-altering decision for someone else and expect it to stick. Gaining control over your health and well-being is one of those times in your life that you get to be completely selfish and not feel bad about it. If you want to meet your goals, you have to make it about you. You have to make it work for you and you alone. Anything less is a setup for failure.

Listen, I have been through this weight-loss roller coaster a few times over the years. I have been there and back and there and back again and again. I had everyone on the planet tell me that I needed to look a certain way or be a specific size if I wanted to make it as a singer. I have been rejected from more jobs than the ones I've gotten simply because of my appearance. If I had listened to all of those people, maybe I would have become a broken-down, overweight, out-of-work, *American Idol* castoff has-been. But I didn't. I was never that insecure. I'm telling you the absolute truth when I say that I genuinely loved my body—fat, thin, and everywhere in between. If I didn't have that confidence, though, I don't think I could have forged ahead and continued to pursue my dreams. Loving yourself means caring enough to make the hard decisions in your life.

I have a friend who is a personal fitness trainer. One day he came to me to say he was getting fed up with a client of his because she wouldn't listen to him to get to a certain weight. We got to talking and I asked him if that number was what he wanted for her or what she wanted for herself. My friend looked at me like I had solved one of life's great mysteries. All this time, he was imposing what he wanted on his client without ever asking her what her goals were. Forget what everyone else wants you to do and figure out what you want for yourself. Here's what I know for sure: The only way you can sustain a permanent change is to create a new way of thinking, acting, and being.

When I decided to become an ambassador for Weight Watchers, I was ready to do whatever it took to get healthy and learn how to finally stay that way. My goals were to feel good, have enough energy and stamina to keep up with my son, get healthy, and not worry about my dress size anymore. And even though I was losing the weight for me, I had the greatest motivation on the planet—my brand-new baby son. Once I welcomed Munchkin into the world, I felt that I had an obligation to be the best mom I could be for him. He deserved to have a mama who could run after him, chasing him around the house without getting winded or tired. I wanted him to have a role model who could teach him to make healthy food choices along the way so he would have the right tools as he went through life. I needed him to grow up with a mama who always would be there for him by caring enough about herself to take control of her health and eating. Everything changed on the day he was born. And now, I had a partner in Weight Watchers to help me get to my goal, for life.

The program is designed so that members can expect a one- to two-pound drop in weight per week when following the program. Of course, there can be some fluctuation in terms of the amount of weight you may lose, especially in the beginning. You tend to lose a bit more during the first couple of weeks due to mostly losses in fluid. One of the biggest challenges to continued weight loss I had was planning my meals around my very full schedule. Liz helped me to take a look at a typical week for me and see where I was making my mistakes.

Was I missing meals?

Was I overeating?

Was I starving and then bingeing?

I now knew I was making mistakes in terms of volume, so that took some time to understand and fix. Since my eating is often sporadic and done on the fly, it was important to come up with meals that were filling and able to hold me over long periods of time. It is not unreasonable for me to go eight, ten, or even twelve hours in between meals, especially when I am on a movie set or in the studio recording. While I once thought that was desirable, through Weight

Watchers I learned it was actually hurting me. So when I did sit down to eat, the question that kept coming up was, "Where and how can I make this meal better for me?" I asked myself that question before every meal—especially in the beginning.

Better awareness became a project and an exercise in discipline that I created for myself so I could study my eating habits—good and bad. Doing this forced me to evaluate what I was about to put into my body. It also gave me the chance to check my *PointsPlus*® so I could make sure I wasn't using up the bulk of my daily allowance in one meal. It eventually helped me learn to use my Points wisely, something that really made a difference in my weight loss.

The real secret to my success on Weight Watchers was tracking my *PointsPlus*® values. I am super-strict about tracking every little thing I eat. Weight Watchers made it really easy for me to stick with the program because everything you need is available online. I even downloaded their application onto my iPhone so I can easily keep track of my Points all day long, no matter where I am. I never skip logging something in because I am only fooling myself if I don't keep track. I want to know exactly where I am with my Points throughout the day so I can budget them wisely for future meals. I've gotten so disciplined that I can now tally my *PointsPlus*® values in my head. After a while, I began to memorize specific *PointsPlus*® values for the foods I regularly ate. Even so, I still use the Weight Watchers tracking system every day to keep me on the right path. If you consistently do that, you cannot fail on this program.

Although it is a fairly new passion of mine, I discovered that I actually like cooking my own food. So throughout the program, I didn't eat any prepackaged foods of any kind. Although Weight Watchers makes a variety of food products, the *PointsPlus®* plan doesn't require you to eat them. It is all about real food in the real world. My goal was to learn to pick foods that were healthy choices, and since I travel a lot, they had to be readily available most anywhere I go. Although I resisted the notion at first, I eventually learned that it was desirable to have a certain amount of carbohydrates because they're fuel for your body. I also began eating more fiber because it helps move things out, if you know what I mean. I also discovered the importance of cutting back on salt and sugar. When I was a little girl, salt was a food group to me. I used to put salt on everything, including my ice cream. (Don't knock it until you've tried it! Salted caramel is a little bit of heaven!

Eating a diet filled with added sugar, unhealthy fats, and refined grains can make it easy to gain weight and at the same time not get the necessary vitamins, minerals, and other nutrients that you need for good health. These foods are also not as filling and satisfying as nutritious foods like fruits and vegetables. I never thought about any of these things before starting Weight Watchers, but they can have an impact on the scale and are equally important to maintaining good health. Weight Watchers does a great job of teaching their members these valuable lessons through their literature, on their website, and in the meetings.

A funny thing happened on the way to losing my eighty pounds. Foods that used to taste good to me no longer do. For example, if I take a sip of a regular soda now, all I can taste is the sugar. I also learned that processed food tastes better because it contains a lot of artificial ingredients that are unnecessary. Foods that contain a lot of artificial flavors often include a lot of fat, sugar, or salt to increase the enjoyment of that food, but they are not filling, and no longer part of my diet.

Since I've lost all of my weight, people always want to know what I eat. Here's the amazing thing about the Weight Watchers plan—you can eat what you've always eaten as long as you are eating the right portion amounts. While I don't have a set weekly menu, I do have some favorites that have helped me get to my goal.

A typical breakfast for me became one of three meals: grilled chicken breast fajitas with brown rice, an egg-white omelet with smoked salmon, or a chicken and vegetable omelet. If I am feeling it, I might add some cheese to the eggs, but otherwise, I go without. It is critically important to measure out the right portions or you will make the common error of eating the right foods in the wrong amounts. I make sure to use only a half to a full cup of chicken per serving, which ranges from two to four Points on the plan, depending on how hungry I am. Once I learned about the dangers of eating too much salt, I stopped adding salt to my omelets, especially the smoked salmon omelet because there is already enough salt in the fish. If I am especially hungry that morning, I might add some

Weight Watchers plain no-fat yogurt and twelve smoked almonds to my menu, too. The Weight Watchers yogurt is one of the only prepackaged foods I eat. I really like the flavor and texture of their yogurt, and unlike other brands, theirs is low in sugar. I highly recommend it as an excellent addition to any meal.

If I don't eat the yogurt with my breakfast, I will usually make it my midmorning snack. I don't believe in wasting my Points on things like juice, which I consider to be nothing but extra sugar and empty calories. The only time I will drink a glass of orange juice is if I feel like my body is craving the vitamin C and there is nothing else available to satisfy that desire. Otherwise, I know I am going to be hungry later in the day and would rather use those two to six Points on something that will fill me up and sustain me a lot longer than a glass of OJ. Instead, I will choose to drink water, Crystal Light, or occasionally, a Diet Coke.

Another secret to my weight loss was learning to make lunch my biggest meal of the day. One of my favorite choices is a turkey burger. I love them, especially the turkey burgers from the Cheese-cake Factory. The problem, though, is their portions are ridiculously huge, so when I order one, I eat only half. And believe me, that's plenty!

I get so frustrated with restaurants that make it hard for a person who wants to make the healthy choice by over-serving its portions. The temptation is often too great to stay strong, so most people will overeat. When it comes to intake, there really needs to be a sense of "too much of a good thing." Even a turkey burger can throw your entire Points for the day off if the serving size is for four instead of one. This becomes a slippery slope when eating out, especially when you order a salad thinking it is the healthier choice but because of the excessive amounts of salad dressing, that salad can contain as many as fifteen hundred calories or more!

Looking at a menu through Weight Watchers' eyes changed my entire perspective on eating out. The Weight Watchers program allows me to eat at any restaurant. One of my favorites now is a chain called Texas de Brazil. They not only offer a buffet of food but also serve you selections at the table. They offer everything from steak to sushi, and black beans, rice with gravy, and so much more. David and I used to eat there before I started Weight Watchers, and I hated going because I didn't think there was anything on the menu I could eat. I don't eat steak, so we mostly went there because David liked it. However, once I got acquainted with the dos and don'ts of the Weight Watchers program, I discovered there were lots of options for me on their menu.

Since I eat mostly chicken, turkey, and fish, what I discovered was that most restaurants are happy to accommodate special requests for how you want your food prepared. These days, I have no issue telling my server that I want my chicken grilled with no sauce, my fish broiled with no butter, and my vegetables steamed instead of sautéed. It's so easy once you know how to make the right choices. And believe it or not, it is still delicious!

Dinner varies for me because it depends on how many Points I have left at the end of my day. My favorite home-cooked meal is one of my childhood favorites. My mama used to make the most delicious turkey wings with roasted sweet potato fries or mashed sweet potatoes. Eating that meal reminds me of my mama's and grandma's houses growing up. It smells like home to me. I don't eat a lot of fried foods, but I still like my turkey to crunch, so I boil the wings and then I put them in the oven where they can get as crispy as they can. I then take the juice from the bottom of the pan and sauté some greens in it to go as a side dish. Now this is some good old-fashioned home-style cooking!

Naturally, I can't eat like that all the time, so another favorite dinner dish is salmon. I was fixing dinner for David one night when I accidentally grabbed cinnamon instead of paprika to put on the fish. I didn't realize my mistake until we sat down to eat. It turned out to be so good that now, I *only* use cinnamon and lemon when I cook salmon. The cinnamon with lemon creates a glazelike finish on the fish that's a little like sweet teriyaki with no sugar. David loves it and I feel like I've got my B. Smith on when I make this dish for him.

Let me be really honest. I can get extremely bored eating the same old things over and over. It has always been one of my biggest pitfalls in dieting. My old cycle was to break my routine by eating something that wasn't a good choice. Now I've learned that I can change things up by getting creative with my meals and snacks. The Weight Watchers website offers thousands of meal ideas, recipes, and even snack options from other members. Snacks are an important part of the Weight Watchers plan, because working healthy snacks into your day means that you keep your hunger in check and don't overdo it at mealtime. One snack I love is almonds, and they are a really good healthy snack choice. On the Weight Watchers plan, they don't have a high *PointsPlus*® value, so I often turn to almonds as a favorite treat. When I am in the mood for something salty and crunchy, I will eat smoked almonds to satisfy my salt craving in a healthy way.

When it comes to making choices for my snacks, my general rule of thumb is to go for the real thing over an imitation. I especially love mixed fruit and melon. If I want orange sherbet, I'll reach for an orange instead of the ice cream. It's the flavor I'm going for so why not eat something that has fiber and nutrients over something that is full of chemicals and artificial flavors?

Okay, so here's the money question everyone always wants to know about.

Do I eat dessert?

The answer is . . . yes!

I have a terrible weakness when it comes to chocolate and banana pudding. I especially love Walter's banana pudding. When I was living in Miami and recording, I was in the studio most of the time. And when I wasn't, I was running along the beach and exercising in the gym. I thought I was staying on top of my weight until my stylist came to fit me for the MTV Video Music Awards. Not one single thing fit. I was so mad, thinking she just brought all the wrong sizes. No, it wasn't that. You see, Walter was making banana pudding all the time back then. I had tasted it way too much. I put a banana pudding moratorium in place right away. I told Walter he was no longer allowed to come into my house with that evil pudding. My biggest lesson there was that you cannot just work out and then eat poorly and expect to lose weight. It doesn't work that way.

One of the tools Weight Watchers taught me to become consciously aware of what I was eating and when, was to keep a journal and write down everything I ate and how I was feeling at the moment of making a decision. Liz explained that doing this would help me understand my triggers that create a habit. Weight Watchers was as much about building awareness as it was losing weight. The program makes you fully conscious of the food you put into your mouth and helps you to find a balance for everyday real life. Even though the program itself was astonishing in its results, it was this newfound awareness that became the game-changer for me.

Every person has to make the decision that they are ready to create awareness about what they are putting into their bodies and then work at learning to control that choice. For me, tuning in meant I began noticing that whenever I was home alone with

Munchkin, or worse, on my own, I often found myself hitting the refrigerator and then sitting on the sofa mindlessly eating. I was often very tired from staying up at night with the baby and wasn't always thinking about what I was eating so much as just eating. I discovered that I was especially vulnerable toward the end of my day, when I don't have any Points left without going into my reserve. One thing I often went for was chocolate. When I am relaxed and comfortable, I grab for some chocolate. I developed an obsession for chocolate bars when I was filming *Winnie* in Africa. To me, eating a piece of chocolate is as relaxing as a massage. It's an event. And when I am eating it, nobody better bother me because that is my moment of bliss. Some people like to have a glass of wine at the end of a busy day.

Me?

I like to eat some delicious chocolate.

Writing these habits down helped me pinpoint my weaknesses and to become conscious of my behavior. With that awareness, I learned to make better choices. Instead of sitting on the sofa, I got up and exercised to a DVD. Or, if Munchkin was napping, I took a nap, too. If I decided to eat something, I ate something healthy like a handful of cashews and a few slices of apple. Let me tell you— when you put those two ingredients together, it is as good as a caramel apple—for real. And if I was going to have chocolate, I made sure it was really good chocolate, and in the right amount. Quality over quantity.

Another time I find it a challenge to make the right choices is when I am on a movie set. When I was making *The Three Stooges,* I really struggled with all of the sugary and salty foods that were kept out on the craft services table throughout the day. It was like that platter of cupcakes kept calling out my name. I decided the best way to combat that desire was to bring my own food from home and avoid the craft services table altogether. And when I couldn't stand it one second longer, I popped a piece of sugar-free gum into my mouth so I could have something sweet without grabbing for the pastries and such. Avoidance is a great tool to get away from food in my face all day long.

I learned to play little tricks on myself to avoid the trappings that used to keep a stronghold on me in the past. Pinkberry frozen yogurt used to be a passion of mine. Whenever I was in L.A., one of my first stops off the plane was Pinkberry to get a cup of their plain frozen yogurt with coconut, yogurt chips, and almonds sprinkled over the top. Now, instead of hitting Pinkberry when I land, I wait until the very end of my trip to treat myself so I won't have another opportunity to go back again before leaving town. That way I can't set myself up for failure or overdo a good thing. And I look forward to that Pinkberry all throughout my trip.

Even though I understood the benefits Liz was trying to share with me about journaling my feelings and hunger levels, it never really became my thing. Many people learn to use food for comfort or as a stress reliever. When they are angry, they like to chew on something crunchy or salty. Food is tied to emotion and is often used as an escape from those feelings. But I do know that for me, boredom was my biggest trigger. Even though I don't keep a journal, I do know this to be true for myself and I try to find ways to combat my boredom. What I learned from Weight Watchers is that food was meant to be used as fuel for our bodies. If we are using it for any other reasons, it is time to take a step back and ask ourselves what's up.

Once I was on the right path with the eating side of my quest for health, Liz helped me take a look at my exercise routines, too. Like my former diet mentality, my thought was that exercise had to be extreme to be effective. By this time, I had kicked up my exercise regimen to high-intensity training sessions several days a week that were leaving me sore and uncomfortable. I had adopted a "no pain, no gain" way of thinking, which left me mostly in pain with very little gain. Liz helped me realize that I could dial it back a bit and take it from being "work" to once again being enjoyable and fun. She did this by challenging me to stop doing things I didn't like and do only the things I enjoyed. That was a novel concept for me because even though I hadn't realized it for myself, somewhere along the way, exercise became a chore instead of a pleasure.

Although I always liked to exercise, at this time I had fallen into the extreme trap that took all of the fun out of it for me. The only real reward I was getting was the satisfaction of knowing that as long as I exercised hard, I could go out and eat whatever I wanted. Wrong! Liz explained that extreme exercise doesn't save you from poor food choices. It can be difficult to exercise and erase away that chocolate cake or pizza pie. It doesn't work that way. There is no such thing as a balanced equation with those things. If you're not eating the right foods in the right amounts, all the exercise in the world won't combat the caloric intake.

What was really hard to adjust to was that after I had my baby it became much harder to get out of the house to exercise. Even if I wanted to hit the gym, there were so many days I was too tired or tied to the house because Munchkin was sleeping. I started using that as an excuse not to do anything. Well, that didn't last long once I started the program.

Liz helped me embrace that the goal with exercise is to have as many options as possible. My close friends often call me "Random" because my workouts are never the same. I like doing fun things that I enjoy, from biking to basketball. Yeah, this sista's got game! I figure that as long as I am moving, I am burning calories. Some days I will choose to run outside or sprint up hills in our local park while others I'd rather use the treadmill at the gym. When I'm on the road, I still exercise to DVDs, especially when there isn't a gym available or when time is short. I like to run up and down stairs, too. I used to live on the twenty-sixth floor of my apartment building in Chicago and often took the stairs instead of taking the elevator. When your schedule is as busy as mine gets, you have to find windows of opportunity to do something active. Even if it's just going to and from the car—I'll take the harder, longer way to get there.

I'm a woman who likes progress. I want to see positive results for all of my efforts. If I am working out, then I expect to see a difference in my body. I'm definitely impatient, though. I hate waiting for anything, so the harder I work, the less time I need to wait to reap the rewards.

Like me, my fiancé is a workout fanatic, too. It's such a blessing to have a partner who shares your same beliefs in getting healthy as opposed to someone who is constantly trying to sabotage your efforts. David is a bodybuilder looking to bulk up his muscles and create mass while I am looking to slim down and elongate, so our workouts are completely different. When it comes to exercise, David never imposes his beliefs on me because we are going after two totally different looks.

The important message I heard about working out and what I want to share is that you create your own opportunities and your own limitations.

When I was assessing a diet plan that was right for me, I looked at many options—none of which made sense for my life. Every program I looked at was nothing more than a food plan. Either you are getting preprepared food delivered via the frozen-food section of your local grocery store or through a home delivery program or you had to read a book and follow their preset menus. N.F.J.—Not for Jennifer.

What the Weight Watchers *PointsPlus®* program does so well is it expands your options by teaching you to eat real food in the real world. It's so easy. You really can eat anything you want and it allows you necessary flexibility to keep you on the plan. And it teaches you how to implement activity that fits into your daily lifestyle without telling you that you absolutely have to hit the gym. It teaches behavior modification by helping you become aware of the bad food habits you've created that are holding you back. And finally, the program offers a tremendous amount of support through its meetings. For many, the meetings are where the rubber hits the road. They can make the difference between staying with the plan and leaving it.

While I wasn't able to attend as many traditional meetings as I would have liked to, when I did, I often found those to be truly inspirational. I was finally able to sit in a room with other people who were having the same struggles and challenges I was having. Hearing their stories was so helpful to know how other people were troubleshooting their problems and how they were receiving support from others. I found it so inspiring to meet other members who had been struggling with their weight for as long as I had been because it helped me come to a better understanding of my own journey. One member told me she had rejoined Weight Watchers fifteen times over the years. I couldn't believe it because I had become such an advocate for the program I could never imagine leaving! Still, she never gave up. She eventually came back and has finally found her stride. That is dedication.

Permanent weight loss doesn't come with an on and off switch. It is not something you do for a little while and think it is going to change your body. My schedule is as jam-packed as one can get and I still found the time to make the program work. You have to want weight-loss success so badly that no mountain, river, or ocean could keep you from reaching your goals. If you have that drive, passion, and commitment, there is no way you won't get there.

Whenever I couldn't make a traditional meeting, I always made time in my schedule to talk with Liz about my progress and my occasional frustrations. Amazingly, Liz was even able to meet me in South Africa for a few days when I was on location for four months shooting *Winnie*. There she introduced me to South African Weight Watchers leaders I could call on if I needed extra support. Liz was available when I needed her.

When I signed on to do the role of *Winnie*, I agreed to conform to the character, which meant losing weight before shooting and learning the proper dialect. I was already well on my way with the weight loss, so I wasn't concerned about meeting that requirement. I was, however, utterly terrified about learning the accent. I started working with a dialect coach two months before filming began. I wasn't familiar with the South African accent Winnie Mandela spoke with, but as an actress, I felt the burden of responsibility to get it right. I thought about Meryl Streep and all of the amazing characters she convincingly played throughout her career and used her as my inspiration to nail the language.

I never had the opportunity to meet Mrs. Mandela in person, but I knew she was an important figure in history and I wanted to honor her many worldly contributions. Playing her was not to be taken lightly, especially as an American actress portraying an African woman. I needed to be completely in the role, and for the first week or so, I was struggling with that. If I couldn't make that commitment, I wanted to do the right thing and pull myself from the film. Making *Winnie* was a huge and scary time in my life because of the immense nature of the character and because this was the first time I was separated from my baby for an extended period. My son was too young to make the trip to South Africa because going there requires a series of vaccinations. Also, David didn't want him to travel, which I completely understood. It was very far away, and not always terribly safe for such a young baby who is more vulnerable to infections and who cannot have the necessary inoculations. When I signed on for the project, I didn't have a family. But now I did. Being away from them was by far the hardest part of making the film.

When we started filming, I believe Darrell Roodt, the director of the movie, could tell I was struggling. He came to me one day to acknowledge that playing Winnie Mandela was a lot for anyone to take on. He said, "After everything you've been through and all that you've experienced—you're still here and that lets me know that you want to be here."

At the time, I couldn't see the forest for the trees, but I listened to Darrell and heard what he was trying to say. Whenever I'm in a situation, whether it was being eliminated from *American Idol* or up against 782 other actresses for a role, I have to fall back on my faith that God has a plan for me. God put me here, so I had no choice but to go with it. I will take that ride because I know it's my destiny. It took me another solid week to immerse myself in the role of Winnie, but once I did, I was in it to win it.

We shot the entire movie on location in South Africa, including Cape Town and Victoria. My days were long and deeply trying because the role was extremely emotional. I got up very early in the mornings, usually between 4 and 5 A.M. and didn't return back to my hotel until very late at night. If I had a day off, I used it to catch up on my sleep or take in the culture of the cities and tiny villages that surrounded me. Although the producers offered to take the cast on safari, I didn't want to do that. I was there to do a job, and when I wasn't working, I wanted to experience the local communities and meet the people. When I did, the conditions that I saw were beyond my understanding of poverty. On my way home from shooting one day, I looked out the car window and saw a little boy who was only slightly older than my baby, washing his underwear in a river. He seemed so happy and content. Despite his situation, I was struck by how joyful this boy appeared.

I saw townships where people lived in mud huts with thatched roofs, had no running water, no plumbing, no electricity, and no vegetation. I noticed smoke coming from one of the townships one day—that seemed odd. I thought there was a fire burning, but there wasn't. The smell of the smoke was so strong that it gave me a pounding headache. When I asked someone about it, they explained that this was the way those people warmed their homes. I was only exposed to the fumes for a short time and it made me sick; I couldn't imagine how the people who live in that township felt living with the smell every night. As we pulled away I saw two little girls out of the corner of my eye. They were both barefoot, walking on glass and dirt. I couldn't imagine letting my baby walk on the city streets of Chicago with no shoes, let alone the filth-laden roads these children were on. And still, those little girls just smiled and waved as we drove away. I asked someone from the crew if they could help me arrange to send shoes to all of the people in that area. And we did. When we returned to give them away, one woman fell to her knees crying because she finally had her own pair of shoes. In that moment, I suddenly realized how spoiled and shallow most people really are. Shortly before going to Africa, my makeup artist and I were in France for a fashion show and we were fussing over the fact that our hotel didn't have electrical outlets in the bathroom. After seeing how these people lived in Africa, I feel so foolish for acting that way. We live like royalty compared to the conditions I saw in Africa. In many ways, the experience there made me grow up. I learned so much about myself through the eyes of Winnie Mandela.

Aside from being away from my family, the hardest part of being in South Africa was trying to stay on the Weight Watchers program. This was the test of all tests on my weight-loss journey. Between the time change and the nature of my demanding production schedule, it was very hard to adjust to being there. The schedule hugely impacted my eating habits because my waking hours were much longer than when I am home, which meant I had to make my Points stretch throughout the day. This took some getting used to, especially because I was eating on the fly, and in between takes.

Thankfully, the portion sizes in this part of the world are much smaller than the enormous American sizes, their food production is less processed, and how food is delivered is so different. Instead of distributing overprocessed foods that can keep on a shelf longer, suppliers invested their money in better refrigeration and smarter packaging so they can package fresh foods. This worked to my advantage and was a real eye-opening experience for me. Because their emphasis was on offering fresher foods instead of foods laden with preservatives, I could continue to move away from the processed foods I had sometimes relied on before Weight Watchers and eat fresher, healthier foods. Even the food labels in South Africa were very different than the ones we have back in the United States, so I had to spend some time figuring out ingredients and calories. Because their country is on the metric system, the labels don't carry the same numbers I was used to, which meant I also had to learn to calculate my Points in a whole new way. But I did.

Winnie was challenging on so many levels. I was making a film that was filled with so much darkness and was deeply investing myself into my character. I was away from my family and found myself feeling sad, lonely, and depressed. As a result, I actually stopped eating enough food to maintain my weight. I was unintentionally losing more weight than I wanted to.

At the time I was actually as scared to lose more weight as I was to gain it. It was so outside of any scenario I had ever played out in my head. I didn't think there would ever be a day that Jennifer Hudson would be afraid of being too *skinny*. Thankfully, the Weight Watchers team was right there by my side helping me to figure out things so I didn't face a diet disaster. It took some convincing, but I actually had to start adding extra Points to my plan so I could maintain a healthy weight and look consistent on camera. I was eating more, but it was healthy food this time around.

I was so determined to get this—and not use being on location as an excuse to fall off my program. I understood the principles of Weight Watchers inside and out by now. There was no reason I couldn't take everything Weight Watchers had taught me and all of my experiences with me and make this work. If I could rise to the challenge, I could take my weight loss to the next level.

I really believe that it was my time and experience in South

Africa which solidified me as a person who actually lives a healthy lifestyle and no longer allows my environment to get in the way. And because of that, I finally *trusted the plan*. Completely. There was no doubt it works.

"*I got this*," I said aloud.

And I did.

As I grew more confident, I began to notice that people from the cast and crew were starting to pay attention to what I was doing. Several people began asking lots of questions about Weight Watchers and my personal program. The script supervisor used to bring me chocolate every single day on the set. She kept asking people how I could eat chocolate and still be so skinny. Someone finally told her that I track my food and then keep a tally of my Points. By doing this, I stay within my limits and won't fall away from the plan. Intrigued, she came to me to find out more about the Weight Watchers program. Before I knew it, I had several people from the movie following the plan, too. I suddenly felt like the pied piper leading the way.

After navigating my way through eating in South Africa, I now know that I can travel anywhere and stick to the program. It doesn't matter where you are because conscious eating is the same all over the world. Saying you can't because of where you are physically is just an excuse—covering up something going on emotionally or psychologically.

When I returned from South Africa, I was asked to shoot my

second commercial for Weight Watchers. I wanted to play a joke on the Weight Watchers people by wearing a fat suit in to the shoot so they would think I gained back all of my weight while I was on location. I couldn't get a convincing fat suit in time, so I did the next best thing. I wore a prosthetic pregnancy belly in to the shoot and had them all believing I was having another baby. Even my manager wasn't in on the joke, so when everyone saw me, they freaked, but no one said a word. I was sitting in a chair rubbing my tummy like I was ready to pop at any minute. When I got to wardrobe, the stylist took one look at me and said, "We may need to let your clothes out a bit. . . ." She was panicking because I was supposed to come in with a brand-new size-6 body. Instead, I came in looking nine months pregnant!

I couldn't believe that everyone was being so polite, especially because we only had that day to shoot the commercial.

Finally, the stylist looked at me and asked if I was pregnant.

"No. It's a joke." We had a good laugh over it, even if no one else did!

Me at age seven—I was always tall for my age.

The picture says it all!
Walter and me at prom.

Prom night with Walter. Big brother was definitely watching.

Rate $ 25 per Song

Jennifer Hudson
Soloist

Weddings
Funerals   773-874-6613
Church Functions   Pager 773-903-7203

$25 a song . . . now that was a bargain!

My dramatic velvet and silver gown
from my talent show days.

Walter Williams III

Walter Williams III

On the football field in Atlanta waiting for
my first *American Idol* audition.

Ready to rock my first
American Idol audition.

Walter Williams III

Feeding my face!

Walter Williams III

Waiting to audition for the judges—do you like my big hair?

American Idol Season 3 top 24
contestants, Ashley Thomas,
me, Fantasia Barrino, and
Diana DeGarmo.

With Mama touring L.A.

Dreaming of someday
having my own star—
still waiting!

My sister Julia and me.

Celebrating my win for *Dreamgirls* at the Golden Globes.

Walter Williams III

David and me in Boston.

Backstage at the Staples Center for Michael Jackson's memorial service with Usher, Stevie Wonder, and Magic Johnson.

David and me shortly before the birth of our son.

Derek Blanks

My baby and me.

At David Jr.'s christening—a blessing for all of us.

Derek Blanks

Clive Davis and me.

Something about this picture reminds me of Twiggy.

Walter and me now. We've come a long way together.

On the beach in the Hamptons, enjoying a rare day off.

Thomas Blue

I loved my Versace gown that I wore to the 2011 Oscars.

Ready to rock the Grammys.

Getting ready for the Met Ball, wearing a Vera Wang gown.

I think I look hot!

CHAPTER TEN

DON'T LOOK DOWN

O nce I got into the groove, being on Weight Watchers actually became fun. I wanted to tell everyone I knew about how great I think this plan is for losing weight. Everywhere I go people stop and want to ask me how I lost my weight. Not long ago, I was in a park playing with my son when a young heavy-set girl came over to me.

"Wow. You look so skinny!" she said. "So, that Weight Watchers thing really works, huh?"

I was thrilled to take the time to talk to this young girl and tell her all about the virtues of the program. Even though I was at the park to spend time with my baby boy, if it meant that five minutes of my time could change a life, I was happy to share my journey with this perfect stranger.

"So, this is how it works. All you have to do is keep track of your Points. You get a certain number of Points to use each day. When you've used those up, you're done eating for the day. That's it. That's how I did it." I was trying to keep it as simple as I could.

"That sounds too hard," she said.

As soon as I heard her response, I knew this girl wasn't ready to make the commitment to change. One thing I know for sure is, you can't force the issue. When someone wants to lose weight, they will do whatever it takes. They can't do it for anyone else but themselves. It has to be for them alone. Without that understanding, they will fail.

As my weight loss progressed, I shared my newfound love for healthy eating with my sister and several other members of my family. My family has always been supportive of everything I do, so when I told everyone that I had started Weight Watchers, several of them decided that they wanted to try it, too. And for those who wouldn't get on board, Lord knows, I did what I could to try to convince them to join.

JULIA, MY SISTER

Our family is a family that eats. If you go to anyone's house for a visit, they will always try to feed you. That's the way it has always been. When my sister, Jenny, decided to go on Weight Watchers, she came to me and begged me to start the program with her. Jenny was always the skinny-mini in our family. Maybe it's because Jason and I were so much heavier than her that we never noticed that Jenny was heavy, too. She told me all about Liz, her weight-loss leader, and offered to set up a consultation between us. I wasn't all that into going, but I told my cousin Pam about my meeting, hoping she might want to come with me. Before I knew it, several other family members decided to join us, too. I was still reluctant, but since the family was getting on board, I agreed to give the program a try. I was very successful for the first two months. Before I knew it, I was down forty pounds, and after years of insulin dependence, I noticed that when I was eating according to the Weight Watchers plan, I really didn't have to take my daily shots. You might think that that was enough to keep me motivated to stick with it, but it wasn't. Aside from the change in my blood sugar levels, I didn't really feel any different from the weight loss, plus my old eating habits were really hard to break.

I know that no one is holding me back but me, and still, I couldn't seem to follow through. You see, I am an expert excuse-maker, so I came up with a thousand reasons I didn't want to stay with the plan. I drive a bus, which means I sit on my rear end all day long. Most everyone I know who drives a bus for a living gains weight. Since I have to get up really early in the morning to make my shift, I don't have enough time to prepare my food for the day. I'd stop at the gas station on my way in and buy chips and donuts to eat for breakfast. Truth be told, I enjoy eating junk food. I've always been that way and don't have any plans to give it up. The funny thing is, I am the most competitive person in our family. If I really gave my all, I know I'd be the family's biggest loser. My head is just not there. I don't like it when someone tells me I can't do something, so restricting how much of my favorite foods I could eat just didn't work for me.

I think about going back to meetings. I see the progress that Jenny and so many of my other relatives have made, so deep down, I know the plan works. If I ever go back, I will have to commit to getting it together, and right now, I don't really have the willpower to do that—at least not yet. One thing is for sure, if our mama were here, she'd be fussing over Jenny's weight loss. She'd say something like, "Now, Jenny, you just got too skinny and don't be losing any more weight!" That would be our mama.

My sister and I have always been close but we couldn't be more opposite—especially when it comes to taking care of our bodies and our health. She loves her junk food, and though I love my food, too, these days I like it healthy. I've always been known for my strong beliefs, but my sister has that dangerous combination of being both strong and stubborn. I tell her all the time that she needs to try a new way of looking at food and change her eating habits or she will not be around to enjoy life. She's so feisty when she is telling me she is "fine," and that she doesn't need my advice. But the reality is, she is very overweight and suffers from diabetes. She is completely insulin dependent, in part due to her obesity. I love my sister and want her to be around for a long time. I had hoped that she would somehow get inspired by my weight loss and give Weight Watchers a try for herself. I begged and begged until one day she finally said she would do it. Julia stayed on the program for two months and lost a little more than forty pounds. But then she quit.

I was so proud of her effort and disappointed in her decision to stop. If she really gave it her all, Julia could blow my results right out of the water because her weight loss would be far more dramatic. She knows she's the only one holding herself back, and when she gets sick and tired of feeling the way she does, she will come back. I know it.

I think Julia is like a lot of women who want to lose weight. They give it their all for a while, but they don't fully change their habits. Anyone can lose a few pounds, but not everyone has the tools to stick with it. I don't judge my sister for giving up. I understand her feelings, and I feel her pain and frustration. I know how hard it is to undo everything you know and are comfortable with doing—especially when you have a lot of weight to lose. It feels like a huge mountain you have to climb. But we can't let our insecurities own or destroy us. We have to face them head-on. That was part of the challenge that motivated me to take this journey. I wanted to see what I could do and, more important, I wanted to understand everything that was holding me back. That took some soul-searching and spending some time alone asking myself the hard questions we all avoid.

"What makes me feel this way?"

"Why do I choose to make poor food choices?"

"What is my core problem?"

Until you can answer those types of questions, you will keep making excuses that only you view as your roadblocks to success. We all make up excuses as a way of avoiding something we don't want to do. Excuses are our way of making a decision okay for ourselves.

How do I know this?

Because I was once there.

I was that person.

I had that mind-set, so I am well aware of why that type of thinking only holds us back.

When my very first Weight Watchers commercial came out, people freaked out because I was sitting in a chair wearing a blazer.

"She didn't lose weight."

"She's sitting down. Who can tell what she looks like?"

These were the types of comments people made about me. But in reality, these were just excuses they were making for themselves. They are the same excuses Julia is still making and the ones I made for myself over the years. That is why I can identify it for what it was.

When the second commercial came along, my stylist kept me in that damn jacket, so people still doubted my progress. It reminded me of getting the role of Effie in *Dreamgirls*. I heard so many people say, "She got the part, but I bet she can't sing the music," and, "She can sing, but can she act?"

People! Stop!

For all of those doubters, haters, and excuse-makers out there— listen up because I've got something to say.

Hear this loud and clear.

I am completely in charge of the choices I make about what I am doing to lose weight and get healthy.

And you know what? We *all* have this power.

Don't be angry with me for something good I've done for myself. Be angry with yourself for not having the courage to do the same in your own life.

At the end of the day, you're not hurting me—you're hurting yourself.

So, stop pointing the finger at everyone else.

Stop making excuses about why you "can't."

And start taking action.

The same frame of mind that is keeping you from doing it is the mind that will help you to achieve what you want to do.

If you're at home reading this book and asking yourself why I have this success and you don't, don't be angry with me—stop and ask yourself what your issues are that are holding you back. Don't be afraid of the answers. Be afraid of not asking the questions.

My cousin Gina started Weight Watchers the same time I did. Every time I saw her, I was losing weight and she wasn't. She'd make comments like, "You're skinny and I can't stand you," while complaining that the program wasn't working for her.

"Girl, you know you're not working the program. If you were, you'd be skinny, too!" Then I told her to stop her complaining and get into the right mind-set so she could do it. When she finally made up her mind to lose the weight, it fell off just like that. If you can break down those walls you've spent so many years building to protect yourself, you can achieve anything.

Are you still making excuses or are you ready to make a change?

And speaking of change, I never thought I'd see the day that my entire family would gravitate toward something like losing weight. It still blows my mind. I often ask myself, Is this the same family? Everyone from the women and the men, the young and the old, is finally consciously aware of what they are putting in their bodies and want to make the right choices. Remember, I come from a family where food was a major part of every gathering and where the women would get on your case if they thought you were getting too thin. A family that loved a table full of fried chicken, pork chops, biscuits, and gravy.

Our biggest success story so far is my cousin Pam, who we lovingly refer to as our "biggest loser" because she has lost more than one hundred and five pounds so far (and counting). It had been a while since I had seen Pam, so after she lost around seventy-five pounds, I invited her to come see me at one of my shows. I saw this girl trailing me backstage but didn't realize it was *my cousin*. I was only able to recognize her by the sound of her voice. I told her how amazing I thought she looked—and she did.

PAM CURB, MY COUSIN

Like a lot of women, I had slowly put on weight throughout the years without totally noticing just how much I'd gained. One morning I stepped on the scale and much to my surprise, it read 337 pounds! "No way!" I said out loud. The scale had to be wrong. I was expecting to see somewhere around three hundred pounds, but not 337.

Now you might think that weighing three hundred that an extra thirty-seven pounds wouldn't much matter, but it did. Every time I went to the doctor over the years, I always let them weigh me, but I never allowed them to tell me the number on the scale. I'd avoided it for so long that I lost track of my weight.

I didn't think it was possible that I had gained more than one hundred pounds since my wedding day thirteen years back. I didn't realize that I was that big. I got a little weepy-eyed because I had let myself go that far without paying any attention to how I looked or felt.

The truth is, I was tired all of the time. I chalked that up to getting up early for work, taking care of my three children, and running around all the time. I didn't have the energy to do any of it with gusto. When my three-year-old wanted me to play with her, I couldn't. She became intentionally defiant when I was scolding her. I'd say, "Come here right now," but she wouldn't move because she knew there was no way I was going to chase her. I couldn't.

We were all at a family gathering when Jen walked through the door looking like a model. "Girl, what are doing? Tell me now!" She said she had gone on Weight

Watchers. I had been on their plan before and didn't believe her because I hadn't lost a pound when I tried. But Jenny kept telling me how easy the program was, and by looking at her, it obviously works.

A few months later, I saw Jenny again. This time she had lost even more weight. I was mesmerized by how she looked.

"Pam, if someone gave you a book and told you to stay within these Points and you will lose weight while still eating anything you want, would you tell them no?" Jenny asked.

"I guess not," I said.

That same night, the Lord spoke to me. "You aren't going to be here for your kids."

When I told my husband, Mario, about the message I had received, he said, "We want you to be here, Pam, and if you don't make some changes, you won't be." He was right.

Shortly after that, Liz came to meet with some of our family members to get us all started. I was eager to jump on the bandwagon and give it a try. Liz explained the program to me in great detail. I immediately thought there was no way I could ever do it because I didn't have time to count my Points. The reality is that I wasn't sure I was ready to give the plan a chance. Liz assured me that I was feeling like many of her members—overwhelmed. And she was right. "Then just change one thing, Pam. Weight Watchers is a lifetime journey. Tell me one thing you are going to change for this week and I promise that you will see results." I had to think about it for a second. When I told Liz that I ate chips for breakfast, she said, "That's not breakfast food." And she was right. For the next week, I made a conscious decision to eat better. I told my husband, Mario, that I was going to give Weight Watchers a try and if he wanted to help me lose weight, then he had to help me with the plan. So he woke up at 3:00 in the morning to fix me a bag of food to take to work. He boiled eggs for me, gave me apples, carrots, and all sorts of healthy choices to pick from. I wasn't used to preparing my breakfast or lunch, so Mario's help meant the world to me.

Mario had noticed I had gained the weight over the years but he never said a word. He wanted me to lose the weight but never really pushed me. He encouraged me to get healthy, which I didn't understand meant losing weight. He inspired me every day by reminding me that I didn't have to be full, only satisfied. He helped me curb my desire to go back for second helpings, something I never thought twice about before starting Weight Watchers. These days I have to make sure that I measure out my portions or I will still overeat.

I told my mother, husband, and children that I wanted to take a year and focus on taking care of myself so I could finally get healthy. They were all on board with that decision and said they would do whatever they could to help me get there. My husband got me started on taking walks around the neighborhood. He was committed to helping me on my journey any way he could. I was the luckiest wife on the planet because some husbands aren't as supportive or involved. My mother helped out by making healthy dinners for us after I put in long days at work and didn't have the time to cook for us myself. If I didn't have everyone's help, I am not sure I could have stayed with the program all on my own. My success has come from the love and encouragement I've received from all of my family.

Once I started exercising, I realized that I had to make the time to do that every day. It didn't matter where or when as long as I got ten minutes of movement in. Since I drive a bus, I knew I had time while waiting in the lineup. I started running up and down the aisle of the bus until the passengers started loading. Sometimes I'd park the bus while waiting and walk around it for those ten minutes. My passengers began to notice what I was doing and were encouraging me to keep up the good work. The more I worked out, the better I felt, and my results were even more significant. I eventually joined a health club to take my fitness to the next level. My husband joined, too, so I would have a workout partner to keep me motivated.

Weight Watchers is the easiest plan I have ever been on. I didn't have to deny myself anything. If I wanted to eat a piece of cake without feeling bad, I could as long as I calculated in the Points for my day. Over the course of a year or so, I lost seventy-five pounds and felt great. My knees were no longer an issue; I had more energy and could breathe a lot easier. It was right around that weight that I hit a plateau in my loss. I began getting careless with tracking my Points. I was messing up every day and couldn't seem to get back on track. Liz reminded me that every day was a new chance to start over, so once I could get my head back into the game, I was able to focus and get back to the plan. As Liz so often reminded me, eating healthy is a lifetime journey. People think of Weight Watchers as a diet, but it isn't. It is a way of eating you want to commit to for life. Not long ago, one of my co-workers saw me eating lunch and asked, "Are you still eating healthy?"

My answer was simple: "I have made a commitment to myself to turn my life around and this is part of it."

To date, I've lost one hundred and five pounds. I've got fifty more to go. I don't have a set weight goal, but I want to get down to a size 12 or 14. When I get there, I'll be happy. My husband is grateful, too, because as he says, "I've got my wife back."

My aunt Bae Mae is in her seventies and has lost more than forty-six pounds. I had only ever known Aunt Bae Mae as a big woman. She was so inspired by my weight loss that she decided to give it a try, too. I think she's the true inspiration for making a decision to take control of her health and weight so late in life. If she can make that decision at her age, there is simply no excuse for anyone else to say they can't do it. I was especially stunned when I heard that my uncle Charles, who is known as the barbecue man in our family because his brother once owned his own barbecue restaurant, is sitting in weekly Weight Watchers meetings, losing weight, too. These two relatives are living proof that it is never too late to get control of your health.

AUNT BAE "BABY" MAE

Age 74

I began my journey with Weight Watchers in May 2010 after one of my cousins called me to say she had started on their program. At the time, I wasn't thinking about losing weight. I've never been a big eater, but I like rich food. I rather enjoy eating grits, greens with salt pork or ham hock, but most of all, I really like butter. And as they say, "Everything is better with butter!" Still, I'd been a big woman my entire life and at my age, I thought, What's the point? She tried to entice me by telling me that the Weight Watchers people were coming to talk to everyone in the family and we were going to have our picture taken to track our progress. "Picture? I don't want any pictures taken!" I told her the only way I would join her was if she took a bus trip with me to an upcoming family reunion. She said, "If I go with you, will you try the program with me?" I reluctantly said I would try it for a week or two.

So many members of our family had started on the Weight Watchers plan that they held their own meetings every week at our church. I really enjoyed attending those meetings because they inspired me. When I heard other people's stories and saw how well my family members were doing on the plan, I felt like I could do it, too.

I lost two or three pounds the first week on the plan. That was enough to get me to go back to another meeting and see how I could do better during week two. I gave up drinking excessive amounts of cola like I used to and replaced it with water. I was amazed that I could eat all types of food as long as I ate them in the right portions. It took me some time to realize that I could no longer go back for a second hamburger, but at least I could still eat one if I wanted to. Today I still eat my beloved grits, but now I'll have a half of a cup instead of a heaping spoonful serving—I get the flavor without all of the unwanted extra Points. I won't bring my old favorite foods into the house, and though my husband still drinks his soda pop, I keep it in the basement where it is out of sight, out of mind, so I won't be tempted. And even if I were, as a senior person, I am not walking those stairs unless I have to!

I'm a Christian woman, who believes that the Lord always has a plan. When I joined Weight Watchers I realized that, like my faith, the door is open for all those who will come. You have to accept the plan and realize that if you slip, and you might, you can't use that as a reason to give up or stop. Even if you go a week without losing a pound, be happy that you didn't gain one. Eating healthy is a continuous way of life. We're all human, which means we will make mistakes. Don't dwell on that—focus on getting back to eating right and you will feel so good.

Even my twelve-year-old cousin Star has benefited from the program. Her story is very near and dear to me because she is a young girl with a bundle of talent who has always been a little chubby and didn't have the self-esteem to see herself as the beautiful girl she truly is. Her mother came to me awhile back to ask my thoughts on how to break her daughter into the music business. I knew from my own experiences that there is so much competition out there, and like it or not, my cousin was going to be judged on her appearance before her talent. Lord knows I had lived through that scene too many times in my life. I encouraged her mother, who was also a Weight Watchers member, to share with Star the new healthy habits from the program. That way Star could face the competition that she was up against with a fair shot of breaking out. Star said she was scared to make changes. Discouraged by Star's refusal, her mom asked me to talk to her, hoping that I might be able to convince her to listen to the advice and learn how to eat healthy.

I spoke with Star for about an hour. I reminded her of all of her positive assets. I told her that no one is perfect—no one. We always think the grass is greener on the other side, but the reality is that everyone struggles with something. I laughed as I shared my thoughts on how everyone has a shape. Some girls have great shapes while others are built like boys. Both are still shapes. Some are built like two-liter bottles of soda and others are built like single cans.

"You know what? I was once that bottle!" I said. I think she knew what I meant.

As we talked, I assured her that no one needed to know she was changing her eating habits and that she could go at her own pace. Before we went our separate ways, I committed to becoming her mentor throughout her journey and promised that she wouldn't go through any of these changes alone.

I didn't have anyone to guide me like that when I was her age, but I was determined to break that cycle in our family by making myself available to anyone who had the desire to get healthy. I managed to talk her into listening to what her mother had to say, and guess what? It worked! She is a whole new person; she can see herself for the amazing girl she is. While her outer appearance has definitely changed, it is her inner beauty that is finally shining through.

Altogether, seventy-five of my family members have gone on the program and, as of the writing of this book, they have collectively lost more than *two thousand* pounds. They attend a weekly

Weight Watchers meeting where they all get together to support one another through their journeys. One of the most valuable lessons I learned from Liz was the importance of having a solid support system. That lack of support is one of the biggest reasons people gain back the weight they have worked so hard to take off. Weight Watchers was so impressed by my family members and their commitment to the program that they actually put two of my cousins in a television commercial for the company in an effort to make their weight loss real for everyday people. Ultimately, weight loss and getting healthy have become a real family affair.

It blows me away to see these people taking control of their health because our family has always loved food—especially unhealthy food. It's such a change in lifestyle for everyone, especially the elders in my family, who never dieted a day in their lives. When I threw my son's second birthday party, almost everyone attending asked me to plan a special Weight Watchers–friendly menu so they could stay on the plan that day. As I walked around the party, we all began talking about our personal weight-loss journeys, and we created a spontaneous Weight Watchers meeting on the spot.

"Jenny, how many Points are in this burger?"

"Can I eat this?"

"Help me not fall off today . . ."

I suddenly felt like I was a Weight Watchers leader, and I loved every minute of the joyful experience. Seeing so many of my relatives enthusiastically embrace these changes makes me feel like Jesus has a bigger plan for me outside of music.

Sharing this moment was amazing. I felt more proud that day than I did receiving my Oscar. For real. Part of my drive to keep at it myself is so I can continue to set a positive example for my family and others.

Healthy eating is a choice, a lifestyle, and a decision only you can make for yourself, but once you do, you'll never want to go back to the way you used to feel.

Even though I have been extremely public about my commitment to Weight Watchers, some people still think I lost the weight by some other means. Some even believe that I had gastric bypass surgery. Here's the thing. I am all about doing things in a natural way. My sister came to me awhile ago to say she wanted to have her stomach stapled. I was all over her before she finished the sentence.

"Julia. That's cheating. It's the lazy way out and I won't let you do that. You have to want to lose the weight and then do the work for it to truly mean anything." And that is how I really feel. So when people ask me how I took off my excess pounds, I tell them I did it the old-fashioned way—with determination and commitment. And just so we're completely clear about what I am saying, whenever you see my stretch marks and excess skin—that is to let you know that my weight loss is real. I am proud of those reminders of how I once looked. They are my war wounds, my battle scars, and they're there to remind me of what used to be the truth. A truth I created and a truth I changed. If I had any type of cosmetic surgery, don't you think I'd get that stuff fixed, too? Of course I would! But I didn't. I didn't do anything but eat right and exercise. You can take that to the bank. And you can do it, too.

According to a recent OECD study, in the United States, the cost of treating obesity-related diseases, such as diabetes, heart disease, and stroke, will increase $66 billion per year by 2030, and represent a 2.6 percent increase in overall health spending. The increasing rates of obesity would mean 7.8 million extra cases of diabetes, 6.8 million extra cases of coronary heart disease and stroke, and 539,000 extra cancer cases by 2030. Losing just a little weight could offset those increases. The report noted that a 1 percent population-wide decrease in body-mass index (just 1.9 pounds for an average 198-pound adult) would prevent more than 2 million cases of diabetes, roughly 1.5 million cases of heart disease and stroke, and 73,000 to 127,000 cancer cases in the United States.

Not only did Weight Watchers change the way I thought about food, it altered my entire way of thinking. I became a much more organized person because I had to practice structure about my meals and keep meticulous notes on what I ate every single day. And even though many experts will tell you not to weigh yourself daily, it's now the first thing I do every morning. I weigh completely naked so there is nothing that can mysteriously add an unexpected pound here or there other than my food intake. This routine helps me to control my fluctuations in weight. If I see a small gain, I know I can do something about it that day. I can drink more water and make smarter food choices to move the needle on that scale back down. I try to weigh myself only in the morning because doing so at other times of the day can have slight fluctuations. Doing this helps keep the circumstances the same each time, so I feel as if I am getting an accurate weight. I know I'm not alone in this—it is just a human compulsion.

If I don't get on the scale every day, I feel as if I am not on top of my progress or lack thereof. If I check into a hotel and my room doesn't have a scale, I call housekeeping to bring one up. Call it a habit or an obsession—either way, I have to know where I am on the scale at all times. If I've gained a pound or two and don't know it, there is nothing preventing me from continuing to gain weight, especially if I am unaware of that movement in the first place. I also do my weekly Weight Watchers weigh-ins like all members, just not usually at meetings. Everyone has their own method of gauging where they're at. Some people never get on the scale and merely go by how their clothes are fitting, while others obsess over the number they see at their feet every day. I am one of those obsessed people. Hello. My name is Jennifer and yes, I am addicted to the scale.

By late 2009, I was back in the studio recording my second album, *I Remember Me.* The title track is based on a poem I wrote one morning because I wanted to share how I felt about all of the experiences I have had, including the highs and the lows and everything in between. The song was written to allow people to get to know and then embrace the new me. I had been through so much throughout my career, in my personal life, and during my weight loss that I wanted to reconnect with my fans by giving them some insight about how all of that felt. I felt like a new person, but I was still the same girl.

While recording the album, I got to work with the incredibly talented R. Kelly, who wrote my first single "Where You At." R. Kelly really got me. Although we both live in Chicago, we had never met while making the album. Even so, he somehow understood me.

I also got to work with the fantastic Alicia Keys, who wrote "Angel" and cowrote "Don't Look Down" and "Everybody Needs Love"; and one of my favorite songwriters, Diane Warren, who I had previously worked with on "Still Here" for my first album, but made it onto my second album instead. "Still Here" was originally dedicated to my grandmother, but it really relates to my whole family. It's a way to remember and keep them in my life.

Diane's songs are the type of music I love to sing. When it comes to songwriting, she is in a league of her own. We recently collaborated on a song for the sound track of *Winnie* called "Bleed for Love." It is such a beautiful song. Give me a Diane Warren song any day of the week and I will smother it with Jennifer Hudson singing love.

I had purposely kept a pretty low profile while recording my second album. The first time I publicly revealed my partial weight loss was when I was asked to participate in a tribute to Whitney Houston at the 2010 BET Honors, held in Washington, D.C. As you can imagine, that was a treat for me. I was finally able to show my appreciation for Whitney by singing one of her biggest hits and most difficult songs to perform—"I Will Always Love You." That song meant so much to me that I told producers they had to let me do that song or I wouldn't perform at all! At the time, I had lost about thirty or so pounds. Although it wasn't that much, the change in my appearance was drastic. I wore a custom-made dress that hugged my body and showed off my brand-new shape.

When I came out onstage, I received a standing ovation based on my look alone. I hadn't even begun to sing. I had to look behind me to see if someone else had come out on the stage, too, because I couldn't understand why they were on their feet. I didn't realize it was just me they were screaming for. I think everyone was shocked by the change in my appearance. It felt unreal.

Ironically, before that night, there had actually been rumors circulating that I might be pregnant again. Those were quickly put to rest the moment I stepped out on the stage. It was one of the first moments I realized the tables had turned—audiences were still looking at me before listening to me, but for the first time in my career, my image was competing with my talent in a positive way.

I killed the song and gave Whitney every ounce of my blood, sweat, and tears that night. When I finished, the crowd went crazy, standing and cheering for me again for several minutes afterward. It was a wonderful feeling because this time, they were clapping for my art.

CHAPTER ELEVEN

I REMEMBER ME

I didn't realize how special growing up in Chicago was until I stepped out and lived someplace else for a while. At the end of the day, Chicago is my home. In many ways, it represents who I am, where I come from, and where I got started, and it gives me a sense of comfort I don't get anywhere else on the planet. When I'm in Chicago, I can just relax and be my old self, Jenny Kate. I can shop, walk the streets, and be myself without anyone making an unnecessary fuss. I know the good people of Chicago and they know me. And that familiarity helps me to feel safe, secure, and stay grounded in an otherwise crazy world that isn't known for those values.

Since David and I come from Chicago, both of our families are there, and family is something that is extremely important to both of us. That is why we made the decision to pack up our baby son and our three dogs, Oscar, Grammy, and Dream, and move our family back to our hometown in October 2010. I want him to have the same sense of family, tradition, and support that I grew up with. It was definitely time to go home.

Although Liz and Weight Watchers had somewhat prepared me for the physical changes I could expect to see in my body and then how to maintain those changes, no one really told me about the emotional acceptance, or even rejection, of losing weight and all of the emotional changes that would take place. She said that some people have such a hard time adjusting to their weight loss that they actually prefer to go back to the way they used to be by gaining back the pounds they lost and, for many, packing on even more. I am lucky that I have a good support system to help me deal with these feelings.

I knew there would be challenges along the way, but I welcome the opportunity to learn and grow from the experiences. "Bring it on!" That is always my attitude.

> *In the United States, about one-quarter of all men were obese in 2008 regardless of their race, while 46 percent of black women, one-third of Hispanic women, and 30 percent of white women were obese.*

First, let me say that I love the way I look. I always have. But I am extremely proud of the hard work I've put into my weight loss and the effort I've given to getting healthy for my family. Nothing prepared me for the attention I now get as a result of losing weight. Even people I'm close to have had a hard time accepting my new shape, including my fiancé. If David had his way, he'd keep me dressed in flowing mumus all the time. To be honest, he doesn't really like it when I wear something that shows off my body. If I try to put on a pair of shorts that he thinks are too short, he freaks out. I think it's kind of funny because my man makes his living wearing drawers and nothing else. Why is it okay for him and not for me?

David has always been the type of man who tells me what he thinks, that I am beautiful, and that he loves when I don't wear makeup. He likes me best when I am plain.

Every now and then David will make comments that "his old girlfriend" never dressed in tight clothes or wore a lot of makeup. Of course, he is referring to me before I lost the weight. Sometimes, when we go out to eat, he'll occasionally offer me bites of whatever he's having, knowing I don't want to add the extra Points into my day. Sometimes I think he'd love to stuff me back to my old weight because it was what he was used to.

In all fairness, even I had to get into a new mind-set when it came to my body. I'd go shopping and reach for the same old sizes I've always grabbed for. Walter usually stopped me by saying, "That won't fit you—you're not a size twelve anymore." And he was right. Like I've said, I always had a shape, but this was the first time in my life that I had a skinny waist and a bra size that was smaller than I'd been since I first grew breasts!

Ever since *Dreamgirls,* designers have graciously sent me dresses to wear on the red carpet, but it was tricky because it was much harder then to find something to wear that fit, let alone flattered my body. The designers that made dresses in the larger sizes wanted to clothe me because they hardly ever got the chance to fit a "big girl." You can bet that Gwyneth Paltrow or Angelina Jolie and I were never fighting over the same dress.

These days, it's hard to pick out which dress I'm going to wear because they all look and fit amazingly. Still, I find it a little intimidating at times because I am not used to someone like Vera Wang asking me to wear one of her dresses at an event, Donatella Versace dressing me for the Oscars, or Michael Kors calling me up to see if I would like to wear one of his gowns at a private dinner in Rome. All I had to do was fly to Italy, put on his gown, have dinner, and mingle among the guests. Mary J. Blige was going to be there performing, too. Talk about coming from the whole other side of the rainbow.

I was someone who grew up never being looked at as a fashionista. And now, for the first time ever, I was actually going to be a model talking about what I was wearing! While you know I always saw myself as a supermodel, I must admit that I worried I might be a complete disaster if the dress didn't go over well. If I agreed to do it, I was purposefully and willingly putting myself in a place where I only was being judged on my physical appearance and nothing else. While I certainly had my share of dealing with that, it was never an intentional decision. It was a lot of pressure to consider. I thought, What the hell? I told Michael it would be an honor to wear his gown and had the best time ever doing it.

People who I knew before I lost weight started looking at me in a whole new way. My friend and stylist Eric Archibald kept trying to dress me in the same type of clothes as he did before I lost the weight. He wanted to cover me up by putting me in a suit jacket. I felt like I was back on *American Idol*.

"I could have worn that jacket eighty pounds ago!" I loudly protested. "From now on, I only want to wear clothes that have a shape to them. That decision is final!" It is a good thing that Eric and I get each other and I know his heart is always in the right place, even if his clothing choice isn't!

Eric had been a fan of mine since I did *Dreamgirls*. He has the most amazing fashion sense of any stylist I have ever worked with. He gets what I like and what I don't like and how I feel about my body. Still, it took him a little while to come around to my new shape because he had grown so protective over my former body size. He used to refuse to put me in tight, form-fitting clothes because he was concerned that I would be too self-conscious wearing them. What I discovered was, when I was heavier, he had his own insecurities about my size that he was inadvertently imposing on me. Honestly, I never felt self-conscious about my body. Never. My decision to lose weight was about being healthy for my son, not about changing my appearance to fit into some preconceived idea of what I should look like. I'd get so mad when Eric refused to bring me figure-flattering dresses because it was his way of telling me he didn't think I could wear that style. And y'all know I don't like it when someone tells me I can't do something. There's nothing that will make me put that dress on faster than someone telling me I shouldn't.

When I was picking a dress to wear to a 2011 pre-Oscar party, it seemed everyone had an opinion on whether I should wear the one I chose or not. Granted, it was short—even for me, but I didn't think it was *too* short.

"You can't wear that!" Walter said as he shook his index finger at me in total disapproval.

"Why not?" I knew what he was thinking, but every now and then I like to play with Walter to see him squirm.

"It's too . . . short!"

We bantered back and forth for a few minutes before I made

him take a picture with my iPhone so we could send it to my sister for her opinion. If Julia said it was too short, I'd agree to change into another dress. If she said it was fine, I had my outfit for the party.

"It looks great," she texted back, and with her approval I proudly wore that sizzling dress.

What was fascinating about this was that Walter is with me most every day. Even though he was a part of my weight-loss journey, like Eric, he also hadn't adjusted how he sees me. My sister has mostly seen the changes in my body from afar. Every time she saw a photo of me in a magazine or on the Internet, she saw drastic differences in my shape. I think the distance gave her a fresh perspective that the people closest to me on a daily basis simply didn't have—yet. They'd eventually come around, but oh, it wasn't easy. Walter is still trying to dress me like his grandma!

Even though I have lost a lot of weight, I am still the same girl who felt self-conscious having to kiss Jamie Foxx in my first scene in *Dreamgirls*. I am still the same Jennifer I always was. I don't want to go and put everything out there on display just because I'm proud of the work I've done to lose weight. When I shot my music video for "No One's Gonna Love You" from my second album, I worked with a director who wanted to put me in super-sexy skin-baring outfits. She thought I would want to be exposed and show off my body. Now, I had never met this woman prior to the shoot, so she didn't know anything about me before making this decision.

Big mistake.

Big.

No one is going to make a decision about what I wear without running it by me first.

When it came time to do the first shot, she walked over to me and said, "Jennifer—for this video, you are so in love with your man that you just want to sleep with him."

Say what?

So here's how this goes. I hadn't been very involved with the planning of this particular video, so I didn't really know what the full story line was until I got to the set. My record company had hired the production team and created a storyboard with the director without my input. There had never been an instance in my career where I worried that someone would want to put me in a compromising position that didn't mesh with my image or brand— until *that* day.

The notion of me playing a sex kitten was a real eye-opener. Was my record label actually trying to repackage me and change how people saw me now that I had lost weight?

I had never done anything like that before my weight loss and I wasn't about to do it now, either. I changed every scene as we went along. I told them I would not cooperate with anything that didn't feel right to me. I made that pretty tough for everyone, all in the name of not compromising who I am. I'm not sorry. I am an adult, a mother, and a woman in charge of herself.

I am in control of all decisions that have to do with my image, which means that no one will decide what's right for me except me. I'm not special. We should all feel this way about ourselves. Sadly, so many women don't, and in the process they compromise their value to please someone else.

Sure, some people want to step out there and expose themselves by using their body to get ahead. That's not who I am. I know my value and wasn't about to taint my image for a record. I didn't need a sexy body to land the role of Effie, I didn't need a sexy body to win an Oscar, I didn't need a sexy body to win a Grammy, and I surely don't need a sexy body to make a music video.

I may have a new body but I am still the same person.

There are a whole lot of people out there who have applauded me for taking control of my weight and health. I've met so many women who have come up to say how much I have inspired them to take control of their health, too. They see my decision as strong and fearless because I stepped out of my comfort zone to reinvent myself. To those women, I want to say thank you. But I didn't really reinvent who I am so much as how I appear.

When I step out onto the stage, I can see and hear people react.

"Oh, my God—she looks amazing!"

"I had no idea she lost so much weight!"

"She is fabulous. I am so happy for her." And so on.

I actually open my shows with me behind a curtain in silhouette so the crowd can see me, get their comments in and done, and then I can do what they came there to see—entertain. For the most part, once they've checked me out, it's all good and the show goes on as usual.

But there has been another reaction people have had to my weight loss that came as quite a surprise to me. They say some very negative things. I'm serious. They are rejecting me instead of embracing me for getting healthy. Even the media began writing articles that I had taken my weight loss too far by losing way too much weight. One article accused me of "pulling a disappearing act," saying that I was "so svelte in my tangerine orange Versace dress at the 2011 Oscars, I nearly vanished when I turned to the side." Well, at least they didn't say it was too tight!

Apparently, there is a fine line in the media between being thin enough to succeed and being so thin that nutritionists I've never met actually worry about my health in the press. While I wasn't seeking publicity for my weight loss, it appears there are those who find it necessary to comment about me. Just as I had to go through a transition period, I guess they did, too. The funny thing is, I know my people, the fans who come see my shows, and up until I lost my weight, the audience was always filled with love and support. Now I've got people looking at me up onstage thinking they don't know me anymore. They see a thinner version of the girl they once knew and appreciated and are now disapproving of me—all because of what I have achieved with my weight loss.

In the summer of 2011, I performed at a show and was barely out on the stage before I had the feeling that the audience was not entirely on my ride. I sensed the negative energy coming from the crowd as soon as I walked out.

"Who does she think she is coming out here looking like that?"

"Girl don't look *that* good."

"She must think she's all that now because she lost weight . . ."

"I heard her voice changed when she lost all the weight. I'll bet she can't hold a tune."

I just felt like the audience was standing there thinking these things. I could see their heads shaking, arms crossed, hear their lips smacking. You would have thought they never heard me sing before, let alone know anything about me. I never had an audience treat me like this.

Why were they acting so angry?

I began to sing "I Got This," a song from my second album, as a way to connect with the crowd.

I was doing everything I knew to grab ahold of the audience and take them on the ride, but they wouldn't take my hand. And then, it hit me. They no longer saw me as one of them. But you see, to me, I am the same person I've always been. Granted, I might look different on the outside, but I am still that same girl from the

South Side of Chicago who overcame adversity and found a way to do things right by staying positive and finding myself along the way. And yet, I was feeling rejected.

I felt like there were one thousand voices inside my head saying all of the negative comments coming from the audience. There was a point when I wanted to stop singing, stop my show, and say, *"Y'all, it is me. It's still Jennifer."* But I didn't. What was the point? I wasn't going to change anyone's mind that night.

Later that night, some friends who were in attendance told me they were hearing the negative comments from the audience, too. At least I confirmed that what I was feeling was true.

I felt so hurt by this experience. The only thing that made me any different that night was my choice to lose weight and get healthy. I mean really. Why would anyone rebel against me for that? Was my choice to lose weight somehow touching a nerve for those who think they can't do it?

Folks started using Twitter as a platform for sharing their views about my weight loss. I originally got on Twitter as a way to stay connected to my fans. I wanted to get to know them and give them a chance to know the real me. I don't read every comment that gets posted to my account, but whenever one catches my eye— I'll take the time to address it.

At first, Twitter was an adjustment for me because the people writing had the freedom to say whatever they wanted—good and bad. Naturally, the negative comments are always the ones that get my gander up. I'm a very outspoken woman, and I've spent a lifetime defending myself for one reason or another. My first thought is always to answer back. All of the negative comments started to make me so mad that I stopped checking my account for a while. But I always ended up coming back to Twitter because I liked the interaction with my fans so much, and the positive outweighed the negative.

When it came to discussing my weight loss, people in the Twittersphere had a lot to say. Their Tweets felt more like personal attacks that were rooted in misinformation more than anything else.

Here's a typical Tweet.

"When you get money that is when you lose weight."

I wrote back, "My weight loss has nothing to do with money. It's about having the will to do it."

"My mama said when people get money, they don't need will, they use their money to buy everything."

My response? "Where there's a will, there's a way."

"I guess you think you're the shit now because you lost all of the weight."

Huh? Uh, no.

I wrote back, "I didn't lose weight to impress anyone. I lost the weight so I could be healthy for my son."

———

At the end of the day, I simply couldn't understand how any-one could be mad at me for a goal I set for myself and worked hard to achieve. That isn't about money, fame, or power. It's about will, dedication, commitment, and knowing your self-worth. You can be poor as dirt and have those traits. Money can't buy you val-ues. You just need to know what is important to you and then feel secure in your pursuit to achieve that. The only difference between the haters on Twitter and me is that my will and what I value is what is important to me. Weight loss may not be someone else's goal, but that won't stop me from working toward mine.

The hostile rejection I received was the single biggest hurdle for me to overcome because:

a. I didn't expect it, and

b. I didn't know how to handle it.

I was really upset by this rejection. It reminded me of a friend I had back in high school who told me that he could no longer be my friend because my confidence in myself somehow made him feel like less of a person. I was so hurt that the way I felt about myself made him uncomfortable with who he was.

I decided to speak to Liz in an effort to understand what the rejection to my weight loss was really all about. I figured she might have some firsthand experience in dealing with this type of reaction.

Liz explained that most people see themselves a certain way their entire lives. When they go through a massive change, such as losing weight, they have to learn to see themselves in a new way. It is one of the biggest struggles her members deal with on their journey.

When that gets layered with getting negative energy for doing a positive thing, it oftentimes leads to disastrous results. She told me that she sees this type of reaction in almost every member she works with. They have friends, family members, coworkers, and even mere acquaintances who react in a negative way. She shared that sometimes things get so bad that marriages break up and long-term friendships are lost over this lack of support. I was very relieved to know that what I was feeling and going through wasn't just happening to me. This type of rejection can happen to anyone who is successful in their weight loss, from Jennifer Hudson to Jane Doe.

People get comfortable with the way you are—they have formed their opinion of you based on everything they see and know about you as a person. When you change that up by losing weight, they no longer understand you. Even though you are the same person they've always known, some see you as different. Their perception of who you are has changed based on how you look. Maybe they no longer feel safe, secure, or comfortable with you anymore. Their insecurities get fed by your newfound security with yourself. Liz taught me that when other people reject positive changes you make for yourself, there is always some nerve to get to the root of in those other people. It usually ends up being about fear and lack of self-esteem.

As a way of illustrating just how common this response is, Liz gave me a scenario of four girls who have been best friends since grade school. They went through everything together, including boyfriends, breakups, weddings, babies, and gaining lots of weight. Since they all got heavy together, they supported one another's heaviness. And then one day, one of the girls decided to change her life by taking control of her health and losing the excess weight she'd been carrying around for years. She can't be friends with those people anymore because they can't handle the change. She doesn't want to be around them because everything they do together is centered on eating. They don't exercise, they want to eat out all the time, and they choose all of the wrong foods. Those activities are simply not a part of her life anymore. The rest of the women feel jealous, envious, and angry with her for no longer fitting in with the group. Worse, they are frustrated with themselves because they are still exactly the same. Little by little, they push her out of their circle, until one day they have completely gone their separate ways.

This happens all the time, and as it turns out, is a much bigger problem for women than it is with men. For whatever reason, men don't seem to have as hard a time when one of their buddies loses weight as women do when a girlfriend decides to shed some pounds. Interestingly, men seem to be the majority of the people who come to my rescue on Twitter, often writing, "Why can't you leave her alone?" or "I think what Jennifer has done is terrific. She looks great." And by the way, there are plenty of girls out there who have supported me, too. And to all of you supporters, here's a great big thank-you!

Liz did a great job guiding me through my confusion on this issue by reminding me that I was solid and right in my decision to get healthy. And I was. There was never really a time in my life where this type of rejection would have rocked my world before. No way.

"Would you trade your weight loss for acceptance from others?" Liz asked me.

"Not a chance." I didn't even have to think about my response.

"Would you ever go back to your old weight?"

"Oh, hell no." My answer was that quick.

When Liz framed her questions in that way, it was easy for me to realize that my decision to lose weight was for no one else but me. And when you come from that place, no one—and I mean no one—should have the power or ability to push you back to where you came from.

After giving Liz's questions some thought, I know that truthfully, I would be willing to gain back weight for a film role, but only if I had to. Now I know I can control it. I would never carelessly go back to my old weight—it would be a choice, a short-term commitment to gain and then lose that weight. This realization was big because I really feel like I've got ahold of my eating and health without any doubt that I would be able to lose the weight again if I gained. You see, Weight Watchers isn't a diet—it's a commitment to eating for health. Once you've got that, you'll never go back to your old ways again.

After I discovered the positivity in my new and healthier body, I began to notice that I wanted to surround myself with other positive people, too. An organic shift began to take place in my entire life. If I am going to be a role model that inspires others to get healthy, then I want to live as the very best example. I didn't learn how to eat for health until I was a grown woman, but I'm going to be damned sure my son grows up making the right choices from the very start. I wish the principles of healthy eating and exercise were a requirement for kids in school, just like math or reading. Society puts such an emphasis on being thin and looking good, but so few people are given the tools early in life to adhere to these expectations. So when those people walk out into the world, like I did when I got to Hollywood, it can be a real struggle to accept that sometimes appearance can be more important than talent or intelligence. If I had been given the education growing up, I would have started my journey to health at a much earlier age. This is why I am so eager to share all of the information

I've been given. I want you to know that there are options out there. If given the right tools, you will be ready and equipped to make your own informed decisions. Where there are options, there is a way. Choices lead to success.

My mama used to tell me that I could do or be anything I wanted as long as I was happy. That was her number one priority for her children. And that is how I want to encourage my son, too. I've seen a glimpse into my son's future—he loves to sing and dance almost as much as he loves to wrestle like his daddy. He is a born performer. He comes to life when he is in front of an audience. Whether it's stealing my spotlight by sneaking out onto the stage and holding his own microphone during a concert in Barbados or insisting he come out with me during an interview on *The View*, my son really knows how to work a crowd. I was exactly like that as a child and now I get to experience what that was like for my mama through my son's eyes. Seeing him shine like that makes me feel so proud. Growing up, I always dreamed of having a sibling I could sing with. Now I get to sing with my son. Munchkin and I sing together all the time, especially when I am putting him to bed at night. He knows his mommy's voice, whether he hears it on the radio, television, or in his bedroom when it's just the two of us together. To the outside world, I'm Jennifer Hudson, singer, actress, and weight-loss ambassador, but to my son, I will always be just Mama. I can't think of a better title!

Becoming a mother is by far my greatest accomplishment. My

son has helped me put everything into perspective and figure out what is really important in my life. Even though I had made up my mind to lose weight before I knew I was pregnant, having my son gave me the best reason not to fail. My mama taught me to always see a cup as half full, and I want to teach that positive perspective to my son, too. I want him to know there is a whole world out there beyond the block he grows up on. Even though he'll grow up in a more privileged environment than I did, he'll still face the world having to make his own decisions. All I can hope for is that I'll do my very best to provide him with the right information and guide him by setting the example by how his father and I live so he will make the right choices.

After becoming a mom, I am most proud of my newfound role as an ambassador of health. There have been such great rewards in seeing how the changes I've made in my life have empowered and inspired others to do the same. I know I touch people's hearts when they see me in an emotionally charged role like Effie White or Winnie Mandela, but nothing had empowered me to help change people's lives until I joined forces with Weight Watchers. I let the world in on my progress by allowing them to monitor my journey to health. I never dreamed that my actions would have such a powerful impact, but God did. He is using every part of me to make a difference in people's lives by spreading my message of health any way I can.

I will never forget a letter I received from a fan shortly after

Dreamgirls was released. He wrote me to say that he thought God gave me my acting career because I embraced my gift of singing and shared it with others. Every time I enter a new realm in my career, I realize that there is so much more I am supposed to be doing with my life. And that is why this journey has been so rewarding. It isn't that I've lost eighty pounds and kept it off. No, it's *because* of that accomplishment that I can see people come together—whether it has been my family, fans, or the people on the street—and be inspired by something I did to make a positive change in their lives. *That* is the true meaning of feeling good!

CHAPTER TWELVE

I GOT THIS

"Jennifer! Over here!"

"Jennifer, can we get a photo?"

"Jennifer, whose dress are you wearing tonight?"

"Jennifer, Jennifer, Jennifer . . ."

Walking the red carpet has taken on a whole new dimension these days. I get to stand next to the skinny supermodel talking about what I am wearing, about my eyelashes, earrings, and even the color of my toenail polish! Years ago, the only thing anyone wanted to talk about was if I felt insecure as a big girl in Hollywood. And now all they want to focus on is how great I look. Any way you slice it, the emphasis is still about my physical appearance instead of my talent. Does it frustrate me? Sure, but I also know it is part of the game we all play, especially in the looks-obsessed world of Hollywood. Just once I wish someone would make it about being healthy instead of being thin. I've always been comfortable with my size, but I haven't always felt healthy like I do now.

Well, allowing myself to be overweight and unhealthy is a habit I've gladly left in my past—I've got more energy, stamina, and drive than I've ever had. When I am singing "Feeling Good" in my Weight Watchers commercials, that's for real. They couldn't have picked a better song to describe where I am on the journey. And if I can do it, anyone can.

And when I say anyone . . . I mean *anyone*.

I was asked to sing at a very small and intimate holiday gathering at the home of Carole Bayer Sager in late 2010. She has collaborated with everyone from Burt Bacharach to Neil Diamond, Marvin Hamlisch, Michael Jackson, Quincy Jones, Michael McDonald, James Ingram, Donald Fagen, Babyface, and even Clint Eastwood. I was a surprise performer that evening in a room full of billionaires, including Barbra Streisand, David Foster, Diane Warren, and *American Idol* executive producer Nigel Lythgoe. Although it wasn't planned that way, it felt as if everyone there had something to do with my career. I had to kill it with the two songs I was there to sing or there could have been disastrous results.

Earlier in the day, producer and composer David Foster had invited me to his beautiful home in Malibu to work on the arrangements for my performance. We spent a couple of hours together and came up with something absolutely amazing. Because of David, I went into the evening with enough confidence to get me through what could have been the most intimidating and terrifying performance of my career.

Before my show began, I was seated next to Barbra Streisand for dinner. I was nervous to sit next to her because she is such a powerful influence on my singing, of course. I had met Barbra earlier in the year at a pre-Grammy party that Clive Davis hosted. Ever since I signed with Clive, he has asked me to perform at the parties he gives. Clive's gatherings are events more than they are parties. He always makes me feel so special by including me in the evening. For this particular pre-Grammy show, Clive asked me to sing two Barbra Streisand songs: "People" and "The Way We Were."

"And Jennifer," he said, "Barbra is going to be there."

Now hold up.

He was asking me to sing two of Barbra Streisand's biggest songs . . . for Barbra Streisand? I knew that both songs were challenging for even the best singers, so I was terrified. To make matters worse, he gave me this task with less than seventy-two hours to prepare. But when Clive asks, you don't question, you just do it. I had no choice but to do what I always do—rise to the challenge and learn those songs cold.

So when I sat next to Barbra the night of Carole's Christmas party, I was hoping she had liked the pre-Grammy performance.

Things could have gotten pretty awkward if she didn't. From the moment I sat down, Barbra and I began chatting like we were long-lost best friends. She said she was fascinated by my experiences with Weight Watchers and asked me to tell her all about it.

Seriously.

I began talking with such ease as I told her how simple the plan is.

"I don't think I could ever do that because I need to have my pasta," she said.

I just smiled because that's how I felt, too, before I started Weight Watchers.

"You can eat pasta. You can eat anything you want as long as you stay within your Points," I responded back.

In that moment, we were just two girls talking about weight. I have no idea if she ever gave the program a try, but I know I did my best to lead her toward that choice.

Barbra and I were still talking when Carole came by the table to ask me if I minded that Babyface sang first.

"He said he doesn't want to follow Jennifer Hudson . . ."

We both laughed and I happily obliged her request. Babyface was amazing and would have been just as good whether he followed me or not that night. And then it was my turn to sing. As I did my rendition of "O Holy Night," I looked into the small crowd and felt like I was singing in a dream. I was thrilled to be there but extremely relieved when I was done so I could relax and enjoy the rest of the night.

Toward the end of the evening, Nigel Lythgoe came over to say hello. Nigel hadn't seen me since I lost my weight. His jaw was on the floor as I stood in front of him looking like a brand-new woman.

"I had no idea . . . ," he kept saying over and over to me as he shook his head in total disbelief.

I wanted to say, "I could have always changed this." But in that moment, we both acknowledged that my weight was no longer an issue.

So many people miss out on true talent because they can't get past a look. At the end of the day, losing weight was easy, but finding talent? Now that's hard. I didn't say what I wanted to that night, but I think Nigel knew exactly what I was thinking. I just smiled and said good night.

As the old saying goes, *success is the best revenge.*

It's not that I really had a need to get revenge on anyone—I just wanted to be a breakout example of how no one should be judged on or limited by their looks. Appearance can always be changed, but the talent stays the same. I don't regret all of the things I missed out on by not being given certain opportunities, because my path has led me to who I am today. And for all of that, I am made extremely proud and grateful by the people I meet on the street, in elevators, on airplanes, and everywhere else I go, who tell me that I have inspired them to make a change in their lives. There is nothing that gives me a greater sense of fulfillment than knowing that how I am living my life has a positive impact on so many others. Being a role model comes with a great responsibility, but one I will gladly take on if it means getting other people to the same place that I am. And inspiring others is where I find my inspiration to carry on this lifelong and life-changing important message of health. That is the greatest reward.

In February 2011, I received a call to appear on the final season of *The Oprah Winfrey Show*. I had been a guest several times before, but this visit would be the most poignant because it would be my last as Oprah's show was ending. My schedule was as busy as it had ever been. I don't drink, smoke, take drugs, or party. Working is my vice. I have a tendency to spread myself a little thin because I hate to say no, especially to someone like Oprah.

When her staff called to book the show, I had already committed to an event in Dallas for Jerry Jones, the owner of the Dallas Cowboys, which Jamie Foxx had called and asked me to do as a personal favor to him. Although there had been some talk about a blizzard in Chicago that week, I thought I could fly to Dallas, do the show, and make it back with enough time to do Oprah's taping the following day. The snowstorm, dubbed by the press as "the blizzard of the century" came and went two days before I flew to Dallas. By all standards, I thought it was a safe bet to go.

I went to Oprah's studio for a rehearsal and sound check on Thursday morning. As soon as I was done, I caught a private plane to Texas, where I was met by a helicopter that was waiting to whisk me off to the venue. Everything was falling perfectly into place.

I did the show, thinking it was all good—that is until I saw my tour manager giving me the signal to wrap things up early. He was mouthing the words, "It's snowing."

Snowing?

In Chicago?

No . . .

In Texas!

That hadn't happened for years.

The weather had gotten so bad that the private plane I had flown in on would not be able to take off. We sat on the plane for an hour before the pilot came out of the cockpit to break the news to us. Apparently, we would not be going anywhere that night. I wanted to tell the pilot to just fly the damn plane, but I remembered something my mama used to say: "Without your life, you can't do anything." And she was right.

Oprah would understand—right? *Right?* I was trying to convince myself of that for the rest of the night. I was supposed to be back in Chicago by 5 A.M. Friday morning and I was still sitting in Texas trying to figure out how to make that happen.

"Can we take a train?" I asked. But there were none that would get me there on time.

"How about driving to the next city where it isn't snowing so I can catch a flight back from there?" I was getting desperate.

One thing was for sure. We couldn't just sit there waiting for it to stop snowing.

Finally, my tour manager found a commercial flight from Dallas-Fort Worth International Airport that was taking off within the hour, but we still had to drive through the snowstorm to get there if we were going to make it.

Somehow, we were able to get to the airport with enough time to go through security and board the flight. The only seats they had left were the last row in coach. I didn't care. They could have put me in the baggage hold if it meant getting back in time to do the show. As luck would have it, I was on the cover of the in-flight magazine that month, so as I made my way to the back of the plane, I could see every single person look at their copy of the magazine, then look at me and say, "It's her."

"Yup. It's me all right. How ya doin'?" I was trying my best to find the humor in the situation. I was fine, too, until I heard the pilot announce that this flight was going to be delayed.

Unfortunately, the lines of communication kept getting mixed up. Oprah's producers were being given different stories about why I was late. So Oprah was hearing a whole bunch of different things from her team. I have found that you get a lot further saying things the way they are instead of trying to hide the facts. Eventually, the truth comes out, so what's the point of trying to cover it up? I had been adamant about being honest with Oprah's team. "You will not lie to Oprah!" I was very clear in my intention.

These types of situations get frustrating because issues get created that could have otherwise been avoided. If her producers knew

the reality of our situation, I am sure they would have done whatever they could to work around it.

We finally arrived in Chicago late Friday morning, which
meant we were already delayed several hours for the taping. My
manager arranged to have my hair and makeup people waiting in
a car at the airport so I would be camera-ready when we got to
Oprah's studio. They did the best they could given the bumps and
turns along the way.

When we arrived at the studio, I rushed to my dressing room
to finish getting ready. About fifteen minutes later, I looked in the
mirror to find Mama O standing behind me.

I swear, you could hear ominous soap opera music in my head,
like something dramatic and bad was about to happen.

"Umm, what happened?" she rightfully and respectfully asked.

I told her the truth. I explained that I had been to Dallas to do
a show for Jamie Foxx and Jerry Jones. I thought we would make
it back in plenty of time until it started to snow in Texas. Oprah
was incredibly kind and understanding. She said she knew something had to be wrong because I had never missed a commitment
and I am almost always on time. She told me that all I had to do
was let her team know what was really happening so they could
make arrangements on their end. She was upset with my team for
not being candid. I completely understood and respected where she
was coming from.

"Jennifer, you have all the power you need, but it is up to you to decide what you're going to do with it." She spoke to me like a loving and caring mother.

I listened to what she was saying very closely because I knew she was talking from experience. I learned a valuable lesson that day, and I told her so.

Oprah was right. You see, we *all* have the power to choose how we are going to handle every situation we are faced with throughout our lives. We are in control of the decision we make whether it's about work, relationships, parenting, or our health.

No matter what I have done in my life, whether singing, acting, or becoming a role model for taking control of my health and well-being, it all comes from an extremely authentic place. I wrote this book because I want you to have a sense of who I am, where I've come from, and what I've been through so you know my journey has been totally real.

God blessed me in so many ways, but I don't think my true calling was to be famous or to make a lot of money. I feel like God put me on this path to be a positive influence by helping others find their true selves. If I can't make a difference in someone's day, then all of my fame means nothing because if I am not serving God's purpose, then all of this will have been in vain. Our culture is obsessed with three things—fame, fortune, and appearance. I dreamed about being famous, about making my dreams come true, and about being thin. I've been on both sides of all of those things.

I've struggled. I've been an unknown trying to make it. I've been overweight. I could easily live without the fame and the fortune—but the one thing I could never give up is how healthy I feel now that I've lost what was weighing me down.

The most important things to me on this earth are God, my family, and last but certainly not least, my health. I can't really imagine living without any of them. There have been many times throughout my life when both my faith and will have been tested. That's just life. I've always been able to push on and persevere when even the darkest of clouds hung over my head. God gave us free will, which means we all have the option to make the right choices in our lives. I've never cared whether the majority of people agree with what I believe because if I don't believe in something, I can't get behind it. But if I do, you can be sure that it's the real deal.

For me, gaining control of my health was a long-term struggle that, for many years, I didn't even realize I had been battling. Now that I've got it under control, I realize that I wasn't living in the way God intended for me. But you know what? I'm okay with that because without all of those experiences, there's no way I could fully appreciate everything that I now have as a result of losing weight and living healthy. It would be insanely greedy to ask for more. I'm grateful for everything that's happened along the way. All I want is to be healthy and happy so I can be around to sing and act for decades to come.

———

S o, here we are—at the end of our journey together. Isn't it time to believe in yourself enough that you are willing to take chances in your life like the ones I've taken in mine? What about loving yourself enough to give it everything you've got and make the commitment to get rid of the things that have been weighing *you* down? Will you finally give yourself permission to break free from the chains that have bound you or will you stay exactly where you are, thinking it's fine? Look, if you don't like what you see in the mirror, don't break the mirror. If you're tired of being on that diet roller coaster and are finally ready to get off that ride forever, you have the power, the choice, and now the tools to make that happen. Life isn't about what cards you are dealt—it's about how you play that hand. Take it from me. I truly know.

I want to wish you my love, support, and inspiration in your journey. Remember, you're making a lifetime commitment to health. It won't happen overnight, but if you stick with it, I promise, it will come to pass.

In Good Health,

Jennifer

ACKNOWLEDGMENTS

To my family. You are amazing and my reason for being.

To my JHud team, including Allison Azoff Statter, Stefanie Tate, Damien Smith, Lisa Kasteler, Samantha Hill, Marla Farrell, Graehme Morphy, Teri Martin, Matt Johnson, David Lande, Jamie Young, and the incomparable Walter Williams III. Thank you for not limiting me and allowing me to be who I am and for supporting my every dream and effort to continue to grow. That gift is what makes you all such a great team!

To my editor, Carrie Thornton, and everyone at Dutton for allowing me this fantastic opportunity to spread my wings and for giving me the chance to share my story through my own words. Thank you to Brian Tart, Christine Ball, Amanda Walker, Stephanie Hitchcock, Monica Benalcazar, Carrie Swetonic, and the entire Penguin team for your support and guidance to get my message out there. Also, thank you to Mel Berger, my literary agent, who helped take this vision to a reality.

Thank you to Weight Watchers, Weight Watchers, Weight

Watchers! There is not a day that goes by that I don't say Weight Watchers is the greatest thing ever created! It really is! And I want the world to know it. To Liz Josefsberg, David Kirchhoff, Cheryl Callan, Donna Fontana, Danielle Korn, Veronica Bertran, Joyce King Thomas, Kathy Love, Sharon Ehrlich, and Danny Rodriquez—I love you guys!

Now, I had to save my family and fans for last because you have lived with me, you have watched me live, and through it all y'all have stayed next to me. I love you all so much for that! I'm so proud of all of my family, friends, and fans who have decided to make a life change, too. You amaze me.

Finally, without God nothing would be possible.

Weight Watchers Online offers members thousands of recipes and helpful tips. I've included some of my favorite Weight Watchers recipes for you to enjoy.

Weight Watchers Recipes

Main Meals

Desserts

★ MAIN MEALS

Tex-Mex Scrambled Eggs

Course: Breakfast
PointsPlus® Value: 4
Servings: 2
Preparation Time: 18 min
Cooking Time: 10 min
Level of Difficulty: Easy

Jalapeño and cumin give these scrambled eggs a bit of heat. They're topped with a homemade spicy salsa for even more flavor.

Ingredients

14½ oz canned diced tomatoes, fire-roasted variety
¼ tsp chili powder, chipotle variety
2 Tbsp scallions, green part only, minced
2 Tbsp cilantro, fresh, minced
1 Tbsp fresh lime juice
¼ tsp table salt
⅛ tsp black pepper
2 large eggs
3 large egg whites
¼ tsp dried oregano
¼ tsp table salt
⅛ tsp black pepper
⅛ tsp ground cumin
1 spray cooking spray
2 small shallots, minced
1 medium jalapeño pepper, seeded, minced (don't touch seeds with bare hands)

Instructions

To prepare salsa, pour tomatoes into a fine-mesh strainer set in sink; press on tomatoes to drain off all liquid, leaving about 1 cup of diced tomato. Spoon tomatoes into a medium bowl; stir in chili powder, scallion, cilantro, lime juice, salt, and pepper. Stir salsa; set aside while making scrambled eggs.

To make eggs, in a medium bowl, beat together eggs, egg whites, oregano, salt, pepper, and cumin; set aside.

Coat a medium nonstick skillet with cooking spray; heat over medium heat for 30 seconds. Add shallots and jalapeño; cook, stirring occasionally, until shallots are tender, about 3 minutes. Pour egg mixture into skillet; cook until eggs are almost cooked through, scrambling occasionally, about 4 to 5 minutes. Serve eggs topped with salsa or salsa on the side. Yields about 1 cup of eggs and ½ cup of salsa per serving.

Notes

If you can find canned tomatoes with chipotle chiles, use them and omit the chili powder in the salsa. You can also save time by using your favorite spicy jarred salsa instead of making your own.

To make this recipe truly Tex-Mex, top with some baked tortilla strips (could affect *PointsPlus®* values).

Bacon, Egg, and Hash Brown Stacks

Course: Breakfast
PointsPlus® Value: 4
Servings: 4
Preparation Time: 8 min
Cooking Time: 14 min
Level of Difficulty: Easy

This is a nice twist on the usual potato and egg breakfast. Leave an extra "stack" in the refrigerator for a quick, microwave-reheatable meal.

Ingredients

2 sprays cooking spray
4 frozen hash brown potato patties, prepared without fat
2 large eggs
3 large egg whites
3 oz Canadian-style bacon, finely chopped
1 Tbsp scallions, minced, green part only
⅛ tsp hot pepper sauce, optional
⅛ tsp table salt, or to taste
⅛ tsp black pepper, or to taste
8 tsp ketchup, hot and spicy variety (optional)

Instructions

Coat a large nonstick skillet with cooking spray. Place hash brown patties in skillet; cook over medium heat on first side until golden brown, about 7 to 9 minutes. Flip patties; cook until golden brown on second side, about 5 minutes more.

Meanwhile, coat a second large nonstick skillet with cooking spray; heat over medium-low heat. In a large bowl, beat together eggs, egg whites, bacon, scallions, hot pepper sauce, salt, and pepper; pour into prepared skillet and then increase heat to medium. Let eggs partially set and then scramble using a spatula. When eggs are set, but slightly glossy, remove from heat; cover to keep warm until hash browns are finished cooking.

To assemble stacks, place 1 hash brown patty on each of 4 plates. Top each with ¼ of egg mixture and serve with 2 teaspoons of ketchup. Season to taste with salt and pepper, if desired. Yields 1 stack per serving.

Notes

Finely diced turkey bacon makes a nice alternative to the Canadian bacon in this recipe. Just make sure to cook the bacon before adding it to the eggs (could affect *PointsPlus*® values).

Italian Pepper
and Egg Sandwiches

Course: Sandwiches
PointsPlus® Value: 5
Servings: 4
Preparation Time: 10 min
Cooking Time: 12 min
Level of Difficulty: Easy

This comfort-food sandwich is great for breakfast, lunch, or dinner. It's made with a lot of pantry staples, perfect anytime you need a quick meal.

Ingredients
    2 tsp olive oil
    1 small onion, thinly sliced
    1 large green pepper, such as a cubanelle, thinly sliced
    1 tsp minced garlic
    4 large eggs
    3 large egg whites
    ½ tsp table salt, or to taste
    ¼ tsp black pepper, freshly ground, or to taste
    4 reduced-calorie hamburger rolls, toasted if desired

Instructions
Heat oil in a large nonstick skillet over medium heat. Add onion and pepper; sauté until tender and light golden, about 7 to 9 minutes. Add garlic; cook, stirring, until fragrant, about 30 seconds. Set vegetables aside.

In a medium bowl, beat together eggs, egg whites, salt, and pepper. Scramble in same skillet over medium heat until almost cooked, about 1 to 1½ minutes. Add vegetables back to skillet and gently mix; continue scrambling until eggs are set but not dry, about 30 seconds to 1 minute more.

Top each roll bottom with about ¾ cup egg mixture; cover with roll tops and serve. Yields 1 sandwich per serving.

Tropical Chicken Salad
with Orange Vinaigrette

Course: Main meals
PointsPlus® Value: 7
Servings: 2
Preparation Time: 18 min
Cooking Time: 0 min
Level of Difficulty: Easy

Tropical fruit and cucumber make this main dish salad super-refreshing. The next time you're grilling chicken breasts*, make extra for this recipe.

Ingredients

- 2 Tbsp orange juice
- 1 Tbsp rice wine vinegar
- 2 tsp olive oil
- ¼ tsp table salt
- ¼ tsp black pepper, freshly ground
- 4 cups mixed baby greens
- 5 oz chicken breast, stewed, without skin
- ¾ cup pineapple, fresh, cut into chunks
- ¾ cup mango, fresh, cut into chunks
- ¾ cup cucumber, seedless, cut into chunks
- ¼ cup mint leaves, fresh, cut into thin strips
- ¼ cup red onion, thinly sliced

Instructions

In a large bowl, stir together orange juice, vinegar, oil, salt, and pepper until blended.

Add salad greens, chicken, pineapple, mango, cucumber, mint, and onion; toss to mix and coat. Serve immediately. Yields about 3 cups per serving.

Notes

*You can buy precooked chicken strips if you prefer.

Give this salad a Cuban spin by adding a sprinkle of cumin to the dressing and swapping out the mint for fresh cilantro.

Chicken and Cheese Quesadillas

Course: Main meals
PointsPlus® Value: 9
Servings: 4
Preparation Time: 12 min
Cooking Time: 10 min
Level of Difficulty: Easy

A Mexican classic with endless variations: Try Monterey Jack cheese and, jalapeños, pico de gallo, and black beans or shredded jicama and mango salsa.

Ingredients

2 cups (chopped) chicken breast without skin, roasted, chopped, or shredded
1 tsp fresh lime juice, or to taste
¼ tsp Durkee ground cumin, or other brand
¼ tsp table salt
8 medium whole wheat tortillas, about 6 inches each
½ cup fat-free black bean dip, spicy variety
6 Tbsp low-fat shredded cheddar cheese, sharp variety
2 medium scallions, green part only, diced
4 sprays cooking spray
½ cup salsa
2 Tbsp reduced-fat sour cream

Instructions

In a small bowl, combine chicken, lime juice, cumin, and salt; toss well to combine.

Place 4 tortillas on a flat surface and spread each one with 2 tablespoons of bean dip. Top each with about ⅓ cup of chicken and then sprinkle each with 1 tablespoon of cheese; divide scallions over top. Cover with remaining tortillas and gently press down on each one.

Coat a very large nonstick skillet with cooking spray; place over medium heat. Cook quesadillas in a single layer until golden brown on bottom, about 2 minutes. Flip quesadillas and press down on them with a spatula; cook until golden brown on second side, about 2 to 3 minutes more. Remove to a serving plate and cover to keep warm (or place in oven); repeat with remaining quesadillas.

Slice each quesadilla into 4 pieces; serve with salsa and sour cream. Yields 1 quesadilla, 2 tablespoons of salsa, and 1 teaspoon of sour cream per serving.

Notes

For even greater flavor, look for a low-fat seasoned Mexican cheese blend.

If you want to make the chicken from scratch, marinate it in a mixture of lime juice, cumin, and chipotle chili powder for 30 minutes before grilling or pan-frying (with cooking spray); then shred with a fork.

Feta-Stuffed
Chicken Burgers

Course: Main meals
PointsPlus® Value: 7
Servings: 4
Preparation Time: 15 min
Cooking Time: 16 min
Level of Difficulty: Easy

Olives, roasted peppers, and feta add great flavor to these burgers. Complete your meal with our light Greek Salad.

Ingredients

- 1 pound uncooked extra-lean ground chicken breast
- 1 Tbsp fresh oregano
- ¼ tsp garlic powder
- 7 Tbsp feta cheese, crumbled
- 4 items reduced-calorie hamburger rolls
- 1 cup lettuce, romaine, cut into thick strips
- ⅔ cup roasted red peppers, sliced (without oil)
- 5 small olives, black, sliced (about 4 tsp)

Instructions

Preheat grill or broiler.

In a medium bowl, combine chicken, oregano, garlic powder, and feta; divide mixture into four balls and then press them gently into patties.

Grill or broil patties until internal temperature of burgers reaches 165°F, about 7 to 8 minutes per side.

Serve each burger on a bun with ¼ of lettuce, ¼ of peppers, and 1 teaspoon of olives. Yields 1 burger per serving.

Grilled Yellowfin Tuna with Teriyaki Sauce

· ·

Course: Main meals
PointsPlus® Value: 5
Servings: 4
Preparation Time: 8 min
Cooking Time: 9 min
Level of Difficulty: Easy

A summertime pleaser. The teriyaki sauce is simple to make and so full of flavor: rich, tangy, and thick.

Ingredients

1 spray cooking spray
3 cloves (medium) garlic, finely minced
2 Tbsp ginger root, fresh, finely minced
1 Tbsp sherry cooking wine, or mirin
½ cup low-sodium soy sauce
½ cup orange juice
¼ cup water
3 Tbsp packed brown sugar, dark variety
1 Tbsp cornstarch
16 oz yellowfin tuna, 1-inch thick

Instructions

Coat grill rack with cooking spray; preheat grill to high.

To make teriyaki sauce, in a small saucepan, combine garlic, ginger, sherry, soy sauce, orange juice, water, sugar, and cornstarch. Boil for 5 minutes, stirring constantly, until thick.

Coat all sides of tuna with teriyaki sauce. Grill, flipping once, brushing on more teriyaki sauce as fish cooks, about 4 minutes for rare, or longer to desired degree of doneness.* Serve with arugula tossed with your favorite salad dressing, or some oil, vinegar, salt, and pepper (could affect *PointsPlus*® values). Yields about 3 ounces of tuna per serving.

Notes

*Grill 3 minutes per side for a 2-inch tuna steak cooked to rare. Or cook longer until desired degree of doneness.

You can also broil the tuna. Just preheat the broiler, along with the pan, to high.

Spicy Beef Tacos

Course: Main meals
PointsPlus® Value: 7
Servings: 4
Preparation Time: 12 min
Cooking Time: 13 min
Level of Difficulty: Easy

You get two tasty tacos in a serving. Add your own touch with fresh chopped cilantro, scallions, or tomatoes.

Ingredients
   3 sprays cooking spray, divided
   2 cloves (medium) garlic, minced
   ¾ pounds uncooked lean ground beef (with 7% fat)
   1½ tsp Durkee ground cumin, or other brand
   1½ tsp ground coriander
   ¾ tsp table salt, or to taste
   1½ cups canned diced tomatoes, with jalapeños or green chilies
   8 small corn tortillas, lightly toasted just before serving if desired*
   2 cups lettuce, shredded
   ½ cup low-fat shredded cheddar cheese, sharp variety
   ⅓ cup salsa

Instructions
   Coat a large skillet with cooking spray; heat over medium-high heat. Add garlic; cook, stirring, until fragrant, about 30 seconds to 1 minute. Add beef; cook until browned, breaking up meat as it cooks, about 5 to 6 minutes. Add cumin, coriander, salt, and diced tomatoes; cook, stirring occasionally, until liquid is almost absorbed, about 5 to 6 minutes.

   Place tortillas on a flat surface. Top each with about ¼ cup beef, ¼ cup lettuce, 1 tablespoon cheese, and 2 teaspoons salsa. Fold tortillas in half and serve. Yields 2 tacos per serving.

Notes
   *To toast tortillas, coat a baking sheet with cooking spray. Place tortillas on top and coat with cooking spray. Heat in a 300°F oven until slightly crisp but not too crisp that they break when folded.

Shrimp with Zucchini and Tomatoes

Course: Main meals
PointsPlus® Value: 4
Servings: 4
Preparation Time: 8 min
Cooking Time: 10 min
Level of Difficulty: Easy

Keep a bag of large frozen shrimp on hand for this quick and easy sautéed meal. The juices from the tomatoes add a wonderful flavor to the sauce.

Ingredients

    1 Tbsp olive oil, extra-virgin, divided
    1 medium zucchini, cut into ¼-inch slices
    1 pound shrimp, large-size, peeled, and deveined
    1 cup grape tomatoes, cut in half
    ½ tsp dried oregano
    ½ tsp table salt
    ¼ tsp black pepper, freshly ground, or to taste
    1½ tsp minced garlic
    ¼ cup water

Instructions

Heat 2 teaspoons oil in a large nonstick skillet over medium-high heat. Add zucchini in a single layer; increase heat to high and cook until bottoms are golden, about 2 minutes. Flip zucchini and cook until golden on other side, about 2 minutes more. Using a slotted spoon, remove zucchini to a plate.

Heat remaining teaspoon oil in same skillet. Add shrimp; sauté 1 to 2 minutes. Add tomatoes, oregano, salt, and pepper; sauté until shrimp are almost just cooked through, about 1 minute. Stir in garlic and water; sauté, stirring to loosen bits from bottom of pan, until shrimp are cooked through and tomatoes are softened, about 1 to 2 minutes more. Return zucchini to skillet; toss and serve. Yields about 1¼ cups per serving.

Notes

Try this with fresh basil instead of, or in addition to, the oregano (just stir it in right at the end).

Grate some lemon zest over top and/or sprinkle with fresh lemon juice, if desired.

DESSERTS

Frozen Mud Pie Sandwiches

Course: Desserts
PointsPlus® Value: 3
Servings: 10
Preparation Time: 15 min
Cooking Time: 0 min
Level of Difficulty: Easy

Low-fat coffee frozen yogurt gives this childhood favorite a grown-up taste.

Ingredients
20 chocolate wafers, or vanilla wafers
1¼ cups low-fat coffee-flavored frozen yogurt, softened
10 tsp fat-free fudge topping

Instructions
Spread 2 tablespoons of frozen yogurt on top of each of 10 wafers.

Drizzle 1 teaspoon of fudge topping over each yogurt-covered wafer. Cover with remaining wafers and gently press together to make sandwiches. Wrap each mud pie in plastic wrap and freeze for 1 hour. Yields 1 per serving.

Cookies and Cream
Freezer Cake

Course: Cakes
PointsPlus® Value: 5
Servings: 12
Preparation Time: 12 min
Cooking Time: 0 min
Level of Difficulty: Easy

Our lightened-up version of icebox cake is a summer crowd-pleaser. It'll hit the spot on hot, humid days.

Ingredients

3½ oz ready-to-eat vanilla pudding, about 1 cup
3 cups Cool Whip Whipped Topping Lite, aerosol, or similar product
9 oz Nabisco Famous Chocolate Wafers, or similar product (should be about 3 inches in diameter each)
1 oz bittersweet chocolate, shavings

Instructions

Line bottom and sides of a 13- to 14-inch-long pan with plastic wrap, making sure you use a big enough piece so that you have enough extra wrap to cover prepared cake.

In a medium bowl, gently fold pudding into whipped topping.

Take a wafer and spread about 1½ tablespoons of cream mixture over cookie surface. Top with another wafer and spread about 1½ tablespoons of cream mixture over second cookie; repeat to form a stack of about 6 cookies and cream. Carefully turn stack on its side and place in pan so cookies are standing on their sides. Repeat with remaining cookies until you create 1 long row of cookies and cream in pan. (Reserve any broken cookies to crumble over top as a garnish.)

When cake assembly is complete, use a spatula to scoop up any cream that has oozed out of sides of cookies and place back on top of cake.

Wrap plastic tightly around cake in pan and freeze immediately for a minimum of 2 hours.

DESSERTS

Slice cake on a diagonal into 12 pieces and sprinkle each piece with shaved chocolate. Yields 1 slice per serving.

Notes

Feel free to swap chocolate pudding for the vanilla, if desired.

Mini Chocolate-Chip Cookies

• •

Course: Desserts
PointsPlus® Value: 1
Servings: 48
Preparation Time: 10 min
Cooking Time: 6 min
Level of Difficulty: Easy

Go ahead and grab a few of these bite-size cookies. They might be little, but they pack a big chocolate punch.

Ingredients

2 Tbsp butter, softened
2 tsp canola oil
½ cup packed brown sugar, dark variety
1 tsp vanilla extract
⅛ tsp table salt
1 large egg white
¾ cup all-purpose flour
¼ tsp baking soda
3 oz semisweet chocolate chips, about ½ cup

Instructions

Preheat oven to 375°F.

In a medium bowl, cream together butter, oil, and sugar. Add vanilla, salt, and egg white; mix thoroughly to combine.

In a small bowl, mix together flour and baking soda; stir into batter. Add chocolate chips to batter; stir to distribute evenly throughout.

Drop 48 half-teaspoons of dough onto one or two large nonstick baking sheets, leaving a small amount of space between each cookie. Bake cookies until golden around edges, about 4 to 6 minutes; cool on a wire rack. Yields 1 cookie per serving.

Notes

Indulge your craving for an intense chocolate experience. Buy a 3-ounce bar of fine chocolate with a percentage of 75 or higher on the

DESSERTS

label. The percentage indicates the combined amount of cocoa bean and added cocoa butter in the chocolate. The higher the percentage, the greater the chocolate taste and the less sweet the product. Chop up the bar and use it instead of the chocolate chips (could affect *PointsPlus*® values).